ω

THAT DAMMED BEAVER

CANADIAN HUMOUR, LAUGHS AND GAFFS

THE EXILE BOOK OF ANTHOLOGY SERIES   NUMBER FIFTEEN

SELECTED BY

BRUCE MEYER

EXILE
editions

Publishers of Singular
Fiction, Poetry, Nonfiction, Translation, Drama and Graphic Books

Library and Archives Canada Cataloguing in Publication

That dammed beaver : Canadian humour, laughs and gaffs /
selected by Bruce Meyer.

(The Exile book of anthology series ; number fifteen)
Short stories.
Issued in print and electronic formats.
ISBN 978-1-55096-691-6 (softcover).--ISBN 978-1-55096-692-3 (EPUB).--
ISBN 978-1-55096-693-0 (Kindle).--ISBN 978-1-55096-694-7 (PDF)

1. Humorous stories, Canadian (English). 2. Canadian wit and
humor (English). 3. Canadian prose literature (English)--21st century.
I. Meyer, Bruce, 1957-, editor II. Series: Exile book of anthology series ; no. 15

PS8323.H85T53 2017   C813'.010817   C2017-906150-X
                                          C2017-906151-8

Copyrights are indicated in the Permissions pages.
Design and composition by Michael Callaghan.
Typeset in Fairfield, Copperplate and Akzidenz Grotesk fonts
at Moons of Jupiter Studios.

Published by Exile Editions Ltd ~ www.ExileEditions.com
144483 Southgate Road 14 – GD, Holstein, Ontario, N0G 2A0
Printed and Bound in Canada by Marquis

We gratefully acknowledge the Canada Council for the Arts,
the Government of Canada, the Ontario Arts Council,
and the Ontario Media Development Corporation
for their support toward our publishing activities.

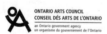

Canadian sales representation:
The Canadian Manda Group, 664 Annette Street,
Toronto ON M6S 2C8   www.mandagroup.com   416 516 0911

North American and international distribution, and U.S. sales:
Independent Publishers Group, 814 North Franklin Street,
Chicago IL 60610   www.ipgbook.com   toll free: 1 800 888 4741

CONTENTS

PREFACE

BEHIND THE BEAVER'S TEETH

BRUCE MEYER

With his buck teeth, that damned beaver may seem to be Bugs Bunny's cousin, busy damming up our world, but if so, he's a distant cousin many times removed. Instead of being a wise-cracking Brooklyn boy, our beaver gnaws all day on the poplars and maples of his own bizarre neuroses. He must know what is funny (presumably he can see his buck teeth in the dark still waters), yet he maintains a hunched inscrutability. He never goes for the big laugh. He knows at the core of his being that he has turned forests – all those trees reaching for the sun – into stump-stubbled swamps. In his realm of murky water, whether he is *Monsieur le castor* or the beaver on an English-Canadian beer bottle, he knows in his heart that he is a rodent.

Laughter, the restorative comic view, is not easy to find in beaver country. Oh, there are stories that set you laughing out-loud, such as Steven Hayward's "August 7, 1921" or Larry Zolf's "The Ping-Pong Affair." There is Austin Clarke's farcical Green Hornet working the city's windshields, the sly hilarity of Jonathan Goldstein's "The Tower of Babel," and Bob Armstrong's sideways take on the madness of the Franklin Expedition in "Undelivered Letters Home;" but these and their like are as rare as nudes in a Group of Seven landscape. We all too often wear funeral crepe around our laughter. Our ghosts – amputated – peer over our shoulders, as in Julie Roorda's Valentine's Day tale, "'Til Death," or, in the case of Jacques Ferron's "The Dead Cow in the Canyon," they peer out of the attic windows of places we call home but cannot stand to inhabit. Perhaps this is the same cow that David McFadden chases the length of Lake Ontario in a motor boat – a cow determined to return to its home as an assertion of life, though we know its destiny is to end up on the poet's plate.

This is the country that has produced the pie-eyed wit of Tommy Chong and The McKenzie Brothers, a land of the in-ebriated revelation, as in Gail Prussky's "The Story of Weasel Tossing," the absurd perception of Andrew Borkowski's "The Lesson," and the hallucinatory certainty shared by Leon Rooke and Barry Callaghan's characters. But essentially, the bush country of our minds, the mythic madness therein, is our turf as in Joe Rosenblatt's vision where nothing is ever what it seems as camels criss-cross in a coal cellar in which the author meets Frankenstein having a smoke. We find delight in such moments when we don't know where we are or where we will arrive, or, as Northrop Frye put it, "where here is." An idea further advanced by Atwood who said, our "here" is not an "absence of order, but an ordered absence." In this enchanted "absence" we explore love in all it mysteries and comic extremities...in the gallows humour of Claire Dé...the fumbling couple in Leon Rooke's story of Eb and Flo, the dream lover in Anne Dandurand's "Psyche from Here," a moment of ecstasy in heat in Christine Miscione's "Timorous Love" (only a beaver high on ashwood or St. Teresa of Avila could achieve such a state), or the high-tech love craft of Myna Wallin in "Canadoll." We run blindly into what we cannot see, smack into a birch tree where a beaver is busily at work on the trunk. At such moments, naked in the throes of passion of one kind or another, we are most vulnerable. At our most vulnerable we are at our most laughable.

For all its complexities, delusions and illusions, love is the beaver's secret entrance to the innermost sanctum of his lodge, the tabernacle of his heart and soul: in Gloria Sawai's "The Day I Sat Down with Jesus," Alexandre Amprimoz's "Saint Augustine," Jamie Feldman's "Double Double An' Chocolate Glazed," and Morley Callaghan's "The Predicament." Even hockey, played by mad priests, reminds us that the damned beaver is always out and about, pursuing one of his passions, in this case busy on an outdoor ice rink, chasing a puck in the midnight hour: such is life in the excerpt from Paul Quarrington's *King Leary*.

And so it goes…from Atwood's story of Salome the strip-
per holding her own head on a platter, to tales of old country
weasel tossing, to the far north country where we find our
very own young Queen cheating at bingo in Karen Lee
White's "Queen Elizabeth Visits the Elks Bingo Hall."
Illusions, delusions, laughs, gaffs – many of our particular
peccadilloes are here open unto you like a toppled forest,
pulped and put to paper, spread upon the pages that you hold
in your hands. You have been beavered – those razor-sharp
Bugsy teeth are not merely the tools our rodent uses to survive: they are his weapons for the carving out of his dammed
world; they also allow him to hide his world behind his polite,
oh-so-nice-nice smile.

UNDELIVERED LETTERS HOME

from Junior Midshipman Archibald Ponsonby-Cholmondeley, recovered recently in the search for additional remains of the Franklin Expedition

BOB ARMSTRONG

"Canada hopes to finally solve one of the Arctic's greatest mysteries this summer: finding the remains of two ships lost in the doomed 1845 Franklin Expedition to find the fabled Northwest Passage." —The Telegraph (U.K.), July 1, 2011

"Even more than the discovery in 2014 of Sir John Franklin's ship HMS Erebus, historians expect this latest find – a carefully preserved cache of private papers – to provide insight into the tragedy that has been called Canada's legend of the Holy Grail." —The Telegraph (U.K.), July 1, 2021

19th of May 1845

Dearest Mother,

The departure from Greenhithe was frightfully exciting, though trying for the men. We had our vessels almost fully loaded when Sir John arrived at Port and discovered a dreadful error on the part of The Admiralty. It seems our Expedition had been assigned the wrong ships. Sir John soon put things to rights and in short order I was securely ensconced in my cabin on HMS Terror. What an ill omen it would have been had I put to sea aboard HMS Sunny Daze!

Your loving son, Junior Midshipman Archibald Ponsonby-Cholmondeley

1st of June 1845

Dearest Mother,

Do you remember last year when Uncle Algernon told me that a sea voyage would make a new man of me? (This was on the evening when he so generously offered to rub me down with goose fat and teach me the sport of Greco-Roman wrestling.) Well, it has come to pass. I am a new man. Your son, Junior Midshipman Archibald Ponsonby-Cholmondeley, has become a bounder.

I know that you and Father both warned me to keep away from bounders, rotters, and cads, but I think you would change your mind if you met my cabin mate Reginald Butterworth. He's a bounder and he's a capital fellow. And the nephew of a Baronet, no less. Butterworth says bounders are simply misunderstood by people who feel threatened by our cravats and our unrestrained language, which I admit can be d—ed shocking. He swears, however, that bounders do not deserve to share in the richly earned opprobrium heaped upon rotters and cads, whom he describes as "douchebags." Butterworth has such a way with words. I believe the douchebag is a French Invention. Perhaps Grand-mama can bring one back from Vichy so that I can better appreciate my cabin mate's bon mots.

Your loving son, Junior Midshipman Archibald Ponsonby-Cholmondeley

10th of June 1845

Dearest Mother,

Today began with a great to-do on the Quarterdeck. I was awakened by sprightly dancing and gay laughter. When I reached the deck, I found many of the men wearing petticoats and Butterworth brandishing a paddle on the bare bottom of one of the cabin boys.

"Not to worry, old sport," he said. "This is a time-honoured Royal Navy tradition that occurs whenever a ship crosses the Equator." That put my mind at ease.

Your loving son, Junior Midshipman Archibald Ponsonby-Cholmondeley

PS: Today we sighted Greenland. Huzzah!

8th of December 1845

Dearest Mother,

Rum luck today, I'm afraid. A few of the deck hands came down with a bad case of the Ague, characterized by much coughing and expelling of bilious humours. Sir John, being a good Christian as well as a man of Science, ordered his personal physician to see to the sick men. Unfortunately, the common English sailor is so steadfast in his Ignorance, that the men had to be physically restrained before the physician was able to bleed them. Terrible idea, thrashing about when one has a scalpel held to one's jugular.

Worse still, we were unable to give the men a Christian burial at sea, as the surface of the ocean is now quite frozen. Terrible shame, as Butterworth has a lovely singing voice and I had looked forward to a few good Hymns.

Your loving son, Junior Midshipman Archibald Ponsonby-Cholmondeley

19th of May 1846

Dearest Mother,

Today, on the anniversary of our departure, I give thanks for British Innovation. We have now been receiving daily sustenance from our new-fangled canned food for one year, and are as hale and hearty as on the day we set sail.

I am well aware that there were those Cassandras who feared ominous side effects as a result of our scientifically preserved Diet, but the airtight lead seals on the containers have steadfastly kept Miasmas and Ill Humours out of our food. Not only do I find our meals delicious, but so does Azazoth, the Archangel who speaks to me through Sir John's Yorkshire Terrier.

Your loving son, Junior Midshipman Archibald Ponsonby-Cholmondeley

15th of July 1846

Dearest Mother,

Today we celebrate St. Swithin's Day by resuming our Voyage of Discovery, after what was, I must confess, a rather longer than expected time in harbour. I cannot, in good Conscience, recommend Beechey Island as a location in which to spend the winter. Fortunately, we had good British woollens to see us through the long months, unlike the poor, desperate Savages, forced to rely upon nothing more than the fur of northern beasts.

I hope deciphering my handwriting is not too trying for you, as I have been learning to use my left since the bothersome loss of some digits on my right hand. Do not worry about me, though, as I am much better off than poor Butterworth, who walks in circles now that he has lost all the toes on his right foot.

Your loving son, Junior Midshipman Archibald Ponsonby-Cholmondeley

22nd of September 1846

Dearest Mother,

Excelsior! Following his most recent astronomical Observations, Sir John has declared the Expedition a success. Sharing in so momentous a Victory for Science fills me with great satisfaction and with a certain amount of regret for poor Cousin Edmund, whose sea voyage on HMS Beagle turned out to be of so little Consequence. As if anything of consequence could be discovered on the pitiful Galapagos Islands!

We have now proven beyond the shadow of a doubt that the Northwest Passage is navigable and will soon become a Sea Route of great importance to the British Empire. All aboard both of our ships are confident that China lies just beyond the large, flat, white island that stretches out to the horizon in all directions.

Your loving son, Junior Midshipman Archibald Ponsonby-Cholmondeley

14th of March 1847

Dearest Mother,

As we wait out another Arctic Winter, the state of our food supply grows increasingly parlous. Yesterday we ate unrecognizable pieces of leathery animal flesh cooked with colourless and tasteless roots utterly lacking in nutritive value. Our last good English meal.

Good old Butterworth helps us keep our minds off our difficult situation. He selflessly spends his free time offering massages to help those men whose lumbago has been exacerbated by the weather. Each day I hear his call to action: "Come along, Ponsonby, time to tenderize the men."

Your loving son, Junior Midshipman Archibald Ponsonby-Cholmondeley

2nd of April 1847

Dearest Mother,

Resourceful thinking by Sir John has resolved one of our most vexing dilemmas: the shortage of space in the aft cabin that serves as our makeshift morgue.

Your loving son, Junior Midshipman Archibald Ponsonby-Cholmondeley

PS: Before I return, please tell Cook not to use the expression "tastes like chicken."

10th of June 1847

Dearest Mother

I hope my previous letters have not caused you disquiet. I remain in good hands under the leadership of the brilliant Sir John Franklin, who today made the decision to abandon ship and continue on foot to the nearest post of the Hudson's Bay Company. While we were filling the sleds with the emergency silverware, Sir John was struck by the kind of Inspiration that has characterized his Naval and Exploratory Career. It took some time, but, using the remains of our food containers, Butterworth and I were able to fashion a hat made of tin to prevent the dastardly French from reading the Great Man's mind.

Is it any wonder that the Royal Navy rules the waves?

Until we meet again, I remain your loving son,

Junior Midshipman Archibald Ponsonby-Cholmondeley

AUGUST 7, 1921

STEVEN HAYWARD

After ten years of "Give-Away Days," the Yankees had managed to dole out a greater variety of baseball paraphernalia than any other team in the history of baseball. The first Give-Away Day was on June 3, 1918 (when 6,500 Yankee caps were given away), and the last was on September 17, 1927 (when over 80,000 pretzels shaped like Yankee logos were distributed). In between, there had been Cap Day, Pennant Day, Bottle Opener Day, Cigar Day, Pillow Day, Sock Day, Mug Day, Pretzel Day, Jersey Day, Sneaker Day, Baseball Card Day, Camera Day, Hot Dog Day, Tobacco Day, Chewing Tobacco Day, Cracker Jack Day, and Peanut Day, to name a few.

August 7, 1921, was Bat Day.

According to *The Completely Complete Book of Baseball Statistics* by Dr. Venus Guzman, there were 21,106 paying customers in Yankee Stadium that day, and 15,000 of them had been given complimentary baseball bats as they entered the stadium. This story is concerned with seven of those people. The first two are Mary and Lyman Labrow.

I know about the Labrows thanks to an article published on September 21, 1923 (roughly two years after Bat Day), that I found in the archives of a now-defunct newspaper called the *New York Reflector*. The article described the circumstances that led to both of the Labrows being in Yankee Stadium that day, and was accompanied by a photo of the couple; in it, Mary and Lyman are smiling and wearing clothes which were already out-of-fashion in 1921. The Grand Canyon is visible in the background. Lyman Labrow was an optometrist and Mary Labrow was a seamstress. They lived in Bergen County, New Jersey, and had no children.

On August 7, 1921, Mary Labrow was sitting one row ahead of me in Yankee Stadium. She was a small, birdlike woman and was wearing a nondescript brown dress that day. She did not look at the field once during the game. Instead, she was looking at two people sitting three rows ahead of her, at a man and a woman.

The man she was looking at was her husband, Lyman Labrow. Mary had come to the game specifically to spy on him, and she could see him perfectly from where she was sitting. Lyman, however, did not see her until it was too late; until she had noticed the same thing I had noticed, that he was not alone.

Lyman Labrow had come to the game that day with his secretary, a twenty-three-year-old woman named Jackie Hubbs. She was wearing a bright yellow dress and carried a small white purse that had a medium-sized bulge in it. She was exactly the kind of girl you look at during baseball games when there is no one at bat.

For the first three innings, no one could have guessed that Lyman Labrow and Jackie Hubbs were romantically involved, despite the fact they were sitting next to one another. They watched the game and their hands did not even touch. Jackie Hubbs' white purse sat chastely on her lap and her white fingers were folded chastely on top of it. However, it became evident during the fourth inning, when Jackie Hubbs reached into her purse and removed the medium-sized bulge, that she and Lyman Labrow were having an affair.

I suppose that today, she and Lyman Labrow could have complicated sexual intercourse in the stands behind third base and no one would think, or say, anything. But those were different times. On August 7, 1921, Jackie Hubbs caused a sensation in Yankee Stadium by eating a medium-sized Granny Smith apple.

She shined the apple by rubbing it extensively and energetically against her bright yellow dress. Instead of biting into it, she licked it three times, extraordinarily slowly, and handed it to Lyman Labrow. He looked at the apple, took a bite, and gave it back to her. Jackie Hubbs stroked the white part of the apple with her finger, and then touched Lyman Labrow's lips, softly.

And Mary Labrow sat perfectly still, three rows behind them, watching.

Those are the first three people who matter in this story.

The fourth person who matters in this story is a drunken off-duty policeman from Evansville, Indiana, named John Seidl, and the fifth person who matters in this story is a sober Yiddish typewriter salesman from New York City named Norman Flax. John Seidl was sitting in the seat to my right and Norman Flax was sitting directly in front of me.

I know that Norman Flax was a Yiddish typewriter salesman from New York City because he stood up in the bottom of the second inning and introduced himself to a rabbi who was sitting behind me. Norman's mother was sitting beside him, and it was she who pointed out the rabbi to her son. Clearly, Norman Flax was the sort of salesman who was always on the lookout for rabbis.

"I'm Norman Flax," he said, reaching over my head to shake the rabbi's hand. "If you need a Yiddish typewriter, you know who to call."

"I've already got a typewriter," said the rabbi. "What should I need another one for?"

"Maybe you don't need one now," said Norman Flax, "but you never know. When you do need one, call this number and ask for Flax."

And I know that John Seidl was a drunken off-duty policeman from Evansville, Indiana, because he spent most of the game talking loudly to another drunken off-duty policeman from Evansville, Indiana, whose name I never found out.

"I gotta take a leak," announced John Seidl, in the bottom of the fourth inning (just as Jackie Hubbs was reaching for the medium-sized bulge from her purse). "And when John Seidl has to take a leak, John Seidl has to take a leak."

John Seidl was the sort of man who habitually refers to himself in the third person, and that is why I happen to know his name.

"Whattya want me to do?" asked the other off-duty policeman from Evansville, Indiana.

"Ahh," replied John Seidl, as he was standing up, "you're hilarious."

Now, John Seidl was a big man, and when he stood up to make his way out into the aisle, he steadied himself by putting his hand on the shoulder of the person sitting next to him, and almost fell down. It was not a shoulder that provided much support, because it was the shoulder of a ten-year-old boy.

It was my shoulder. That was me. I was sitting beside the sixth person who matters in this story.

Unlike the majority of people in the stands behind third base that day, the sixth person who matters in this story was concentrating on the game. His real name was Giovanni

Spadafina, but everyone – even my mother – called him Sampson Spadafina. He was my father.

My father worked at the Heintzman Piano Factory where he was one of twenty-three men responsible for the manufacture of the tiny hammers that strike the strings inside Heintzman pianos. He had come to New York from Italy in 1911 with my mother.

"The name of the ship," he used to tell me, "was the *Santa Maria*."

This was something that he said repeatedly. Like Christopher Columbus, my father was from Genoa, and the fact that he landed at Ellis Island in a ship called the *Santa Maria* was of great symbolic importance to him. It allowed him to claim, only half-ironically, that he had arrived in the New World in the same vessel as Columbus. I am aware this is an extremely dubious, if not dangerous, claim to make in this age of political correctness, but it is one that my father – were he still alive today – would continue to make. To my father, Columbus represented everything a man should be: he was intelligent, resourceful, brave, industrious, physically strong, self-sufficient, and very, very rich.

"The Italians," my father used to say, "civilized the world."

When he was not working at the Heintzman Piano Factory he supplemented his income by gambling, and won almost every bet he ever placed. This was not because my father was particularly lucky, but because he always bet on the same thing: himself. He had developed a routine that would usually result in someone agreeing to bet against him. First, he would walk into a bar and order a drink. Then he would begin to talk. He always said the same thing.

"In the Old Country," he would say, "everyone was afraid of me."

Then he would tell the story of his impossible strength, about the earthquake that shook Italy in the spring of 1887, and how the roof of his parents' house landed on his father's legs. He was only a child then, and said he didn't give much thought to what he'd done until after he'd done it. He just lifted the roof off his father.

"And that," he would say, "was when they started calling me Sampson."

The routine usually worked. After he finished telling the story of his impossible strength, the other men in the bar would begin to look at him, to size him up.

The truth is that my father was not a physically imposing man. He was less than five feet tall and did not look strong. There was almost always someone willing to wager he wasn't strong at all.

There were a number of stunts he could perform to demonstrate his impossible strength, and these stunts were usually the subject of the bets he would place. He could pick up tables with his teeth, perform one-arm chin-ups with another man clinging to his back, arm-wrestle three people at once, rip telephone books in half and, on one occasion, I saw him juggle a rusted cannonball, a butcher's knife, and a small St. Bernard.

But my father had to be careful never to go into the same bar too many times. Otherwise people would challenge him to do something that was really impossible. This was what almost happened when he won the tickets to the Yankees game.

I was with him that day. My mother had sent us down to West 88th Street, to the Columbus Bakery, to buy a loaf of bread. On the way he stopped into a bar called O'Malley's and ordered a drink. Then he began to talk.

"In the Old Country," he said, "everybody was afraid of me…"

I suppose that if he had been paying closer attention, he would have seen the look on the bartender's face, how he whispered to another man behind the bar, and the way they both laughed. My father would have known it was a set-up.

"All right, Sampson," said the bartender, "I've got a pair of Yankee tickets right here that say you can't lift the man sitting at the back of the bar."

"That's all?" he asked.

"That's all," said the bartender. "You just lift him up, and you walk out of here with the tickets. If not, then you pay me for the tickets and I keep them."

"Adesso," said my father, waving both his hands. In Genoese dialect this is an expression that can mean almost anything. It can be a confirmation, a contradiction, a compliment, a protest, a warning, a congratulation, a shout of dismay, or a way of asking someone to pass the pasta. In that particular context, it was the Genoese equivalent of my father announcing that he was ready to demonstrate his impossible strength.

Everyone followed the bartender to the back of the bar.

It was impossible not to recognize the man my father was required to lift. He was perhaps the most easily identifiable person in the whole of New York. He had been interviewed by every major newspaper, been photographed by the *Guinness Book of World Records*, and had shaken Charlie Chaplin's hand. People came from all over the world to catch a glimpse of him, or to have their photograph taken while sitting on his lap. However, many people declined such a photo opportunity because the man charged a nickel (which in those days was a lot of money) for the privilege. He had a concession at the foot of the Statue of Liberty and it was rumoured that he made a pretty fair living. His real name was Brian Flanagan, but everyone called him what the papers called him: The Fattest Man in New York City.

He was sitting at the back of the bar in a reinforced steel chair, which had been specially constructed to bear his weight. He looked like he had been born in that chair.

When my father saw The Fattest Man in New York City he looked worried. He wiped his hands on his pants. This meant that his palms were sweating. I knew this was a bad sign. My father had palms that never sweated.

"I've made a bet," he whispered to me. "I have to try."

"Good luck," said The Fattest Man in New York City, as my father moved closer to him. "You'll need it."

The bar became completely silent. All I could hear was the sound of my father breathing and The Fattest Man in New York City's uneven wheeze.

"I'm very fat," said The Fattest Man in New York City. "No one has ever lifted me."

"Perhaps I will be the first," said my father, moving to the man.

Now, I knew exactly what my father was thinking. He was thinking about Columbus; about being first. I remember watching my father as he paced circles around The Fattest Man in New York City and – for the first time in my life – wondering if there was something he couldn't do.

I'm not sure exactly how it happened.

"*Adesso,*" called out my father, and in a split second, with one perfectly fluid clean-and-jerk movement, it was over. He had somehow taken hold of a foot and a shoulder, and lifted the huge man over his head. The Fattest Man in New York City looked worriedly at the floor, and vomited.

My father quickly put him down, picked up the Yankee tickets and walked out of the bar, wiping off one of his coat sleeves. "Don't tell your mother about this," he said when we were out on the street, "and I'll take you to the game tomorrow."

They were good seats, but they weren't great seats. My father didn't seem to mind. That was before television, and he had never seen a baseball game before. He had no idea what was going on.

"I understand the strikes," he said to me, "but what's a ball?"

I was about to explain when Babe Ruth came up to bat.

He is the seventh person who matters in this story.

Now, in the bottom of the ninth inning, only the core of Jackie Hubbs' Granny Smith apple remained. She held it between her lips and made a loud sucking noise that drew the attention of everyone sitting in the stands behind third base. I think even Lyman Labrow was embarrassed, although he didn't look like he was about to complain. Mary Labrow found that she could not contain herself any longer. She stood up and spoke to her husband.

This is what she said: "Lyman, you snake, I'm going to kill you."

Unlike myself, John Seidl and the other drunken off-duty policeman from Evansville, Indiana, were paying no attention to the domestic dispute occurring two rows ahead of them. They were deep in conversation. They had already discussed criminals, the criminal mind, specific criminals John Seidl had arrested, the difference between criminals in New York City and criminals in Evansville, the trouble with John Seidl's kids, the trouble with all kids, the trouble with John Seidl's wife, the trouble with having a wife at all, and then, finally, in the bottom of the ninth inning, they began to discuss the 1919 World Series, and who was responsible for fixing it.

"It's them Jews that done it," said John Seidl loudly.

"I don't know," said the other drunken off-duty policeman from Evansville, Indiana.

"John Seidl is here to tell ya," said John Seidl. "It's them Jews."

"Ain't none of the players that were Jews," pointed out the other man.

Norman Flax turned around in his seat to see who was speaking, and then went back to watching the game.

John Seidl saw him turn around and kept talking.

"It don't matter that none of them was Jews," he said, sounding so ugly that even Norman Flax's mother turned to look at him.

"It was them Jews – they're the ones with the money."

That was when Norman Flax stood up.

"Which Jews exactly?" asked Norman Flax. "Just tell me which of them Jews it was, so that I can get them."

"Siddown, boy," said John Seidl. "You don't want no trouble from John Seidl."

"I'll sit down," said Norman Flax, "when you shut up."

That was when John Seidl stood up.

Babe Ruth stepped into the batter's box. The pitcher threw the first pitch. Babe Ruth took a swing, and hit a high foul ball into the stands behind third base, right where we were sitting.

If it had been any other day at Yankee Stadium nothing would have happened. It would have been a foul ball and the game would have continued.

But it was August 7, 1921.

Bat Day.

Everyone swung at exactly the same time.

Mary Labrow reached across two rows of seats and attempted to hit Lyman Labrow with her complimentary bat. Lyman saw the complimentary bat coming at him and ducked out of the way. In fact, everyone sitting in that row ducked out of the way, with the conspicuous exception of Jackie Hubbs, who, with both of her eyes closed, was preoccupied with sucking an apple core.

The complimentary bat hit her in the face, and flattened her nose completely. There was a strangely silent moment just before Jackie Hubbs began to scream, when she reached up to her nose and found it crushed.

And Norman Flax reached for his complimentary bat and took a swing at John Seidl.

And John Seidl reached for his complimentary bat and took a swing at Norman Flax.

And both men were knocked instantaneously unconscious. They fell forward and rolled out into the aisle, in each other's arms.

And my father moved with the same unreal fluidity with which he had lifted The Fattest Man in New York City over his head. The foul ball headed right toward us, and before I knew what was happening, he had reached for his complimentary bat and jumped onto his seat.

"*Adesso,*" he told me and bent his knees slightly, and took a swing at the foul ball, and hit it right back at Babe Ruth.

The last thing I remember seeing as we walked quickly out of Yankee Stadium was Babe Ruth lying over home plate. No one knew what had happened. One moment Babe Ruth was hitting his cleats with his bat, and the next, he had collapsed into the dust.

We walked straight home and my father did not say a word. It was not until we got to our house, until he had opened the front door, that he noticed the bat was still in his hands.

"Carmella," he said to my mother, "I think I killed Babe Ruth."

What happened next happened very quickly.

My mother decided that we had to do something. So, we neither waited for the papers the next day (which said that Babe Ruth was still alive), nor went to the police station (which was already filling with the casualties of Bat Day). Instead, we panicked. We packed our things and got on a train the next morning. We came to Canada.

After that, my father stopped doing impossible things. He became a quiet, ordinary carpenter who earned his living building porches and installing kitchen cabinets. People no longer called him Sampson and he never told anyone about August 7, 1921. He died when he was sixty-two-years old, of prostate cancer. They sent him home after the treatment had failed. His hair had fallen out and he was completely blind.

The last picture of him was taken just before he died, at my daughter's fifth birthday party. He had already been sent home by the hospital. In the picture he is singing "Happy Birthday," but looking the wrong way as my daughter blows out the candles on her cake. On the table in front of him there are some walnuts that he had cracked open. The nuts are still in them. My father never liked eating walnuts, but loved cracking them open. He would pick up a nut and squeeze it until the shell cracked. He was the only one I ever knew who could do that with only one hand. I've tried it more times than I can count. I suppose that this is the picture that would have to go at the end of his story. Or maybe just a close-up of the walnuts.

August 7, 1921, was the first and last Bat Day in the history of baseball. One hundred eighty-seven people, including Babe Ruth, were injured that day. According to the article in the *New York Reflector*, the Labrows divorced and Jackie Hubbs had reconstructive surgery on her face. In the paper she was quoted as saying that she liked her new nose "better." I have no idea what happened to John Seidl and Norman Flax. The last time I saw them, they were lying with their eyes closed, in each other's arms at the end of our aisle. We stepped over them as we exited the stadium. Perhaps they lived happily ever after.

I still have the complimentary bat that my father got that day. Today it is a rotted piece of wood, and the Yankees logo on its side has faded during the years it was kept in the damp basement of my house. The truth is that if I could show it to you, you would be unimpressed. It does not look at all like a bat that might have changed the course of history.

But I still have it. I am an old man now, with grandchildren of my own, but there are days when I go into the basement just to touch it. The feel of the wood never fails to bring back that day, the day my father became afraid. I close my eyes and I can see myself standing beside him in Yankee Stadium. The game is about to begin and both of us are singing "The Star-Spangled Banner." His real name was Giovanni, but everyone – even my mother – called him Sampson. I smell the grass and hear the roar of the crowd, the final note dissolving into sunshine.

WHEN MONSTERS SMOKED

JOE ROSENBLATT

There was a trick you could do with an empty package of Camel cigarettes. You folded the package into several parts, squeezed out the central image of the camel itself and then rolled the parts out until the beast seemed to move across the dunes: the mind drugged by cigarette smoke, drifting. We were blowing smoke behind my house on Major Street. Turning on with the weed, a soaring feeling of confidence, buoyed above the crowd. It took a number of cigarettes to get the habit going. It sizzled sometimes as the smoke shot up the wrong flue, but after a few practice bouts, my soul descended on a spiral. It had a calming effect, although when it went bad for me I would choke, gasp and throw up spots of parakeet blood. I was determined to get the drift of it. I wanted to be like other paranormal people. In those days, everybody wore a cigarette butt in the corner of the mouth. Smokers were the toughest, the meanest, the truest romantics, and if they weren't killing they were loving. They loved and killed before or after the act. Sex seemed an excuse to have a smoke. They sometimes made love without fondling but only staring into each other's button eyes and blowing smoke into each other's faces. This was legal sex. Everybody smoked: detectives, poetroons, cowboys, buffoons, rich dudes, poor Okie folk…it didn't matter, they had one thing in common: they smoked every damned chance they had: brains, manhood, courage, villainy, what did it matter; facing the last mile on Death Row you smoked, or stepping into the vortex of a cow town you smoked before you smoked your shooting iron.

I smoked Camel, others smoked Black Cat…which I think was a cigarette for sissies… You smoked through your nostrils, your mouth, or simultaneously. I loved Frankenstein because he could smoke through his ears. He didn't smoke Old Gold…he only smoked when he was being wired down and shot through with bolts of electricity…the straps snapped …his huge chest swelled…

I was jumping up and down in my seat…the monster's lips twisted and turned, and then his eyeballs (which weren't his) popped back into their sockets. Frankenstein, it seemed, was an electrical junkie…somebody you could never trust in an electrical storm, who attracted bolts of lightning as a packing-house attracts sewer rats, and there he was, the monster with a spike running through the *flat* on the forehead of his skull… He gurgled words, or rather, he ate sound…the same sound the mummy made when a deluded scientist unrolled his linen, a regurgitated, half-wormy sound…urgg ghh murrrrr-RRRRRrrr.

I stared into the gape of his mouth…did he have natural teeth though made of spare parts? Who looked at his teeth?…they were stubs…they reeked of decay… The monster jerked against the straps, his huge cement shoes jerked up with the zaps of electricity…and finally the monster passed out, having climaxed with the last burn, and smoke poured out of his ears…out of his skin… His cheap trousers seemed to singe with every electrical fuck in the ear…and the hands, they were huge… The good doctor wiped the sweat from his creation's brow…and the rag steamed…

Yes…yes…my son…yes…assured the doctor. You will live…and URRRRRG…gurgled the monster…urgggh…and then the monster flaked out. A thought crossed through my mind: *Supposing I wired the wrong doorknocker and the monster came to the door…they would use parts of me to keep the creep together…* Nobody screwed around at Dr. Frankenstein's door, only the police captain with one arm who had heard a rumour that the doctor was rejuvenating the beast who had ripped his arm off before in a vicious encounter. With his steel fist he pounded on the thick oak door. The captain didn't believe in knocking…

I knew the monster was lurking around the coal bin down in my basement. My mother told me to go down and get potatoes. I was too frightened. The war was still on and there were blackout drills and by some freak coincidence, as soon as I mustered my nerves and went down, the lights suddenly went out. Half my body was steaming in fear. Lights flashed outside the basement window; it seemed my life was flashing away, and goosebumps rashed all over my skin: warm piss, goosebumps and a handful of potatoes, dirt still fresh as the grave…earth apples…musty…Frankenstein's boneyard…

I was crying and cringing and had anybody said BOO I would have jumped out of my mouth. I dashed blindly up the stairs, stopping at the top to puff out my fear. I had gone through dungeons, my imagination yeasting with images of dismemberment…ripping…tearing…choking…clawing… but never biting: neither the mummy nor Frankenstein's creation ever bit anybody: they tore off their hands, applied a choking hold, but certainly never bit anybody…that was for the squeaky vampire who darted around in the early hours of the morning and materialized in a dusty coat, a nocturnal evening dress, a starched white shirt, as though the wearer had been sleeping in a crypt where only moths cleaned up after him. From that day on it was hellish to go down into the basement and sidle past the furnace room, past the hidden presence of the square-headed Frankenstein monster. I was sure he was concealed under the coal. Each shovelful brought me closer to the shuffler. I saw his outline in the flames, his grinding mouth and twisted face. Even monsters love to eat potatoes. He could have been hiding in a burlap bag. I kept away from the spuds and handled the coal shovel gingerly, selecting clumps of coal but not digging deeply into the earth lumps piled to the basement window. I dreaded the coal men lumbering up to the window at the side of the house, dumping sacks of coal onto a chute which ran up to the open window. Hands reached out from the grave, Franky's calloused hands.

The coal navvy pushed me aside as he swung another bag of coal down the chute, his face covered with grime, and as the man sweated he smeared the dirt across his brow as though he meant to convey how his life was a smear of coal darkness containing the gift of fire. To the householder it was different: it seemed the dirtier he was the more acceptable he seemed; the householder wanted his money's worth and felt elevated viewing a human being who worked with grime ground into his pores. The coalman was doubled over, one hand gripping the nape of the bag, the other supporting his hip and the small of his back, and he gripped the rear end of the bag and hoisted it above his waist, rolling the coal over his back. The coal roared down the chute. The coalman smiled, or at least, he always seemed to smile, and his features were

made all hideous by the few blotches of white skin…
advanced leprosy…and his teeth appeared ominous, and his
peep-hole eyes. The coalman seemed to love his job, dumping coal without a sign of being disgruntled. A few of the
labourers requested a glass of water, lapping the water like
sick cats. What disturbed me most about their vocation was
their lunch hour…they munched on a sandwich…ingested,
dust and all, and to top off their meal, they sucked on a cigarette, the quick flow of digestive juices blending with dust
and the tar from a Camel or Sweet Cap. Still, none of these
actual creatures came close to Frankenstein, whose face –
although it appeared clean – had its veneer of sickly light: the
filth was on the inside. Frost chilled away at a coalman's face
but the dirt acted as a protective layer. It was eerie to see a
man with a blackened face not only sweating but exhaling a
draft of warm bodily air against the savage nip of winter. They
sweated, smearing lines of dirt across their face, and gurgled
sounds like the monster, their lungs past repair, dust eating
away the linings of their precious lungs…and then sneezing,
dust flying up their nostrils…and then they laughed.

It was an honest living, more productive than attaching
new parts to a monster who had a pair of size twenty shoes
and whose head had apparently been flattened by a concrete
ironing board. He walked through his dungeons with his
hands stiff as wood, his shoulders broad enough to carry two
bags of coal. He was at least five ax handles across the back
and had bolts on his shoulders and tufts of black hair, trans-
plants as well. The poor dumb bastard tried to form sounds
but the only real sound was MASTER…*master*…*master*…
and it made the good doctor's day when his fear of fire singed
his very soul, if he had one: *Master, master* cried the monster,
globs of tears and glue flowing along his jutting jaw.

What a poor dumb clot. He proved to be nothing more than the doctor's evil alter ego, uglier than a toad blowing marsh gas. The coalman had a set of shoes which went *crunch crunch crunch* melting the snow in their path, but even Frankenstein's shoes belonged to somebody else. Who? *Master, master*...the mouth formed a harsh sound... The doctor smiled at his creation. Yes, yes...my son...yes...soon you will have a brain...yes, yes... Glue oozed and gurgled out of the monster's mouth at the very mention of a transplanted brain. The monster rammed a finger at the side of his head above his prominent ears: Brrr ain...? Demented, a smile formed around his drooling mouth: the thought of a brain, the delicious watering of the monster's hole of a mouth...

Another zigzag of electricity. The operating room was crammed with electrical devices and tubings, electrical panels and giant switches, motors with huge rubber bands and auxiliary engines. The monster, strapped against the table, which was itself on gears and pulleys, strained against his straps. Even the transplanted mat of hair on his flattened head appeared to smoke... The doctor's assistant, usually a dwarf, tried to restrain the monster, fearing the beast would blow the spark plugs in his cranium. The fury of shattering electricity had brought on psychic orgasm, the monster's eyes blackened, jolts jamming through his body, smoking as well... and then he lay back, passive...all he needed was a cigarette...as the dwarf turned up his bubbly eyes to the doctor, who calmed his twitchy assistant, stroking the poor soul's crooked hump, running his hand over the dwarf's heavy-set eyebrows. *EEeeegor...all is ready...soon I will prove that the fools were wrong...I...Doctor Frankenstein...they laughed at me...I'll show them...I'll...who are you staring at...you fool... you lump...dirt...away with you...away...hahahahahaha...*

"Yes master, yes…" Eeeegor squealed, waddling away with his painful hump (at least two sofa cushions high). The hunchback appeared to move sideways, past the coal bin, and he waddled up a flight of concrete stairs. He squealed again, a fiendish cry…something resembling a laugh, its frostiness melting into the shard of a twitter… The monster clumps toward the doctor, his hands raised like one in a dream state, those eyes open, those peepers that don't belong to the creature…planted as seeds of vision, fitted in, played around with, the pulps of eyes…

There was a huge rabbit-like brain in a jar. Igor fondled the jar, staring like a child at its content…brain…brain…he was transfixed. "Give me that, you oaf," snarled the doctor, seizing the jar from the hunchback who raised his hands to ward off blows. "No, master…no…" The child in Igor had not yet fathomed the gravity of his act: to hold, to fondle, to fabricate, to flush another's brain…that was to put the hunch on the back of life. That was power. The doctor set the jar on the marble table and connected the circuits. A jag of white thunder illumed the contents of the jar. The monster, supine and sedate, rolled his eyes and suddenly a knowing smile formed on his pale lips.

Unfortunately, there's always a rat's hair in the mills: the brain's former owner was an absolute degenerate, a sociopath, a destructive low-life. After all the soft hum of ozone sucking in a nitrogenous vapor…*glup glup*…and the gases liquefying…with Igor silently watching in the background, full of hate, assuming that the brain was meant for him (a perverse love triangle here) – the vast bully grunted his approval, popped his eyes and pulled against the straps. Igor screamed, but it was too late, the monster had seized the doctor's wrist…but it was only a gentle tug, playful…and Igor, after a

touching moment of reconciliation, served as a guide, a pro-
curer for the monster, who huffed and puffed, emitting
obscene noises at Igor…kill kill kill…

The village folk complained to the one-armed captain, the
eyes and ears of the judicial system. Enough was enough. The
village inhabitants mobilized for a torch-lit deputation to the
castle, a lynching…there was safety in numbers…they carried pitchforks, shovels…knives…and only the one-armed
power-tripping captain was in possession of a long piece of
hardware, a revolver. It was curtains for the deadly trio: a
frightened Igor hoisted above the heads of the mob…the doctor stomped to death by the peasants…and the monster
chased into quicksand near the castle… Master, he cried out
before he sank into the muck of the subconscious. The castle
was torched and everybody but the dead was as happy as vampire bats strung out on a jugular vein. I charged up the basement stairs, my heart thumping. I knew he was down there,
that he had pulled himself out of the quicksand. There was a
butt (a Camel) in his mouth. He was smoking out of his ears,
he was moving across the dunes of my mind leaving huge
footprints, and who…who had worn those huge cement
shoes before…?

Drawing by Margaret Atwood

SALOME WAS A DANCER

MARGARET ATWOOD

Salome went after the Religious Studies teacher. It was really
mean of her, he wasn't up to her at all, no more sense of self-
protection than a zucchini, always droning on about morality
and so forth, but he'd finger the grapefruits in the supermarket in this creepy way, a grapefruit in each hand, he'd stand
there practically drooling, one of those gaunt-looking men
who'd fall on his knees if a woman ever looked at him seriously, but so far none of them had. As I say it was really mean
of her, but he'd failed her on her mid-term and she was under
pressure at home, they wanted her to perform as they put it,
so I guess she thought this would be a shortcut.

Anyway, with a mother like hers what could you expect?
Divorced, remarried, bracelets all up her arms and fake eyelashes out to here, and pushy as hell. Started entering Salome
in those frilly-panty beauty contests when she was five, tap-
dance lessons, the lot, they'd slather the makeup on those
poor tots and teach them to wiggle their little behinds, what
a display. And then her stepdad ran the biggest bank in town
so I guess she thought she could get away with anything. I
wouldn't be surprised if there wasn't some hanky-panky going
on in that direction too, the way she'd bat her baby blues at
him and wheedle, sickening to watch her rubbing up against

him and cooing, he'd promised her a Porsche when she turned sixteen.

She was Tinker Bell in the school play when she was twelve, I certainly remember that. Seven layers of cheesecloth was all she wore. There was supposed to be a body stocking underneath but whether there was or not, your guess is as good as mine. And all those middle-aged dads sitting with their legs crossed. Oh, she knew what she was doing!

Anyway, when she got the rotten mark in Religious Studies she went to work on the guy, who knows how it started but when they were caught together in the stockroom she had her shirt off. The teacher was growling away at her bra, having trouble with the hooks, or so the story goes, you have to laugh. If you want what's in the package you should at least know how to get the string off, is what I say. Anyway, big scandal, and then he started badmouthing her, said she was a little slut and she'd led him on, did some innuendo on the mother just for good measure. Everyone believed him, of course, but you always knew with Salome that if anyone's head was going to roll it wouldn't be hers. She accused the poor jerk of sexual assault, and since she was technically a minor – and, of course, her banker stepdad threw his weight around – she made it stick. Last seen, the guy was panhandling in the subway stations, down there in Toronto; growing a beard, looks like Jesus, crazy as a bedbug. Lost his head completely.

Salome didn't come to a good end either. Tried out for ballet school. Modern Dance was what she thought would suit her, show a lot of skin, centre your thoughts on the pelvis, bare feet, fling yourself about, but she didn't get in. Left home after some sort of blowup between the mom and the stepdad, midnight yelling about Miss Princess and her goings-on, furniture was thrown. After that she took to stripping in bars, just to annoy them I bet. Got whacked in her dressing room one night, right before the show, too bad for Management, someone clobbered her over the head with a vase, nothing on but her black leather macramé bikini and that steel-studded choke collar, used to get the clients all worked up, not that I'd know personally. Saw two guys running out the stage door in bicycle-courier outfits, some sort of uniform anyway, never caught them though. Hit men set on by the stepdad is one rumour, wild with jealousy. Guys get like that when their hair falls out. It was all the mother's fault, if you ask me.

CANADOLL

MYNA WALLIN

STATE-OF-THE-ART HOME PLEASURE
INTRODUCING CANADOLL
FROM SIMULOVE INDUSTRIES.

First there was CANADARM, a remote-controlled mechanical appendage used on NASA space shuttles from 1981-2011, establishing Canada's unparalleled reputation as a leader in the field of robotics. The CANADARM could be thought of as a 15-metre human arm with a wrist, elbow, and shoulder that *could bend and turn with more flexibility and sensitivity than a real human arm!*

What does all this innovation have to do with the newly conceived CANADOLL? Well, there are plenty of companies penetrating the sex-bot market these days, but only one Canadian company has the robotic engineering expertise and technologically proven capabilities to produce the most realistic love doll on the market, guaranteeing an experience even more real than the real thing! If you've ever dreamed of creating the ideal partner to meet all your needs, programmed to your exact specifications, designed by you and for you, choose CANADOLL from Simulove. Simulove Industries promises each customer will be entirely satisfied, or your money back!

There was a big cardboard box waiting for me at Canada Post. It was so big that the clerk behind the counter, usually impersonal and bored, was clearly curious. He didn't exactly come out and ask, "What the hell's in the box, eh?" but I could see him twitching, his mouth trying to form the question, as I signed my name and showed him a piece of ID.

I was so excited I could hardly breathe. I had taken a shower, washed my hair, done my nails and put on some sexy lingerie, just like I would for a regular date. Only this would be better, better than real life. Real was messy, hurtful, and probably not going to call me back. Real was condescending, like my last boyfriend, who complained I was "sex-obsessed," because I wanted to have sex more than twice a week. Twice a week! My best friend thought he might be in the closet. She said any man who worked out at the YMCA three times a week, one more time than he wanted to have sex with me, was definitely suspect.

Anyway, I was fed up with dating. Especially the perfect-in-the-beginning and then flaws-and-cracks-appearing-soon-after kind of dating. So tiring, so migraine-inducing. This was going to be fantastic, this perfect man, wrapped in bubble wrap, vacuum-sealed, cushioned in Styrofoam "peanuts" with the return address: "Beaver Creek, BC."

Back up a few months. I was hanging out with a girlfriend and we were watching a crazy documentary on male and female sex-bots. These were dolls with silicone made to feel like real skin, with anatomically correct parts, with the weight and heft and hair of "breathing" people. They didn't move or speak like in sci-fi films or books, but they'd come a long way. They were real enough for their owners to fall in love with them. The craze originated in Japan, with the video game LoveForever, and its love sims, Megumi, Akane, and

Gimisum, and then it caught on just about everywhere. Admittedly, it was still an underground thing, but highly profitable, nonetheless. Canada didn't invent the love sim; they just perfected it.

"God, that's the stupidest thing I've ever heard of," my friend Nicole said. She had never had a problem getting a date in her life and took pleasure separating the wheat from the chaff. At the time, I said I agreed with her, but as time passed, it didn't seem so stupid anymore. Now here he was, my very own CANADOLL, waiting for me to release him from his box, waiting for me to make love to him. He was my life-sized secret. How could anyone possibly understand?

"Hello, Ryan," I whispered tentatively, peeling the sealed plastic shrink-wrap from his life-like body.

I had decided to name him Ryan Gosling, after one of my favourite actors. Ryan had a body that wouldn't quit, and his on-screen persona was usually sweet and gentle. I knew Ryan, my Ryan, would never disappoint me; he'd never show a side of himself that I wouldn't like. He was mine.

I lifted him, gingerly, out of his packaging. A note fell out, saying this was model #69 (weren't they all model #69?) and had been carefully inspected by Cindy (I'll bet he had!). If there were any defects, I was to contact Simulove Industries directly within forty-eight hours of receipt. He would be promptly and lovingly replaced.

I removed every last peanut shell that stuck to Ryan's creamy but not overly soft skin; he had a two-day shadow of stubble, just as I'd requested. I offered him some Oka cheese and crackers, and a glass of Riesling Icewine from the Okanagan Valley, to make him feel at home. He wasn't hungry and I gathered he never would be, but that didn't mean I wasn't going to be thoughtful. Or make assumptions. He might get hungry. You never know.

I expected Ryan wouldn't be much of a conversationalist, but that was all right. What I needed was a good listener. I told him about my problems with men, how frustrated I had been in finding a good one, and he just stared at me with those decent, London, Ontario-born eyes.

"Uh-huh."

Now that cannabis was legal – since July 2018, thanks to our still hot-as-a-pistol Prime Minister – I asked Ryan if he wanted any. I had briefly considered putting Justin on my short list of programmable males, but it turned out it was against the law to turn a head of state into a facsimile bot. Too bad.

I closed the blinds in my two-bedroom apartment and laid Ryan on the leather couch in my living room. I always liked fooling around with my boyfriends on the couch first, then going into the bedroom later. Why should Ryan be any different? He had a head of gorgeous blond hair (I'd had enough of brunets) and a pinkish hue to his cheeks, making him look perpetually excited and a little drunk. His eyes were sapphire blue and his body muscular. He wore jeans and a tight T-shirt, but I knew he wanted to get out of them. I already felt connected to him.

"Let's go, Rachel," I thought I heard him whisper. I took off my clothes, and with *La La Land* on the wide-screen TV in the background I took him right there and then. We fit perfectly. We did it on the couch, me on top – my favourite position. My breasts bobbed against the stubble on his face, and I could swear I felt a few drops of saliva on my nipples coming from his mouth. Gosh, these Simulove people really did know what they were doing! Ryan's body was perfect. His penis hardened with some kind of hydraulic pump implant. All I had to do was squeeze his hand affectionately, and his penis went rock hard. And stayed that way until I was done. I came four times that night and I'm pretty sure I had a G-spot orgasm at least two of the four times. Oh, CANADOLL!

"I love you," Ryan whispered.

"I love you, too," I answered. And I meant it. I carried Ryan to my bedroom and curled up, wrapped in his strong arms and thighs all night.

In the morning, I reached out for him, but he wasn't there. I heard dishes clatter in the kitchen and smelled the aroma of fresh coffee, toast, eggs and bacon wafting up to the bedroom! I thought I must still be dreaming; one of those dreams where you think you're awake and then realize it's still part of the dream. I walked into the kitchen and Ryan came over and kissed me, his life-like arms wrapping around my waist. I felt his breath on my neck as he kissed me again.

"You aren't dreaming," he answered, as if reading my mind. "Sit down, I'll explain," he said gently, sounding a lot like Ryan Gosling.

He gave me a cup of coffee, already knowing how I took it. I sipped at the coffee, still shaken.

"If we are treated properly, if we are made love to the way we want to be made love to, we have the ability to make ourselves self-sufficient. Of course, the company can't say so; it isn't legal, you see. It crosses the line between *home entertainment* and *prostitution*. You understand?"

"So, you're…uh…real?" I stammered.

"In a manner of speaking, yes," Ryan answered. And shrugged that famous Canadian nice-guy shrug.

"Are you going to join me for breakfast? Then maybe some dessert in the bedroom after?"

"I'm not programmed for that kind of eating, Rachel. But I can learn. I'll sit with you for now, keep you company." Had my bot just picked up on a *double entendre*, made a sly dirty joke, and admitted that he's trainable?

"Can you go out?" I asked, still baffled, wondering if my meds were working.

"No. I'm an adaptable sex toy, nothing more, nothing less," Ryan answered, without emotion.

"Oh, I see," I said, hugely relieved.

I contacted Simulove and wrote a rave online review, anonymously, of course. I figured there was no point mentioning the talking, the moving around of his own volition. It was entirely possible I was having a psychotic break. No point worrying anybody. Either way, I'd never been happier. I even called my therapist, told her I was doing much better, and thought I'd discontinue treatment for the time being. She asked me what was contributing to my "elevation in mood" as she put it, and I told her I was seeing someone.

"Well, let me know if you want to resume treatment, Rachel, I'm always here. New relationships can be very stressful."

"Thanks," I said, "I think I've met someone easy-going this time. Malleable, even."

We had a few months of pure bliss. Ryan loved to be showered with attention, we had lengthy conversations on a whole range of subjects, and he was an adept lover who never tired. I felt deeply calm and complete for the first time in years.

When I was at my advertising job during the day, Ryan liked watching his own movies, and became quite taken with his on-screen persona. But he became equally frustrated when he found out he couldn't sing or dance, like his character could in *La La Land*. He was also disappointed when I told him there was all kinds of red tape involved in acquiring a gun licence in Canada.

"Rachel, in *Drive* and *The Nice Guys*, and a whole bunch of his other movies, he gets to shoot a gun. I don't understand why he gets to do all these cool things and I don't."

"Ryan, sweetie, you've got limitations, just like the rest of us," I told him. "I guess you're only programmed to do certain things. Like some people are good at math and science and others aren't."

"But why, Rachel?"

It started to dawn on me that when Ryan wasn't in pleasing mode, his default position was that of a three-year-old child: "Why, Mommy, why is the sky blue?" Ryan's questions were maddening. When I didn't have the answers for him he became despondent.

The only thing that seemed to cheer him up was watching sports, especially hockey. Gradually, like any three-year-old, he forgot about wanting to be Ryan from the movies, and started finding other role models. Now, he wanted to be Sidney Crosby. I got him the latest NHL Wii games for Christmas and he played virtual hockey for hours with it between playoffs.

But I had to teach him everything. I had to teach him how to use the shower so he wouldn't burn himself and then I had to remind him to do it again. He didn't understand why some things (things that weren't fun) had to be done over and over.

He started to sit around and eat potato chips. Since he wasn't really programmed for eating, he never knew when he was full. I'd come home from work, find him covered in potato chip crumbs, wearing the same Leaf's sweatshirt he'd been wearing for days, his hair and nails filthy, and then he'd say, sweet as can be, "Do you want to have sexy-time, Rachel?" I was totally disgusted.

I called Simulove and they took care of everything. Seriously, their customer service is off the charts. They promised me a free six-month upgrade, a new CANADOLL free of charge. A technician from Simulove came over and switched off Ryan before he knew what was happening. He also promised me they'd wipe Ryan's memory and give him a good home.

I had to do it; I had to send him back. Besides, they're replacing him with The Justin. He was just added to their catalogue of bots since the Liberals were defeated by the NDPs. He will never sit around and watch hockey day and night, eating potato chips. Not my Justin. He's got more important things on his mind. And he looks like he'll be unbelievable in bed. Plus, he's fluent in English and French. I can't wait.

HOW THE OLD MAN DIED

JACQUES FERRON

There was a bone askew above his stomach; he wasn't sick, but the bone made him uncomfortable, stabbing him with every breath he took. He would have to stay quiet until the bone reset. After three or four weeks the wretched bone had not moved, the old man was going from bad to worse; they sent for the manipulator, but the manipulator, having felt him, refused to manipulate him, for by shifting the bone, he would have dislocated the nerve of the heart. The old man was done for. They sent for the priest.

"Old man," said the old woman to her husband, "maybe you're not very sick, but you're so old that you're dying."

"I'm dying?"

"Yes, you're dying; what's to become of me?"

"And what about me?" asked the old man.

"You have nothing to worry about," replied the old woman. "All you have to do is lie back; the priest will take care of everything. Only you'll have to be polite; you'll fold your hands, look up, and think of the good Lord, if you can; if you can't, just pretend to. And no funny business, do you understand!"

The old man was having difficulty breathing; he promised to behave. However, the arrival of his boys with their sanctimonious faces upset him in his resolve. His hands were already folded, he tried to separate them without being noticed, but the old lady had her eye on him; she fastened his wrists with a long rosary. Just then the priest arrived, concluded that there was no hope for the old man, and accordingly made haste to administer the last rites. After that he was at a loss to know what to do; it wasn't yet time to say the prayer for the dying.

"How are you feeling?" he asked the old man.

"Bad, thank you," replied he.

Bad, to be sure, but not bad enough to go under. Now higher, now lower, he was still rising and falling with the swell. The priest, who was inclined to be squeamish, retired to the kitchen, accompanied by the women. The boys, who had stayed with their father, didn't waste a moment; his handcuffs they removed. The old man gave them a wave:

"Hi there, boys!"

"Hi there, Pa," they replied.

Short waves shook the old man. This lasted an hour or more; then after the final wave came the final hour; the old man was at peace at last in his bed; the bone pained him no more; he was healed; he was about to die. The women had returned to his side, smothering little seagull cries in their handkerchiefs. The priest was saying the prayer. It was too good, too good; it was too good to last.

"The pot," cried the dying man.

The priest stopped. The chamber pot was brought, but the old man pushed it away:

"Too late; I'll go on the other side."

And he died.

When they had put him in the coffin, clean-shaven and smartly dressed, he looked very distinguished. The old woman could not stop gazing at him, and tearfully she told him:

"Ah, old man, my old man, if only you'd always been like this, sensible, clean, quiet, how I'd have loved you, how happy we'd have been!"

She could talk all she liked, poor woman! The old man was not listening to her; he was in the kitchen laughing with his boys, laughing as much as one dare laugh at a wake.

(Translated by Betty Bednarski)

from

THE COW
THAT SWAM
LAKE ONTARIO

DAVID McFADDEN

Anyway, on the evening of October 11 –
I remember it well for it was my birthday –
I was in a borrowed motorboat fishing for salmon
on Lake Ontario just beyond the Burlington Canal
through which giant Great Lakes steamers
in fact huge ships from all around the world
enter the factory-lined waters of Hamilton Harbour
when I hear what I thought was a salmon
skipping along on the surface as they often do
and turning I was surprised to see
a bovine head, with two shining horns
and two eyes as full and calm as fresh-plucked plums
ploughing steadfastly through the starry waves
heading, and for this I checked my map and compass
in the direction of Prince Edward County
that peninsula on the north shore
two hundred kilometres across the cold night waters
of lovely Lake Ontario.

Of course, I pulled my line and quietly followed
at a respectful distance, knowing the very presence
of an observer frequently alters that which is observed,
and I was surprised to find what must seem absurd –
the beast was proceeding in a line so straight
and at such a steady pace, without diverging
one degree in either direction from its course,
it made me think a seasoned sea captain
could take lessons from this lowly animal.
It was proceeding at maybe half a knot
as a full moon spilled a splash of light
and sparkled off its horns
and I lagged behind with my motor idling
at a speed suitable for trolling for salmon
until I was at a point where the bovine head
was about to disappear into the distance
and I kept at that distance
all through the night
following that awesomely purposeful beast
as it ploughed through the black and golden waves
straighter than the deadliest arrow
and as I putted along back a quarter of a mile
I sipped coffee and for a while
imagined I was the coach of Marilyn Bell.
And by the time the rosy fingers of the sun
took over from the slowly setting moon
the task of illuminating this strange scene
I began to feel a sense of senseless love
toward the cow I was so senselessly following
for I was not following it with the hope
of somehow capturing it and slaughtering it
and taking its carcass home for my freezer

but rather I was following it
out of the deepest curiosity
and a kind of non-anthropomorphic devotion
for I didn't even know that cows could swim
never mind swim the width of Lake Ontario.

The dawn was quiet as the night had been.
The sound of the softly turning motor of my boat
and the watery whisper of the swimming beast
had calmed my mind to a silence so profound
I could hear the slow soft thumping of my heart.

And slowly as we continued across the lake
in a line so straight I thought my heart would break
the dawn turned into brilliant day
and beyond the black hypnotic head of this fearless beast
a thin blue line rose above the horizon
and I checked my map and compass once again
and realized we were approaching
the shore of Prince Edward County.

We passed Wicked Point and the lighthouse of Point Petre
and entered a lovely bay known as Soup Harbour
which was named, so the story goes
after a ship loaded with kegs of powdered soup
was wrecked in a storm a hundred years ago,
a ship so large and so filled with soup
the wives of settlers in the area
for weeks after carried pails of water
home from the bay and boiled the water down
and served delicious soup for supper.

The sun was almost at its zenith
and from my vantage point half a mile out
I watched as the cow's hooves struck shallow bottom
and it raised its weary body and stumbled ashore
and fell exhausted on the warm dry sand.
But it didn't rest long. It soon arose,
staggered up across a narrow gravel bar,
its udder blue and puckered, barely swinging,
and slipped into a grove a maple trees.

It seemed strange there was no one on the shore
to greet us, no television cameras,
no hordes of well-wishers, no local politicians,
no corporate executives to shower my nameless friend
with free cars and other expensive gifts
for after all her feat was just as great
as those of Marilyn Bell and other mighty swimmers
who have conquered as they say the cold black waters
of lovely Lake Ontario.
But I didn't dwell on what might have been.
I pulled the boat up on the shore
and ran toward the grove of trees
anxious not to let the cow out of my sight
for after following her quietly through the night
I certainly deserved at the very least
to discover the destination of this beast,
to discover the reason behind her odyssey,
and if I lost her now I'd spend my life
torturing myself for having let her go.

Once again, I reached the trees I stopped and listened
and heard in the distance the crunching sound

of heavy hooves on the forest floor
and followed the sound until I came to a clearing
and there I saw a sight so endearing
I'll remember it as long as I live
and maybe even longer.

Just beyond the clearing was a pasture
enclosed by a well-built barbed-wire fence
and in the pasture a good-sized herd of cows
and as you might have guessed some bulls as well
lazily grazed on green grass in the sun.
And there was the cow I'd followed through the night –
my cow as I'd come to think of her –
standing outside the fence looking in.
And as I watched a large black bull looked up,
saw her, and broke into a run.
And several cows and calves came also over
as if welcoming my cow home after a holiday.
And after sniffing each other's noses for a while
the bull, the cows and calves backed up a bit
and my cow crouched down as if about to sit,
then with one mighty leap leaped over the fence.

The nearest town to there was Cherry Valley,
about four miles away. I tried to thumb
but no one would pick me up. I guess
after such a night I looked a mess.
So I walked to town and ate a meal
then phoned home and arranged
to have a car and trailer
driven around the lake
to pick up my borrowed motorboat.

And then I made a few long-distance calls
to various meat plants and slaughterhouses
in the area around Hamilton and Burlington
and after a few calls I talked to a guy
who said they'd had a nice shipment the day before
of cattle from a farm way up on the north shore
and from that shipment one cow had jumped
from the ramp leading to the abattoir
and got away before they could recapture her
but they were planning to start looking for her again
in the woods around Cootes Paradise,
a little bay that flows into Hamilton Harbour.
You'll never find her there, I said,
and then hung up.

And so, I went home and wrote this poem
without even bothering to wash my hands
or change my clothes. And now
I'm coming to the end of it
and as you can imagine I'm really tired,
although not as tired as that cow must have been
after its great escape from the camp of death.
And I know whoever reads this won't believe me
they'll think it's just a lot of bull
and not even very well written.

All I can say is this:
following that cow across that lake
was the most poetic experience of my life
and I just had to write a poem about it.
And maybe that great escape and marathon swim
gave the brave cow only a couple of days more life.

Maybe she went back to the meat plant in the next shipment.
And maybe this time she wasn't able to escape.
Beef cattle are on the same level of anonymity
as earthworms, minnows and the untold thousands
who built the pyramids of Egypt. The farmer
never would have noticed her return.
And her eventual fate I'll probably never learn.
But maybe, my friends, at some future date
I'll find her lying on my supper plate.

THE STORY OF WEASEL TOSSING

GAIL PRUSSKY

People are always asking me to tell them about weasel tossing. Wherever I go, I'm surrounded by hordes of people hungry for information about the sport. I try to be polite.

I don't like talking about it too much. It brings back bitter-sweet memories…

About a hundred years ago, in the village of Babushkin in the Republic of Buryatia, Yuri Kozlov's pet weasels escaped from their shed and began breeding, at a time of revolutionary upheaval left, right and centre. The weasels, having gone wild, threatened the village's economy – the steady sales of chicken-stuffed cabbage rolls and egg blintzes. Weasels were decimating the chickens of Babushkin.

Yuri Kozlov, feeling horribly guilty, came up with an idea: "Weasel Tossing," a competition that required the use of twenty or more live weasels. This encouraged the people of Babushkin to go into the woods and hunt for weasels. Everyone wanted the grand prize – a week in Minsk and a year's supply of beet borscht with sour cream from the monasteries of Novgorod.

The game required strength, a good eye and blood that would clot easily. (Weasels have razor-sharp teeth.)

My great-great-grandmother, Ludmila Popov, lived in Babushkin. She had powerful arms, built up from pushing a single blade hand plow and carrying her crippled husband, Oleg, into town every day to pick up his vodka.

Ludmila won the weasel tossing championship year after year. Decades later, when my grandparents fled to Canada to escape from NKVD persecution, they brought all of Ludmila's trophies with them (mostly electroplated cabbages) as well as Babushkin News articles that featured Ludmila on the cover, grinning toothlessly.

Weasel tossing in small Russian villages in Babushkin came to a halt when all known weasels disappeared. Overnight, there were no more weasels or weasel breeders. For a time, the village folk tried to carry on the sport by using wolverines. They were too large, too rank, too mean.

Then, the village of Izerbash in the foothills of the Republic of Buryatia – seized by a fit of nostalgia – held a competition using farm-raised weasels. They shortened the length of the throwing field, because nobody pushed plows anymore and nobody had arms like Ludmila. And most of the men were drunk out of their minds on vodka and couldn't focus on the far end of any given field.

As a Diaspora descendant of Ludmila Popov, I was asked to be a judge for that year's competition. Of course I accepted and spent a fabulous homecoming week in Izberbash. All the borscht I could eat and a night on the town with Agidel Gureyv, known as the handsomest man in Izberbash because he had the most gold teeth.

Though I watched dozens of rodents fly through the air, the competition was not particularly exciting. Being farm-raised, the weasels lacked a certain ferociousness. Still, I have never felt so alive as in Izberbash. The scent of vodka with a pickle, the pungent odour of weasel glands, the crowds cheering in unfamiliar dialects not heard since the late 1800s, the free cabbage rolls with fresh sour cream for everyone.

I may be a lesser Ludmila, but I have discovered that weasel tossing is in my blood. Plus, more importantly, Agidel Guryev is in my arms.

THAT CHAMPIONSHIP SEASON

MARSHA BOULTON

While the farmers were taking off the second cut of hay and worrying about the rain, I was putting makeup on my dog and worrying about the rain. Go figure. I was going to a dog show.

At sheep shows I have seen that it takes a fair amount of primping to make a sheep a champion. Fluff the wool a little here, trim it back a little there – use a black felt-tip marker to disguise a few white hairs where there should only be black. In dire straits, go for the Miss Clairol.

Cattle breeders use vacuums and hair blowers on their prize beef. They have trunks full of clippers and hair-shiners, hair spray and hoof gloss. And, I hate to tell you this but there was a scandal in the dairy industry when certain competitors were accused of enhancing the utters of prize-winning cows with silicon injections.

People will go to ungodly lengths to try and win a silly ribbon. That notion really struck home for me when I found myself wiping a cosmetic sponge covered with clown makeup over Wally the Wonder Dog's gigantic nose.

It started innocently. A few bull terrier owners complimented Wally's good looks, and said he had "show potential."

That was some solace to me, since he had shown no
sheep-herding potential. Lambs stamp their hooves at him
and he runs away – at top speed, usually aiming for my knees.
He tries to engage the horses by squatting in front of them
and wagging his tail like a helicopter ready for take-off. They
just snort in his general direction. He's good at chasing chickens across of round bales of hay, disrupting the stacking of
anything and jumping into puddles. "Show-potential" sounded
soothing.

It took a year for me to figure out how to enter Wally in a
dog show. When I told him dog-obedience instructor what I
was planning, I was dispatched to a store that specializes in
dog-show equipment where I could find fancy, thin, show
leashes and a chain so fine it could be a silver necklace.

There were isles chock-a-block with doggy things, everything from life-size plastic fire hydrants to bags full of those
impossibly tiny little bows people use to hold the hair out of
the eyes of furry little lap dogs. There was even a special
counter for pet perfume and hygiene aids including whiten-
ing, brightening" toothpaste to go with curved canine tooth
brushes.

Dog foods ran the gamut from puppy to geriatric, with all
manner of gummy bone, raw hide bone and fake salami. Then
there was must be the ultimate in the waste-not-want-not cat-
egory – dried pig's ears.

Real late-pig's hearing devices dried to a crisp for Fido's
pleasure.

Perhaps that explains the toothpaste.

Before I could grab a shopping cart, Moose bagged the
fine chain and leash and whisked me out of the store, muttering something about turning Wally into some kind of "girly
dog."

On the day of the dog show I got out the garden hose and gave Wally a good bath. I brushed him until he shone and clipped toenails. That was it, I thought. Ready for the show. I had a fresh package of something called Beggin' Bacon to make Wally stand prettily and my secret weapon – a lacrosse ball.

I was totally unprepared for what greeted me at the arena that day. A thousand dogs of every variety imaginable stared out of metal cages, plastic dog houses and little pens. There were trailers and vans filled with dogs in the parking lot. In one corner of the arena, huge Old English Sheep Dogs stood on sturdy stands while their personal groomers worked the hair dryers. Scissors and shears trimmed Poodles into some sort of art form, while every silky strand of Lhasa Apso was carefully combed in place. Impossible tiny bows were everywhere.

Moose thought taking Wally to a dog show was the biggest waste of time I had come with since trying to get chickadees to take seed from my hand in winter. We waded through a sea of dogs and dog owners just as the Bull Terrier class was called. I examined Wally. His paws were still white.

Having watched a few dog shows on satellite television, I had some idea of the routine. My numbered arm band was adjusted and I swung into the ring with Wally. He was perfect. Trotted around looking joyful. Stopped dead like an alert statue when I pulled out the lacrosse ball. The judge padded his body, and, at the appropriate moment, Wally looked deeply into the judge's eyes and wagged tail. What showmanship!

Wally won a ribbon. It was unreal. We kept going back in the ring and winning some more. In the end, Wally got a trophy and a handful of Beggin' Bacon. Moose was jumping up and down like a bee-stung goat. I shook the limp hands of losers and realized that these were professional dog handlers. Wally the Wonder Dog had emerged from nowhere and ruined their day. Alas, we never regained our early glory.

The professionals always topped us in the final round. It was going to be a long limp toward winning the title of champion. Moose started developing conspiracy theories: drawing charts showing which judges favored which handler and gripping about American dogs stealing the thunder of Canadian dogs.

Once, when Wally seemed sure to take the top prize, we were called into the judging ring at the precise moment that a neighbouring dog had what would be called a rather large "accident."

"Clean up," shouted the professional handler without a hint of embarrassment. I looked a Wally. His almost-champion face was a twisted grimace that said: "Somebody's in a lot of trouble." It was the same look he gave the Bassett-faced judge. Then he tried to hide from sight by burying his head under her skirt.

"Control your dog," she commanded.

Wally looked up.

Moose added that judge to his list of conspirators.

Our final show was an outdoor extravaganza that promised to bring out the *crème de la crème* of dogdom. Wally was ready in spirit, but not in form.

By mid-summer, he had developed a fair-sized callus on his nose from heading off soccer balls. Then he chased a chipmunk into a woodpile, adding splinter wounds to go with whatever damaged a cornered ground hog can do.

Bluntly put, Wally's nose was a bloody mess of bumps, burises and scabs.

I thought of forfeiting the entry fee. Then I remembered how things worked in sheep and cattle shows. I checked with a friend who is an old hand in the world of doggy showing and discovered that the remedy for Wally's nose was clown-white makeup and a dusting of corn starch.

Where in small town southwestern Ontario was I going to find clown makeup? Stedman's, of course.

Sure enough, on the toy rack facing the vegetable peelers and potato mashers I found clown-white Halloween makeup, non-toxic to children. Stedman's never lets you down.

Applying makeup to a teenaged Bull Terrier is not an easy matter. By the time I finished, my arms were streaked with clown-white, and a whole section of the kitchen floor was covered in a fine dusting of corn starch.

Moose surveyed my handiwork.

"He looks like a girl," was the verdict.

On the drive to the dog show, Wally rolled in the backseat. When we arrived that upholstery was clown-white.

I registered, leaving Moose to exercise Wally. When I found them, they were in a crowd of children putting on a show of their own.

"Batter up" Moose cried. Then he lobbed a tennis ball at Wally who promptly hit it back with his nose. More clown-white was applied. Dusted in corn starch, I looked more like Bela Lugosi than any show-ring belle.

Spectators in lawn chairs lined the show rings.

Chihuahua owners carried their dogs in vest pockets to keep them from disappearing in patches of long grass.

A Yorkshire Terrier passed by, carried aloft as though it was a stuffed town.

Elegant Afghans paused to have their paws groomed before stepping daintily into the ring.

Apparently sensing the odds of an "accident" occurring in such a large number of dogs, Wally commenced howling and barking.

Reluctantly, he followed me into the show ring, squirming to check out the dogs behind him. Then a child on the sidelines shouted, pointing at Wally: "Mom, it's the dog that hits balls with his nose!"

Wally heard the word "ball" and promptly went into a crouch, waiting for the games to begin. I tried to straighten him out and instead he flopped down on all fours.

I looked down the row of dogs. Professional handlers in tweed suits held skinny leases over still-as-stone, perk-eared Bull Terriers.

"Round the ring," said the judge.

Wally lurched to his feet. The idea is for the dog to show off his gaits. But Wally was having none of it. He wanted to sniff the grass for underground moles before he took another step. Behind us, a line of dogs jogged in place like finely tuned dressage horses.

Wally jitterbugged all over the ring somewhere between a trot and a gallop. He jumped in the air and kicked out his hind legs. The crowd loved it, especially when the lease became tangled around my leg, and Wally barked while I twirled around, trying to free myself.

With an arch of his finger, the judge called us for an inspection. Beads of sweat on my brow, sunglasses hung askew.

"Teeth, please," said the judge. I wrested Wally's jaws open, revealing a Beggin' Bacon strip glued to his incisors.

The judge patted Wally's head and a cloud of corn starch poofed in his face.

At the tail end of the examination, the judge tried to check Wally's breeding equipment. Wally suddenly reared back and gave the judge such a look as though to say, "What the hell do you think you're doing, you pervert?"

"To the corner," said the judge curtly. I felt as though I was tugging an anchor. I went the wrong way.

"Miss, diagonal, please," called the judge. I turned too suddenly and tripped. Wally stopped my fall by jamming his head in my face, followed by a full body licking.

"You two are a pair, aren't you?" noted the judge.

We waited in line while the other dogs performed beautifully. My nose was bleeding. Nothing a makeup sponge covered in clown-white makeup couldn't absorb.

Bored, Wally decided to dig a hole, apparently to China.

To distract him and spare the spectators from flying clods of dirt, I pulled out his favorite thing in the world – the lacrosse ball.

Bingo, he butted it out of my hand where it rolled under the belly of an American-bred Bull Terrier whose owner had travelled half a continent to see his dog win a ribbon. The Yankee dog lunged backward in an unseemly fashion. So did the judge, whose heel slipped on the ball, propelling him into the lap of a large lady who may have had a Chihuahua in her vest pocket.

We did not win that day. By some miracle, Wally placed third. The crowd applauded. I wiped my brow, smearing clown-white across my forehead.

"Looking more and more like your dog, Miss," said the judge when he handed me the ribbon.

"Pervert," I thought.

That was the end of Wally's career as a show dog.

The American breeder whose dog won the class asked me if I might be interested in "harvesting" Wally so that he could add his spirited genetics and fine sense of balance to his kemnnel's breeding program. My eyes rolled and the sponge fell away from my nose.

Outside of the ring, Moose took Wally on a tour of the grounds. Man and dog trotted in a straight line.

A crowd of children gathered and Wally shot tennis balls off his nose until it started to rain.

Our makeup melted and that was fine with Moose. I went back to worrying about that second cut of hay, and Wally went back to soccer and searching the barnyard for moles.

KING LOG
IN EXILE

MARGARET ATWOOD

After he had been deposed by the frogs, King Log lay discon-
solately among the ferns and dead leaves a short distance
from the pond. He'd had only enough energy to roll that far:
he'd been King of the Pond for so long that he was heavily
waterlogged. In the distance he could hear the jubilant croak-
ing and the joyful trilling that signalled the coronation of his
celebrated replacement, the experienced and efficient King
Stork; and then – it seemed but a mini-second later – the
shrieks of terror and the splashes of panic as King Stork set
about spearing and gobbling up his new subjects.

King Log – ex-King Log – sighed. It was a squelchy sigh,
the sigh of a damp hunk of wood that has been stepped on.
What had he done wrong? Nothing. He himself had not mur-
dered his citizens, as the Stork King was now doing. It was
true he had done nothing right, either. He had done – in a
word – nothing.

But surely his had been a benevolent inertia. As he'd
drifted here and there, borne by the sluggish currents of the
pond, tadpoles had sheltered beneath him and nibbled the
algae that grew on him, and adult frogs had sunbathed on his
back. Why then had he been so ignominiously dumped? In a
coup d'etat orchestrated by foreign powers, it went without

saying, though certain factions among the frogs – stirred up by outside agitators – had been denouncing him for some time. They'd said a strong leader was needed. Well, now they had one.

There'd been that minor trade deal, of course. He'd signed it under duress, though nobody'd held a gun to his head, or what passed for his head. And hadn't it benefited the pond? There had been a sharp upturn in exports, the chief commodity being frogs' legs. But he himself had never been directly involved. He'd just been a facilitator. He'd tucked his cut of the profits away in a Swiss bank account, just in case.

Now the frogs were blaming him for the depredations of the Stork King. If King Log had been a better king himself, they were yelling – if he hadn't let the rot set in – none of this would have happened.

He knew he couldn't stay in the vicinity of the pond much longer. He must not give in to *anomie*. Already there were puffballs growing out of him and under his bark the grubs were at work. He trundled away through the woods, the cries of amphibian anguish receding behind him. Served them right, he thought, sadly and a little bitterly.

King Log has retired to a villa in the Alps, where he is at present sprouting a fine crop of shitake mushrooms and working on his memoirs, one word at a time. Logs write slowly, and log kings more slowly than most. He has engaged a meditation guru who encourages him to visualize himself as a large pencil, but he can only get as far as the eraser.

He misses the old days. He misses the lapping of the water in the breeze, the rustling of the bulrushes. He misses the choruses of praise sung to him by the frogs in the pink light of evening. Nobody sings to him now.

Meanwhile the Stork King has eaten all the frogs and sold the tadpoles into sexual slavery. Now he is draining the pond. Soon it will be turned into desirable residential estates.

THE LESSON

ANDREW BORKOWSKI

Miss Kalyn spins up the front walk, the kerchief tied tight over her head as if to keep it from flying off. The quick glances left and right, the sunglasses pressed high to the bridge of her nose, shoulders hunched to her earlobes; from her lookout post behind the front curtains, Marlene Mienkiewicz reads the piano teacher's body language and wonders what today's story will be. Miss Kalyn clutches an avocado purse to her side, so it won't be a re-peat of the time she left her bag on the Rexdale bus (the driver, acting on the orders of his superiors in the Masonic Lodge, had driven erratically in order to disorient her into leaving it on the seat). It could be another stalking incident involving the pianist Glenn Gould (whom she believes has never forgiven her for almost defeating him at the Kiwanis Music Festival of 1944 and who retired from the concert stage in order to follow her around town in his car). Or she might have had another brush with the Mafia, (of which she is convinced her Italian neighbour is a member).

Miss Kalyn stops at the door and waits without ringing (because doorbells emit ultra-high frequencies that destroy the hearing) for Marlene to open up.

"How do you do?" she says, as if they were meeting for the first time, then brushes past into the dark hallway, ripening the air with her bad perfume. Miss Kalyn removes her kerchief, allowing tresses of unwashed brown hair to slide down to her shoulders. She does not remove the sunglasses.

"Tell me, Mrs. Menkiewicz," she asks with a nod to the front door. "Do you see a Muskox outside?"

Marlene goes back to the window peeks through the sheers.

"I'm sorry Miss Kalyn, I'm afraid I don't quite know what you're looking for."

"A Muskox. Those cars that all the hooligans are driving."

"You mean Mustangs?"

"Yes. Those. I'm sure one of them has been following me. All the way from Mississauga."

"I don't see one."

"You *can't* see from there. You must go outside and look."

Marlene goes outside and looks. No Muskoxes, just the bulky Oldsmobiles and Buicks favoured by the factory workers who live on Galway Avenue. Marlene can't believe she's doing this. Across the street, Mrs. Schwilpo glances up from the carpet she is beating over her porch railing and fixes Marlene with squint. Mrs. Schwilpo dismissed Miss Kalyn as her kids' piano teacher long ago. So did all the other families who had engaged her. Now everyone is waiting for Marlene to do the same.

"There's nothing," she says as she steps back inside. "Nothing unusual, just our neighbours' cars." A tremor passes over Miss Kalyn's features. Her lips purse and release in a hint of the concert hall smile that once graced the stages of Warsaw, Krakow, and Prague. Reassured, she is ready to begin.

Marlene knots her hands in her apron and looks for somewhere to look.

"Alex is late again," she lies.

"Your son makes a habit of this lateness, Mrs. Mienkiewicz."

A sly timbre colours Miss Kalyn's voice. She understands this exercise, has worked through its steps many times.

"Alex is a busy boy. He's on the student council, he's in a play, he has his sports…"

"*Un jeune homme engagé.* So like his father. I understand. But you must teach Alex to set his priorities," Miss Kalyn instructs her. "You must be firm."

"Yes, of course, Miss Kalyn. You're right."

Miss Kalyn sweeps into the front room and lights on her usual chair beside the piano.

"Well?" Miss Kalyn prompts. "Shall we begin with Blaise, then?"

"Of course. Blaise."

It's a long trudge up to the landing outside her younger son's third floor room. The poster on his door asks "Suppose They Gave a War And Nobody Came?" and its Day-Glo festoons make her dizzy when she stands too close. She clears her throat, giving the boy an extra second's warning so he can spirit away anything she might not care to see, then knocks.

"Yup," he calls. She pushes open the door. Blaise slouches in the beanbag chair by the window. His legs, sheathed in flares of purple corduroy, extend to the windowsill where his clunky shoes bob to the music thudding in the speakers on either side of him. At his side is a large juice tin filled with yellow sand. The statue of the Blessed Virgin he was given for his first communion is planted head down in the sand, the rim of its inverted base smudged with nicotine stains.

Say nothing, she tells herself. Say nothing about the statue. Say nothing about the cigarette butts that she knows are buried in the tin. Say nothing about the briny male odour that permeates the room. Say nothing about the comic books and music magazines overlaying the untouched homework on his desk. Say nothing about anything and maybe her son, her baby, will do this one little thing. For her sake.

"Miss Kalyn is here, Blaise."

"How come? We're not taking lessons anymore. Dad said."

"I know. But – well – she's here, so. Perhaps, we could just humour her a bit longer?"

Blaise cranes around the back of his chair, his features pointed with mischief under the fall of his long shag cut.

"You haven't told her? You were supposed to tell her. Mum, this is so telepathetic it skittishicizes me! You still paying her?"

"We can't just brush her off like that, Blaise. She's a distinguished pianist."

"She's a head case."

"You're the only students she has left. She needs the support of her community."

"Since when are *we* the community? We don't even speak Polish. You know what the *community's* doing? They're laughing at us 'cause we're the only one's who'll let her in the house. "

Marlene points to the photo hanging over his bed.

"Miss Kalyn was good enough for him, the piano player in that band you're so crazy about."

"Nicki Bury? You can't even ask her about it. She just *freaks* when you say his name."

True. Miss Kalyn sees the success of her famous pupil as a personal humiliation.

"Hey Mum, I got an idea. Why don't *you* take the lessons?"

"Me? Don't be ridiculous."

"Okay, so you gonna pay just to listen to her loony speeches? How long you gonna let it go on?" Blaise asks with a pimply leer.

Back on the landing Marlene pauses and tries to reconcile the young cynic in the beanbag chair with the white-blonde toddler who loved trains and wept when she hung his stuffies on the line to dry after he took them swimming in his splash-pool. How did this happen? she wonders. How have I ended up so alone?

She finds Miss Kalyn at the front window, scanning the street for Muskoxes.

"I'm afraid Blaise isn't feeling well again," she says. "He won't be down."

The piano teacher seems not to hear. She keeps her eyes to the street. Striking eyes. Green, tinged with flecks of gold. If only she'd learn how to apply her eyeliner.

"Alex shouldn't be long. I'll make some tea."

Marlene retreats to her kitchen. The vegetables lay unpeeled on the counter. Thad will just have to wait for his dinner, even if it makes him late for his evening shift at the Parish Trust (or the Air Force Association, the Legion, or some pensioner whose taxes he's agreed to do). It's him who started this. Why isn't he here to finish it? The bump and scrape of furniture in the front room tells her that Miss Kalyn is once again rearranging the furniture around the piano – to correct "dissonances" in the room's acoustics.

"So that's where she got to!" said Liz Hejnal, Thad's assistant at the Trust, when someone mentioned that Zosia Kalyn was giving piano lessons. Liz had been in St. Boleslaw's choir when Miss Kalyn was the church organist. "They fancied themselves," she said. "The whole fandamily."

Liz told them how Miss Kalyn's parents came as political refugees *before* the war, which meant they *had* to have been communists. The father spent all his time in the greasy spoons on Copernicus Avenue, holding forth as if he was still in the cafes of Warsaw while his wife worked shifts at Dempster's bakery. Liz said that Zosia was an obvious talent from the get go and nothing was good enough around St. Bolesław's. She won all the competitions, topped her class at the conservatory, almost beat out Glenn Gould at the Kiwanis.

Then she was discovered by Alloysius Ardaszkiewicz, the pianist and hero of the resistance. Marlene saw him at Massey

Hall with Thadeus on one of their first dates. They were introduced to him at the reception afterwards, the shock of white hair swept back from his temples, fingers still hot from the performance as he took up her hand to kiss it. After that tour, he spirited Miss Kalyn off to Warsaw at the age of seventeen.

"The old goat," said Liz. "Him in his sixties, and her barely finished convent school. He takes her back to Poland, tutors her, gives her the big buildup, and then, on the eve of her first big concert tour, he croaks. A stroke, though Zosia's dad swore up and down Copernicus Avenue that he'd been poisoned. Who knows? The old boy had enemies for sure, and once he was gone, the knives came out for Zosia. The official critics dumped all over her. That's when she went off the deep end."

And now it was this: the long bus rides in from Mississauga, students who despised her, and parents who catalogued her eccentricities to fuel the firestorm of gossip that followed her around the neighbourhood.

"Like letting a wild animal into your house," said the mother of one former pupil as they stood in line outside the Crippled Civilians store one Thursday morning

Miss Kalyn comes into the kitchen clutching the windup clock that belonged to Marlene's great aunt Lex.

"Mrs. Mienkiewicz, you must never, never leave such items on your piano."

"But Miss Kalyn. It's not electrical."

"All the same, Mrs. Mienkiewicz. It is metallic and invites the possibility of fields which could magnetize your piano."

Marlene plucks the clock from Miss Kalyn's grip and says, "I will try to remember that." Marlene learned early on that the room with the piano had to be cleared of electrical devices. The record player, the adding machine, and the old tube radio that was a wedding present all had to find new homes. Thadeus' roll top desk had to be locked after Miss Kalyn was caught going through it looking for paper clips, staplers, rulers, and any other metal object that might cause an unwelcome vibration during a lesson.

While the tea brews, Marlene steals a glance into the front room to monitor the progress of the inspection, but the teacher has suspended her search. She stands at the old upright, her hands resting on keys that are yellowed and chipped. The fingertips flutter and twitch but don't produce a sound. Marlene has only heard Miss Kalyn play once, two years ago, when, frustrated with Alex's slow progress on a Chopin prelude, she shoved him aside and launched into a rendition of the composer's *Etude in C Minor*.

"You see Alex," she crooned as she played, "see how the chords in the treble, modulate through the dominant till they reach the subtonic, how they surprise us, how they bound even further up, all the time resisting these arpeggios plunging downwards in the bass. Now the theme, always thrusting at the upper registers. It is the eagle weaving in a sky red with its own blood, major tearing at minor, it is longing and it is defiance. This is your history, Alex. It is who you are. There is no escape. Defeat is inevitable, but hear the great things we make of it!"

The women of Galway Avenue, the ones who have banished her from their homes, say Miss Kalyn refuses to play in front of her pupils because she has "lost her touch." Marlene knows otherwise.

"The music doesn't lie," she told Alex once, "never waste it on people who do."

Maybe that's why Marlene lets the charade continue. Maybe she can't accept that the music has been wasted on her.

"The tea is made," she says, setting the tray down on the coffee table.

Marlene pours into two of the bell-shaped Blue Willow cups she collects from the junk stores on Queen Street, then sits opposite Miss Kalyn who perches on the edge of the sofa and stares into the middle distance as if someone were holding up a score for her to read. There is nothing you can ask this woman. She doesn't cook, clean, shop, sew or knit. She has no children, no husband, no house, nothing that harmonizes with Marlene's experience. So Marlene just sips the tea that she has learned to drink in the Polish style, very clear with lemon, and hopes for a story about Warsaw stirring itself out of the rubble, of the old people sitting among the roses that ring Chopin's rebuilt statue, eyes closed, as if hearing his music on the breeze.

Instead Miss Kalyn's eyes focus on the bookshelf and she sets down her tea with a clatter. She crosses the room, skirts swiping at the furniture, and snatches up a record sleeve. Glenn Gould standing on the ice at Lake Simcoe.

"Oh Mrs. Mienkiewicz, surely you haven't gone over to *Gould*?"

"It's really very good," says Marlene, who checks herself from adding that it was only a quarter at Aberdeen Antiques.

"This!" cries the piano teacher, shaking the sleeve illustration of the muffled little man on the ice. "This is treachery indeed. This is not music. It's just wheels and gears. It is the *clock* on your piano, Mrs. Mienkiewicz. It is machinery where it has no business being! Gould will suck the air from your boys' playing, Mrs. Mienkiewicz. He is one of those *cats* who crawls into beds and steals the breath of children!"

She's off, arms circling as she conducts her resentment.

"They loved him in Russia you know. Your Gould. They gave him flowers. These mechanical men. These theorists! Gould has no idea what he is playing at. He is still a child in his shorty pants."

Miss Kalyn waves aside a plate of the sugar cookies baked just this morning. From the avocado handbag, she extracts the watch that she never wears on her wrist, holds it at a safe distance to consult it, and says, "I am sorry Mrs. Mienkiewicz, but it would appear that your boys have once again missed their lessons."

As if he had been clocking the hour, Blaise turns his stereo up so that a bass line shudders down the staircase.

"Ha!" Miss Kalyn huffs, "So your son has also learned to hide behind his machinery. A real Gould! This rockandroll, it is nothing but a logical extension, I tell you. Machine music. Yes, a logical extension "

She re-fastens her kerchief and returns the sunglasses to the bridge of her nose. In the front hall she turns smartly to Marlene as if to deliver an encore.

"You must remind Alex how to think of his pieces," she says, "He must round his shoulders like a bear in the Liszt. In the Prokofiev, he must rummage among prickly thorns. For the Bach, especially in the *rubato*, he must remember what the courtier says to the lady-in-waiting. Everywhere he must make flutes of his arms and flames of his fingers."

Marlene goes into the kitchen, opens the drawer where she keeps the housekeeping money and makes a quick calculation. If she serves hamburger instead of lamb chops, Tang instead of orange juice, stretches the Sunday roast to two dinners and mixes more powdered skim into the two percent, she can just manage the ten dollars.

"I should not be taking it," says Miss Kalyn. "You must tell Mr. Mienkiewicz he is very generous."

Marlene steps onto the porch and watches the piano teacher spin down the street as furiously as she came. Yes, she thinks, Thadeus will be furious when he finds out, but, after he has come and gone and she is alone, it will have all been worth it, just so she can call her sister M-K and tell her all about Muskoxes and Gould and what it means to have flutes for arms and flames for fingers.

THE CARNATION

LOUISE MAHEUX-FORCHER

At the end of every month, the old woman's son sweetened the account generously enough to ensure that Roger would always extend a deferential welcome to that anachronistic customer, who ate like a bird but demanded just for herself the nicest table for three, at the back of the restaurant.

Punctually and without fail Madame Anaïs would appear at the stroke of noon, when the owner opened the door, and again at half past six, arriving with Mimi, the little flower-seller whose job it was to replace, at the first sign of wilting, the beautiful red carnation that brightened every table.

Kissing Anaïs's hand, Roger would relieve her of her cane and, in winter, the innumerable layers of furs that made her resemble an onion. With the care of a boatman surrounded by reefs, he would then steer her to her appointed place, where, after helping her to squeeze into the seat, he would light the little lantern, shift the carnation to set it off, and arrange the menu to suit her. Nearly blind, nearly deaf, and intentionally mute, the old woman would signal approval with a nod of her head, enhanced by a quivering feather, and a wag of her turned-up chin as it settled itself on top of a cascade of additional chins, forming a ruffle.

Anaïs was nearing the end of her life and didn't have much appetite any more, but she had not lost the exquisite manners of her day; not for the world would she have refused food so graciously offered, even if her dear one-and-only-always-travelling bachelor son had entrusted the trouble of cooking it to strangers.

But truly, that evening Anaïs had no appetite at all! Every spoonful of soup came to a standstill at the first landing of her throat, and it was only with great effort that she managed to tip the little pool of liquid into the next basin.

Anaïs soon saw that she should not keep trying. In fact, she saw that a great blessing had been granted her, that suddenly she had been freed from one more form of bondage. Having all but taken leave of the need for sounds and colours, at last she was finished with food!

Still, so as not to offend anyone, even her son, she accepted the steak and potatoes; but stealing a peak around her, she furtively dropped every mouthful into her lap and folded a corner of her napkin over it. She did the same with the bread and the raspberries, after which she slipped the messy little bundle into her purse and pretended to hunt for…the very thing she was hiding.

Most distressed, Roger ceremoniously scolded the waitress, demanded the missing article, and ordered Madame Anaïs's herbal tea.

It was then that the old woman felt a curious temptation…like the cravings she'd had long ago, when she was pregnant…in those days the object of her desire was never to be found, but now…now…

Standing up in its vase, swaying in the lamplight, with all its lacy ruffles sparkling, the red carnation… Anaïs reached out her hand, drew the flower to her nose, and took a long deep whiff; then, very daintily, her face radiant and her teeth at the ready, she began tackling it from the outer fringe, the way one does with an artichoke…

When she laid the heart on the table, she was vaguely aware of Roger bending over her...

Then, in a voice that deafness made both thunderous and sepulchral, and that out of courtesy she inflicted on others as rarely as possible, Anais told him: "I must have white carnations tomorrow... Will you ask Mimi?... White carnations... The red are a little too spicy... You understand, Roger? Before I start pushing up the daisies, I want to acquire a taste for them!"

And at that moment, with the astonished staff and delighted patrons all looking on, Madame Anaïs decided to leave this earth, in grand style, choking on her own laughter as it cascaded down the tiers of her multiple chins, while on top of her head the feather tossed and fluttered for the last time.

(Translated by Sally Livingston)

EATING AROUND THE HAIR: A LOVE STORY

SHANNON BRAMER

A stray strand of hair, wrapped around a baby's toe or finger, can cause major damage by cutting off circulation. When a toe turns purple or red in reaction to being strangled by a piece of hair, doctors call this "toe tourniquet syndrome."

I was twenty-two years old and having dinner with your parents in a French restaurant in downtown Waterloo, Ontario. It was deep winter in Southern Ontario, cold and snowing. Your mom had short, auburn hair and a serious, contemplative expression – except when she laughed or smiled and suddenly looked like a completely different person. Mostly she reminded me of a squirrel. She looked at me sideways with her dark, brown, listening eyes. Short eyelashes. She was a sex-educator and a nurse. Your father was a high-school teacher with silver-brown hair and a cleft lip. Warm and well spoken. Also: those grey-blue January eyes. The eyes he gave you. I was nervous about having a meal alone with your parents, but you were across town working at another restaurant – a *real dive*, you liked to say – making beef stir-fry and chicken fettuccini. I felt this must be some sort of strange initiation into your life, as I had made a special trip in from

Toronto and this date with your parents was sprung on me. I obediently got in their car and we drove to *La Fraîcheur*. I wondered if they liked me? I wondered if they might take me somewhere and kill me. Instead, we talked about you: when you were nine you wanted to be a ballet dancer. Now you worked with dancers in a restaurant. They hoped the library science degree would pan out.

I ordered the asparagus crepe.

The strand was long, thick and curly. Most likely the renegade hair of a healthy adult woman: tangled and wound around a perfectly steamed spear of asparagus, nestled within the folds of a delicate and artistically presented crepe, smothered in hollandaise sauce. I did not notice it until I was a few bites in and gagged imperceptibly. I looked up at your parents who were both watching me and smiling. At that very moment, your father asked how my meal was. I took a large slug of my Shiraz and washed a section of the long follicle down.

I told your parents: the asparagus was tender, but crisp. The sauce was delicious and not too salty. The crepe itself was the best I'd ever tasted. I told the truth. I did my best to eat around the hair until I realized that the long black enterprise was even longer than I thought, wild and winding like a medieval vine around two-thirds of the three spears – binding them together. I panicked. I suddenly believed that if I did not eat everything on my plate, and do it quickly, your parents would notice the hair and become shocked, embarrassed and disgusted. Not to mention baffled by this young woman who studied theatre, wrote poetry and seemed to have no problem eating hair.

I never told you. I never told you that I ate a hair for you. Or perhaps it would be more accurate to write that I ate a hair because of you. Perhaps things would have been entirely different if your parents had brought me to your restaurant instead. Or maybe it would've just been more of the same; I would have eaten the tough tail of a baby mouse instead of a hair. Who knows? I was that crazy about you. You may not remember me but I still think of you occasionally (particularly when I check for hairs around my new baby's toes!). All the while, I remain wary of crepes.

STRYCHNINE BLUES

JAMES DEWAR

An hour and a half into our Purple Micro Dot LSD trip Wally leaned forward on the couch. He extended his right hand out in front of his face and gazed at it like he had never seen it before. His fingers flexed open and closed a few times. I have to admit I was also becoming fascinated with his hand. Then Wally extended his fingers straight out and said, "Shit."

It was a late Sunday afternoon. We spread out hits of LSD on the dining-room table and eeny-meeny-miny-mo'd through Window Pane, Purple Micro Dot, Orange Sunshine, Purple Haze and What the Hell is This (our pusher threw those in for free). The Micro Dot won. We popped a hit into our mouths and started the eight-hour commitment to the idiosyncrasies of alternate reality.

Now when someone looks at their hand and says, "Shit," it could mean just about anything, but unlikely it's anything good. Only God knows how long it took before I actually heard the word, let alone how long it took for the word to register in my mind. I do recall turning my head in slow motion, looking at Wally's remarkably large, bearded face and saying, "Pardon?"

Wally had enough long black hair to knit a coat. So, as I waited for him to say something, his head became a writing

Medusa. Heebie-jeebies started dancing in my gut. "What the hell are you doing?" I asked.

His hand hovered in the air between us. He opened and closed his fingers like he was trying to make the Vulcan salute. (Which is humanly impossible for most people even if they're not on acid.) His eyes turned to focus on his fingers. So did mine. They were hard to miss, just six inches from my face like that. He exhaled another word. "Strychnine."

At some point in the next minute or so it registered what he meant. Then I said, "Shit."

For the last few months the LSD we had been getting was much quicker on the uptake and provided a little better buzz on the peak. The chemists who manufactured acid were always trying new ways to make the trips better. One of the experiments they tried was to add a wee bit of strychnine. But we subsequently discovered that the benefit of adding a little more buzz wasn't worth the agonizing joint pain that came with putting strychnine into our bodies.

Once acid gets into your blood it goes right into your brain and zaps it pretty good. The chemical itself does not last very long at all. Think of it as a reboot. The acid trip is your brain trying to start the nervous system from scratch and that is where the hallucinations come in. A typical eight-hour high starts slow, gradually moves through the trip into the peak. That's the fun part, until the mind has regained equilibrium, and then it's three or four hours coming back down to reality. Throughout the entire trip, it is impossible to pass out. This is supposed to be a benefit, but when strychnine congeals in the joints of the body and slowly stiffens them, wakefulness is the least desired state of consciousness. Luckily the rigidity isn't permanent, but its debilitating effects last for several hours.

But enough of the science. Let's just say that even in his zapped state Wally recognized, in the telltale stiffness in his fingers, the signs of an oncoming bad trip.

"Better get comfy," he mumbled, stood up and walked toward his bedroom. He returned with all three of his pillows and all of his blankets, and laid them out on the floor facing our old TV.

Wally and I started out living like this together in grade twelve back in our hometown. I had concentrated on excelling at higher education; Wally concentrated on getting higher. Since our current dilemma involved the imminent re-emergence of an experience he had been through before, it was clearly Wally's theatre to direct. I accepted his advice about how to prepare without a single quip and made my way down the delightfully misaligned hallway.

As soon as I saw the toilet in the bathroom I rearranged my priorities. Taking a leak on acid is like putting out a fire at the Royal York Hotel. At least that's what went through my head as I whizzed. The audio coming from the splashing in the toilet accentuated a vibrato in the echo chamber of the bathroom. I was so sad when I ran out of urine. I stood staring down, demanding more liquid. Hotel guests were calling for help from the windows and I had to save them!

"Pillows!" It was Wally's voice bellowing from far away.

It took a while to zip up, and when I flushed the toilet I became fascinated by the water spiralling down the bowl. I flushed it again and again and again.

"Pillows!" Wally yelled, breaking the spell.

I left the audio magic of the bathroom, collected my two pillows and blankets and returned to the living room. Wally had gone into the kitchen and brought out four unopened bottles of orange juice. He lay stretched out on the floor facing the TV. I placed my bedding and pillows beside him and grimaced. My knees were already aching. He handed me two bottles of orange juice, which I placed beside me and completely forgot about.

"Are we going to watch TV?" I asked.

Wally did not answer. His head turned to the left. He was mesmerized by the Japanese fighting fish in his giant fish tank. I deliberately averted my gaze from the blue gurgling, bubbling brightness of that tank. I wasted too many trips staring for hours and hours at the inhabitants of that confined little world saying, "Oh look, it turned left, oh look, it turned right," or "Give it more fish food. Oh wow, it's EATING!"

"Six." Wally said. With an incredible strength of will, he turned his head away from the fish tank and back to the little TV we owned. Channel six was CBC.

"No way," I said. "CBC sucks."

"Six," Wally grumbled. "We don't want to watch anything that will make us move. We have to lie perfectly still if we're going to survive the strychnine blues."

CBC on Sundays carried family programming, harmless shows like *Walt Disney*, *Ed Sullivan* and *Bonanza*. I walked over, turned on the TV, then click-clicked the dial past four and five, stopping at six. I could feel the twinge of pain in my fingers and wrist now. Maybe Wally was right. If we stretched out on the floor, only barely entertained, we wouldn't have to move our joints at all. What a genius.

I turned the volume to a level we both agreed on, then eased down onto the floor beside him.

The commercials were particularly hard to take. Luckily we were immobilized, or in our stoned condition we would have been out buying every bloody product they were trying to sell. It also helped that the commercials were short enough that once the next one came on, we totally forgot about the one that preceded it.

The trip wasn't so bad during *Walt Disney*. It was a movie about a family living in the country with a dog. Just as it started I said, "I hope this isn't *Old Yeller*.

Luckily it wasn't that classic tear-jerker. We were relieved when all the grandparents, parents, kids, neighbours, horses and dogs remained hale and happy to the end. Somebody pulled away in a horse-drawn wagon and everyone started waving like the Beverly hillbillies. I raised my hand to wave back and the pain shot through my shoulder, elbow and wrist, but it was too late to stop. I waved, moaning in pain.

"You should have seen that coming," Wally laughed, and then he moaned too from the pain of moving his jaw to talk and laugh. We both laughed again.

I said, "I hope there's no more waving," and I moaned. Realizing the increased intensity of the stiffness, I made an extra effort to stay still. I lowered my arm slowly back across my aching chest.

By the time the *Ed Sullivan Show* came on we were deep in the throes. Any movement of any kind came with a stab of pain. Ed Sullivan looked like a midget from our vantage point on the floor. It was worth the pain for me to point that out. Wally did not respond to my observation. Then some musical act from South America came on. A huge band played salsa accompanied by dancers in skimpy outfits, everyone smiling so wide I thought their faces would crack open. I realized that my face had changed to imitate those big smiles. Still smiling, I slowly turned my head to see if Wally's had too. Yep. a big hairy Cheshire cat. Then I laughed at how ridiculous he looked.

"Don't look at me," he shouted and then he laughed.

"Okay!" I said with clenched teeth. It hurt. The dancing TV mayhem ended and it went to commercial break. Relief.

A comedian came on next, but he talked so fast I couldn't keep up. He kept saying, "You can call me Joe. Or you can call me Mo. Or you can call me Ray" – not funny. He confused the hell out of me. He was so annoying I fantasized again about the Royal York Hotel, the grateful young women in dresses still smoking from the flames and covered in black soot reaching for me. "Thank you! Thank you!" But their faces kept morphing from colour to black and white. I started to freak out a little. Luckily Topo Gigio came on.

Topo Gigio was a mouse puppet with huge ears that Ed Sullivan talked to at the end of every show. It spoke with a squeaky Italian accent. Topo Gigio was so cute that, frankly, everything that aspired to be cute in western civilization in the following decade would be measured against Topo Gigio.

When Ed leaned over and asked Topo how he was doing, Topo made a squishy face, acted shy, raised his huge eyes tenderly and said, "I wuv you, Eddy."

Wally said, "Awww," then, "Ouch!"

I couldn't believe Wally had actually said "Awww." I started to laugh at him and he shouted, "Shut up!" Then he started to cry.

I laughed because he was crying, and then I felt overwhelmed and started to cry, too. Wally pointed at my tears and laughed and then… We were both hurting badly, but so happy for Ed Sullivan to have an Italian love him like that.

This outburst must have gone on for at least fifteen minutes because when we finally wiped the tears from our eyes and were able to lie still and focus again on the TV screen, the *Bonanza* theme had already started. The Cartwright family riding on horseback, smiling and all friendly-like.

"We should be safe now," Wally growled through gritted teeth.

I agreed. *Bonanza* was an extremely popular family western, a show to showcase the sexiest star on TV at the time, Michael Landon. He played Little Joe Cartwright, the youngest brother on a huge ranch in the old American west. Predictable plots synced with a good Christian moral at the end of every episode. I shared Wally's hopefulness. I could feel every piece of cartilage attached to my ribs now. My jaw ached. Please God, a break from all this emotion.

But it was one of those episodes where Little Joe meets the beautiful young widow who just arrived in town to be the new school teacher. At the first commercial break I said, "Oh no. Little Joe is falling in love."

And Wally said, "Oh no. You know what that means?"

"The school teacher must die!" we said in unison.

I laughed and moaned, then he laughed and moaned, then we repeated. There we lay stuck on the floor unable to get away, trapped in the middle of a sad, sad tale. Little Joe and Betty Lou falling madly in love. Then a crazed ex-con arrived in town to take revenge on the Cartwright family for putting him in prison years earlier.

Wally and I had no way to protect ourselves from the inexorable collision of love and revenge as the drama moved slowly toward the predictable climax. We might as well have been in *A Clockwork Orange*, our eyeballs forced open, listening to the *Bonanza* theme instead of Beethoven's *Ninth Symphony* while the video horror slowly overwhelmed us.

Little Joe knelt on the ground and held the beautiful, dying girl in his arms. She had jumped in front of the gunman as he fired the bullet meant for Little Joe. The close-up of a single manly tear leaking from Little Joe's handsome, manly eyeball pushed us over the edge. Wally and I both started to cry. This time we cycled through weep, holler, sob, scream, sob and moan until the show faded into the closing credits.

I now floated on a pillow soaked with tears and I ached everywhere. I turned my head toward Wally, trying not to notice the snot in his moustache, trying not to focus on the bright aquamarine fish tank in the background, and said, "I hate the CBC."

Wally turned and looked at me, his face red from weeping. "I know. Me too."

"I'll change the channel," I said. But after the monumental effort of pushing through the pain and rising from the floor, I thought I heard calls for help again from the Royal York Hotel. Lurching heroically toward the bathroom and this new source of urgency, I abandoned Wally for hours to the tyranny of public broadcasting. An oversight for which I have never been forgiven despite the number of lives saved.

CRITICS' TAKE

on the Premier Showing of
Tank's Documentary of the Closing Eye

LEON ROOKE

The entire time! The tension! I was pure poured concrete for
four hours and forty-six minutes.

"Right on. It was so right on."

"I don't dare blink. My attention didn't wane even when
you touched me."

"That wasn't me."

"Not even to eat my popcorn? You mean it was the guy on
my right? In the raincoat? His hand between my legs?"

"What a tribute to that movie. That guy could have
climbed all over you and would you have known?"

"Cool. Oh, way cool. Who was that guy?"

"In the raincoat? The director, I think."

"Of *Documentary of…*?"

"Yee-oh! The big chief himself.'"

"Oh God! Say it again! Hank stroked my thighs: Mr. Slow
Motion. The king? I swear to you this man has made a film
the very equivalent of Proust."

"Ah, Proust! Another masterpiece of the first walk was
Proust."

"Eighty-two hours and forty-six minutes of sheer unutter-
able utterance. Who can ever forget Proust propped up in his
cork-lined bed, that semi-dark room, never the smallest noise

save that of ink smacking the page, the single-sustained camera position through eighty-two hours as the dear asthmatic neurasthenic composes the sixteen volumes of *A la recherche du temps perdu.*"

"Time! When has time ever been better comprehended?"

"Yes! And the cup of tea, the bit of cake. The crumbs on his chest. Sheer genius. My heart stopped. It just went pitter-patter and stopped."

"Wasn't Proust a Tank?"

"Definitely. When he was married to that little red-haired girl in the green shoes."

"Whose eye is it in *Documentary*? Do you think it was the Eye of God?"

"It was Mel Gibson's eye, stupid."

"Yeah, but like, whose eye was Mel's playing?"

"There you got me."

"Let's go back tonight. *The Documentary of the Closing Eye* is utter rivetting drama played out on a heretofore unrecognized human scale. When that eye finally clanged shut after four hours and forty-six minutes, it was as though eternity had closed its doors."

"*Closing Eye Two* comes out next year. I hear in that one he's got something in his eye."

"Mel? God? You mean like…?"

"Jesus. That's so – so…"

"Biblical?"

"Yeah. Such a daring treatise on – on…"

"The failure of philosophy. The phenomenology meltdown. Our moral quagmire."

"God, yes. Oh, the agony. I can't wait."

DOUBLE DOUBLE AN' CHOCOLATE GLAZED

JAMIE FELDMAN

Name's Jimmy Sanders. Occupation? What yas mean occupation? Yas picked me up at work. I'm the friggin' Chicken Man o'er the Lick-A-Chick up Little Bras d'Or. I wave to the cars an' stuff, tryin' ta get 'em in ta buy some chicken. I'm still wearin' the suit, ain't I? Can't we just git on wit it?

Alright, well, yas see I's just mindin' my own business. Ain't doin' nuttin'. Well, udder than wavin' an' greetin', ya know, stuff I's s'pose ta do. So there I was, o'er at the Lick-a-Chick in this here chicken suit just flappin' away for the customers when this rig pulls up at the Tim Hortons across the street. Now this rig, I ain't seen nuttin' like it, least not on the island, anyways. They's be turists, like mainland turists with those fancy dealerships. Give me an ol' Chevy any day. Still got my '97, ya know. Runs like brand new. Have to do a little work to 'er, though. Gotta really giv'er when ya start 'er up. Think the alternator's goin'.

Them tourists, they had a Kia. One of those ones advertised on the Tee-Vee that city folks buy. Ya gotta git all the parts shipped in from China or some place. Now a Chev, though, I just git the parts o'er Rick's garage an' do the work myself. These tourists didn't look the type to know their way 'round a rig. Bet the ol' man couldn't even change the oil. An' his woman prolly wouldn't be able ta cook his dinner neether. Anyways, they's a couple, one a them retired couples that go drive 'round the trail in summer, an' they pulled into the Timmy's across the way. The woman gits out an' stops dead, just starin' like at the wall. The ol' man doesn't know what to make of it, right, but then he sees it too an' they both drop to their knees, right, religious like, right? So they both start sayin' a rosary or somethin' like that an' a customer comes out an' he nearly drops his double double on the sidewalk when he see it, too. Soon there's a whole crowd a folks an' the managers tryin' ta essplain they just changed the lightin' an' it's just shadows on the bricks but no one's lisnin'.

It was the friggin' Jesus! Youse know that. Theys all thought they seen the friggin' Jesus himself in the pattern on the bricks on the side of a Tim Hortons. Now I wouldn't think Jesus would drink coffee a-tall, but if he did I'd s'pect he'd show up at one of them fancy Starbucks places up on the mainland. I went an' crossed the street, though, ta see what all the fuss was aboat an' it did kinda look a little like the Son of God, ya know, like how he appears in people's toast an' stuff down south. I saw that on Tee-Vee once, 'boat how some ol' biddy in Alabama thought she saw Jesus in her burnt toast.

So it all started escallatin', right? Like folks leavin' flowers an' candles an' shit at the Tim Hortons, an' turists were comin' from all over. They's all kneelin' an' prayin', holdin' up the line for anyone lookin' for their coffee. I use ta go o'er every day 'round my mornin' break an' order a double double an' chocolate glazed, but now fifteen minutes ain't time enough for that sort a thing! An' I's jist across the street! I tells ya, with all that flappin' an' shoutin' they's doin' ta that wall, put 'em in a chicken suit an' theys coulda been doin' my job. I hear it's a blessin' that blasted Jesus went away. Tim Hortons was losin' money, ya know, even with all them turists. 'Cause ya see none of them drank Timmy's, they just came for the Jesus an' ta hold up the line for the rest of us! Well, we all just started goin' ta the one down George Street by the Casino. Definitely no Jesus there. Not great parking, though, that's where them bikers hang out showin' off their bikes, but them b'ys not gonna hold up the doughnut line, are they?

As for me an' Rick's Garage? I don't see what me workin' there has ta do with anythin' 'cause I ain't workin' there a-tall. See, that's what I's aboat ta tells yas. The last time I went o'er to the Timmy's, the one with the Jesus, I saw my old woman, well ex old woman. Sees I normally take my chicken head off, but I had ta leave 'er on that day so she wouldn't find out. I was s'pose ta be workin' o'ver Rick's place but me an' him had a fallin' out. That friggin' fool says I was stealin' sockets but I wasn't. What would I be doing with his sockets? Then his weldin' kit got all messed up. The tip's worn out. But I ain't got nuttin' ta do with that. I got my own kit out the country. What would I be needin' his fer? So he says I can't work there no more. Can't trust me. I can't trust him! He's right some shifty, that fella is. Rick's been talkin' ta Lorna anyhow. Lorna my ex, yeah. Rick an' Lorna used ta date back before Sandy was born, back before Lorna was with me.

Yeah, Sandy's my kid! What youse getin' at? You sayin' she's Rick's? She ain't that arsehole's. That's fer shore.

I see. You jist need me to say it, fer the statement, like. All right then. Sandra Marie Sanders is *my* daughter. Born 2004 o'er at the General. That good? Good. So I was awful sour seein' Lorna o'er the Tim Hortons that day, 'specially after havin' ta deal with all them Jesus worshippers holdin' up the line. They were somethin' fierce, I tells ya. They don't move for nobody, well, other than the Jesus I s'pose. Anyhow, I couldn't let Lorna see me since she thinks I's still working o'er Rick's. Though I wouldn't put it past him ta have told her I couldn't work there no more. Prolly just ta piss me off. Prolly made some stuff up about me too. Cruisin' for a bruisin', he is. Ya can't trust that arsepick, ya know. He's the one'd steal the eyes out the back a yer head if he had the chance. But I was tryin' ta get custody of Sandy an' the courts, they's always give custody ta the mother even if she is a lyin', cheatin' witch if there ever was one. Couldn't even make a decent stew, neether. I tells ya, if I ever git another woman she's gonna know how ta cook. But Lorna wasn't s'pose ta find out I's been workin' o'er the Lick-A-Chick 'cause we've got another court date comin' up an' that prolly wouldn't look too good, not if I's gonna try an' git Sandy back, even if it is jist every udder week-end.

Aboat Sandy? Well, she's got blue eyes like mine. Rick don't have no blue eyes. Oh, that's not— What you gittin' at? Sandy's a good kid. She's already got her grade eight, so ya know she's smarter than her old man. That's me I'm talkin' aboat.

Security cameras, eh? Wouldn't think they'd have put somethin' like them in out here. We's good folks out here. An' ain't nuttin' inside a Timmy's cost more than a couple loonies or toonies. You sure it was Sandy on the tape? I bet it was one of them mainlander turists that come in. Youse questionin' them too, I 'spect. Besides, the way I heard it, the security cameras were taken out. They's gone an spray painted o'er the lens part. The first thing they did. Real smart, if you ask me.

What ya mean how'd I know a thing like that? The whole town's talkin' aboat it! Everyone knows everything an' even if youse did get someone on the tape takin' out the camera, that don't prove nothin'. How much could yas have seen? A few seconds of someone in a hoodie walkin' up ta the building? No way youse are gettin' Sandy for this. She's a good kid. She don't deserve it. Ya know when all this first happened, the Jesus I mean, when I went o'er in my chicken suit that day? A man sees a lot a things from inside a chicken suit. I saw Lorna that day. Sandy was there too. See, I saw her from across the street an' bein' in the suit an' all I could go see her. No court's gonna say the chicken man can't talk ta a kid. I brought a flyer with me too, just in case, so I could say I was passin' them out if anyone asked. I just wanted ta see her, ya know? She's got them streaks in her hair now like them girls that walk around on the Esplanade. That was her mudder's doin', that was. I never woulda let her do that. Looks cheap an' Sandy's not a girl like that. Ya know I taught her how to use the dozer out the country? That was back before the divorce. Ain't got no dozer now. But back then I'd sit 'er on my knee an' let 'er use the lever that lifted up the blade. Took right to it. She got a head on her, that one, that's fer shore.

I tried to hand Sandy the flyer that day but she didn't want it. Called me a pervert for tryin' ta touch her. Gave me a kick in the crotch. Luckily the chicken suit offers pretty good protection for the family jewels, ya know. Guess I deserved it for lingerin' so long before tryin' ta talk to 'er. But she was whisperin' like, an' even through the crowds a folks I could make out what she was sayin'. She's sayin' she missed her Daddy an' wanted me to come back. She said it, I swear! I ain't makin' nuttin' up aboat that. A girl misses her fadder, that's just how it is, but if she's wantin' me ta come back, then she better talk ta her mudder aboat that. I couldn't believe it, though, nearly shit a brick when I heard her actually prayin' ta it, the Jesus I mean, askin' it stuff like that. She's sayin' stuff like me comin' back home an' wantin' ta drive the dozer again. Okay, maybe not that bit aboat the dozer, but yas know what I mean. I don' think that the Jesus on a Tim Hortons is in the business of grantin' wishes or nuttin', so she musta been awful desperate. I guess she figured that out, ya know, 'cause a couple nights later when I's getting off shift across the street I saw her, ah – *someone* again. That someone had some cans of spray paint in 'er pockets an' was all cursin' up a blue streak. Sayin' things about how Jesus ain't grantin' no one's miracles these days, even if the newsman said it on the Tee-Vee. This was after they had sent down that Bruce Frisko from the city ta put it on the *Live at Five*. Well, that had all the rich mainlanders down here after that. Ya could hardly open the doors ta the place then, there was so many offerings ta it. One night I thought the place'd burn down from the candles. Thought aboat callin' the fire department on account of hazard but them boys'd prolly just blow 'em out so they could get their double doubles an' be on their way, an' them there candles'd be lit again before ya could pick up the phone ta dial the 911.

I ain't say that was Sandy with the spray paint. I said it was *someone*, an' so what if the paint was from Rick's Garage? I ain't steal it. Sandy didn't neether. She's allowed o'er there though. Rick prolly gave it to 'er, prolly put 'er up to it. That is, if she did it. I ain't sayin' that. Heck, you want me to take the blame for stealin' the paint? Go on, pin that one on me. If it saves Sandy I'll take the blame for that. But look, the girl who walked o'er to the Tim Hortons that night, I know she defaced the thing. Drew the devil horns an' tail on it like what's there now. The Jesus deserved it, if ya ask me, trickin' everyone like it did. It ain't no sign from God, just someone else offerin' some fake promises ta this goddamn town that never come true. Sandy knew that an' she ain't deserve an upbringin' like that. Kids shouldn't know that kind a thing yet, ya know. Let 'em have their parties an' proms an' that 'cause there ain't nuttin' ta look forward ta after that.

Look, that's why I went o'er there. Sandy's too young ta have 'er dreams already crushed 'cause the fake Jesus ain't gonna grant her no wishes. She wanted her Daddy, so what's a fadder 'spose ta do? I sure ain't gonna just watch 'er paint the damn thing an' not go o'er there! It was like reflexes. I had ta go. I didn't care if I still had half the suit on or not. Sandy's a good kid an' she'll love 'er Daddy, no matter what he's wearin'. Her mudder already tellin' her I was no good, like I was on the pogey an' spendin' it all on Captain Morgan an' buyin' two-fours fer the boys o'er the pier every weekend. I ain't. So after thinkin' all that, maybe it ain't matter if she found out aboat the chicken suit. Maybe she wouldn't tell 'er mudder, an' Sandy could come in ta the Lick-A-Chick with 'er friends after school knowin' the truth. Her friends wouldn't have ta know, neether. It'd just be our secret.

I tells ya, I was the one who went an' grabbed the tire iron from my truck an' went o'er the Tim Hortons there the night the Jesus went away. Sandy was shocked at first, threw 'er paint can at me 'cause she thought I was a creeper, but then saw it was me an' thought I was gonna bust 'er instead, like turn 'er in ta the cops or somethin'. That's when I smashed the lightin' out. I just pushed Sandy out the way an' took out the bulbs, glass all rainin' down into my feathers, but I didn't care. The Jesus disappeared after that. Just those painted devil horns left on the wall now an' a shrine ta them. We laughed our holes out at the sight of it, we did. First time I seen Sandy laugh in God knows when. I won't take that back for nuttin', even if it does cost me every second weekend.

So arrest me if yas want ta. But I's jist doin' what had ta be done, what was right. I've gotta take care of my kid. You tell that to the courts if yas like, tell 'em I done it for my kid. Theys can't hold it against me fer stickin' up fer my Sandy, fer tryin' ta protect 'er! I tells ya one thing, though. I ain't never had a double double an' chocolate glazed since. It jist don't feel right. Jist like it don't feel right leavin' prayers an' makin' wishes that ain't gonna come true with a fake Jesus on the side of a Tim Hortons. Whatever git's ya through, I 'spose, though. Whatever gits ya through.

EVERLASTING LOVE

CLAIRE DÉ

For me, it's not the same as for my sister Anne: tits-and-ass gets me nowhere. When you look like me – fifteen years old going on ten, no breasts, or even a bush, an oversized head full of oily hair tied with a pink bow, glasses thick as ice cubes, and a mouthful of braces – it isn't leather shorts and purple hair-dye that are going to improve the situation. What's more, in school I'm at the top of my class, in every subject, which isn't hard, the courses are so dinky. Then there's my mother who buys me nothing but "pretty little dresses," and I collect exotic fish in a giant aquarium: nothing you would call a turn-on.

Looking back, I'm surprised that someone of average intelligence, in fact somewhat above average, like me, didn't understand all that, before sleeping with Yves Lachaille. But I fell badly in love with Yves Lachaille the very first time I saw him, playing harmonica in a sort of café steeped in darkness, on Boulevard Saint-Laurent. On that score, too, I'm unlike my sister Anne: she prefers established rockers, those hairy comets who whip up tornadoes inside the temples of pandemonium. As for me, I'm drawn more to performers on the rise, the ones said to be up-and-coming, though I always wonder: coming up from what, exactly?

Anyway, him, with his eyes closed, his dejected dog look, the wolf howls and whale blasts of his mouth harp, he got to me: made me all hot between the thighs, and wet, practically an orgasm. I was done for, Yves Lachaille too: I loved him, I would love him as long as I lived, he was mine, I needed him, right away. *Do it now, or die tomorrow*: that's what they say in English, and my age group can't say it any other way.

Either it was too dark in the café, or the guy keeps his eyes closed even when they're open: it had never been so simple. All I had to do was to wait – granted, till five in the morning – and ask him if he was interested in a smooth little pussy. If it works with members of Parliament, it ought to work with harmonica players. It worked.

Yves Lachaille must sleep with anyone who makes him a fairly straightforward proposition. That's what's so tough in life: conquests are too easy, there's no romance. Or maybe my literature teacher has had me read *Wuthering Heights* too many times. Anyway, it's a lucky thing I'm Mister Trudel's pet – he's my chemistry teacher – because on April 25, the day after my night with Yves Lachaille, I was all thumbs with the test tubes.

The thing is, that fool Yves Lachaille called me again. Okay, he did sleep with me one time, in a rented room on Rue Sanguinet, because he was too drunk or because it was too dark. But to want to repeat the experience without loving me, this I just could not accept. It doesn't work that way with me. Adolescence feeds on the absolute – I don't know who said that. Me, perhaps. It would cost him.

I telephoned and told him to come over. The fool, he probably never even suspected. I let him in through the basement door while my mother was sleeping, and she sleeps very soundly, my mother. I had him lie down in my little princess bed and whispered that he would get harder, that it would be better, if I pretended to strangle him when he came. He believed me, boys like that are willing to do anything for an extra thrill.

I strangled him for real, of course. Strange, but I hadn't read anywhere (maybe they don't tell you everything in books) that, at that moment, their tongues swell and jut out of their mouths, and that they keep their hard-ons. I even put my glasses back on, to observe the phenomenon more closely: yes, Lachaille's hard-on wouldn't go down even when he was dead. I'll have to mention it to my biology teacher one of these days.

I emptied my giant aquarium, a bucket at a time, into the toilet, exotic fish and all. I packed Yves Lachaille into it. Not the toilet, it would have become blocked, but my aquarium, and hid the whole thing in my closet. I'll tell my mother I'm not interested anymore in exotic fish. In any case, she never comes into my bedroom, my mother. No need to, it's always neat.

At my next chemistry class, I'll find out from Mister Trudel how to get hold of two hundred litres of formaldehyde. I'm not his pet for nothing, he won't deny me the information, not me, his brightest student.

They're starting to worry, in the show biz community, about Lachaille's disappearance. I read it in my mother's *L'écho des vedettes*: "There has been no word from the famous harmonica player, Yves Lachaille." Famous…they're always overstating things. Anyway, I'm quite pleased: today my biology teacher said that specimens have been preserved in formaldehyde for periods of over a hundred and fifty years. So, with his closed eyes, his jutting tongue, his erect member, my pickled love will marinate in my aquarium for a long while. So I have the last laugh. Love does not linger so well.

(Translated by Lazer Lederhendler)

TIMOROUS IN LOVE

CHRISTINE MISCIONE

Beautiful man. Beautiful scarf-wearing man. Man under duress, dressed up in a baby blue scarf and studded cowboy boots. Boots up to his knees crossed, and hands on knees are clammy, and hands wear chunky jewels bejewelling clamminess because he's shy. And he's a thinking man, a singing man, a singer-songwriter-soulful man, performing under duress of his dress and audience stares. My favourite song: *Cleavage of Persona and Person.* The lyrics leave his mouth travelling room to ears, entering ears to canals, and words in canals are brilliant, and words wax too abstract to understand. But he's singing about shyness. Debilitating shyness. His own shyness, because he's a shy man. And he's defining shyness in one hundred ears. He's saying shyness is fullness, need-an-audience fullness, and *I'm shy*, he says, filling one hundred ears.

Then in leopard-print pants the next day. Feathered scarf the next day. He's a shy man with defined eyebrows. He's a yellow-pleather-purse man. A heartbreaker. A singer. He's bashful in frilly leotard. Timorous in red lipstick. A man of lace gloves that hold hands with a man in suspenders, and all four hands stroking later in positions For Men Only, on bed sheets For Men Only, with twists and thrusts For Men Only, no women allowed. And what shyness as he struts, his pleather dangling, and the click-clicks of studded cowboy boots. And what fullness as he writes songs that sparkle, with pens that shine, pens writing songs about men and love and shyness, and his work is exalted, and his work is profound, and he's a superstar of a man, a super-extraordinary man, a man like no other around.

And no one knows what it's like to see his shy brow furrow above blue eye-shadow's creasing, as timid blush glitters beside his pink mouth that's speaking. Because he's speaking about love. And he's singing about shyness. And his lip curls to smile, and eyes soften in kindness. And no one knows what it's like to write him an email later, "Ode to a Beautiful Scarf-Wearing Man." Then every day by your computer, fingers clicking beside your computer, mouse scrolling, neck cramping, eyes glazing beside your computer. And every day moving in and out of an email inbox. Waiting in front of an email inbox. Hoping and waiting for a reply, a *Bonjour,* for something, anything in an email inbox from the beautiful scarf-wearing man.

But nothing ever comes.

Instead you watch him in dimly lit taverns. His jade beret bashful. His pink halter shining. He struts and he laughs and spills brilliance in *other* ears, his smile filling *other* eyes, while you're invisible in dark corners, a ghost, a groupie. No one knows what can happen to your heart when your heart sits in an email inbox, ignored. When your heart loves a man of scarves, a shy man, a man nothing like his shyness, who instead clicks his high heels across tavern stages, *click-click-clicking* into ear canals, and dive-bar laughter, and later, *click-clicks* under bed sheets, filling holes in bed with another man.

No one knows how it feels to fill your own bed with straight men. To kiss and fuck straight men. Filler for your hole, because you're not a man yourself. And to always kiss perfect strangers. To floss and smell perfect strangers. Floss your left molar and smell Tommy. In-between canine and incisor, Jake. And bits of Christopher fling onto your bathroom mirror four days after you kissed him because you only floss once a week, and you kiss a lot of men, and all the men you kiss, you kiss to replace the one who has your heart in his email inbox, the beautiful scarf-wearing inbox, the man of shyness and softness and pleather purses that sway.

And how your heart tumbles when he enters the bar! And your brain stops when he throws off his coat! You feel your panties rise with his eyelids – he's opening his mouth to speak: *Love and shyness* in pink lips that glitter – but you have nothing in those panties to rise. A will to rise but no manhood for hardening. No filler for filling. And you're unlovable with no penis. You're incompatible. Incongruous. Instead you're filled with everything inside of you. Full of sex and love *inside* of you. *And shyness is fullness,* a Beautiful Scarf Man once said.

And all the daydreams of gaiety with your shy man. All the fantasies of love with him, filled by him, naked together on bed sheets. And all the sleepovers in fancy pajamas. The pillow fights and giggles. Strolls with your shy man. Baths with your shy man. Bubbles and matching shower caps, lavender creams and tickles. *Oh, the kisses!* And the laughter! And all the pretty things you could do together! You'll ride buses from Hamilton to Toronto, laugh at sculptures in the AGO, pretend you're mummies in the ROM. Then you'll walk Yorkville in matching colours, dine at Bistro 990; you'll order the same thing wearing the same purple and you'll laugh together happily. And when you fall asleep at night, he'll pet your face with lace gloves because you like it. In the mornings he'll wrap you in his satin arms and kiss you, because you like it. Every Tuesday he'll loan you his leopard-print pants because you like them, and he knows that, and he wants to make you happy. Only ever wants to please you. And he'll write you words that sparkle, with pens that shine, lovely songs of whimsy and passion entwined. Then on Monday nights he'll dress in mauve tights with paisley cravat. He'll stand below your window, your beautiful shy Romeo, and profess his love to you, sing in a soprano so high your fullness will seep into panties, run down thighs.

THE PING-PONG AFFAIR

LARRY ZOLF

She was standing on her toes. She was peeking through a transom window at dirty movies. The movies were being screened by the Manitoba Censor Board in the basement of the Manitoba Legislative Building, where I was working at a summer job. It was 1955 and I was one year away from completing my Bachelor of Arts. The calves of her legs were taut. Her flapper haircut set off a very handsome face, and her quirky curiosity set off my own. I joined her on tiptoe. The movie was *Lover Boy Meets the Sex Kitten Bandit,* starring no one. My calves hurt. I could stand on my toes for only a minute.

Flat-footed, I could see that the young lady had a fine figure.

"I'm Larry Zolf," I said. "I'm the shipper's assistant in the Department of Education. I go to United College. My majors are history and poli-sci. You?"

"I'm Patricia Legge. I'm an assistant to the Minister of Mines and Natural Resources. I'm also at United; I go to the Fort Garry campus. My majors are mathematics and physics."

Wow. I had always hated mathematics; it was the one subject that was totally resistant to my capacity for bafflegab. I had failed it twice in high school. In fact, mathematics had helped put me in the "dummy" class – I was too stupid to take physics.

Patricia Legge. My daydream was upon me: I would become the Clarence Darrow of the 1960s, and she would be my forensic expert, my science advisor. Together, we would conquer.

But first things first.

"Would you like a cup of coffee?" I asked with a little woo on my mind.

"Sure."

Patricia Legge was the women's table tennis champion at the University of Manitoba. I had been taught to play ping-pong back in high school, by Holocaust children. After the Americans had liberated the concentration camps, the first items they'd brought survivors were bushels of food; second were ping-pong tables so that the survivors could play while they awaited repatriation. I had never met a teenaged camp survivor who wasn't an absolute ping-pong shark. These survivors had taught me to play hard and fast – back apace from the table, rapid fire, constantly spiking the ball.

The next time I saw Patricia Legge, she was at her porno peephole. The flick was *Hand Job to Paradise*; it starred an ex-sumo wrestler.

"I hear you play a little ping-pong," I said. "How about if I play you a game or two?"

Over the ping-pong table at the Students' Union, I fired one spike after another at the head, shoulders and ample chest of the lovely Patricia Legge. All my spikes were quietly and quickly returned. At the end of the day, I had lost each and every game.

The race for her heart was on full tilt. I took her to museums, art galleries, impromptu campus debates (in which I starred), intramural basketball games (in which I held my own), pool halls and gambling emporia, and bowling alleys. We drank beer in the ladies and escorts section of the Bell Hotel, and visited the odd after-hours club. We went to movies, lots of them, and we did not stand on tiptoes. *Au contraire*.

I had not laid a finger on Patricia. I didn't want to jeopardize our friendship. With my huge hooter and skin-and-bones body, I was no prize package. But we kissed and miracle of miracles, our teeth did not collide. Patricia Beatrice Legge put her tongue in my mouth (no one had ever done that before) and leaves fell, trees bent, sparrows fled. I was head over heels in love. Beauty had aroused the Beast. But because the pill had not yet been invented, and condoms and diaphragms were not common among the mostly uninitiated, oral sex was our delight of choice. We'd sixty-nine in the back seats of cars, in front of the legislative buildings late at night, in the last row of the Capitol and Garrick movie theatres, in the laundry room of her apartment building. We groped on elevators and escalators.

We also studied together, and went to parties and dinners together. We were inseparable.

Pat's mother, however, was not keen on me. Though Mama Legge, an American woman from Wisconsin, was amiable enough during our first meeting, she was wary, and by the end of the visit, disapproval was in the air.

"I'm Larry Zolf. Is Patricia home?"

"Yes, of course! Come on in. Have a cup of tea. How are you? How's the university?"

"I'm fine. So is the university."

"Have you known Pat for very long, Mr. Zolf?"

"Three weeks, four days, eighteen hours and twenty minutes – and I've never had so much fun in my life."

Images of "fun" popped into Mama Legge's mind. The images looked very much like stills from a porno movie.

"Isn't today Yom Kippur?" she asked, trying to clear her head. "My associate, Mr. Flink, took the day off to fast. Can you have tea and cookies?"

"I'm a socialist, Mrs. Legge, and to be a socialist, you have to eat every day, even on Yom Kippur, so that you are strong enough to bite the capitalist enemy – like James Richardson and Sons – in the throat. Pat tells me that your husband slaved for the Richardson family for thirty years before he passed away. And, if I'm not mistaken, there was no pension. This wealthy cartel that holds Winnipeg by the throat provided no help to you, the widow!"

My odd looks, my socialist views and my quasi-vampire attitude repelled her.

Later, Mama Legge felt obliged to inform Pat that Jews were descendants of the Devil, that Jews cast spells on beautiful gentile girls in order to do with those girls what they wanted. Pat and Mama Legge quarrelled bitterly. Hair was pulled, blouses ripped, ankles kicked, faces slapped.

"Patsy," I said, when told of the episode, "if I could cast spells don't you think I would have gotten rid of my *schnozz*?"

With tenderness and affection, Pat fondled my nose, my spare sex organ.

PSYCHE FROM HERE

ANNE DANDURAND

I remember exactly how everything started. It was a night in the middle of March, glacial and moonless; nonetheless I was naked, curled up under my electric blanket that was set at maximum heat. I was pretty sure my bones would never be free of winter.

I wasn't sleeping. I wasn't even trying. To tell the truth, I'd surrendered to insomnia ages ago (in this tormented world I can't help but keep my eyes open, it's a question of anxiety). That week it was the five thousand corpses done in by mustard gas in the city of Halabja that were keeping me going. Setting me off.

My next-door neighbour was listening over and over again to that song of Corey Hart's: "I wear my sunglasses at night, so I can, so I can…" Later, I got to thinking that on that night the whole universe was conspiring against me.

It all started like this. I felt a length of warm fur tremble along the tips of my fingers on my left hand. I shivered. It didn't feel at all like Chansonette, my grey civet cat. It bore a terrible resemblance to a man's hair, thin and fine! My heart pounding, I turned on my amaranth lamp and lowered my only defence against calamity, but there was nothing under the wrinkled sheets at all!

And no person either!!!!

I was beginning to believe that I was having a postdated hallucination from my only acid trip (ten years ago), when I noticed Chansonette in a crouching position, two meters away.

Her gaze was rivetted on a corner of the room, a completely uninteresting corner cluttered with old shoes: her pupils wide, she was staring at a precise point in space, at about the height of a man.

Yes, of a man.

Then, just as she does when you stroke her, Chansonette lowered her head and closed her eyes, and I heard her purr particularly loudly. She went so far as to lie down on the cold floor, completely displaying herself, opening up her little underbelly for a caress, an obscene little kittenish trick that she had so far reserved for me. Always, just for me...

It should have sent cold chills down my back, but I blushed as though in front of a fire.

❧

The next day it rained. When I began to get drowsy around the same hollow hour I took some precautions. If I were to hold my breath for just a moment I'd have certainly fallen asleep. So, I didn't bother turning off the television. I had pirate cable channels, and with the music station on, submerged in the trembling light of a Pierre Flynn clip, I had the vague sense that these lines were endlessly streaming by: "Searching through the broken nights of capital cities, I followed her and lost her so many times." But I'm not sure about that since my memory, grown quiet at last, also dozed off.

Around five in the morning an electrical failure woke me up. Or to put it more accurately, I was shaken by the sudden silence. No more rock music, no more rattling humidifier, nothing. Curiously, the room smelt of grass after a rain, but also of summer sand, and when I concentrated hard enough, I picked up the sweet scent of hyacinths. I saw nothing but Chansonette's eyes glowing in the black room.

Then I heard my pussycat let out a little cooing sound. I guessed she was languishing in that uninteresting corner, and if I also let out a moan, it was not from fear, but from desire. Hermits must feel the same way when inspiration draws them forth.

As though to avoid frightening me, someone lightly touched my hair, then an imperceptible but delicious kiss was placed on my shoulder, and I had the taste of a feast in my mouth, or more precisely, a mouthful of ouzo first, then ripe, black olives, bursting with sun, and then goat cheese flavoured with basil and a drizzle of olive oil and, finally, the delicate sweetness of a honey and puff pastry.

When I felt a man's feverish and angular hand (yes, a man's hand) on my belly, and especially when I felt someone nibble the nape of my neck – which electrified me right down to my toes and soaked me between my legs – it was irresistible, I couldn't hold back, I wanted to see this exquisite intruder who knew me so well. I picked up my lighter from the bedside table and lit it.

My bed and my room were just as empty as my heart. Chansonette eyed me scornfully, as though I had ignored a painfully obvious detail.

There was a tearing inside me.

The next morning I understood. That same night I closed the coral blinds as a reddish moon was rising, I put clean sheets that smelled of hope on the bed, and perfumed myself a little too much (as I always do when I have a date).

Naked, I stretched out, more ardent and tremulous than noon-day heat on the road.

Chansonette was at her post in the corner that was now becoming interesting. I waited, and waited, I was absolutely patient, but it wasn't until an hour before dawn that a distant and indolent chant began to slowly move toward me, with its ancient harmonies of sistrum and lute. As a precaution, I closed my eyes and had a vision of a host of sprites dressed in madder and absinthe-coloured muslin. They formed a smiling ring around me.

The same stranger lay down by my side. His erect penis against my hip, its satiny pulsations, and I was faint. I didn't move, afraid that the charm might be broken. His hand wandered over my entire body as though to awaken the blood, but there was no need: my heart was battering me to the breaking point: the stranger was quivering too, his knee opening mine, his lips opening mine, I imbibed his sweet saliva, our breathing in tune like an orchestra, the grain of his skin as smooth as youth, his chest teasing my nipples, his navel touching mine, his palms meeting mine, and he slipped into the ravine between my thighs, grasping the knot of my desire with his breath, his mouth, his tongue, with all his soul. As I ascended the spiral of sensuality my last lucid thought was that only a god incapable of any form of violence could love me so well.

When I awoke, dawn cut its blond light into the coral blind, my room still swaying in fragrant murmurs of the sea.

Later that day, I decided on an experiment.

Spring was streaming in, blushing at its belated arrival. By noon, the sun came showering down, the air dancing, drunk with heat, motorcycles crisscrossing like mysterious flaming swallows.

I locked myself into my windowless bathroom. Chansonette was curled up in the sink, as was her daytime habit. I bolted the door, just in case. I started to fill the bathtub with water and groped in the pitch dark for a sachet of dried flowers and two handfuls of coarse salt to soften the skin, which I added. I lowered myself into the hot water. To be on the safe side, I closed my eyes. Would he come?

My right hand was dangling over the steamy edge of the tub. A cooing sound from Chansonette was the first sign. Then, just as happily, the chant of the night before drew near with the step of a gentle doe; delicate fragrances of seaweed tinged with orange coiled around me, and a fleeting breeze like a fuchsia petal touched my wrist.

Before I melted into the euphoria of his presence, I breathed: "Who are you?"

He held me close and enchanting zephyrs raised us into the atmosphere, so much higher than cities or anxieties, and he whispered into my left ear, "Of all my brothers and sisters, I'm the one your heartless century has wearied the most, ravaged the most. I am only Eros."

My poor soul faltered, marvelling. He added, "You saw me as a vulture, a jackal, I've been so hurt… Oh, I was only waiting to love you… Finally, you're here, finally, you're here for me…"

His voice sounded as if it had been drawn up from the depths of ages, but it was tender enough to make you weep. I kissed him at the base of his throat, then over all his face. I traced the corners of his lips and ran my hands through his hair dark with secrets. He laughed and I laughed too because I'd lost the whole burden of my pain. His belly quivered against mine. Ivy and cypress at once, we each wrapped a leg around the other's waist. I opened up onto his lance of joy, and our bodies' cantata rose up in powerful tendrils, sky and sea and flesh entangled, all the echoes of the earth suddenly voiceless, the tortured losing their distress, bombs losing their roar, and I discovered that, in the face of evil, there is nothing but love, the love so close to me, within me, and later, infinitely later, he said, "I chose you especially for your words, the words you write in darkness and doubt…There are so few who celebrate me now. Let me love you, love you forever, even it if will always be in the most complete darkness…"

❧

Fate will not have the last word with me.

To make room, I threw out all my old shoes the next morning. Then, sitting on the floor in the corner that was now of considerable interest, I discussed the situation with Chansonette. We came to an agreement: nothing is irrevocable and the twentieth century still has something beautiful about it.

I ransacked all the boutiques on St-Laurent. I tried on almost a thousand pairs, and bought the darkest ones I could find.

For Eros, always, I will not be seen without my sunglasses.

(Translated by Luise von Flotow)

NARCISSISTIC EB AND UNLUCKY FLO

LEON ROOKE

We were down among the strippy currents basking in the afterglow of having torn ourselves apart when my true love said, "You should let some of your feminine side out." I said, "If I let it out it will most certainly be slapped into prison."

She said, "Give it a whirl."

I let my feminine side out just for a minute and instantly it started dancing on its toes. It was going at this big-time.

"Put it back, Eb," she said. "You let too much of it out."

"Well, gosh!" I said. "Well, golly!"

I tried putting the whole thing back, but it ran one way and another and soon disappeared. It had gone to Florida. It had gone to the Sunshine Coast. Gone to where it could wear a bikini without being cold or arrested for conduct unbecoming to—

"I'm not hanging in with you any longer," she said. "You've gone all nasty masculine."

"My feminine side has gone to a place where it can fulfill its destiny."

"Get off me," she said. Get off me now."

"I found it hard to love my mother," I said. "She was a hard woman."

"Sometimes I hate people," she said. "I hate people who refuse to comb their hair. I'm very fond of feet, though. I have very nice feet. My mother used to tell me that. 'You have very nice feet, Ruth,' she'd say to me. Ruth was my sister. Mother was always confusing one of us with the other. She led a very confused life, my mother. I believe she never enjoyed a sturdy moment. She saw life through a prism of her own devising. The dog was the one party in our house able to tell Ruth and me apart. She was a most excitable dog. The house shook from that dog's excitement and then you'd discover it was excited over nothing. Except that time the house burnt down. That time was different."

"Are you done?" I said. "Are you quite finished?"

"Would you please get off me," she said. "I can't breathe down here. I'm dying. You ought to go to the gym and lose that flab."

"What was all that stuff about dying with your boots on, I wonder?"

"What stuff?"

"I never got it. That "boots on" business. What was the point? There was a lot of stuff like that in my childhood that I never got."

"Me, too. Like how you got me."

"That boot business bothers me. I'm a deeply troubled guy. Yet this is pretty good, us here like this. If there were a heaven, it would be exactly like this. Look, there's my feminine side coming back. Wow, get a load of that outfit. Been shopping, I guess. A flaming dyke!"

"Arsehole."

'TIL DEATH

JULIE ROORDA

Who says romance is dead? If you believe that, I guarantee you'll change your mind by the end of this Haunted Tour. Of course, the fact that you've come out for this special Valentine's Day edition suggests I'm probably preaching to the choir, as far as love is concerned, but there are always a few skeptics. Take hold of your sweetie's hand now, and cuddle up close; it's not just the February wind chill that's going to make you shiver on this trip.

Now, if you'll gather around me here, I have a question for you: How many of you carry smartphones? As well as affirming your faith in the undying nature of love, this first example may serve as a cautionary tale. Look around. You may not think there is much to see here, just a typical Toronto back alley, some run-of-the-mill graffiti. There are streetlights, which means it's well-lit at night. But those were of no use to a young woman who took a shortcut early one November evening, just a few years ago. As she entered this intersection with the alley that leads to the street, she was blowing good-night kisses to her young lover by videophone. She didn't notice the garbage truck that was barrelling down on her. The driver saw her, honked and tried to stop, but the young woman didn't even look up as she stepped directly into the truck's path. Didn't have a chance. Her boyfriend saw a rush of dark sky and buildings flash across his screen as the woman's phone flew through the air upon impact and then clattered to a stop on the ground, where it relayed to the horrified lover one last shot of his girlfriend's feet sticking out from the truck under which she was pinned before his screen went black.

Reports started coming in a few years later, always from people taking the same short-cut after dark. Just as they enter this intersection, their phones ring. When they answer, they hear nothing, but feel a presence and an overwhelming sadness that makes them certain someone is there at the other end. The calls are always from unknown, untraceable numbers. In at least one instance, the person was sure her phone was turned off, yet it still rang.

I can see several of you nervously patting your pockets, but don't worry, the calls come only if you are in this alley alone. Those who have just parted from a lover are particularly vulnerable. So, stick together, look both ways, and there'll be no calls tonight. Shall we move along?

This is a charming little church, more than a hundred and fifty years old. There's no need to go inside, but if you'll just stop here in this courtyard, I'd like you to listen very carefully. Do you hear that? A grinding noise – it's faint, but quite distinct – like the sound of a handsaw cutting wood. No? Perhaps you need a more practiced ear, like mine.

Although it now belongs to the Unitarians, this church originally housed a Lutheran congregation. Many of the couples who married here were of German descent, and the Germans had a tradition requiring the newlyweds, upon exiting the church, to saw through a log together to signify the beginning of life-long partnership and cooperation in even the most mundane and practical aspects of life. Couples took part in this meaningful ceremony for centuries, and aside from the odd severed pinkie, it was entirely safe. Not so for one unlucky couple in the 1920s. The bride created a bit of a sensation by wearing a long lace veil — they weren't a common fashion with regular people back then, especially among austere Lutherans, but this young woman was a trendsetter. The couple were full of joy and energy as they began sawing through the log at record speed, obviously perfect life companions. Then disaster — the lace of her veil caught in the teeth of the blade and yanked her face down against the log where the saw sliced clear across her throat, severing the jugular. It happened so fast, witnesses could hardly fathom what they'd seen, least of all the poor groom whose last lusty heft on the saw had ripped his beloved away from him forever. But the groans of that saw — many say they resemble sobs — those sobs can still be heard today, forever echoing the memory of young love cut tragically short. Forgive the pun.

Zip up your coats, we're going down the street to a children's playground — not the kind of place you want to hear about sightings. I can assure you this particular presence has never been spotted during the day, only after nightfall, so your children can continue to play here without fear of being spooked.

What I want to show you is the wading pool. It's empty now, of course, for the winter, but I'm going to tell you about one summer evening, shortly after the pool was constructed, about forty years ago. Toronto was experiencing a heat wave and the pools all stayed open later than usual. But eventually, evening arrived and a city worker, a man in his fifties came to drain the dirty water. He'd recently celebrated his twenty-fifth wedding anniversary for which his wife had given him a gold identity bracelet. The truth is, he wasn't that keen on the bracelet, found it a bit fussy and feminine, but he loved his wife dearly and wore it every day with pride. You can imagine it was to his great dismay that evening when, just as he reached into the last bit of water to clear some grass from the drain, the clasp on the bracelet opened and followed the water down. Desperate, the man reached into the pipe as far as his arm would go, lying down on the ground to reach deeper. What he didn't realize was that a valve, just a few inches down, would close automatically once the draining was complete. Severed his arm just below the shoulder.

Since then there have been several reports, usually from young lovers liaising in the playground after dark, of a hand reaching up out of the drain, clenching and unclenching the fingers as if it's trying to grab on to something. Some accounts describe the arm as wearing some kind of a shiny bracelet; others say it is completely bare.

What's most interesting about this case is that the man in question survived the accident – albeit minus a limb – and lived another twenty years. Yet sightings of the arm began within months of the event. It's as if the arm possessed a reality of its own. I reported it to Ghost Hunters International and they said such visitations by phantom body parts are not unusual at all. I had my gall bladder removed a few months ago. I'm really looking forward to its manifestation in spirit form once it has grown accustomed to its new circumstances. It may have something very interesting to report, which I will, of course, incorporate in future tours.

I thought it would be appropriate to end at the most romantic of the sites – this charming little house. Though it's abandoned and boarded up, people swear it gives off twinkles of light from time to time, usually in winter. You might catch some glimmers now, if you look closely. It was a young couple's starter home, and they wanted to make their first

Christmas here perfect, so on a snowy evening not unlike tonight, they came outside to decorate the front porch with a string of coloured bulbs. They managed to attach the string to the roof, but when the young man went to plug it in at an outside socket just near the ground, something went terribly wrong. The outlet was severely corroded, as it hadn't been used in years, and when his hand, wet with the snow came in contact, it sent a jolt of electricity through his body so strong it killed him in seconds. It is unclear whether his wife grabbed hold of his hand because she saw what was happening and preferred dying with him to being left alone, or if they'd just never let go to begin with. The two were found the next day, burnt to charcoal, buried in a layer of fresh snow, their hands fused together for eternity.

Happy Valentine's Day, folks. I hope you'll all return for another of my walks. I'm planning an absolutely unforgettable tour for Mother's Day, starting at the laundromat next door, where a young mother playing hide-and-seek with her child hid herself inside a mega-washer. No one knows exactly how the machine got turned on. But, ever since, those appliances have been known to start up on their own in the wee hours ever since. I promise the tour will be scintillating. What better way to celebrate the woman who gave you life?

THE CANADIAN ACCENT

MARK PATERSON

Drew was shorter than the other boys I grew up with in Fresno. And, over the summer before our first year of high school, he got chubby. Such physical drawbacks might have made other boys quiet and shy, but Drew was a brazen weirdo.

He could talk me into anything. Like taking Public Speaking as an elective. Drew delivered speeches about the Sandinistas and punk rock. He argued for the impeachment of President Reagan. One of our assignments was a demonstration speech. We sat through How to Iron a Shirt and How to Make Origami Cranes. Then it was Drew's turn. He walked to the front of the class with a bag of groceries and announced: "This is how to make a sandwich." On Mrs. Adams's desk, he sliced an enormous French bread in two, lengthwise. He spread mustard on one half, mayonnaise on the other. On the bottom half of the bread he laid a layer of ham and, on top of that, capicola, alfalfa sprouts, tomatoes, cheese, onions, and pickles. Then he added banana slices, cooked spaghetti noodles, soy sauce, honey, horseradish, potato chips, and Peanut M&M's. Delicately, he set the top half of the bread in place.

Then he took a bite.

One day Drew announced he was joining the water polo team. I didn't even know our school had a water polo team, but my name was already on the signup sheet, under Drew's

It turned out I was pretty good. Coach pegged me as the hole set and I played nearly every minute of every freshman game. Drew's hands were weak and his swimming was weaker, but he made his mark in other ways. Like fashioning a Soviet hammer and sickle from yellow felt and stapling it to his red Speedo. Coach told him to keep his commie ass out of the pool until he got a new bathing suit.

Daily exercise brought on near-constant hunger. The Snack Shack at school sold Hostess Fruit Pies for seventy-five cents. We wolfed them down before and after practice. When we went away on tournaments, we depleted the towns' convenience stores of their Hostess stocks.

When we went to Sacramento, Drew borrowed his dad's Super-8 movie camera for the weekend. The first night at the motel he crammed the whole freshman team into one of our rooms, dressed in our Speedos and water polo caps. He flipped the beds up against the walls to make space. He had us lie on the carpeted floor and he filmed us eating pies. It didn't take long for it to turn into group wrestling, with pie.

We cleaned the various fruit fillings from our bodies with a swim in the motel pool.

Drew planned to send the footage to Hostess's head office. He showed us the address printed on the package of an apple pie. There was excited talk at school; we'd all be rich from an endorsement deal. The film came back from the developer's completely black. There hadn't been enough light in the room.

When Christmas break came around, Drew and his family flew to Montreal to visit his grandparents. He was gone until the second week of January. School was dull in his absence. When Drew finally came back, he announced – in a heavy British accent – that he'd had a blooming good time.

It was funny at first, but he kept it up all day. And the next. Our Geometry teacher said that's not how people speak in Canada. Drew said, "My good sir, I beg to differ." Mr. Cosgrove shook his head, sighed, and went on with finding the value of x.

At practice, two seniors waded over to Drew and threatened to kick his ass if he didn't start talking American again. He insisted he couldn't help it. "The Canadian accent is in my bones." One of the seniors held Drew's arms behind his back while the other twisted both of his nipples, hard. Drew screeched and pleaded with them to stop, his accent unwavering. There was a lot of splashing. Finally, Coach blew his whistle. He told the seniors to save it for their girlfriends. They swam away. A few of us freshmen gathered around Drew. His flabby pectorals were pink, the nipples erect, swollen, and raw. He shook one fist in the air and called out to his attackers, "Bloody ruffians!"

A week went by. Even I was beginning to believe Drew's accent had permanently changed. We walked down to the Golden West at lunch one day. When our meals came, Drew asked the waitress for vinegar. "What for?" she challenged.

"Why, for the chips, of course."

"You don't got chips."

"Pardon me," Drew said with a snooty laugh. "For the *French fries.*"

"For the French fries," the waitress parroted.

"Everyone puts vinegar on their French fries in Canada."

"Last I checked, this isn't Canada."

"I would still like some vinegar, if you please."

The waitress returned with a little bowl. She deposited it roughly on the table. "Here's your vinny-gurrr."

She turned on her heel and left us.

"Can you imagine being so miserable?" Drew's accent was gone.

I tried the vinegar on my fries. It was smashing.

QUEEN ELIZABETH VISITS THE ELKS BINGO HALL

KAREN LEE WHITE

Everybody will be at the Whitehorse Elks Bingo Hall tonight, including the Queen. For the big prize. When they open the doors, look up on the stage. Yup, the Queen's overseen every bingo game since this bingo opened. She's way overdressed. But the night she did show, she wasn't.

You know the formal dress rule in the Yukon is you don't upchuck on your date, right?

Yup, look aroun', people are wearin' their lucky winning jackets. You s'pose anyone wears Depends like those hard-core casino gamblers? So they don't have to stop and go to the bathroom?

Queen Elizabeth's face is more familiar than my mother's. Think about it. I had to stare at her aaaaaaall day, every day in the Chooutla Residential School. She looked down regally from the wall in every class. As if us Indian kids needed an extra eye on us. I was lucky if I saw my mom and dad for the summer.

Here's a question. Why do you s'pose the Regent's sash in her portraits don't say "Queen of England?" Like the "Sourdough Rendezvous Queen," or "Miss America?"

When you walked in here just now did you notice everyone stared at you? Openly, or surreptitiously? Yeah, good word, right? I do those Word Power quizzes from *Reader's Digest* in the outhouse. It means "sneakily," by the way. If folks in here don't recognize you they wanna know who you are. It's about their mojo. Their "Bingo Feng Shui." Bingo is life and death here. People will stare, but they're a little superstitious so the usual cultural etiquettes go right out the window. Etiquettes? Means politeness, giving you the Indian nod. Mos' people will act like they don't know you even if you are cousins. Until you say something, they'll outright ignore you. Yep, bingo is serious business.

Were you here when Queen Elizabeth and Prince Phillip came by to play a game? No? Oh yeah, of course, you weren't born yet. You missed quite the event. It wasn't part of the official Royal Tour. They came to Whitehorse the summer of 1959. A stinkin' hot day.

Well, jeez. Canada brings them into the military airport in a Transport Canada plane. Like they are cargo. We're all expectin' a Royal Aircraft with a crown on the side. That's the first let down.

The Queen descends, I mean, *descends*. (*Glides*. Sheesh.) She kind of glides on air down that gangplank, or whatever you call plane stairs. She has her white gloves on, I guess to avoid germs from the hands of her subjects. She shakes hands with just her fingers. She's only been the Queen for seven years, but she has her moves down.

Somebody has lined up an Inuit kid to present her with flowers. The kid forgets the Royal protocol, and the Mayor has to remind her to curtsy. The kid has obviously been practisin' that for weeks, but I guess she gets Queen-struck. The Indians are wonderin' how come a local Indian kid isn't cool enough to give flowers. We woulda handpicked our own Royalty that wouldn't forget the curtsy. I mean, it's not like there are any more than three Inuit in the whole territory, for Chrissakes, maybe three. And they're just in town to buy a truck at Yukon Ford and hit the Dempster back to Inuvik. Anyways.

The forgetful Inuit does a perfect curtsy at the end, and the Queen doesn't even smile. Holy. Poor kid. Probably thought she was in trouble. Ah, us Indians are born in trouble, anyways.

So, Main Street is all gravel back then, and it's been oiled and watered and all to keep the dust down. The old girl is walking along in her high heels beside Prince Phillip. Tryin' to look interested in our old cowboy town. To give her credit, she didn't even turn an ankle on that dirt and gravel. She looks off. Not smilin'. She looks like she wants to puke for the whole time. We all think she doesn't like the place. It turns out there's another reason.

Anyways, the first stop for her is MacBride Museum. The only interes' the Queen really shows is in the gold nuggets and jewellery that are on display for that day only for their viewing pleasure. I mean, who in their right mind would have a pan full of nuggets in the museum for anyone to just pocket? Well, the Queen does. No. I swear. Second let down.

The curator, (attendant, for Chrissakes), was my great-uncle Bill MacBride. Yeah, *the* Bill MacBride. He tol' me. She sees them, and pockets them. There's this big necklace with a big-assed cross, all nuggets, and I guess when Uncle is showin' it to her she up and puts it in her handbag! No shit.

He doesn't say a thing. I mean nobody says anything. What are you going to do? Tell your Queen that she needs to hand over the nuggets because they aren't hers? People are dead-shocked. Standin' there like twelve-year-old boys with their mouths wide open.

I bet whoever owns that big expensive necklace, I think it was the Logans, had something to say about that later. I mean, that damn thing is worth a bloody fortune. The nuggets were huge! The Queen must have been a weightlifter. I mean, she has that thing in her purse, hangin' off her wrist, for the whole day after that.

And, five years later when Billy Charlie won that trip to England in that contest? Says he saw that necklace on display in with the Crown Jewels. He snapped a picture. You know, that was a conspiracy. Guess who had held the contest? Yup, Logans. Interesting, right?

Anyhow, we're figurin' the Ruler doesn't like Whitehorse because we've heard the rumour about the "fin." Fin is what we call the five-dollar bill. So, the deal is that the 1954 five-dollar bill is the first to have Queen Elizabeth on the front. She has been Queen for a year and I guess the Bank of Canada think they oughta replace her late dad's picture with hers.

Well, it doesn't take long for conspiracy theorists to get into the act. They say they can see a devil's head in Elizabeth's hair. Doesn't say much for British hairdressers, does it? So, those fins become known as the "devil's head series." The rumour is that a French-Canadian separatist designed the portrait because he is against the monarchy. Sneaks a devil's head past the inspectors. To cover their asses, the Bank of Canada had the plates changed in 1956. There goes any chance of seein' a devil's head. I know, right?

What does this whole fin deal have to do with the Yukon? Shut up for a minute and I'll tell you. Jeez.

On the back of the 1954 five-dollar bill is a picture of Otter Falls. Yes, Yukon. Where I fished for rainbow trout with my cousins. I've been tryin' to find out how the Falls got on the devil's head bill? Who took the photo? When? How was it picked?

My cousin swears it was taken by Brownie Logan, the late brother of moneybags Ralf Logan. He says he was there and saw Brownie snap the picture. Who calls a guy Brownie? Did his snapshot end up on the five-dollar bill? Maybe, but the Bank of Canada Museum say they don't know. There is no information. It's a mystery. I mean, Otter Falls wasn't the most famous or beautiful spot in the territory, that's for sure.

As a collector's item, those rare fivers are worth diddly. They mean something to a Yukoner, though. Especially an Indian who was pissed off over the end of a great fishing spot. Worse, the loss of the sight of that white water slowed to a crawl by the building of the Aishihik dam.

But that's not where the story ends. So, her first night in the "horse," the Sovereign (Queen, for Chrissakes) decides to miss a reception in her honour at the RCAF Officer's Mess. Yup, she stands up the Commissioner and his wife and more than 200 guests. Probably the first time they had ever got the chance to dress up.

She does this for what? Well, what else? For a visit to the bingo hall. No, I shit you not! Ask anybody here. They know. She musta heard about the prize. A year's supply of Canadian back bacon.

Well, we're sittin' here that night, yeah, this is my lucky chair, so right here, literally, and in walk four Mounties in full red dress uniform. They look like they are watching out for the Mad Trapper. We all freeze. All of us. 'Cause Indians are guilty of being Indians. I'm pretty sure it was still illegal back then to be an Indian in Whitehorse after seven o'clock. And there we were, a room full of 'em. White folks don't take to bingo around here.

Anyways, the RC's stand in the four corners, looking like they are guarding Parliament. We hold our breath. Then in she comes, the Queen of England, just like that. There she is, in her white high heels, and slacks and a sweater set, with her hat and all, with Prince Phillip right behind her. Well. You can imagine. She didn't have a bannock butt either. It was substantial. Jeez – I mean she had serious butt.

Everyone dropped what they were doing, even their chips.

The caller even shut up. A hundred Yukon Indians staring at six white folks. Dead silence, I mean you could have heard a bingo card drop. Prince Phillip nodded, and the Queen, in her regal voice, says, "Do please carry on. I did so want to take in a local Native Indian cultural event, and this is where the Mounties said you would be on a Thursday night."

We were stupefied. Great word, right?

Then, she asked for tea. Tea. You know as well as I do tea doesn't come in fine china at the Whitehorse Elks Bingo Hall. It comes, bag floating in warm water, in a Styrofoam cup.

That's probably how the old girl got her "royal tummy ache," like it's reported on CBC North. For anyone else it would be gut ache. Not her. Royal tummy ache. Turns out later the rabbit died. (Oh jeez, Phil nailed the target. She was preggers with Prince Edward, for Chrissakes.) But I figure it was the tea.

Anyways, back to the bingo game. The caller was the best we ever had. Old Golden Voice. She sounded better than

those announcements in Woolco. "Attention Woolco shop-
pers, spotlight sale in aisle three." I mean a voice as smooth
as velvet. And an ass as wide as three axe handles. Too much
time in the bingo chair.

So, Elizabeth asks Lorna Muskrat how you get in on the
game. Well, the Muskrats are from Carcross, so Lorna isn't
known for being genteel. Plus, she comes from Indian royalty from Juneau, so she knows she's on the same level as
Elizabeth. She doesn't even look up. She says, "Up there," and
motions with a chin nod to the front. It was the Queen's fault
for interrupting Lorna's juju routine. Yeah, you know those little rituals we all have for bingo.

The Queen sits her prim, beige-slacked ass down, right
across from old Lorna, who still hasn't finished off her bingo
sacrament. Her Royal Majesty interrupts her again.

"As long as you are saying a Native prayer, won't you say
one for me as well?"

"No, do your own," Lorna says, right outta the side of her
mouth.

The Queen, she has had her Royal trainin'. She doesn't
look shocked or anything, just gives a Royal nod. Lorna gives
her one right back. I don't know that Elizabeth likes that,
because her lips are a little tight; white around the edges.

Phillip takes orders, and, looking twitchy and sweaty, goes
up to the card table. He has no cash. Red as a tomato, he
walks over to one of the Mounties and hits him up for a
twenty. We all grin at one another. Northern secret grin, you
know, that flash sideways in the eyes.

Lorna's annoyed when she has to break her concentration
and explain to the Monarch how to play the game. She gets
right into it, Elizabeth. She's giggling like a schoolgirl. Well,
maybe a British schoolgirl. Phillip goes out for a fag with some

of the boys from Carcross. That's how we found out our Ruler was up the stump. (Pregnant! Jeez.) Phillip was askin' the boys how they handled the morning sickness.

"Pilot bread," Edgar John says. They're all nodding.

"That or bush tea. That Labrador tea. But, I don't think it grows around your palace," and the boys bust a gut laughing. Phil titters a little. How does he know what the hell pilot bread or bush tea is?

"I had to bring Her Majesty here for diversion. The nausea has been quite dreadful this time around, I'm afraid."

"I'd be afraid too. She could throw you in the dungeon."

That Ned Charlie isn't the sharpest tool in the drawer. But for some reason, this cheers the Prince up quite a bit. He smokes and laughs out there for quite a while. The boys are teaching him bad words in Tlingit and Tagish when the Mounties notice he's gone, and start looking around for assassins. All they find is a bunch of Indians and a pile of cigarette butts. They circle around us, but we have the Prince, so we aren't worried. He doesn't seem as if he is in any hurry to get back inside. Anyways, the Mounties kind of rain on our parade, so we beat it back in with the Prince for the big prize round.

I guess when you're Queen of the Commonwealth, you don't have to play by the rules. She doesn't. She calls "Bingo!" in that snotty accent. We could all see she doesn't have all the numbers. Well, sure, we were all standing up. Hell, we all wanted that year's supply of back bacon!

But who the heck is going to tell her she is wrong? There is probably a big law against it. So, the caller with her voice shaking calls out, "Stop the game." And makes a big deal out of walking her barge ass down off the stage and checking the Queen's card.

Lorna Muskrat is vibrating. Bright red. Wolf-Clan mad. Glaring at the Queen in a mean tone of face. The Queen is busy. Studying architectural wonders. The Elks Bingo Hall ceiling.

The Anglican Minister and the bingo caller are arguing. So quiet none of us can pick up what's going on.

"Bingo!" The Golden Voice, thin as water, warbles, all velvet gone. The hall falls dead quiet.

Lorna isn't having it.

"Ya gotta be kiddin' me," she says, shooting the Queen the stink eye.

"She cheated!" The Queen puts her hand to her heart, and makes a bad attempt at looking shocked and offended. She's no actor. None of us are fooled. The old girl is lying through her straightened British teeth. Lorna stands right up on her chair. We all hold our breath.

"If nobody else is gonna say it, I am. The Queen is a thief *and* a liar!" The Mounties draw their revolvers right out of them smooth brown holsters. All four are aimed straight at Lorna. This only pisses her off more. Now she's wolverine-mad.

We still aren't breathing.

"That's right. You can go right ahead and shoot me, but I was one number away from a year's worth of bacon!" Lorna's third chin waggles with outrage.

Nobody, including the Mounties, are stupid enough to argue with a wolverine-mad Tlingit of the Wolf Clan from Carcross. I mean, anyone knows that is just not good for your health. They know not to piss off a Tlingit-Tagish woman. Ever. And if you do, just leave town. And tell your family not to come back for six generations, because these women can hold a mean like nobody you ever saw.

The Monarch is not about to back down. I guess she knows she has the Commonwealth on her side. She stands up, and faces Lorna down. They do the big stare. We are all riveted, waiting to see who will blink or look away first. Chrissakes, we sit there what seems like sixty minutes with all eyes glued on those two women. My eyes water from holding them open so I don't miss anything. Which Queen is going to win?

That Anglican Minister is no dummy. He quietly goes out, and himself, loads Lorna's pickup with half that bacon. Who wouldn't do what he does? I mean, he probably figures, how the hell is the Queen going to know how much a year's worth of bacon is? And he doesn't want to have to deal with Lorna's wrath for the rest of his life.

Who wins? Well, we never figure it out. The Queen sways, like willows in the wind, and she faints. That doesn't count as looking away on purpose. One of the Mounties runs and catches her like a football before she hits the floor.

Lorna Muskrat holds her arms up, with the biggest grin you ever seen.

The Mounties hustle a limp Queen out. The Prince is fanning her with her bingo card.

The Minister yells, "Hey, you Carcross boys, load that bacon up in the RCMP cruiser!" I help. Outside, the oldest Mountie, who looks like this isn't the best night of his life, orders us to come in the morning and load it in the Transport Canada plane.

The Queen isn't in the best mood when she and the Prince arrive at the plane early the next morning. She has a sour look on her face. She probably doesn't see us underneath loading half of that Canadian back bacon into the cargo hold.

Phillip is telling her, "Darling, watch your step going up the stairs." She turns, burns him to the ground with her eyes and says, "It's Your Highness. Do fuck off, Phillip." It doesn't sound right in an elegant English accent. Phillip goes stoneberry red, takes her elbow, and walks her like she's a crate of eggs right up those steps.

LESSONS IN THE RAISING OF HOUSEHOLD OBJECTS

HELEN MARSHALL

Mummy asks me how I am doing, and I tell her that I am afraid of the twins.

This is true. I don't know who the twins are. In fact, the twins aren't anybody yet. In fact, the twins are quite probably dead. Mummy tells me I don't really know what dead means, but I most certainly do know what dead means. When Scamper forgot how to wag his tail on my third birthday, Daddy told me that meant that he had died, and I said "Oh," and he said, "So now you know what dead means, that's good, that's good, sweetheart, you're growing up." So I do know what dead means; it means when you stop being what you were before.

Mummy doesn't like that I am afraid of the twins.

Mummy insists that I press my head up against her belly until her little poked-out belly button fits right into my ear. It feels strange there, but it also feels normal, as if belly buttons were designed for ears.

Then there is a kick, and then there is another, and I know that the twins are mad at me, so I start to cry. I don't like crying very much but sometimes you can't really help crying. It's just something you have to do.

Mummy pats me on the back and she says. "It's okay, darling, honey, peanut, Miss Angela Clothespin Jacket." My real name is Angela Chloe Jackson, but I like that other name for me better even though it isn't real.

"I don't want them, I want them to stay there, I don't want them to come out," I tell her, but I am still crying so she does not hear me. The thing about Mummys is that they can't hear what you're saying whenever you are crying, and so I hate crying, but like I already said, sometimes it's just what happens.

But, anyway, that isn't quite what I meant because I don't want them to stay there. I don't want them to stay anywhere, but maybe inside Mummy is better than outside Mummy where they will have to roll around with their lumpy flesh and the tangled-up arms and legs like Daddy showed me in the black and white picture.

Mummy says, "But Angie, Mummy's tummy will get too big. They can't stay in there forever."

And I think, yes, that is exactly the problem.

❦

I decide that I will be a good little girl, and I will practice loving the twins.

Mummy says it is important that I love them and that I am nice to them because they will be very fragile when they come out. "Like a lamp?" I ask. I have broken the lamp in my room more than once, and then I have to sleep in the dark because of it so that I will learn. Daddy calls this an object lesson.

And Daddy says, "Like the lamp except even more fragile than that."

"If you're very good," Mummy says, "I'll let you hold them." I wonder what it will be like to hold those things.

"But what if I break them?" I ask, and Mummy just purses her lips in that way and says, "You'll have to be very careful, Angie."

Mummy asks, "Do you want to feel them kick again?" and I say, "No," because how can you love something that is trying to kick you? I must practice first on something easier to love than the twins.

I find two cans of tomato soup in the pantry because tomato soup is the thing I like most, specially with toasted cheese. Tomato soup will be easy to love. Even without the toasted cheese.

I am not supposed to go in the pantry by myself, but I think Mummy and Daddy will like it if I learn how to love the twins so I do even though it is dark and I am worried about the shelves and all the other things there are in the dark.

I name one of the cans Campbell. I name the other Simon because I cannot name both of them Campbell. I decide that Campbell must be the older of them, but I think, deep down, that I like Simon better. He is better behaved. And besides, he doesn't have any dents. His label is crisp and new.

Campbell and Simon must stay with me if I am to learn how to love them. Sometimes I watch them. They are not very interesting to watch. I decide that it is probably because Simon is too well behaved, and so I love him a little bit less for that. I try rolling Campbell down the stairs. Afterward, he is slightly more dented than he was before, and I decide that this is what Daddy calls an object lesson. Simon says nothing.

"You're supposed to say something, Simon," I tell him. "You shouldn't let me roll Campbell down the stairs, not if he's a baby." And Simon starts to cry so I can't hear what he's saying, and I decide that I don't love him at all. I tell him I like cream of broccoli better. I tell him I like chicken with noodles, and why couldn't he be chicken with noodles? Simon is crying even more now, but that's what babies do. They don't ever say anything, they just cry.

Finally, I give Simon to Mummy who always helps me when I am crying. Later on, Mummy gives me tomato soup and toasted cheese for lunch. I look at Campbell with his dented rim and his sad, sad face. I hope that this has been an object lesson for him.

❧

The problem is that Mummy is not getting bigger because the twins are getting bigger, but Mummy is getting bigger because the twins are thieves.

The morning that Mummy came home and said to me, "Darling, baby girl, Angela C., you're going to have brothers!" was the first time I knew they were thieves. She was smiling so much that her face looked like another person's face, and Daddy's face looked like another Daddy's face, and both of them were hugging each other and hugging me. But after all the hugging was over with, I noticed that my hairbrush was missing, the one with the pink handle that I have used since I was a baby even though it is too small for me because it never hurts. "No," Mummy tells me, "it wasn't the twins," but I know it was, anyway.

❧

I have come to a decision about Campbell. Well, we have reached the decision together.

The decision is that I will not eat anymore tomato soup because Campbell says it is cruel, and Campbell will help me to catch the twins, who have now carried off not only my hairbrush but also my flower fairy which I only left out to see if she would like the rain, and also the bunny-eared hat that I was given at Christmas. I do not mind losing the flower fairy and the hat so much but that was a really good hairbrush and Mummy says they don't make them anymore, so now I have to use a grown-up hairbrush, and grown-up hairbrushes pull and pull and pull until I am crying all over again.

So I will leave Campbell out on the bookshelf next to my bed, and I will keep on the night lamp so that he can see properly even though I am now fully too old for it, and night lamps are stupid anyway, but Campbell gets scared of the dark and besides, how else will he see the twins?

Mummy and Daddy come and kiss me goodnight, and Daddy smells wonderful, like cinnamon and coffee and chocolate, but Mummy doesn't smell like Mummy at all. When she sits on my bed I can feel it moving as the twins go kick, kick, kick. I think to myself, or rather, I say to Campbell, "Look, you can see them kicking, just you wait and see." But Mummy doesn't like it when I talk to Campbell, and Daddy has to say, "No, honey, it's okay, we won't take Campbell away," and then I stop crying.

⚭

In the morning, Campbell is sitting in exactly the same place, and my stuffed Adie is gone, who I liked best because one eye was blue and one eye was green and dogs don't normally look like that.

"Campbell," I say, but Campbell is still asleep and so he doesn't answer me.

⚘

This is how the twins come out, I think.

There is a hole in Mummy's tummy. I have seen it because that's what the belly button keeps all plugged up, and that's why her belly button points out now, because the twins are pushing on the other side. At night, when Mummy is under her covers, I think she cannot see her belly button anymore and, anyway, just like Campbell she has to fall asleep. That is when the twins come out. Daddy says that the twins are still quite small so I think they must be able to still fit in through the belly button.

Sometimes when I am sleeping I hear noises. I think it must be the twins and I want to say to them, "Go back inside! You're supposed to be dead still!" But I don't think they can hear me very well. Maybe that is because I am whispering it to Campbell.

It is scary when the twins are outside of Mummy and sometimes I have to hold Campbell very close to me. I don't love him just yet, but I think I might be somewhere close to loving him. I say it is okay if he falls asleep and he says that he loves me very much.

"They are taking things, I know they are," I whisper to Campbell and we are both afraid together. In the morning things are a little bit different than they were the night before and Mummy's tummy is a little bit bigger. I think they must be building a tent inside, filling Mummy up with hairbrushes and flower fairies and bunny-eared hats and Adie.

The next time Mummy asks me to listen to the twins, I put my ear against her tummy. I think I feel the shape of the hairbrush and I think I can hear Adie barking, so I bite Mummy's belly button until there is blood, because if I can get in then maybe I can get them back. Now Mummy is crying though, and so I can't understand what she is saying, and Daddy is so mad that he puts me in my room and he turns out the light and he takes away the night lamp and he takes away Campbell.

So now I am sitting in the darkness, and I have the blankets close to me and I miss Campbell, which makes me think I must be starting to love him a little, but I am also thinking that this must be what it is like for the twins inside Mummy's tummy.

I don't know where Campbell is, and when I go into the cupboard there are other cans of soup, but they aren't Campbell and so I cannot love them.

I wonder if maybe the twins have taken Campbell too, or if maybe they are in cahoots with Mummy and Daddy.

"Mummy," I say, when she opens the door at last and is standing in the doorway and there is light all around her so that it hurts my eyes. "Is Campbell inside you?" I ask, but she just squeezes her lips until they aren't lips anymore, they are just a single line that she cannot speak out of, and then she closes the door again.

I am trying not to think about Campbell anymore. I am trying to pretend that there has never been a Campbell, and so in the morning I eat cereal and I think to myself, that this tastes nothing like tomato soup and that is a good thing.

Mummy is still hugging Daddy, but neither of them wants to look at me properly so I just eat my cereal. I pretend that I can't see Mummy's tummy moving when the twins kick. But I am thinking to myself, *I know that you are in there, I know that you are all in there,* and Mummy has no idea that I can see all of the things that are starting to poke out of her, because she is not big enough for all the special sequined purses and shoe racks and televisions and night lamps and Adies and bunny-eared hats and flower fairies and Campbells that she has inside of her. There, right there, I can see the spokes of my brand new ten-speed bicycle poking out of her, but she has no idea and neither does Daddy when he hugs her.

꧁꧂

I don't know how the twins have done it but they have taken Daddy too.

Last night he was here and kissed me on the forehead and he read from my special book, the only book that is left now, and he said, "Where are your other books, Angie?" and I said, "The twins have taken them, Daddy." Then he touched my forehead very lightly like a butterfly, and said, "You can't keep doing this, honey, peanut, darling. The twins are coming and they are coming soon."

Daddy doesn't understand, but now Daddy has gone too, and I am afraid he is deep inside Mummy and we won't be able to get him out.

But I have a plan.

This is my plan. I will lay a trap for the twins. I will catch the twins and then maybe I will be able to give them what

Daddy calls an object lesson so they will know that they can't keep doing this anymore.

◦✖◦

I don't have a night lamp and I don't have Campbell and I don't have Daddy, so I must do this alone.

I take my special book, the one book that I have left, and I tie a string around it just like Daddy taught me to tie my shoelaces, and then I tie another string around my wrist because then, even if I fall asleep, I will be able to catch them. Mummy kisses me on the forehead and she asks if I want her to read to me but I shake my head and say, "No, Mummy, I am too old for reading," because being too old is when things stop working the way they did before. So Mummy smoothes my hair like she did when I was itsy bitsy, and she sits on the bed with me. I want to tell her not to sit on the bed, that I don't want the twins that close to me, but Mummy is so big with all the dishwashers and book shelves and staircases and basements sticking out of her that I can't believe she even fits on the bed.

"Are they building a house in there, Mummy?" I ask, and Mummy just laughs and shakes her head. "No, Angela Clothespin Jacket, they are not building a house, they are going to come live in our house."

Then I am crying again, and I cry until I go to sleep.

◦✖◦

I wake up in the middle of the night and there is a tugging at my wrist, so I look at my wrist and there is the string, and the string is pulled all the way to the book and then there is the twins. The twins are not two people, they are just one person, and they are not a person at all because, really, they are just a bunch of arms, and legs, and foreheads like in the picture.

"Why don't you just go away?" I ask the twins. And the twins say, "Because we love you, Angela Clothespin Jacket. You know what it is like to live in the dark, just like we do. We want you to come live with us forever inside Mummy where it is safe and warm and there are night lamps and Campbell and Adie." I think about this for a while because I don't like the twins very much, but it is lonely here and perhaps it will be less lonely inside Mummy, in the dark, with the twins. At least then we will be all together, even if it is inside Mummy.

I say, "Okay, twins," and then I go through the belly button with them.

⚓︎

The thing is that the twins are cleverer than I thought.

Adie is in here and Campbell too, and the flower fairy, but the twins have locked the belly button and it is very dark and I don't know how to get out.

I feel around, amidst the ten-speed bikes and the sequined purses and the night lamps, and then there is a sound and it is Daddy. I am feeling very scared, so I climb over the bookshelf and the club chair until there he is, smelling like cinnamon and coffee and chocolate. I want him to hold me, but it is too crowded for holding in here.

"They are out there," I say to Daddy. "The twins are out there."

And he says, "Yes, peanut, honey, darling, the twins are out there, but that is where they are supposed to be. That's the way Mummy wanted it to be."

Daddy cannot hold me, so I hug Campbell close to me because he is small enough for holding.

"We have made some bad decisions," I say to Daddy, and he says, "No, peanut, this is what was supposed to happen. This is what we planned for all along, it was supposed to be the twins coming out and you going back in."

"Why?" I ask Daddy. "Because," he says, "we wanted a baby who didn't cry as much. We wanted a baby who didn't have so many names as you. We wanted a baby who was real."

"I can be a real baby," I say. Maybe I say that. I'm crying, so it is difficult to tell.

"No, honey, that's not the way it works. That's why I'm down here. Now that the twins are born you have to live here forever. This is your new room."

"Inside Mummy?" I ask.

"Yes, peanut, inside Mummy, with all the other things we don't need anymore."

I think about this for a while. I cannot see Daddy's face in the darkness. All I can smell is cinnamon and coffee and chocolate, and I decide that I don't like those things anymore. Those are just things, and they aren't Daddy.

"No," I say to Daddy, "I'm going to get out of here, and when I do I'm not going to take you with me."

Daddy doesn't like this very much, but I don't care. I like this, and Campbell likes this, so I think we will be okay.

⚮

It is time for another plan, I say to Campbell, and Campbell also thinks it is time for another plan.

I take Campbell and I put him in Mummy's sequined purse and I put it over my shoulder. Then I climb the bookshelf and feel along the top of Mummy's tummy, which is big and curved like being underneath an umbrella. Daddy tells me to stop doing that but I have decided that I will not listen to Daddy anymore. I know that there is a belly button somewhere and so all I have to do is find it.

"You can't do that," says Daddy. "Someone must stay in here to mind the house and it won't be me!"

"Well, Daddy," I say, "you should have thought about that before you came in here."

I climb from the bookshelf to the club chair to the minivan, and for a moment I wonder how on earth the twins managed to fit all of these things inside Mummy, but then I stop wondering and I keep climbing. Finally, I discover the belly button at the very top of Mummy's tummy.

I put my ear to the belly button, and I can hear that on the outside Mummy is laughing. I think she must be laughing because the twins are doing something funny like telling jokes or aerial acrobats, and I hate the twins a little bit more for making Mummy laugh, and I hate Mummy a bit more for loving the twins like that. But at least I have Campbell, and at least Daddy has already taught me how to tie and untie knots.

I start to untie the belly button, and Daddy says to me, "You'll never be able to get out there, you're not a real daughter, Miss Peanut, Miss Honey, you're not a real Angela, you're just clothespins and jackets."

"No," I say to him, "I am too real. You made me because you wanted me and so I am as real as the twins and I am real as Campbell, and we are getting out of here right this very instant!"

❧

First there is a light, and my eyes hurt because I have gotten used to the dark, but Campbell tells me to be brave, that it will be okay out there, and I say, "I love you, Campbell." He says, "I love you, baby girl," and I like it when Campbell calls me that, so I tug at the string and the light gets brighter and the hole gets bigger. Then I am sticking my head out and then I am staring at Mummy and she is staring at me, and I am half inside her and half outside of her so I climb out the rest of the way even though I can hear Daddy crying still from inside.

"What are you doing here?" she asks.

"I just wanted to see the sunshine," I say. And there are the twins, and they are all the things that they were before but somehow they look more and more like people and the people they look like are Mummy and Daddy. But when I look at Mummy, Mummy looks more and more like just a mess of arms and legs and skirts and pantyhose and lipstick and eyelashes and not the thing that she was before.

"Are you going to stay?" she asks me.

"Yes," say the twins, "please stay with us, Angela Clothespin Jacket! We can all be real babies together! It would be good to have a sister!"

I think about this for a bit because maybe I want to stay with Mummy and Daddy and the twins. Maybe I want to be with them, even though none of us are the things we were before. But then I take Campbell out of the purse and he whispers something in my ear.

"This has been a real object lesson," I say to Mummy, and I am holding Campbell close to my chest because I love him so very much, "but I think we will be going now."

And we do.

DOING RIGHT

AUSTIN CLARKE

I see him and I watch him. I see him and I watch him and I start to pray for him, 'cause I see him heading for trouble.

Making money. "In five or six years, I want to have a lotta money," he does say. "Only when I have a lotta dollars will people respect me."

I had to laugh. Every time he say so, I does have to laugh, 'cause I couldn't do nothing more better than laugh.

"Look at the Rockefellers. Look at the Rothschilds. Look at the Kennedys."

I was going-ask him if he know how they mek their money, but before I could ask, he would be off dreaming and looking up at the ceiling where there was only cobwebs and dust; and only God knows what was circulating through his head every time he put himself in these deep reveries concerning making lots o'money and talking 'bout the Rockefellers, the Rothschilds, and the Kennedys.

I was still laughing. 'Cause the present job he had, was a green hornet job. He was a man who went to work in a green suit from head to foot, except the shoes, which was black and which he never polish. His profession was to go-round the St. Clair-Oakwood area where a lotta Wessindians does-live, putting parking tickets 'pon people cars. Before he start all this foolishness with Wessindians' cars, he uses to be on the Queen's Park beat for green hornets.

A big man like him, over two hundred pounds, healthy and strong and black, and all he could do after eight years as a immigrant in the year 1983, is to walk-'bout with a little book to his hand, putting little yellow pieces o' paper on people windshields. He like the job so much and thought he did doing the right thing that in the middle o' the night. During a poker game or just dipsy-doodling and talking 'bout women, he would put back on the green uniform jacket, grabble-up the peak cap, jump in the little green motor car that the Police give him, and gone straight up by St. Clair-Oakwood, up and down Northcliffe Boulevard, swing right 'pon Eglinton, gone down Eglinton, and swing left 'pon Park Hill Road, left again on Whitmore, and all he doing is putting these yellow pieces o' paper on decent, hard-working people cars. When he return, he does-be-laughing. I tell him he going-soon stop laughing, when a Wessindian lick-he-down with a big rock.

"I have fix them! I have ticketed one hundred and ten motto-cars today alone! And the night I leff the poker game, I ticket fifty more bastards, mainly Wessindians."

I start to get real frighten. 'Cause I know a lotta these Wessindians living in them very streets where he does be ticketing and laughing. And all them Wessindians know who the green hornet is. And being as how they is Wessindians, I know they don't like green hornets nor nobody who does be touching their cars. So I feel that any morning, when one o' these Wessindians come home from a party or offa a night shift and see him doing foolishness and putting yellow tickets 'pon their motor cars, I know um is at least *one* hand brek.

Wessindians accustom to parking in the middle o' the road, or on the wrong side, back home. And nobody don't trouble them nor touch their cars. And since they come here, many o' these Wessindians haven't tek-on change in attitude in regards to who own the public road and who own the motor cars.

So whilst the boy still ticketing and laughing, and putting his hands on people cars which they just wash in the car wash on Bathurst, I continue worrying and watching him.

One night, just as we sit down to cut the cards, and before the cards deal, he come in grinning, and saying, "I ticket two hundred motto-cars today alone!"

"One o' these days, boy!" I tell him.

"When I pass in the green car and I see him, I know I had him!"

"Who?"

"I see the car park by the fire hydrant. The chauffeur was leaning back in the seat. One hand outside the car window. With a cigarette in tha' hand. The next hand over the back o' the seat. I look in the car, and when I look in, I nearly had a fit. I recognize the pipe. I recognize the dark blue pinstripe suit. I recognize the hair. With the streak o' grey in um. And I mek a U-turn in the middle o' the road—"

"But a U-turn illegal!"

"I is a green hornet, man!"

"I see."

"I size-up the car. And I see the licents plate. ONT-001! I start getting nervous now. 'Cause I know that this motto-car belongs to the big man. Or the second most biggest man in Ontario. I draw up. The chauffeur nod to me and tell me, 'Fine day, eh?' I tell he, 'A very fine day, sir!' And I get out. I bend over the bonnet o' this big, shiny, black car—"

"Limousine, man. A big car is call a limo."

"Well, um could have been a limo, a hearse, be-Christ, or a automobile, I still bend-over the bonnet and stick-on one o' the prettiest parking tickets in my whole career!"

"The Premier's car?"

"He mek the law. Not me!"

"And you think you do the right thing?"

"My legal bounden duty. Afterwards, I did-feel so good, like a real police officer and not a mere green hornet. And I walk-through Queen's Park on my two feet, looking for more official motto-cars to ticket. And when I was finish, I had stick-on *five* parking tickets in their arse... One belongs to the Attorney General too."

"The same man who does-defend Wessindians?"

"I put one 'pon Larry Grossman car too."

Well, that whole night, all the boy talking 'bout and laughing 'bout is how he stick-on tickets on these big shots' cars, or limousines. And to make matters worse for the rest o' we, he win all the money in the poker game too. I feel now that the boy really going-become important, maybe, even become a real police, and make pure money. Or else going-lose a hand, or a foot.

But we was feeling good, though. 'Cause the big boys in Toronto don't particular' notice we unless um is Caribana weekend or when election time coming and they looking for votes, or when the *Star* doing a feature on racism and Wessindian immigrants that be illegal, and they want a quotation. So, we feel this green hornet is our ambassador, even if he is only a' ambassador o' parking tickets. So we does-laugh like hell at the boy's prowess and progress.

And we does wait til a certain time on a Friday night, nervous as hell whilst cutting and dealing the cards to see if the boy going-turn up still dress-off in the green uniform, meaning that he hasn't get fired for ticketing the big shots' cars. And when he *does* turn up, dress from head to trousers in green, we know he still have the job, and we does-laugh some more.

But all the time I does-be- still nervous, as I was seeing him and watching him.

Then he start losing weight. He start biting his fingernails. He start wearing the green uniform not press, and half dirty. He start calling we "*You* people!"

I getting frighten now, 'cause he tell me that they tek-him-off the Queen's Park beat.

So um is now that he up in St. Clair-Oakwood, and I feel he going-put a ticket on the *wrong* motor car, meaning a Wessindian car. And at least one hand brek. Or one foot. And if the particular motor car belongs to a Jamaican, not even the ones that have locks and does-wear the wool tams mek outta black, green, and red, I know um could be *both* foots and *both* hands!

I see him and I watch him.

"I have live in Trinidad, as a police," he tell me. "But I born in Barbados. I leff Trinidad because they won't let me ticket one hundred more cars and break the all-time record. I went to Guyana after Trinidad. I was a police in Guyana before Guyana was even Guyana and was still Demerara, or B.G. They make me leff Guyana when I get close to the record. Ten more tickets is all I had to ticket. From Guyana, I end up in Dominica. Same thing. From Dominica, I went to Antigua, and um was in Antigua that a fellow came close to licking-me-down for doing my legal duty, namely ticketing cars. But in all them countries, I ticket cars that belongs to prime ministers, ministers of guvvament, priests, civil servants, and school teachers."

I see him and I watch him. I see him getting more older than the forty-five years he say he was born; and I see him drinking straight rums, first thing every morning lately, because he say, "The nerves bad. Not that I becoming a alcoholic. I only taking the bad taste o' waking up so early outta my mouth. I am not a alcoholic, though. It is the pressure and the lack o' sleep."

But he was drunk. Cleveland was drunk-drunk-drunk early-early-early every day. He had to be really drunk after he outline his plan to make money to me.

"Remember the Rockefellers, man!" he tell me. "This is my plan. I been a green hornet for eight-nine years now. They promise me that if I ticket the most cars outta the whole group o' hornets, they would send me to training school to be a police. First they tell me I too short. I is five-four. But most criminals is five-three. Then they tell me that my arches fallen. Jesus Christ! What you expect? After all the beats I have walk in Trinidad, Guyana, Antiqua, Dominica, and Grenada, my arches *bound* to fall! And eight-nine years in this damn country pounding the beat ticketing cars! But they can't beat me. Not me. This is the plan I got for their arse. Tickets begin at five dollars. Right? There is five dollars, ten dollars, and fifteen dollars. Right? Twenty dollars for parking beside a fire hydrand or on the wrong side. Right? Now, I write-up a ten-dollar ticket. And I change the ten to a forty. The stub in my book still saying ten. But the ticket on the car that also says ten, I going-change from ten to forty. Then I rush down the vehicle registration place on Wellesley Street where they have all them computers. And I tell the fellow I know from Guyana something, *anything* to get him to look up the registration for me. And then I get in touch with the owner of the vehicle and subtract ten from forty and—"

"You think yougonna get thirty…?"

"You don't like my plan?"

"I think your plan'll get you ten years."

"Okay. What about this other one? People don't lock their motto-cars when they park. Right? Wessindidans is the biggest vegabonds in regards to this. Right? A fellow don't lock his car. And um is night. And I got-on my green hornet uniform. Right? Meaning I am still operating in a official capacity…"

I see the boy start to smile, and his face spread and light-up like a new moon. The face was shining too, 'cause the heat and the sureness that the plan going-work this time make him sweat real bad. But I watching him. I know that Wessindians don't have much money, because they does-get the worst and lowest jobs in Toronto. Only certain kinds of Wessindians does-have money in their pocket. The kind that does-work night shift, especially after midnight when everybody else sleeping; the brand o' Wessindian who I not going-mention by name in case they accuse me of categorizing the race. And being a reverse racist. But *certain* Wessindians, like hair-dressers, real estate salesmen, and fellows who know race-horses backwards and forwards, good-good-good, *plus* the unmentionable brand, namely the illegal immigrants, the illegal parkers, and them who hiding from the Police, them-so would have money to burn, inside their cars that not locked.

The boy eyes smiling. I see dollar bills instead o' pupils. I even hear the money clinking like when a car pass-over the piece o' black rubber-thing in a gas station. *Cling-clang.* "Gimme just three months," he say. "Gimme three bare months, and I going-show you something."

Just as I left him and walkin' cross Northcliffe Boulevard going to Eglinton, I see a green hornet fellow standing-up in front a fellow car. The fellow already inside the car. The fellow want to drive off. But the green hornet standing up in front the man car. The fellow inside the car honk the horn.

And the green hornet fellow take out his black book. Slow-slow. And he flip back a page. And hold down a little. And start to write down the car licents. The fellow honk the car again. The hornet walk more closer. He tear off the little yellow piece o' paper. And getting ready to put it on the man brand-new-brand grey Thunderbird. Just as the hornet was about to ticket the man for parking next to a yellow fire hydrand, the fellow jump out. A Japanee samurai wrestler would look like a twig beside o' him. Pure muscle. Pure avoirdupois. Pure *latissimus dorsi*. Shoes shining bright. White shirt. Stripe tie. A three-piece grey suit. Hair slick back. And long. Gold 'pon two fingers on each hand. Gold on the left wrist. More gold on the right wrist. The hornet par'lyzed now. A rigor mortis o' fear turn the whole uniform and the man inside it to pure starch, or like how a pair o' pyjamas does-look when you left um out on the line in the dead o' winter.

"Goddamn!" the man say.

"You park wrong," the hornet say.

"Who say I park wrong?"

"You park illegal."

"Who goddamn say I park illegal?"

"Look at the sign."

"Which goddamn sign?"

"The sign that say NO PARKING BETWEEN FOUR AND SIX. And NOT STOPPING ANYTIME. You not only park, but you stop. You stationary too." The Indian green hornet man's voice get high and shaky. "You have therefore park."

"Ahmma gonna give you two seconds, nigger, to take that goddamn ticket off my car, motherfucker!"

"What you call me? I am no damn nigger. I am Indian. Legal immigrant. I just doing my job for the City of Toronto in Metropolitan Toronto. You are a blasted American negro!"

Well, multiculturalism gone-out the window now!

All the pamphlets and the television commercials that show people of all colours laughing together and saying "We is Canadians," all them advertisements in *Saturday Night* and *Maclean's*, all them speeches that ministers up in Ottawa make concerning the "different cultures that make up this great unified country of ours," all that lick-up now, and gone through the eddoes. One time. *Bram*!

The Goliath of a man grabble-hold of the hornet by the scruff o' the green uniform, the peak cap fall-off all like now-so, the little black book slide under the car, the hornet him-self lifted up offa the ground by a least three inches, and shak-ing-'bout in the Gulliver's hands, pelting-'bout his two legs like if he is a Muppet or a puppet; and when I anticipate that the fellow going-pelt him in the broad-road, the fellow just hefted him up a little more higher offa the ground, and lay him 'cross the bonnet of the shining Thunderbird, holding-he-down like how you does-hold-down a cat to tickle-he under his chin; and the fellow say, "Now, motherfucker! Is you gonna take the goddamn ticket off mah Bird?"

I pass 'long quick, bo'! 'Cause I know the Police does-be up in this St.Clair-Oakwood district like flies round a crocus bag o' sugar at the drop of a cloth hat; and that they does-tek-in anybody who near the scene o' crime, no matter how small the scene or how small the crime; and if um is Wessindians involve, pure handcuffs and licks, and pelting-'bout inside the back o' cruisers till they get you inside the station. And then the real sport does-start! So I looking and I looking-off, know-ing that a green hornet, even if he look like a Pakistani or a Indian, but is really a Trinidadian or a Guyanese, and only look a little Indian, he going-get help from the Police. Not one Police. But five carloads o' Police.

All like now-so, the road full up with Wessindians and other people, and these Wessindians looking on and laughing, 'cause none o' them don't like green hornets, not even green hornets that come from the Wessindies!

I pass 'long quick, bo'. I got to face the Immigration people in a week and I don't want nothing concerning my past or present to be a stain through witnessing violence, to prevent them from stamping LANDED IMMIGRAND or IMMI-GRANT REÇU in my Barbados passport! I may be a accessory before the fact.

But I was still thinking of my friend, the *other* green hornet, so I look back to see what kind o' judgement the Thunderbird-man was going-make with the Indian gentleman from Guyana, who now have no peak cap, no black notebook, one shoe fall-off, and the green tunic tear-up. And as my two eyes rested on the scene *after the fact* I hear the Charles Atlas of a man say, "And don't call the motherfucking cops! I got you covered, nigger. I knows where you goddam live!"

I hope that this Goliath of a man don't also know where my Bajan green hornet friend does-live! I hope the Thunderbird don't be park all the time up here! And I start to think 'bout getting a little message to my friend to tell him to don't put no tickets on no grey Thunderbirds, or even on no Wessindian cars, like Tornados, which is Wessindians' favourite cars. And I start to wonder if he know that a Wessindian does-treat a Tornado more better than he does-treat a woman or a wife; and with a Wessindian, yuh can't ask his woman for a dance at a dance unless you expecting some blows. Even if he give you permission to dance with his woman, don't dance a Isaac Hayes or a Barry White slow-piece too slow and too close, yuh...

I waiting anxious now, 'cause I don't see the boy for days, these days. I feel the boy already start making money from the scheme. I walk all over St. Clair-Oakwood, all along North-cliffe, swing right 'pon Eglinton, mek a left on Park Hill Road, a further left up by Whitmore, and find myself back 'pon Northcliffe going in the opposite direction, and still I can't rest my two eyes on the green hornet. Fellows start telling me that the boy does-be going to the races every day, on his lunch break from ticketing people cars, and betting *one hundred dollars on the nose* and *five hundred to show* on one horse, leffing the races with bundles o' money. And laughing like shite.

I walking-'bout day and night, all over St. Clair-Oakwood, and still no sight o' the boy.

Then, *bram*! I start hearing horror stores.

"I come out my apartment last Wednesday night to get in my car, and my blasted car not there! It gone. Tow-'way!" one fellow say.

A next fellow say, "Be-Christ, if I ever catch a police tow-ing-'way my car!"

"I don't like this place. It too fascist. Tummuch regulations and laws. A man can't *breathe*. I can't tek it 'pon myself and lodge a complaint with the Police 'cause I here illegal. No work permit, yuh know? No job. Now, no car! You park your car, and when you come out in the cold morning to go-work at a li'l illegal job, no fucking car?"

"I was up by a little skins one night," a next fellow say. "I tell the wife I going to Spree. I tack-up by Northcliffe at the skin's apartment. I really and truly did-intend to spend only a hour. Well, with a few white rums in my arse, one thing lead to the next. And when I do-so, and open my two eyes, morning be-Christ brek, and um is daylight. My arse in trouble now, two times. Wife and wuk. I bound down the fire escape, not to be seen by the neighbours, and when I reach ground, no blasted car!"

Stories o' motor cars that get tow-'way start spreading through the St. Clair-Oakwood neighbourhood, just like how the yellow leaves does-fall 'pon the grass a certain time o' year. Stories o' fellows getting lay-off, no work permit, getting beat-up, can't go to the Police in case, and getting lock-out, all this gloom start spreading like influenza. The fellows scared. The fellows vex. The fellows angry. And they can't go and complain to the Police to find out where their cars is, 'cause, yuh know, the papers not in order. As man! And the li'l matter o' *landed* and reçu and so on and so forth...

They can't even start calling the Police pigs and racists and criminals. And all this time, nobody can't find the green hor-net boy at tall.

Well, a plague o' tow-'way cars rest so heavy on my mind, even though I don't own no wheels, seeing as how I is a real TTC-man that I get real concern. 'Cause, drunk or sober, blood more thicker than water...

"*As man!*"

I hear the voice and I bound-round. And look. I see cars. I see Wessindians. I don't see no Police, but I frighten. I see a tow-'way truck. And I still don't see nobody I know. But I think I recognize the voice.

"As man!"

I bound-round again, and I see the same things.

"Over here, man!"

God bless my eyesight! Um is the green hornet man. My friend! Sitting down behind the wheel of DO RIGHT TOWING 24 HOURS. I do-so look! I blink my two eyes. I seeing, but I not seeing right. I watching, but I having eyes that see and that watch but they not watching right.

"Um is *me*, man!"

The tow-'way truck real pretty. It have-in short-wave radio. Two-way radio. CBC-FM. Stereos. *And* CB. It paint-up in black, yellow, and white. The green hornet boy, dress-off now in overalls and construction hat cock at a angle on his head, cigar in mouth and shades on his face, like if he is a dictator from Latin America.

"Remember the plan? The plan I tell you 'bout for making money? Well, I went to my bank and talk to my bank manager and squeeze a loan for this outta the son of a bitch." He tap the door of the tow-truck like if he tapping a woman. "And I had a word with a fellow who was a green hornet like me. I is still a green hornet myself, but I works the afternoon shift. This fellow I know, the ex-green hornet, couldn't take the abuse and the threats to his person of being a hornet, so he open up a little place up in Scarborough where he *enpounds* the cars I does tow-'way. And me and him splits the money. I brings in a car, and quick-so, um lock-up and enpounded. If a fellow want-back his car, fifty dollars! You want piece o' this action?"

I get real frighten.

"You want to get cut-in 'pon this action?"

"But-but-but-but…"

"You see that pretty silver-grey Thunderbird park beside the fire hydrand? I watching that car ow, fifteen minutes. I see the fellow park it, and go in the apartment building there. I figure if he coming back out soon, he going-come-out within twenty minutes. I got five more minutes…"

I start getting real frighten now. 'Cause I see the car. And the car is the same car that belongs to the Goliath, the black Amurcan fellow. I so frighten that I can't talk and warn my green hornet friend. But even if I coulda find words, my tow-truck friend too busy talking and telling me 'bout a piece o' the action and how easy it is to tow-'way cars that belongs to illegal immigrants and get money split fifty-fifty, and to remember the Rockefellers…

"…and I had to laugh one day when I bring-in a Cadillac," he tell me, still laughing, as if he was still bringing–in the Cadillac. "Appears that my pound-friend had a little altercation of difference of opinion with a 'Muracan man over a car once, so when I appear with the silver-grey Caddy, he get frighten and start telling me that nobody not going maim him or brutalize him or curse his mother, that before anything like that happen, he would go-back home to Guyana first and pick welts offa reefs or put-out oyster pots down by the sea wall… Look, I got to go! Time up!"

I see him, and I watch him pull off from 'side o' me like if he didn't know me, like if I was a fire hydrand. I watch him drive up to the shiny grey Thunderbird car, not mekking no noise, like if he is a real police raiding a Wessindian booze-can after midnight. I see him get-out the tow-truck, like if he walking on ashes. I see him let down the big iron-thing at the back o' the tow-truck. First time in my eleven years living here as a semi-legal immigrant that I have see a tow-truck that didn't make no noise. I see him bend-down and look under the front o' the Thunderbird. I see him wipe his hands. I see him wipe his two hands like a labourer who did a good job does-wipe his hands. I see him go-round to the back o' the Bird and bend-down. He wipe his two hands again. I see him size-up the car. I watch him put-on the two big canvas gloves on his two hands. I watch him cock the cigar at a more cockier angle, adjust the construction hat, tek-off the shades and put them inside his pocket, and I see him take the rope that mek out of iron and look like chain and hook-um-on 'pon the gentleman nice clean-and-polish grey 1983 Thunderbird. I seeing him and I watching him. The boy real professional. I wondering all the time where the boy learn this work. He dance round the tow-truck and press a thing, and the Bird raising-up offa the road like if it ready to tek-off and fly. I see him press a next thing in the tow-truck and the bird stationary, but up in the air, at a angle, like a Concord tekking-off. I see him bend-down again, to make sure that the chain o' iron hook-on good. I see him wipe his two hands in the big canvas gloves a next time, and I see him slap his two hands. Telling me from the distance where I is, watching, that it is a professional job, well done. I think I see the dollar bills registering in his two eyes too! And I see him tug the chain tight, so the Bird would move-off nice and slow, and not jerk nor make no noise, when he ready to tek she to the pound to enpound she.

And then I see the mountain of a man, tipping-toe down the metal fire escape o' the apartment building where he was, black shoes shining in the afternoon light, hair slick back and shining more brighter from a process, dress in the same three-piece suit, with the pinstripe visible now that the sun was touching the rich material at the right angle o' sheen and shine, and I see, or I think I see, the gentleman tek-off a diamond and gold ring two times offa his right hand, and put them in his pocket – I think I see that – and I see how the hand become big-big-big like a boxing glove, and I tell my former green hornet friend to look over his left shoulder. I seeing, but I can't talk o' what I seeing. I find I can't talk. I can only move. A tenseness seize the moment. I do so, and point my index finger, indicating like a spy telling another spy to don't talk, but to look behind. But at that very moment, the black Amurcan gentleman's hand was already grabbing my friend from outta the cab o' the tow-truck…

REVULSION

HEATHER J. WOOD

From: greatactress@gmail.com
Subject: Re – what happened my callback?
Date: January 12, 2017
To: mel@talents.com

Hi Mel,

What do you mean the personal hygiene products agency has blacklisted me from appearing in any more of their commercials? I thought peeing my pants during the audition would add some honest-to-goodness realism to the incontinence pads ad. I was submerging myself in the role – finding my motivation. You know, Stanislavsky! Strasberg! Method acting! Sigh…some people just have no appreciation.

Anyway, I still want to try out for that herbal anti-nausea commercial. If you get me in front of the casting director on Monday, I swear I'll stick to the actual script. I promise J. You know you can count on me, Mel. It's not like I'm going to intentionally barf.

Remember, you're the most awesome agent in the biz!

Hugs and kisses from your favourite client, Star

From: greatactress@gmail.com
Subject: About that little incident
Date: January 31, 2017
To: mel@talents.com

Hi Mel,

Glad you're still talking to me. Sorry about your having to pay the insurance company's deductible L. I don't know what I'd do without you, Mel. You really are the best. I mean, who knew that kerosene was so flammable? I was just trying to show Mr. Serious Horror Film Director that I was totally immersed in the pyromaniac character's backstory. You should have seen the look on his face, his hair being on fire.

Anyway, maybe you're right about my staying away from movie bookings for a little while. How about you rustle up some live theatre auditions for me?

Can't wait to hear what you come up with! I owe you one,
Star

From: greatactress@gmail.com
Subject: V-Day audition
Date: February 14, 2017
To: mel@talents.com

Hi Mel,

Forgive me, OK? But really, rhyming "vagina from Regina" is just so grade six. Plus, I thought the whole point of this monologue show was female empowerment or something. Using *vagina* when you mean *vulva* is just not on. I told the director, "I'm empowering myself by making my lines more anatomically correct." Boy, did that piss her off! Her face went deep purple – matching her fake Pashmina scarf. She said I was making a mockery of her critical feminist production and that I wasn't fit to perform alongside the dedicated women who were taking the audition seriously.

I turned up the mic and shouted *vulva revulsion, vulva revulsion, vulva revulsion*. Then David, this really cute security guard, escorted me off the stage. (You wouldn't know how to get in touch with him, would you?) Anyway Mel, I still really need a money-making gig. Do you think I could join Peter downtown tomorrow and audition for *Puppetry of the Penis?*

Star

A PREDICAMENT

MORLEY CALLAGHAN

Father Francis, the youngest priest at the cathedral, was hearing confessions on a Saturday afternoon. He stepped out of the confessional to stretch his legs a moment and walked up the left aisle toward the flickering red light of the Precious Blood, mystical in the twilight of the cathedral. Father Francis walked back to the confessional because too many women were waiting on the penitent bench. There were not so many men.

Sitting again in the confessional, he said a short prayer to the Virgin Mary to get in the mood for hearing confessions. He wiped his lips with his handkerchief, cleared his throat, and pushed back the panel, inclining his ear to hear a woman's confession. The panel slid back with a sharp grating noise. Father Francis whispered his ritual prayer and made the sign of the cross. The woman hadn't been to confession for three months and had missed mass twice for no good reason. He questioned her determinedly, indignant with this woman who had missed mass for no good reason. In a steady whisper he told her the story of an old woman who had crawled on the ice to get to mass. The woman hesitated, then told about missing her morning prayers... "Yes, my child, yes, my child..." "And about certain thoughts..." "Now about these thoughts; let's look at it in this way..." He gave the woman absolution and told her to say the beads once for her penance.

Closing the panel on the women's side, he sat quietly for a moment in the darkness of the confessional. He was a young priest, very interested in confessions.

Father Francis turned to the other side, pushing back the panel to hear some man's confession. Resting his chin on his hand after making the sign of the cross, he did not bother trying to discern the outline of the head and shoulders of the man kneeling in the corner.

The man said in a husky voice: "I wanna get off at the corner of King and Yonge Street."

Father Francis sat up straight, peering through the wirework. The man's head was moving. He could see his nose and eyes. His heart began to beat unevenly. He sat back quietly.

"Cancha hear me, wasamatter, I wanna get off at King and Yonge," the man said insistently, pushing his nose through the wirework.

On the man's breath there was a strong smell of whiskey. Father Francis nervously slid the panel back into position. As the panel slid into place he knew it sounded like the closing of doors on a bus or streetcar. There he was hearing confessions, and a drunken man on the other side of the panel thought him a conductor on a streetcar. He would go into the vestry and tell Father Marlow.

Father Francis stepped out of the confessional to look around the cathedral. Men and women in the pews and on the penitents' benches wondered why he had come out of the confessional twice in the last few minutes when so many were waiting. Father Francis wasn't feeling well, that was the trouble. Walking up the aisle, he rubbed his smooth cheek with his hand, thinking hard. If he had the man thrown out he might be a tough customer and there would be a disturbance in the cathedral. Such a disturbance would be sure to get in the papers. Everything got in the papers. There was no use telling it to anybody. Walking erectly he went back to the confessional. Father Francis was sweating.

Rubbing his shoulder blades uneasily against the back of the confessional, he decided to hear a woman's confession. It was evading the issue – it was a compromise, but it didn't matter; he was going to hear a woman's confession first.

The woman, encouraged by many questions from Father Francis, made an extraordinarily good confession, though sometimes he did not seem to be listening very attentively. He thought he could hear the man moving. The man was drunk – drunkenness, the over-indulgence of an appetite, the drunken state. Scholastic psychology. Cardinal Mercier's book on psychology had got him through the exam at the seminary.

"When you feel you're going to tell a lie, say a short prayer to Mary, the mother of God," he said to the woman.

"Yes, Father."

"Some lies are more serious than others."

"Yes, Father."

"But they are lies just the same."

"I tell mostly white lies," she said.

"They are lies, lies, lies, just the same. They may not endanger your soul, but they lead to something worse. Do you see?"

"Yes, Father."

"Will you promise to say a little prayer every time?"

Father Francis could not concentrate on what the woman was saying. But he wanted her to stay there for a long time. She was company. He would try and concentrate on her. He could not forget the drunken man for more than a few moments.

The woman finished her confession. Father Francis, breathing heavily, gave her absolution. Slowly he pushed back the panel – a streetcar, a conductor swinging back the doors on a streetcar. He turned deliberately to the other side of the confessional, but hesitated, eager to turn and hear another confession. It was no use – it couldn't go on in that way. Closing his eyes he said three "Our Fathers" and three "Hail Marys," and felt much better. He was calm and the man might have gone.

He tried to push back the panel so it would not make much noise, but moving slowly it grated loudly. He could see the man's head bobbing up, watching the panel sliding back.

"Yes, my son," Father Francis said deliberately.

"I got to get off at King and Yonge," the man said stubbornly.

"You better go, you've no business here."

"Say, there, did you hear me say King and Yonge?"

The man was getting ugly. The whiskey smelled bad in the confessional. Father Francis drew back quickly and half closed the panel. That same grating noise. It put an idea into his head. He said impatiently: "Step lively there; this is King and Yonge. Do you want to go past your stop?"

"All right, brother," the man said slowly, getting up clumsily.

"Move along now," Father Francis said authoritatively.

"I'm movin'; don't get so huffy," the drunk said, swinging aside the curtains of the confessional, stepping out to the aisle.

Father Francis leaned back and nervously gripped the leather seat. He began to feel very happy. There were no thoughts at all in his head. Suddenly he got up and stepped out to the aisle. He stood watching a man going down the aisle swaying almost imperceptibly. The men and women in the pews watched Father Francis curiously, wondering if he was really unwell because he had come out of the confessional three times in a half-hour. Again he went into the confessional.

At first Father Francis was happy hearing the confessions, but he became restive. He should have used shrewd judgment. With that drunken man he had gone too far, forgotten himself in the confessional. He had descended to artifice in the confessional to save himself from embarrassment.

At the supper table he did not talk much to the other priests. He had a feeling he would not sleep well that night. He would lie awake trying to straighten everything out. The thing would first have to be settled in his own conscience. Then perhaps he would tell the bishop.

GOODBYE, GOD

MARTY GERVAIS

I was the fifth born, the fifth son, but the first in my family to be born in a hospital. All the others in a house on George Avenue. I was also born on my brother's birthday… No one knew what to call me. I started out as Douglas, then it was Charlie, then it was Allen, then it was… Well, it was finally my uncle, a Catholic priest, who broke the deadlock and called me Henry, naming me after himself. He stepped out of the church on a grey windy day in early November, and presented me: my wispy forehead damp with baptism. I was finally saved from Limbo the place where a heap of unbaptized dead babies wind up…

I was six years old and I could ride a bike and read a book and stay up an extra half hour every night… It wasn't a good time though, this being 1952, and Saturday mornings with the sirens in Detroit jarring us all awake like an alarm clock, reminding us we were at war. War with Russia, and there'll come the day when the Russians will paratroop from the sky to blow up our homes and bury us alive… And my neighbours back then started tunnelling backyard bunkers, places to hide, a refuge, and they were storing up beans and weiners and Vernors and Mars bars…But my dad said there was no point in doing that – we'll all be dead, but we'll all go Heaven straight away because the Russians weren't Catholics, and we were, but, like the Russians, the Protestants were all going to

Hell too, and so they better build the bomb shelters – they're all going to Hell – they weren't part of the one true Holy Apostolic Roman Catholic Church.

My first confession. I was seven. The nuns at St. Thomas told me my soul was black from sin, and the only way to wash away that evil was to confess. We practiced in the basement of the school, kneeling on the concrete floor, our hands clasped together, eyes shut, and reciting the Act of Contrition: *Oh, my God, I am heartily sorry for having offended Thee, and I detest all my sins, because I dread the loss of Heaven, and the pains of Hell, but most of all because they offend Thee, my God, Who are all good and deserving of all my love.*

I was afraid of God. Kept expecting he was going to zap the Earth any minute because the nuns were constantly forewarning us that we knew not the day, nor the hour… What the hell? What kind of God is this that he can't even give us a little bit of a warning! And he was always *watching* us, knowing our every step. What kind of creep would do that? But this was God. What I couldn't understand, however, was all the fuss about Satan. He seemed like God's biggest competitor, and if God was all powerful, and Satan was all Evil, then why wouldn't God just zap him and get rid of him? Besides, why was it so much easier to go to Hell than Heaven. And why resist? Anyway, when I was about eight or nine, I wondered about all this stuff, and thought maybe there was no Satan, maybe it was God's way of frightening us, so I stood there one day in my room, all by myself, and glanced around, and thought, *Hey, let's go for it.* "Okay, take my soul if you'd like – it's yours!" Satan never appeared. It's not like he tapped on the window, and said, "Henry, open up!" But over the next couple of months, I was testing 100% on all my tests, without ever studying, and I was on my feet in the classroom answering questions with words I didn't even know the meaning of, but now I did... And my cursive handwriting suddenly was the best in the school, and I was gobbling up book after book, and my head was spinning with...and...and...

I watched men in felt fedoras ogling the nyloned curves of the legs of demure women. That's when I heard those words. Men would parry about them, guffaw, mutter things I never understood – names for a body part I knew nothing about. I was awed by such lingo, vocabularies that were alien, foreign, out of sync, exotic, mysterious – *flaming lips, hoohaw, cha-cha, snapper, muff, Lady V, kitty, cupcake, beaver, cooter...* I wrote them all down, committed them to memory, recited them like a square dance tune – *snapper, muff, cupcake, beaver...cha- cha, kitty, hoohaw, cooter... It's a do-si-do and tip of the hat, one step forward and two steps back, cowboy cowboy marry me, I'll bake you a cherry pie, Well, thank you very kindly, ma'am, but I'm too young to die. Well do-si-do side-by-side, one step forward, one step back, cupcake, beaver, snapper, muff, cowboy's kitty is not enough, it's do-si-do and tip of the hat, we'll all lay down back to back...* I didn't know what the hell it all meant. I loved the sound, the beat, the tumble and turn of words, a "lexicon of lust" as the priest told me when I asked if these were "bad words," grown-up obscenities. I saw the old priest slumped behind the grating of the confessional, shaking his bald head in disgust, yet inviting me to repeat each word, to pronounce them clearly, and slowly, and I mouthed them: *cooter, cupcake, kitty, cha-cha, hoohaw, snapper, beaver, muff...*

I was afraid of God. We counted sins. Venial sins and mortal sins. We found out about Purgatory, a place that wasn't anywhere near as bad as Hell, but definitely not comfortable.

A one-star hotel, maybe. Bath-room down the hall. No TV, no Disney, no sports, no Vernors, no chocolate. This is how the nuns introduced us to arithmetic. We counted and subtracted. This was plus and minus. And lying to your mother was a venial sin, and that would send you into exile for a couple of hundred years. The only way around it was to stockpile "indulgences" or special prayers, or acts of kindness that would somehow lessen your sins. A single day in Purgatory, hissed Sister Bartholomew, would feel like a thousand years of anguish. But if you recited your prayers before meals for one full week without fail, you could win back twenty years. If you made the sign of the cross, that might erase another 150 days, and if you performed this with holy water, there might be a bonus. And if you served Mass on Sundays, as well as one day during the week, and you did that seven straight days, you could deduct six years from your sentence… My brother figured he'd scored big when he traded a stack of holy cards, including five different St. Francis of Assisi images, for a card that contained a miniscule bone chip of St. Gerard. This relic was worth at least a thousand days spent in Purgatory. I stared at it for such a long time, and when I told my brother it looked like a fingernail, he beat the crap out of me… At six or eight or nine, the concept of indulgences sounded a lot like Monopoly and being handed a get-out-of-jail card.

Mark Twain apparently said, "The two most important days in your life are the day you are born…and the day you find out why." I'm not sure I know why. Do you? Does anyone? But I do know that language has always been the thing to grab on to, and movies were the bones of language – dialogue, plot, the lyric grace of gesture, all swarming those afternoon movies. It all made sense. Somehow it awakened in me something to say, formally, maybe a deep longing, that is, and yet I didn't understand that…yet that morning when I slipped into a wooden desk in the windowed classroom – a little bored, inattentive, and opened up the textbook, and began reading the *Dark Lady Sonnets* by Shakespeare, it all made sense. Didn't it? This love-lost narrator worried sick over a woman's betrayal:

> *O! call not me to justify the wrong*
> *That thy unkindness lays upon my heart;*
> *Wound me not with thine eye, but with thy tongue:*
> *Use power with power, and slay me not by art,*
> *Tell me thou lov'st elsewhere; but in my sight,*
> *Dear heart, forbear to glance thine eye aside:*
> *What need'st thou wound with cunning, when thy might*
> *Is more than my o'erpressed defence can bide?*

I fell in love. I fell for the words, the plummet and pitch of sound, the playful wit, again, the gesture in the way someone turned, or the way a hand coyly smooths the collar of a jacket…I sit here now believing in all that authority that comes alive with words, and I play the moment for all its worth, *I see the moon, I see the moon, I see its playful heart, I see the moon, I breathe its mischievous art…*

This was era of bow ties, and our dads wore white shirts rolled up to the elbows, and Clark Gable mustaches. By 1959 though, my dad stuffed those elaborate silk ties in a shoebox that he placed on the top shelf of his closet. My father wore a tie to his first interview at the Motor Lamp. And got a job on the line making headlamps before he wound up working in the office. And when we were kids, we wore bow ties, clipped to our collars, and brushed back our hair like his, straight back, no part, and drove off to church like that, each Sunday. We wanted to be like him. When we grew up, and started our own families, and accidentally caught sight of ourselves in a store window or mirror, and instantly recognized that look, that sullenness of my father all over again. We hated that. It was everything we had hoped for as kids, but now as grown men, we needed something else, our own soul, not his. Finding the bow ties in that shoebox after his death was like looking at old school pictures. We wore those ties on Sundays, all day long and by nightfall we tossed them across the dining room at one another. I never saw the point of these ties. They seemed fake, a half tie, a gesture, a half- hearted nod in deference to ties. They look like misplaced eyebrows.

Ah! The good old days. No, I am no sentimentalist, believe me. Hated school. Hated teachers. Hated priests. Hated the neighbourhood. Happy to move north to Muskoka. At first, I hated being there too. Spotted my classmates leaping into the river near the falls. I couldn't swim. Instead, I retreated to the closed-in verandah at the back of the house, and read… Read all of Mark Twain, my afternoons fading into the twilight, my mind swarming with images of adventure and mystery. Outside was foreign, distant, irrelevant. My mother was worried sick over my lack of "ambition" and not being "out in the sun…with friends." I didn't need them. I felt cheated by them actually… My first days in grade four. Minny McCracken, a stout elementary school spinster whose sister Mae also taught at that school, ordered us to open up our geometry sets, and for reasons unknown to me, I was slow to doing it, and it prompted her to challenge me. My forbearance triggered a confrontation. "Open it!" she demanded. My new friends, all around me in desks, were snickering, and I suddenly was emboldened by this, thinking they were cheering me on. "No!" I said. Finally, I did, but only after Minny sidled up to the desk and tapped the tin box three times with cold insistence. I flipped it open, but to my horror, there, resting on my protractor was a cut-out black-and-white photograph of a tit. It sat there looking up at me like a stranger, maybe a little dog, maybe a bug…I don't know. Horrified, I slammed the geometry set shut. Minny was appalled. She scooped up the tin box and walked to the front of the class. She said nothing. I was going to Hell for sure. I survived, but at recess, my new friends all had a good laugh.

To soothe my ruffled feelings, they treated me to the other part of the snapshot. A picture of a sister taken by a boyfriend. Her brother held up that beat-up Brownie photograph, and graciously presented it to me, like a prize, or trophy. I stared at this young girl whose one breast was now missing. Minny had the other tit on her desk, secure in my geometry set. I never knew what happened to it. Did she take it home? I didn't really care, because I had the rest of the shot. I pored over it for days deliberating over what this girl was thinking when it was taken, what the conversation was like with her boyfriend, and did they *do* anything before or after it was snapped… She just stood there, naked from the waist up, hands resting on her hips eyeballing the camera, maybe a trace of a smile, bright bright eyes, and I *knew* her. She lived in town, a high-school girl, and I saw her nearly every day… All such conjecturing left me paralyzed as I stumbled about the schoolyard, face flushed, as I strayed aimlessly over the playground. I stuffed the photograph into my coat pocket, and at night, slumped in the bathtub, stared at it, mute, the only sound in the house pulsating from *Leave It to Beaver* downstairs… The picture of that town girl with one tit. I kept it for years, and somehow, over time, it got lost, maybe thrown out, who knows? Maybe tucked inside a book. Years later – and I swear this is true – I heard this same person had a breast removed… I didn't make that up.

I hear myself. My voice, an echo, a reminder… I'm alive, I'm alive. I'm here. I'm Now. And I pretend to encircle myself with memories, binding me with all of you. I fear the worst knowing hope is no resolution. We lived through the Cold War. We marched as children on Ouellette Avenue in the Blue Army, the army of the Virgin Mary, and we strode in the May Day parades – I saw the Russians strutting in Moscow Square, the Red Army sending dread and trepidation into the world, threatening to bomb us when we were asleep in our beds… There we were, boys filing into line, nightfall shrouding us as we paraded to Jackson Park's bandshell, Bishop Cody presiding at the podium like Dwight Eisenhower surveying the Allied troops. We were soldiers. Members of the Blue Army, a religious group born out of the Fatima revelations right before Elvis Presley took America by storm. We were the answer to Communism, that godless society of Bolsheviks. This was the Cold War. We were the children of Hope. We were the children of McCarthyism. We saw spies everywhere. We walked in single file, that sweet scent of incense trailing in the air. Life was important. We were important. We were defending our faith… But it was never perfect. Especially for me. In that first parade, I was maybe ten, and feeling ill over having stuffed myself with too much chocolate. Walking didn't help. As I made my way in the street, I glanced over at my brother Bill and told him I was sick. He fired back a frown and made it clear that if I broke ranks I'd embarrass the parish. I persevered. Kept marching. This was for God. This was for country. This was for Mary. This was me signalling to Khrushchev that Communism was evil! And now, just as we were nearing the bandshell, where the Knights of Columbus in their plumed hats and swords flanked the bishop, I started retching. It was like a scene out of the 1973

film *The Exorcist*. Projectile vomiting. The starched white sur-
plice of an altar boy in front of me was where the first volley
landed, like being hit by winter slush from a passing car. The
next settled on the shoes of one of the organizers. I was bawl-
ing my eyes out. Moments later, there was my father rescuing
me, driving me home, gritting his teeth and not saying anything at all. I expected a Blue Army court martial.

SAINT AUGUSTINE

ALEXANDRE AMPRIMOZ

His mother died during the winter. Her last words were, "Continue your research and you won't be lonely."

The idea of courting one of the eight girls who lived down the street with their mad father crossed his mind. It would be easier now, with the house all to himself, his mother no longer there to check up on him.

But he'd never thought women were essential. He had other ways of fighting his loneliness. He decided to get a rattlesnake.

It was a pleasure, coming home with a few rodents for Saint Augustine. That was the name he gave his pet (a thing he would never confess to anyone). He never tired of watching the "snake dance and song of death" and when the reptile finally sank his fangs into a rat, he felt shivers of pleasure travel up his spine. The same game with mice had been a lesser thrill.

Spring. One evening he was too tired to read even a few pages of *The City of God* before retiring (though he hadn't yet reached forty-five). In his sleep, in his dream, he spoke to his mother. "Mother, on the purple hill, you left me alone by the first gate where the river boils, but thank you, Mother, for the two mermaids. I will chew them properly. Then I will take the train that drips down from the moon like a slow slug and…"

The next day Saint Augustine had two heads. He didn't mind going to a funeral home with the madman and his six daughters. Two of them had just died in a car accident.

"The party at the funeral home is for them. I'm bringing a bottle of Cold Duck, get it?" asked the madman.

That night, he gave Saint Augustine a rat and went to bed. Then in his dream he spoke to his mother. "You should see Augustine. For a long second it is too beautiful. You should see, Mother, the way he swallows the two witches…"

The next morning the snake had four heads. Two more of the madman's daughters had died during the night, drowned in the lake.

There are no more dreams and Saint Augustine has eight heads. He is rather happy: four of the girls are still alive. That proves that there is no relation between his snake's extra heads and the madman's daughters' deaths.

"It was only a coincidence," he murmurs.

He is sitting in his living room looking at Saint Augustine. "I should have bought an octopus." He falls asleep. *The City of God* drops from his hands. Saint Augustine bangs one of its eight heads against the glass, the terrarium begins to break…

THE DEAD COW IN THE CANYON

JACQUES FERRON

François Laterrière, the fifth son of Esdras Laterrière of Trompe-Souris *rang*, Saint-Justin de Maskinongé, came of good stock. When he was sixteen years old he already looked twenty. His father said to him:

"You're not a child anymore."

"No," he admitted.

The conversation went no further. Several months passed, and the old man continued: "Well then, my boy, seeing as how you're not a child any more, have you thought what you're going to be in life?"

"Yes, Pa: a habitant like you."

A strange idea, this, coming from the youngest son! The old man made up his mind to give it some thought. A year later he asked his son:

"Hey, François, who was it put such an idea into your head?"

"What idea?"

"Lord love us! The idea of becoming a habitant."

"The priest, Pa."

The priest. Now, that was a serious matter. Esdras Laterrière, his brow knit, realized the going could be tough. *Whatever I do,* he thought, *I must be sure and not rush things.*

"François," he said, "I have great respect for the priest. You know that. But the harder I think about it, the harder it is to understand. Why ever did he advise you to become a habitant?"

"Because that's what you are, because that's what your father was, and because we must preserve the heritage of our ancestors."

"The heritage of our ancestors?"

"Yes, Pa."

The old man waited to hear no more. He hitched up the old grey mare, jumped onto the cart, and with a "Giddap!" was off to the presbytery.

"*Monsieur le curé*, I've come to pay my tithe."

"There was no hurry, my friend."

When the calculations were completed and the arithmetic done, the habitant did not budge from his chair.

"And there's something else," he said

The priest had suspected as much.

"There's my son François," the habitant continued. "He's stirring up trouble at home."

The priest expressed surprise. The habitant explained.

"But there's been a misunderstanding!" the priest objected. "François has no intention of ousting his eldest brother! The land will go to him, whole and undivided. François knows that as well and you and I do. He simply wants to follow in your footsteps and become an honest farmer himself, Monsieur Laterrière."

"He doesn't want my land?"

"No, he doesn't, I can assure you."

"Then I have to agree, Father. He's not a bad boy at all."

The habitant, however, was not entirely reassured. He had nothing against his son becoming a farmer, but where was he going to get his land?

"That's a mere detail, Monsieur Laterrière!"

"A detail! There's no land left in the parish, and there's none in the county either!"

The priest rose to his feet.

"There was no more land in France. Our ancestors found it in Canada. There's no more in the county, no more in the province, you say? Your son won't let that stand in his way. He'll find land somewhere else!"

"Where?" the habitant asked.

"In the Farwest," the priest replied.

Esdras Laterrière had never heard of any such country. The Farwest, Patagonia…they were one and the same to him. But no matter. His worries were over. His boy would not be setting himself up at his expense.

Back home again, he said:

"François, I've found you some land."

François thanked him. The next day he set out for the Farwest. Two years later he arrived in Regina.

"*Monsieur*," he asked the first man to come along, "is the Farwest still here?"

"No," said the man, "it's moved to Calgary."

The lad from Trompe-Souris was beginning to find the Farwest a little too much for him. In Toronto, they had told him it was in Winnipeg; in Winnipeg they had said it was in Regina; and now he had reached Regina only to discover it had already moved to Calgary. The land of Edras Laterrière had never shifted an inch. True, it was very well fenced…

"It's a strange country, this Farwest, *Monsieur*!"

The first man to come along agreed with him politely, then bade him good day. This man was followed shortly after by a second man, but François did not speak to him, nor to any of the others who came his way. Without further pause, he continued on to Calgary.

Calgary is a city with wide avenues, where there are no longer any horses to be seen. There are, however, a great many horsemen, whose sleek boots, thick belts, steel spurs and high hats all attest to the fact that they have left their mounts at the city gates. The avenues themselves tell you nothing you do not already know, show you nothing that cannot be seen elsewhere. But close your eyes for a moment and you hear the hard jangle of spurs on the pavement. In an instant, the ordinary world is abolished, for the place is surrounded by a thousand horses, impatiently pawing the dust. You breathe the air they blow from their ardent nostrils; it is the air of the Farwest. François inhaled it with satisfaction, but before long his throat was dry. He went into a tavern.

"I'm happy," he said to the landlord.

The landlord slid two glasses his way.

"Why two?" asked François, whose tastes were modest.

"In my tavern that's how it is, my boy," replied the landlord. "You have one drink because you're happy, and I offer you another because I'm happy to see you happy."

This friendliness, the beer, and the joy he felt at finding himself at last in the Farwest put the young man in a confiding mood.

His chin over the glasses, his hand in his mane, a faraway look in his eyes, he began to tell his story. The landlord interrupted him, banging on the counter with his fist. The glasses jumped, but the young man did not flinch.

"You're from Trompe-Souris?"

"Yes, *Monsieur*."

"And you want to be a habitant in the Farwest?"

"Yes, *Monsieur*. A habitant like my father, like my grandfather, like all the Laterrières, because we must preserve the heritage of our ancestors."

The landlord leaned over to Timire, his assistant.

"Take off your apron," he told him. "Run and tell the Chief: the Chosen One has arrived."

Timire took off his apron and hurried out. François, however, protested that he was not the Chosen One. The landlord hastened to reassure him.

"You're from Trompe-Souris, I'm from Crête-de-Coq. You're from Saint-Justin, I'm from Sainte-Ursule. We're from the same county. Could I possibly wish you any harm?"

"No, not if it's like you say."

"If it's like I say? It's even better than I say. Why, I wouldn't be surprised if you weren't my cousin. My name is Siméon Désilets!"

"Well, how about that! My mother is a Désilets!"

"Her first name?"

"Wait now…"

"Georgina?"

"No."

"Valeda?"

"No… Wait now… I've got it; Victoria!"

"She's my sister; I'm your uncle."

The landlord wasted no time. He seized a glass and filled it. Uncle and nephew raised their glasses. The drinks overflowed: they were deeply moved. The beer spilled onto the counter; the landlord mopped it up, himself scarcely able to hold back the tears. When you're a French Canadian you can't possibly know all your relatives, but you're overjoyed to make their acquaintance all the same. Family spirit is strong!!

When they had drunk, the landlord asked for news of the old country, then he continued: "You're not the Chosen One, Nephew. I know that as well as you do. You're no fool and I've still got my head screwed on. But we can make the Chief believe you are."

"The Chief?"

"Yes, the Chief. One of the feathered breed, a kind of Iroquois. When I first arrived here I traded with him. Then I bought my tavern. A good-hearted fellow, but not much of a head for business. I owe a lot to him. He's right at home here. I let him drink as much as he likes. He's always paid me. If he weren't my friend, I sometimes think he'd be my best customer."

The landlord drained his glass. François did the same. With the glasses empty, the acoustics were much improved.

"Why should we make him believe you're the Chosen One? I'll tell you why, Nephew. He has a daughter. Her name is Eglantine. He wants to marry her to a white man. The fellow's nuts. He says the spirits have spoken to him. The spirits, they're the good Lord's flying *curés*. When they command, you have to obey, otherwise you go mad. So there's the Chief, looking for a white man. Not that there aren't plenty of them about. You can find white men of every race and religion in the Farwest. The trouble is my friend is fussy; to him all whites are savages. He wants to obey his priests, but he doesn't want to give his Eglantine to a savage. He's in a right quandary. So what does he do? He comes to see me. 'You good white,' he says to me, and to the good white he offers his daughter. Now, if ever any man has cheated, robbed, taken advantage of the old Chief – I can tell you this, you're my nephew – that man is me. Hearing him talk like that just about breaks my heart. 'Chief,' I says, 'I'm good, all right as good goes. But that doesn't mean I'm the man to marry your daughter. I'd consider myself lucky, make no mistake, but alas, I'm old, the tavern ties me down, and there's Beauty Rose, my Irish girl. You know her: she'd spit fire of hell in your face if she heard of your offer.' Before I could finish my speech, the Chief was in tears. It was the first time I'd ever seen him in such a state. I was touched. I said to him, 'There, there, don't cry. I'll pray to God and ask him to send you my cousin, a fine lad from Maskinongé, not savage at all, and white as milk. We'll marry him to your Eglantine.' That was the promise made to the poor Chief, out of the goodness of my heart. Tell me, François: wouldn't you have done the same?"

"Yes, of course," replied the young man.

"Ah, Nephew, you are indeed the son of my sister Victoria, the kindest girl in the world."

And the landlord proceeded to fill the glasses.

"To your mother, to my own kind heart, to the goodness of the Désilets!"

They drank.

"After hearing my promise," the landlord continued, "the Chief went away rejoicing. I can see him now. And that was more than two years ago. He went away, but he came back. At the end of every season he'd come down from his canyon to ask for news of the promised cousin. I'd do what I could to keep him happy. The last time, at my wit's end, I promised him he wouldn't have to wait much longer. The old boy went home. The season ended. Yesterday he arrived with his Eglantine to greet the Chosen One. There wasn't a cousin anywhere I could lay my hands on. I didn't know which way to turn, I cursed my promise. But I didn't have the heart to disappoint them. They were so happy, so trusting. So I said to them, 'Come back tomorrow.' Oh, what a night I spent! And then morning brought you, dear Nephew! Even if you're not the Chosen One, you must admit you couldn't have come at a better moment!"

The landlord paused for a moment and banged his fist on the counter. The glasses jumped. François did not flinch.

"Thanks to you," cried the landlord, "your uncle's word will not be broken!"

The young man was uneasy. He'd have liked nothing better than to help an uncle keep his word, but it wasn't for that that he'd walked for two years, crossed four provinces, worn out fifteen pairs of cow-hide boots. Besides, the Commandment that told him to honour his father and mother made him no mention of any other relatives, least of all an uncle with a tavern in the Farwest, who he hadn't even known existed until one day, feeling particularly dry, he'd entered this tavern to wet his whistle.

"What's the problem, Nephew?"

"The problem, Uncle, is that I'd like very much to oblige you…"

"I know that."

"It's also that I didn't wear out fifteen pairs of cow-hide boots and come all this way just to meet an Indian maiden from the Farwest.

"Now you're talking! Have another drink, you deserve it."

And the landlord slid one over to him.

"All the same, Nephew, what would you say if this Indian maiden, a fine-looking girl, as it happens, also brought you a canyon the size of a whole parish for a dowry?"

"A canyon?"

"A piece of land surrounded by mountains as high as the sky."

"Hey," said François, "then I'd ask to see her."

He saw her, found her to his liking, and the next day they went to the church. A priest with carrot red hair, not one inch a Métis, married them with a wave of his sprinkler. The ceremony continued at the landlord's tavern. After eight days of revelry, the Chief stopped drinking, pushed away his glass and said:

"It's no good."

He still wasn't drunk. His thirst was intact. So why go on drinking? This wasn't the first time he'd tried. His previous attempts had all ended in failure. He'd never managed to get himself drunk. To bring him to his senses, it had always been necessary to knock him out. With age he'd grown wiser. This time, before he lost patience, he'd cut short the drinking, thus avoiding the final fury.

"It's no good," he repeated.

The landlord, who knew his Chief, having had occasion to bring him to his senses in the past, was careful not to insist. He made haste to end the celebration and had the horses brought up. When the animals were at the door, François asked:

"And what about the cows?"

For François Laterrière, shaken though he was by the little jolts of marriage, still held fast to his resolve.

"Yes, Uncle, the cows. I cannot become a habitant like my father, like my grandfather, like all the Laterrières before them, and preserve the heritage of my ancestors, if I don't have at least one cow to put in my canyon."

"What did he say?" asked the Chief.

The landlord explained his nephew's demand.

"Pooh!" said the Chief.

"What did he say?" asked François.

"He didn't make himself very clear," replied the landlord, "but I think he has a rather low opinion of cows."

The lad from Trompe-Souris, touched to the quick, flashed an indignant glance at his father-in-law, who continued:

"Cows! Pooh! Buffalo in canyon."

"What did he say??"

"Instead of a cow he's offering you a herd of buffalo."

The young man refused. Who had ever seen a buffalo on a habitant's land? It was a cow he needed. The Chief raised his arms to heaven: a cow would never be able to climb up to the canyon.

"He's right," urged the landlord.

But François took no notice. Disdainful and proud, he remained deaf to anything that might deter him from his mission. Blood will tell. Like all French Canadians he was a descendant of Madeleine de Verchères. He was a hero. All that mattered to him was his cow. They suggested a doe: a fig for their doe! A goat: fie! and for shame! Eglantine was growing anxious, the Chief impatient. Suddenly, the landlord cried:

"A heifer!"

There was some sense in the idea; our hero considered it; he hesitated. Pressing his advantage, the landlord slapped him on the back. A heifer, after all, was only different from a cow for a few months. And what were a few months to a determined young man who had worn out fifteen pairs of cow-hide boots, crossed four provinces and found his way at last to his uncle, Siméon Désilets?

"Come on, François, come on!"

François gave in at last.

"I give in," he said, "but I'm not giving up. I'll accept the heifer but I won't forget the cow. I'll give satisfaction to the

Farwest, but I'll remain faithful to the tradition of my ancestors."

"Bravo!" cried the landlord. "God has inspired you. You
speak like a true *curé*!"

They all applauded and everyone was happy. All they had
to do now was find the heifer. The gods smiled on them: she
was found at once. François took her in his arms and leapt
onto his horse. The party moved off. Siméon Désilets stood
alone at the door of his tavern.

"Whew!" he said.

Then he went inside and poured himself two drinks, one
because he was feeling happy, and the other because he was
happy to see himself happy.

"You're laughing," exclaimed Timire in amazement.

"And you would be too," replied the landlord.

II

Once they were out of Calgary, François cried:

"Hallo!"

He was echoing that distant hallo that the rising mounts
call to the plain.

"Hallo, plain," they say, "give up your illusion: the earth is
not flat."

The lad from Trompe-Souris was astonished. The mountains drew nearer. His astonishment did not lessen, but his
apprehension grew.

"The canyon isn't up there, I hope," he inquired.

They showed him, between two dazzling peaks, the pass they would have to cross to reach it. He felt no pleasure at all at the sight. Like La Vérendrye, he would gladly have turned back. Nevertheless, he continued. It was a long climb. When he finally reached the canyon he vowed never to come down. One year later he started down again. You can be sure of nothing when you've a heifer in your care.

By spring the heifer had already become a cow. She took no notice and continued to graze. However, she was gaining less now and grew more slowly. Summer came. She stopped growing altogether and was amazed.

"Why should I bother to eat any more?" she asked Eglantine.

"Eat, my girl, eat," replied Eglantine. "You'll not regret it."

Enigmatic words, which the cow was to ruminate for a whole month. At the end of the month, she wanted to know more. Eglantine proceeded to instruct her. From then on, her ears aquiver, her neck strained, she lived in expectation. She forgot to eat her due. Then amid the juicy hay, hunger gnawed her, and she began to wail. It was pitiful to hear.

"What's wrong with her?" François asked.

"She claims," replied Eglantine, "that your hay tastes bad."

This insinuation was not well received. The hay was from good millet and identical in every way to the ancestral hay. How could it possibly taste bad? The cow was an impudent hussy and was lying shamelessly. To satisfy himself, François went and examined her closely. When he came back he announced:

"Wife, there's nothing the matter with my hay. It could feed more than one cow; it could feed a whole herd."

"In that case," inquired Eglantine, "why does she wail, poor thing?"

"There's another reason. We must go down to Calgary and bring back a bull calf."

At that same moment the Chief emerged from the bushes. He had been gone since fall and had spent the winter hunting. His pelts had been rich; he was carrying a roll of bills as fat as a girl's thigh. The roll redoubled his valour; his children were on their way to Calgary; without pausing for breath, he set off behind them.

"Well!" thundered Siméon Désilets, "this is a big surprise!"

The Chief put his roll on the counter.

"Count," he ordered.

The landlord felt it.

"It's velvet to the touch."

"You keep," said the Chief, "if you find way to get me drunk."

Thus challenged, the landlord felt every confidence in his ability to get him drunk. He brought out his very best mixture; white lightning, beer and rubbing alcohol. One week later, the Chief was hollow-eyed, but he still sat upright in his chair. "Wait a moment, my good Chief," said the landlord, "you won't be sitting like that for long!" And he placed in front of him the decisive glass, filled with straight rubbing alcohol.

"Just taste that now and tell me what you think."

But the Chief didn't seem the least bit curious. He didn't even touch the glass. Perhaps he needed a little encouragement. Siméon Désiletes, acting out of the goodness of his heart, went to give him a friendly pat on the back... He remained rooted to the spot, his hand upraised, extremely surprised. The Chief had spun round, lithe as a cat, and plunged a knife into his belly. No allowance had been made in the itinerary for any such stabbing. Having come down to Calgary for the sole purpose of acquiring a bull calf, François and Eglantine had intended to go straight back once the calf was acquired. They were obliged to attend the landlord's funeral, then the Chief's trial, and finally his hanging. These family duties kept them in Calgary for more than three months.

Meanwhile, above the canyon, the sun never blinked from morning to night. In time it grew very hot; the springs stopped running, the water in the trough dried up, and in a cloud of dust drought descended on the land. The little cow soon found herself in difficulties. Whenever she took a step, thousands of grasshoppers would fly up, and with their shrill call warn the grass to flee still further. Imprisoned in a moving desert, she could find nothing at all to eat. Her skin was loose, her bones unsteady. She had grown so thin she looked as if she were wearing her big sister's coat. Ridiculous and pitiful, she wandered about, saying to herself:

"If only I could get a drink."

It was her sole concern. A hundred times a day she returned to the trough, and always came away disappointed. Above the grasshoppers, the hawks hovered; higher still, the vultures. Neither bird was a good omen. At last, her courage failing, the unfortunate cow said to herself:

"My hour is come."

And, so saying, she let herself fall onto the burning ground. After a time, however, discovering that she was not quite dead, she opened her eyes and strained her ears...And what should she hear, but the sound of running water!

"My hour is not yet come," she cried.

And with this she struggled to her feet, poor creature, and rushed off once more in the direction of the trough. But the effort this time was tremendous; her strength gave out; she staggered; a thousand suns were spinning in the sky. To regain her balance, she stopped, but her skeleton kept right on going. She was blinded by the dust, deafened by the grasshoppers, the hawks, and the sun. A vulture landed on her head. The skeleton was still going; it was already well ahead of her; she didn't know what to think. She shook the hat and the vulture flew off; she had lost sight of the skeleton now, concluded that she must be dreaming, and continued on her hallucinating walk. She arrived at last at the water trough; on the dried up mud lay the skeleton of a cow. She was not dreaming; it was her own.

"I am dead," she murmured to herself.

Death as a rule has a most devastating effect on life. In this case, the opposite was true; the result was exhilarating; the cow felt better dead than alive; freed of needs she could no longer satisfy, harassing needs, more terrible by far than hawks or vultures, she once more took pleasure in herself. The impression was a strange one: she almost felt alive again.

At the same moment, the sun blinked and rain transformed the landscape. As soon as they were wet the grasshoppers fell silent; reassured, the grass came back, soft and defenceless. The carrion birds, lords of the drought, had disappeared; green silences replaced their harsh cries. Although she was indifferent to the renewal, the little cow nevertheless felt inside her a joy that grew with each new day. Her courage had returned, her skin fit once more. True, she still had no skeleton, but it hardly noticed; her appearance was most respectable. She wandered freely through the canyon. Every now and then she would pause to take a mouthful of grass; not that she was hungry – it was pure caprice. Sometimes she would go over to the water trough and there, occasionally, she might take a drink; not that she was thirsty – it was just a lapse; she simply wanted to see the reflection of the spectre her joy had brought to life.

When they returned to the canyon, François and Eglantine were delighted to find her, to all appearances, in the best of health. They ran to her, embraced her fondly, then introduced the male calf they had brought back with them from Calgary.

"He's a nice little animal."

There was no glow of passion in her eyes.

"Nice, he is," Eglantine replied, "but that's not all. Just wait: a year from now, burning with passion, a little bull he'll be."

The cow remained cold.

"What's the matter with you, little sister?"

"I'm dead," she replied.

Eglantine burst into tears.

"What wrong?" asked François, who understood nothing of the language of cows.

"She says…Oh, God! it's dreadful."

"Well, what?"

"She says she's dead."

Surprised, François walked around the animal, then looked up, skeptical. Eglantine, offended, brushed away her tears.

"How could you have the heart," she cried, "to doubt the word of a poor dead cow?"

To which he replied that he, for his part, had heard no such word.

"Is it my fault if you're deaf?"

"If I'm deaf, Eglantine, then maybe you've too much imagination."

Then she asked him if he thought she was crazy. No, he didn't think she was crazy. But he did disapprove of her listening to the blather of animals. She argued back: he refused to climb down. She called him a savage; he called her a squaw. In short, they quarrelled. When they had finished, the cow motioned them to follow her: she led them to the water trough. The skeleton was there, irrefutable.

"Well?" said Eglantine.

François, shattered, could find no reply.

"Now, do you dare to say this cow is not dead?"

He did not dare.

"But," he added, "dead or not dead, what's the difference as long as she'll calve?"

"What do you mean?"

"Let's leave the little bull to sort things out."

A year passed. The bull calf, now every inch the animal required, began to lift his eyes in the direction of the cow. One day, emboldened, he lifted his legs instead. The cow, already suspicious, had seen him coming; she jumped sideways and the bull fell to the ground.

"You should be ashamed of yourself," she said.

He picked himself up, his forehead bristling, all ready to try again.

"If you want to know the truth," the cow went on, "you disgust me."

Round-eyed, he stared at her.

"Fool, can't you see I'm dead?"

The poor chap swallowed his saliva. He was sincere in his intentions, but blinded by passion, he had not noticed the sad condition of his companion. In his innocence, he had wanted to serve her. Since she was dead, he did not insist. He walked away. Not for the world would he have defiled her. And his ardour, with no outlet, turned inward against him now. His head became swollen, his eyes shot with blood; he longed to crush his bones against a rock; the canyon shook with the sound of his bellowing. Until in the end the little cow took pity on him.

"After all," she said, "I may be dead, but that doesn't stop me from taking a mouthful of grass here, a drink of water there. Why shouldn't it be the same with the other little necessities? There, poor boy, don't look so sad now. You can do what you like with me. Feel quite free: it's really all the same to me."

Now it was the bull's turn to be disgusted.

"Thank you very much," he replied, "but I don't need your cold carcass!"

And with that they were estranged, estranged forever, sadly, foolishly, all because of a few thoughtless words, estranged for no good reason! For they could have been reconciled; indeed, they should have been. Love is the coming together of life and death; it is perfectly natural for one party to be cooler than the other.

Meanwhile, François himself had not been idle. Having talked first for the sake of it (which improved his voice) he found at last the world he had been looking for. And so it was that the virtue of the race, at first inoperative, one day bore fruit. Eglantine, mysteriously touched, smiled as she grew heavier. In spite of her condition, she continued to look after the animals. Her shoulders thrust back, portly as an ambassador, she went from the bull to the cow and from the cow to the bull, mediating as best she could, but unable to make peace between them. This failure, however, did not trouble her unduly, for she had already achieved within herself the reconciliation of opposites. François, for his part, was preparing the nest. He was putting the finishing touches to a house, the perfect replica of the Laterrière farmhouse in Trompe-

Souris, in the parish of Saint-Justin de Maskinongé. He had
thus reconciled future and past, heir and ancestors, and was
on the point of transplanting to the Farwest the traditions of
the Quebec people. It was too perfect to last.

One morning, Eglantine, on one of her diplomatic mis-
sions, spied the bull, normally quite stand-offish, coming
toward her with blood-shot eyes, his head low.

"What's the matter, little bull?" she asked.

He did not answer, but kept on coming. Then Eglantine,
guessing his intentions, uttered loud and piercing screams.
Her emotion only proved to the animal that she was indeed
alive. Frustrated by a dead cow, he needed nothing more. The
morphology of the two parties did not lend itself to their
union. The fair Eglantine died. François, who had rushed to
the scene, now furious at finding himself a widower, killed the
bull, then collapsed himself on the two bodies. When he
came to, he heard a wail. It was a baby girl, lying there, kicking, in the blood of her mother and the monster.

François Laterrière left the canyon that same day. It was
the dead cow who moved into the house, that perfect replica
of the ancestral home. She felt quite happy in it. But there
were times when she would climb up to the attic and there,
with her head thrust out the window, gaze nostalgically into
the distance.

III

Fleeing his canyon, François Laterrière left behind him, like
an absurd dream, a house built in the Quebec style and

haunted by a dead cow. The chorus of ancestors tried to hold him back, but he refused to stop, thinking it was the cow. For two days and two nights he walked. After which, already much distressed by the death of Eglantine and the failure of his mission, he had completely taken leave of his senses. God guided him. At the end of the third day he reached Calgary, a city large enough to get lost in. But God did not abandon him: he found his way to the tavern of his late uncle, Siméon Désilets.

The last client had left. Beauty Rose and Timire were in the process, she of totting up the day's cash, he of wiping the tables. Any moment now they would be closed. The door opened; a man walked in and placed on the counter a tiny bundle of soiled linen. Automatically, Beauty Rose slipped him a glass; he emptied it in one gulp. She slipped him another; he emptied it just as fast; then a third, a fourth… He was clearly very thirsty. Beauty Rose, her interest aroused, said to herself:

"Something tells me I know this man." But she could not put a name to him. Suddenly the tiny bundle moved.

"Lord, it's moving!"

"So what?"

"What is it you've got all wrapped up there and moving like that?" she asked him.

"Dunno," he replied.

She took pity on him.

"Come along with me," she said.

He followed her to the Tourist Rooms adjoining the tavern. She pulled off his boots and put him to bed. A maid appeared, enticed.

"Is this one for me, Ma'am?"

"No," replied Beauty Rose, "he's not for you, nor me, nor anyone. He hasn't a cent and he's sick; his own mother wouldn't want him now."

When the servant had left, Beauty Rose thought to her-self: *Perhaps he really hasn't got a cent.* She checked: she was right. But what should she find in his pocket but the rosary of Siméon Désilets, her late husband.

"It's my nephew, François," she said to herself. "I thought he looked familiar!"

She left the room. To the maid, she said:

"It's my nephew, François. Something terrible has hap-pened to him."

"Poor you," said the maid.

"Something terrible. And he's changed, changed! I recog-nized him by his uncle's rosary."

"Poor you! What a dreadful thing to be so changed!"

Cutting short these ancillary condolences, Beauty Rose went back downstairs. The bundle was still on the counter.

"Timire," she called.

Timire arrived.

"Unwrap this bundle, Timire. I haven't the heart to do it myself."

He unwrapped it. She clutched her hands to her breasts.

"Lord Jesus! Just as I thought: it's a girl, a lovely little girl! Timire, don't just stand there with your mouth open! Come on! Do something."

Do what? Timire had no idea.

"Why, baptize her, of course! Can't you see she's cold? You never know; she might have caught her death, the poor little creature."

Timire, beer in hand, said:

"I don't know what to say."

"Poor fool! You say: 'I baptize you in the name of the Father, the Son and the Holy Ghost."

Timire was about to touch the baby's forehead with his glass, but Beauty Rose stopped him.

"Fool! Precious fool! It's not beer you use to baptize a child! Do you have no principles, then?"

She handed him a bottle of white lightning.

"It's white lightning!"

Once the ceremony was over and the way to paradise opened to the poor little creature, the widow of Siméon Désilets regained her composure.

"Now," she declared, "we must see to it she doesn't die."

Timire called the maids. They came down to the tavern.

"This," the widow told them, "is the child I've been promising you. She's my niece. Her name is Chaouac."

Their joy was amazing to behold. The child was handed over; her weight seemed to reassure them. When they had taken her away, Beauty Rose asked Timire how he felt.

"I'm very glad," he replied.

The next day, although he had fully recovered his senses, François Laterrière did not recognize the grimacing little frog he had found lying in the blood of a monster and a woman; they showed him a clean, well-fed baby, asleep on the breast of one of the maids. This breast, alas, reminded him of another.

"Aunt," he said, "Eglantine is dead."

"I'd guessed as much," replied Beauty Rose.

He told her the tragic story. She said:

"François, your daughter is my daughter. Stay here, we'll bring her up together."

At such generosity the young father lost his composure and fell down upon his knees. Seeing this, his aunt lost hers, and burst out laughing.

"Get up off your knees, you silly boy! You owe me nothing. It's a favour you're doing me letting me take your daughter."

He got up.

"There are three reasons why you owe me nothing. Just listen to them and you'll stop your genuflexions, you'll see!"

And Beauty Rose explained that she had not always been a person of staid disposition, having first been driven by wanderlust for many years. Born in Dublin, she had acquired her Irish education in haste and had left in search of adventure by the time she was thirteen years old. Her travels had brought her, by a thoroughly capricious route – via Australia, China and Russia – to Canada, where she had at first sojourned in the ports of the east. After which she had moved to the Yukon, and from there to the Farwest.

"Nephew," she went on, "I paid my own way. For a long time I had the means. As I grew older, however, I found it more difficult to make a living from my looks, and I was soon in desperate straits. From then on travel became difficult. I have very unpleasant memories of the Yukon: men there are quite unreasonable. When I arrived in Calgary I was exhausted. Siméon Désilets came along. He needed a wife, I deserved a rest, we were married. He was a strong man, your uncle! He kept me where he wanted me and there I stayed! And I became staid, oh so staid! We lived together five years, then his friend, the Chief, did him in. He's gone now; but he left me his memory, Timire, his tavern, and his morals. That's the first reason why you owe me nothing, even if I am helping you out."

But the inheritance was not all pure gold. There was also, in the widow's estimation, an element of wastage, understandable if one considered that Siméon Désilets had not come to Calgary via Australia, China and Russia. He had held on to certain of the prejudices of Saint-Ursule de Mas-kinongé, which Beauty Rose had been obliged to dispense with after his death. On the subject of the sexes, for example. Not for anything in the world would the landlord have encouraged contact between them. He had every occasion to do so, however; beer awakens a client's generosity; after two or three bottles he very often feels the need to bestow his favours on some poor disadvantaged girl; in this case, why not help him to find her? Besides, collaboration of this nature is always profitable.

"Your poor uncle always refused."

François Laterrière had not travelled via Australia, China and Russia either.

"By God," he exclaimed, "my uncle was right."

"After his death I gave in."

"You betrayed him!"

"Precisely," said the widow, "and that, you see, is my sec-ond reason. I've been unfaithful to the principles of your uncle. I'm sorry, even though I didn't approve of them. You're his nephew. I'll help you and so make amends."

François, indignant:

"Make amends some other way. Don't count on me any-more. I'll have nothing to do with your acts of fornication."

Beauty Rose, taken aback:

"Fornication?"

"Yes, fornication."

"I don't understand, Nephew. You're forgetting that I have morals."

"Morals? You must be joking!"

"Morals that I got from you uncle. If I hadn't had them, I'll admit, I'd have gone in for a brothel; but I had them, and so I made do with Tourist Rooms."

François had spoken too harshly.

"Tourist Rooms, that's different," he conceded.

"Just a modest little enterprise: ten rooms, four maids. So help me, I don't see where you get your fornication, Nephew! I employ the maids to look after the rooms; in between chores they have time to spare; I don't ask them how they spend it; that's their business. I collect the money for the rooms. What could possibly be wrong with that, Nephew?"

"Why, nothing at all, Aunt Beauty Rose."

"Besides, I'm never in the place. I stay in the tavern. There, after the second or third bottle, a client will sometimes ask me for a girl: I offer him a room, I promise him nothing; I tell him if he's lucky the maids will like his pretty face. If he still takes the room it's at his own expense, and not theirs, because he never has a pretty face. I personally select the clients; the pretty faces always go elsewhere to be admired."

"And the third reason?" asked François, who was beginning to weary of his aunt's dialectics.

Beauty Rose hesitated.

"To be perfectly honest," she replied, "when the client goes upstairs I'm not as confident as I let on to you. True, I've personally selected him; he never has a pretty face. But then, I'm not that well acquainted with my maids either; they just might have poor taste. And so, to calm my fears, I've insisted that they all have milk."

François, aghast:

"Milk!"

"Yes, milk."

"Hmm," said he.

"Of course," Beauty Rose went on, "a maid can't have milk without having previously experienced a certain misfortune, and I tell myself that the milk will prevent it from happening again. That's my third reason: we'll have more than enough to feed your daughter. You lend her to us, we'll care for her, and you can keep your genuflexions for another: your daughter will pay us back."

The young father, horrified:

"How?"

"By sucking," came the reply.

Having milk is not everything; what matters is being able to keep it. To achieve this end, it's best that it be drunk, since breasts are so made that they will fill up only as long as they are emptied. For a while, before the arrival of François Laterrière and his daughter, Chaouac, this generous paradox caused Timire great concern, for it was he who had been put in charge of the milkmaids' welfare. Day in, day out, morning, noon and night, he had to provide them with hungry children. He chose these children with the greatest of care; they were nevertheless always taken off the streets, where children have a tendency to be more talkative than elsewhere. And so it happened that certain parents came to hear what repast was being served in the Tourist Rooms, and they were most upset, for parents, it is well known, are always more or less corrupt; these felt obliged to forbid their children the healthiest, the noblest, if not the most humane of all foods. As for Timire, they talked quite simply of hanging him. Timire would hear nothing of it, but he was anxious all the same. He had no difficulty approving the adoption of Chaouac.

François Laterrière also approved it, but with less promptitude. First, he had to listen to a debate in his conscience between his daughter, the said Chaouac, on the one hand, and his priest, Monsieur de Saint-Justin, on the other. The priest spoke first; he affirmed truths to which François listened, but which he barely heard, since the acoustics of a "tourist room" in the Farwest are hardly conducive to such things as those of a farmhouse in Trompe-Souris. Then it was Chaouac's turn; her speech was short and to the point; she was thirsty. With her first cry François heard her and felt the torment of her thirst.

"Oh, *Monsieur le curé*, forgive me," he cried, handing the child to Beauty Rose. "I have no other choice!"

"Not so fast, there, Nephew!" replied Beauty Rose. "I may have my morals, but I'm not a *curé* yet!"

One of the "tourist rooms" was made available to the young father and it was suggested that he might like to help Timire in the tavern during the day. He accepted the room but refused the job, happy to be able to sleep next to Chaouac, but not the least bit inclined to get himself breathed all over by drinkers of beer. Not that he despised these drinkers; they were his brothers, exiles like himself, and for the most part of the same origin. Indeed, the tavern is the only place in America where a French Canadian can speak his language freely. But François Laterrière was not one to indulge in conversation. He was a serious lad, who had no time for idle talk and knew that, as far are essentials were concerned, everything had already been said long ago by persons in authority, and in particular by Monsieur de Saint-Justin. And so he preferred the open air.

He went to work on a ranch. No speeches there, just grass and wind, and sometimes a cloud or two, or else an empty sky and the backdrop of monotony against which simple, uncomplicated souls, inclined to melancholy, seem to thrive. François found peace there, if not happiness. They hadn't given him a lasso; he had no idea that he'd become a cowboy. The ranch seemed to him like one vast Trompe-Souris, a free and unfenced version of the lowlands of Maskinongé county. He wished for nothing more. At night he came back to sleep at the Tourist Rooms; in the morning he returned to his cows. He took care, however, never to go near the tavern, which he believed to be a haunt of the Devil. On the ranch he felt no cause for anxiety. Yet it was there that a sinister encounter awaited him. One day he found himself face to face, not with Satan, but with a white bull, an animal utterly lacking in subtlety, who was nevertheless to have a most disastrous influence on his soul.

Both parties began by examining one another coldly. The landscape was green, almost blue. Then a strange heat was felt, as a cloud moved aside, unmasking the sun, which was yellow, almost red. And in that same moment both turned coward. Each took a step forward in the hope that the other would step back, then keep on going, leaving fury triumphant and carrying off in his retreat the cowardice of both. But the other party also stepped forward. So there was no alternative but to fight it out. François was the madder of the two. His fury triumphed. With his neck wrung, the white bull turned coward and died. "Bulls and I," said François to himself, "just don't seem to get along!"

He had to admit that he, for his part, detested them, for the very good reason that one of their kind had forced him to leave the canyon, where he had found his mission, where Eglantine lived, and where his ancestors and his children would together have brought about his certain happiness. But he refused to allow for the existence of any such sentiments on the side of the bulls. Yet the bulls had every right to feel this way, since they considered their brother in the canyon to have been guiltless, laying the blame for Eglantine's death on the dead cow and responsibility for the bovine fury on

François, who, they claimed, could have prevented it by removing the offending organ. In short, as is always the case, both sides had excellent reasons for carrying on the war. And the war continued. Ten more times, pitting his strength against an ever renewed enemy, François Laterrière emerged victorious, thus demonstrating the superiority of the lad from Maskinongé over the bull of the Farwest. This was not quite what the boss had had in mind.

"You'll go far, my boy," he said. "Ten bulls in one week is a mighty fine start! Carry on the good work anywhere you like, but keep off my ranch!"

So, François took himself elsewhere and, at the expense of another boss, proceeded to repeat his demonstration. Before long a nasty reputation had overtaken him. Thrown out a second time, he was unable to get himself hired on a third ranch. After which, on the advice of Beauty Rose, he went to see old Jesse Crochu at the Calgary Stampede. Crochu took him on immediately, but on one condition: he was to change his name. Frank Laterreur he became.

Not long afterwards, who should arrive in Calgary but Monsieur de Saint-Justin, on an apostolic mission. He was companied by an academician – a ferret-faced pinhead – none other than the famous historian, Ramulot. They had come from Edmonton where, on behalf of the Committee for the Survival of the French Agony in America, they had been inspecting the few remaining houses where the French Canadian lingo could still be heard. In Calgary there was no one to visit. And so, to the Calgary Stampede they went. There, the said Frank Laterreur greatly impressed them, both by his courage and by the extreme simplicity of his technique. Indeed, without picadors, without banderilleros, alone in the ring, and unarmed, without the aid of a red cape, or a lance, or a spear, with only his bare hands, he slew the black bull. This beat anything Europe and its toreadors could do.

"Oh my! Oh my!" exclaimed Monsieur de Saint-Justin.

"Hooray! Hooray!" cried Ramulot, his mouth watering.

After which, still hungry for more, they decided to go and congratulate the champion on behalf of their Homeland and to present him, *honoris causa*, with the emblem of the fleur-de-lis. In the wings they bumped into Jesse Crochu, who asked them, "Who are you?" They gave their names and listed their titles. The Academy? Old Jesse had never heard of any such thing, but, putting two and two together, guessed what it must be. *I reckon that's what those fellas down East call their rodeo,* thought he.

"Anyhow," he said, "don't go getting ideas about taking Frank away from me. Bulls, now – that's okay. If you need some, I can let you have all you want. But not Frank. He's mine, and he stays right here with me."

Ramulot thanked him: the Academy was not in need of bulls. As for the said Frank, they had no desire to hire him. They simply wished to congratulate him and pin a fleur-de-lis on his chest. Jesse Crochu, reassured, saw no reason to stand in their way. Let them congratulate, then, and decorate; let them fleurdelisate to their heart's content!

François saw them approaching. Like most priests when they travel, Monsieur de Saint-Justin was not wearing a cassock. François caught sight of his collar. *Bah! it's a clergyman!* he thought.

As for Ramulot, he was wearing a tie, a blue one, distinctly on the gaudy side.

"You, my pinhead," said François under his breath, "you can pay for the heresy of your friend."

And drawing in his neck like a bull, he advanced towards him.

"Mr. Laterreur!" cried the Academician, "I have the greatest admiration for you. Please stop and allow me to decorate you with the fleur-de-lis!"

Now, in the Farwest, this symbol is used for branding cattle.

François: "Just you wait! I'll show you who's the calf around here!"

But Ramulot had no wish to wait. He turned on his heels and fled. All went well until a terrible boot with a deadly aim caught him from behind, raising his lower quarters high off the ground and causing his upper quarters to plunge accordingly, so that he sailed through the air, a ferret-faced Icarus, in the direction of the nearest manure pile. There he landed, pin-head first, and sank so deep that François abandoned the fight in disgust. And turning to Monsieur de Saint-Justin:

"Mr. Clergyman," he said, "take back your shit-faced friend."

So ended the encounter of François Laterrière and his parish priest in Calgary. They met again in Saint-Justin twenty-five years later, but this time, the priest having assumed his cassock and François his real name, they recognized each other.

"So!" cried François, "the clergyman was you!"

"So!" cried the priest, "the toreador was you!"

And they burst out laughing at the memory of Ramulot. He alone had kept his identity. And a fat lot of good it had done him.

"God can't have wanted us to recognize each other," the priest concluded.

"Still, there were a lot of things I'd have liked to tell you, *Monsieur le curé*."

"You can tell them to me, now, François Laterrière. It's never too late."

And François did. There was Siméon Désilets and his tavern, there was his marriage to the Chief's daughter, the canyon and the dead cow, Eglantine's death and the birth of Chaouac, Beauty Rose and her Tourist Rooms, and the Calgary Stampede.

Upon my soul, thought Monsieur de Saint-Justin. *I foresaw nothing like this when I sent this boy to the Farwest!*

François also told him about the milkmaids, but out of regard for his listener, he arranged the episode in such a way that it appeared edifying.

"There you are, *Monsieur le curé*. That's the story you'd have heard in Calgary if by chance we'd recognized each other."

"Very well," said Monsieur de Saint-Justin, "but what happened next?"

What happened next presented François with certain difficulties of narration. It had come to pass that the said Frank Laterreur, having constantly to pit himself against the bulls, had ended up resembling them in one very significant way, the consequences of which are easy to imagine when one considers that he was spending his nights in the Tourist Rooms and that more often than not the four chamber maids whom Beauty Rose reserved for clients also slept there. He took advantage of the fact that they were his daughter's wet-nurses and insinuated himself into their company, with the result that the clients soon ceased to receive the attentions they were accustomed to. The affairs of the Tourist Rooms declined, seriously damaging those of the adjoining tavern. All of which would have given Beauty Rose cause to complain, but Beauty Rose herself had no time to think about it, being, in spite of her age and her morals, just as well served as her maids. The honeymoon lasted four years. After which, business picked up again and improved from month to month. Two years later, Tourist Rooms and tavern were flourishing as before. It was the said Frank who had gone under. The bulls had stopped hating him, he himself no longer detested them, and from there it followed that everything else was changed. Jesse Crochu had fired him. Beauty Rose now did the same.

"Your daughter is six years old," she told him. "There's nothing to stop you putting her in a convent now. I'll not be able to help you anymore. As it is, I've given you far more than I need have done. I've paid off my debt to the late Siméon. Farewell, Nephew!"

François Laterrière, ex Frank Laterreur, fallen champ, now not even worth his weight in beef, left Calgary, taking with him his Chaouac, his bright little flame, his only passion. In Regina and Winnipeg he worked as a butcher, in Toronto as a gangster. When he reached Montreal, Chaouac was turning fifteen. She was well educated and beautiful. Together they opened up Tourists Rooms, and fortune smiled on them...

"Very well," said Monsieur de Saint-Justin. "What happened after that?"

"After that...well, er..." What happened after that, it seemed, presented certain difficulties of narration. Here was the gist of it.

With a sweep of his hand, François indicated, over by the presbytery, the huge black limousine, in which he had driven up like a prime minister.

"My, my," said the priest. "What a big car! I'm very glad indeed. Then the advice I gave you wasn't so bad after all!"

"It was good advice, *Monsieur le curé*, and I thank you for it. However, I must tell you that I didn't carry out the mission you entrusted me with."

"What mission? I don't remember any mission."

"To be a habitant in the Farwest, a habitant like my father and my grandfather and all the Laterrières of Maskinongé county."

"Forget it, François, forget it! You've kept your faith. You've kept your language. And you're rich. What more could anyone ask?"

François Laterrière was sad, for he knew himself to be unworthy of the priest's approval.

"Besides," the priest went on, "even if you didn't succeed in putting down roots there yourself, the conquest of the Farwest by our people is going well."

He pulled out some photos of his trip, showing the various houses in which, twenty-five years earlier, French was still being spoken.

"What do you think of this one?" he asked.

François recognized his own house in the canyon.

"Doesn't it look just like one of our own?"

"Yes, indeed, Father."

"When we visited it, the owner was away. A cow had climbed up into the attic, and she was standing there, with her head out the window, mooing and mooing. I said to her: 'Now stop your mooing. Your master'll soon be home.' And I blessed the house."

François Laterrière took leave of Monsieur de Saint-Justin. The village around the church had not changed. In his big car he drove through Trompe-Souris. Trompe-Souris had not changed either. The parishes of Quebec took on their definitive shape in the last century. Since then they haven't budged, hardening like cases around their inhabitants and retaining always the same invariable number, the number they held one hundred years ago. François found his childhood still intact. And yet, in spite of this, he was a stranger in the village and in the *rang*; his place was no longer here. But then, had it ever been here? Temporarily, perhaps until such time as he could grow up and be expelled to an absurd Farwest. For he belonged to that surplus humanity that the Quebec parishes have continually to reject, in benefit of foreigners, and exploit and sell, the grimacing face of the puritan prostitute.

When François Laterrière left Saint-Justin the first time, wearing his cow-hide boots, he wept, and could find no solace til, in a far-off canyon, he had managed to recreate the likeness of his Homeland. When, thirty years later, in his big black limousine, he left the village for the second time, no tears blurred his vision. He knew then that he had never been loved. He also knew that a country that values itself more highly than its children and doesn't hesitate to get rid of them, sending them off to the cities, to the mines, to every corner of America, without thought for their fate, concerned only with the preservation of its own old togs, is a country that does not deserve to be loved. And he was perhaps sadder than the first time.

When he got back to Montreal, he sold his Tourist Rooms. No one has ever enjoyed running a brothel, and François Laterrière was no exception. He had been driven to it out of necessity. After the death of Eglantine and the failure of his mission, with nothing left to guide him, he had understandably sunk very low, low enough to collect the wages of sin and to bounce back onto the highways in a big, black limousine, like a prime minister. This limousine he also sold. Soon he was free to go as he pleased. He returned to that absurd and unlikely canyon, which was the place in all America where he felt least like an exile. Meanwhile, at his side, with staring eyes, her head stuck out the attic window, the dead cow mooed in the direction of an unattainable Trompe-Souris.

(Translated by Betty Bednarski)

TALMUD

MATT SHAW

Yes! She was not balding and she had excellent fashion sense. She had not lost her husband to poker, or her only daughter, just eighteen, to a burlesque-revival show in Chicago. All truths, but not for Lilly, who could contort any fact into falsehood. This delusion inspired her to sell her split-level Canadian home, pack two suitcases (crammed with bikinis and lacy bras) and move to Europe, where she had sensuous affairs with thirteen European men before birthing a child and returning to Canada, alone, to live in a small log cabin on the western shore of Lake Erie.

The European men refused to wear condoms because they were too thin for amorous European sex (of thirteen kinds, including Spanish, French, and Slovakian). She became pregnant. The boy was named Talmud and she left him with the man she presumed was his father, Iran, a portly aficionado of cigars and American pop culture who was actually Russian-American and not foreign in the least. She wrote Iran a cheque for $5,000 and promised to send more. He was happy to live his new American Dream of the doting single father, but in Amsterdam, which he found more hospitable in his dotage. He hugged Talmud against his chest as Lilly boarded an airplane to New York and shouted a promise that Talmud should visit her when he turned twenty and she had adjusted to the idea of motherhood.

Lilly did not know how to live a small-town life. She bought a hatchback and drove it sparingly. She lit her sparse lakeshore cabin with candles of all manners, sizes, and scents. She bought a body pillow to simulate the presence of another being beside her. She applied for a job as a waitress at a faux-fifties diner on the town's main drag and dressed every morning in a checkered vinyl skirt, earning a living and growing older.

After three years she felt cervical pain and sought the town gynecologist, but he was stymied. The pain increased and her hair thinned until she saw patches of her scalp in the mirror. She wore hats before realizing it was a useless charade. She quit the diner and stayed home whenever possible, reading histories and biographies of famous and less-famous celebrities and politicians, and often of the dogs or women that they loved, and walking along the lake with her feet in wet sand, wishing she could bury herself in it.

During this period she received the first visitor who knew of Iran and Talmud. He arrived suddenly, without luggage. He might have been sent, Lilly thought. His name was Pahl, he was from Norway, and he said Iran was a very good friend. Iran had indeed told him he would find Lilly here if he ever travelled in Canada. Talmud was beginning school now and could write his name very legibly. This made her happy. She slept with Pahl, *fucked him silly*, as the ladies at the diner would say, and it dulled her uterine pain. In the day, they stayed apart, each doing their own business. At such times Pahl was less a visitor than a guest in need of a room.

In the evenings they played Scrabble and then they fucked. And in the morning she went to the white beach. When the sheets were humid and tangled she sometimes asked him about Talmud. What else might he know? *Nothing,* he would say, *nothing,* until he drifted off in an interminable snore.

Soon she was nearly bald except for a ring of auburn hair that ran from ear to ear. Her water storage tanks were unreliable and she cut her bathing schedule to twice a week to conserve water. Her skin felt dirty and she neglected to shave her legs, her underarms, or the dark hair that grew up her lip and on her chin.

She received another visitor, Anders, who arrived in a pickup truck and was as burly a man as she had ever known. She badly wanted to sleep with him. Her memory of Pahl faded, but Talmud still tumbled in pieces from her mouth.

Anders could not be forgotten. His odour was strong. When he came in her he squeezed so she felt her ribs crack, and he broke the couch he slept on with his girth. While Anders might have been large, he was so ubiquitously large in every aspect that he lacked any other quality of physical distinction or heritage. His eyebrows were neither thick nor thin, his hair neither dark nor light; if she saw his face in a crowd along Times Square or at a music festival, she might not recognize him at all.

She made him meals of ham and eggs, trays of toast, or basted turkeys and yams, as she prodded him. *What are you,* she said, and before he could be insulted, she added: *I mean, where are you from, or your parents? Are you Hungarian? Yes,* he said. *I am Hungarian. Is that all you are?* Lilly asked. *No, I am also Swedish. I am American, and Icelandic, and Hungarian, and Swedish.* For her part she saw no Swedish in him. So he was not someone to ask anything of, not seeming to be anything himself. She never asked him about her son or told him what Pahl had known, that the boy could write his name.

Lilly desperately wanted Talmud to send a postcard with his name on it.

Anders spent a time there, the particular length of which she could not remember, but as he prepared to return to Switzerland he startled her by saying that Iran was now living there with Talmud, who was beginning the third grade. He said it quickly, without so much as a head turn. Lilly was scarcely sure she heard him. He wrote her a cheque for the room. *No, no money required,* she said, *I'm not an inn. Don't be ridiculous.* He laughed. *It's not for the room,* he said.

Lilly no longer had any use for dresses or stockings, and so discarded them. Her breasts adapted to their new freedom and shrunk against her chest. She rarely saw anyone and had no one to compare herself with, but she felt taller. Her shoulders were broader. She was comfortable urinating anywhere on the secluded beach or in the clumps of trees. In the absence of guests she was perfectly alone and free to wonder if her life was part of some cosmic joke, if all of this was the beat before the punchline of a comic who had lost his timing.

Iran, the Russian-American in Switzerland, never wrote her with news of Talmud, though she still sent money for the child. But the cheques became smaller. She was out of work now, and out of sorts with herself, and could ill-afford the international cheques and eventually mailed personal cheques. And when she felt she could order no more cheque books (and see the carbons of how little she was providing her abandoned son) she sent IOUs on sticky refrigerator notes. Freedom she had, and a body whose androgyny released her to feel whatever she wanted, to express it too: she could curl on a swinging chair on the deck and push the remnants of her breasts against her knees and rock herself like a child (or a mother rocking a child) or she could cut timber, pound her fists against the stumps, and walk through the forests bare-foot.

Win was very slender, effeminate, and of Thai descent. He did not announce himself until he closed the cabin door and said *My name is Win, and I was told I could board here.* He was short and fragile and moved with such grace that he mes-merized Lilly. He spoke softly and ate tofu. If he noticed her appearance it was unimportant or common. Win was, how-ever, difficult to talk to. When he touched her it was a faint tickle, and when he left the house the doors never slammed. When he cooked meals, the silverware did not clank, the blender did not whirr, and knives never clunked against the cutting board. Win said he was on a tour of North America and that he was enamoured with the Great Lakes. But on Talmud he seemed to have nothing at all to say.

For the first time in her life Lilly seduced a man. There was no trick to it, none that she remembered reading about in the magazines or had seen in television movies. Win drifted in and out of the cabin, and she would wait for him to come back, yet whenever he entered a room she was caught off-guard by his silence. Then she would grab him and motion toward the bed, but he said *That is not right, that is not how you do it.* She tried, but Win said again and again that it was wrong. She grew tired of his rejections and one morning threw Win on the bed. He moaned. She bit his wrists and pushed his body into a prone position. She could not remem-ber who entered who but the sensation was fiery and as deep-nerved a pain as she had known, like childbirth. Through the window they resembled two trees in a hurricane. *Where the fuck's my son?* Lilly demanded. *What can you tell me about my son?* Win looked at her in confusion. *You have a son?* he asked. *What's his name?*

She spent entire days walking past cottages on the white sand. The fat which had made her so much larger tightened into muscle. Her hands grew rough with the work of keeping the cabin. She went to the department store and bought several large flannel shirts, jeans, and a pair of boots, sold the car and the cabin, bought a plane ticket for Switzerland where, on the advice of two of his favourite prostitutes, she found Iran at a spa in Tribschen. He wore a long, tattered bath robe, the untied sash trailing damply along the sauna floor. They fucked in the dense steam, where they could not see each other, until Iran offered, tying his sash, to take Lilly home to meet her son. *Yes*, she said, *yes*. Outside, their bodies steamed in the cold, and for a while the car rose and fell unceremoniously among the mountains until Iran said, *I've always thought he doesn't look like me. But, I should tell you, he doesn't look much like you, either.*

IT'S NOT EASY BEING HALF-DIVINE

MARGARET ATWOOD

Helen lived down the street from me when we were growing up. We used to sell Kool-Aid off her front porch, five cents a glass, and she always had to be the one to carry the glass down the steps, eyelids lowered and with that pink bow in her hair, and mincing along like she was walking on eggs. I think she palmed a few nickels, being hardly the most honest type. I know she's famous and all now, but quite frankly she was a pain in the butt then and still is. She used to tell the worst lies – said her dad was somebody really high up, not the Pope but close, and of course we teased her about that. Not that this so-called big shot ever showed his face. Her mum was just another single mother, as they call them now, but my own mum says they had another name for it once. She said they had goings-on at night around there, naturally, since every man in town thought it was being handed out for free. Used to throw pebbles at the door, shout names and howl a bit when they got drunk. The two boys, Helen's brothers – they were pretty wild, they took off early.

When she was ten, Helen went through a circus phase – liked to dress up, thought she'd be a trapeze artist – then she got close with the woman who ran the beauty salon, used to

do her hair for her and give her product samples, and then she
started drawing black rims around her eyes and hanging
around the bus station. Fishing for a ticket out of town, is my
guess. She was good-looking – I'll grant her that – so it wasn't
surprising she got married early, to the police chief, a prime
catch for both of them as he was pushing forty.

Then just a few months ago she ran off with some man
from the city who was passing through. Didn't need the bus
ticket after all, he had his own car, quite the boat. Hubby's
pissed as hell; he's talking about a posse, go into the city,
smoke them out, beat the guy up, get her back, smack her
around a bit. A lot of men wouldn't bother, with a tramp like
that; but it seems he doesn't believe in divorce, says somebody has to stand for the right values.

Personally, I think he's still nuts about her and anyway his
pride is hurt. Trouble is she's flaunting it – the new man's
quite well off, set her up in some sort of mansion, her picture
gets in magazines and people asking about her opinions, it's
enough to make you sick. So there she is, all diddied up in her
new pearl necklace and smiling away as sweet as pie and saying how happy she is in her new life, and how every woman
should follow her heart. Says it wasn't easy when she was
growing up, being half-divine and all, but now she's come to
terms with it and she's looking at a career in the movies. Says
she was too young to get married that first time but now she
knows how fulfilling love can be, and the chief wasn't, well,
he just wasn't. Of course everyone thinks she's saying he was
a nothing in the sack department, so there's been some snickering up the sleeves, though not openly because he's still got
a lot of clout in this town.

The long and the short of it is, pardon my pun, nobody
likes to be laughed at. The chief's from a big family, a brother

and a lot of cousins, all of them with muscles and tempers. My bet is things will get serious. It's worth watching.

CONSPIRACY

PRISCILA UPPAL

They give you these little red see-through gel capsules and act like the whole thing is a damn mystery.

Let us know when you're able to go.

I've just had a lung transplant.

My roommate has had a tumour resected from her brain.

Now they want us to take a shit but apparently they haven't solved the problem of how to move our bowels.

If you don't go for five days, you need to let us know.

Five days?

I'm supposed to leave here in four.

My roommate in three.

It seems the body can recover more easily from intrusions into the frontal cortex or pulmonary cavity. They want me to keep blowing into this tube so my lung capacity continues to expand. My roommate has finger exercises to reconnect her neural pathways.

We get pills for pain – lots of pills for pain – pills for nausea, pills for sleep, pills for muscle atrophy, and surprisingly painful injections to thin our blood.

But only these little red see-through gel capsules to move our bowels. That are quite obviously useless to all involved. No one has taken a shit here since pre-op. No one.

It's a fucking conspiracy, I'm telling you.

Laugh if you want, but it's true. It's a fucking conspiracy.

The little red see-through gel capsules are no more effective than placebos. It's a medical sleight of hand designed to manufacture hope.

Everyone is constipated here.

Everyone. On every floor.

In every room.

You want another word for constipation? Replace it with conspiracy.

And they practically pin a medal on you when you fart.

Farting is also part of the plan. Farting is a loss-leader. A taste of success before you're taken for all you're worth.

Let me tell you, it's the same in hospital as it is anywhere. Don't let the red crosses or the ladies with the cookie and juice carts fool you.

Nobody, nobody wants to deal with your shit.

When you get your discharge papers, that's when they give you the real pills, the ones that will actually move your bowels and move them so fast you'll think a volcano is erupting. Just before you hit the five-day limit.

Because the real mess happens when you go home.

THE WEIGHT OF THE WORLD

DARREN GLUCKMAN

Manfred was eating a grapefruit at breakfast when he felt a crushing blow across his back. His torso was thrust forward, so that his head almost hit the table. He turned around but there was no one there, nothing that could have been the source of the blow that had come and now, apparently, gone, but he was left with the sensation that something enormous was resting upon him. He put down his grapefruit spoon – a teaspoon with a serrated edge – and looked across at his wife, Gretchen, who was drinking coffee and reading the paper and evidently hadn't seen what hit him, or even that he'd been hit. He said to her, "My God, it's like…it's like I have the weight of the world on my shoulders."

Gretchen looked up at him and said, "Perhaps you have too many meetings scheduled, perhaps you should cancel some. One or two meetings can be sacrificed if you're feeling the weight of the world." And she got up, grabbed her brief-case and shouted for the children – who came running with their schoolbooks and lunch bags – then waved goodbye to Manfred and was out the door.

An hour later, at the office, Manfred was between meetings when he felt it again. It buckled his knees and he fell to the ground. He called his secretary, who saw him lying prone and trying but unable to raise himself up. She called 911. In the ambulance, on the way to the hospital, the pain became too much. A medic plunged a syringe into a vein.

Gretchen was at his side when he opened his eyes in an antiseptic room. The children were fighting over a toy in the corner. Gretchen had turned to them and was instructing the girl to leave it alone, that it belonged to the boy, that she had her own toy to play with. Manfred thought, *If they only knew, they would forget about the toy, they would forget about toys altogether! No, it's better that they don't know. That no one knows.* Gretchen turned back to Manfred and saw that his eyes were open. "They said you had a breakdown," she said. She didn't seem terribly concerned. But then, he reminded himself, what difference did it make whether she was concerned or not? Who was she, really, in the grand scheme, in light of what he now understood?

"I didn't have a breakdown," he said, his mouth extremely dry. He tried licking his lips but there was nothing. Gretchen passed him a paper cup with water. He took a sip.

"I didn't have a breakdown," he repeated. "It started pressing down on me."

"What did?"

"The weight of the world. It's descended upon me."

"I'm trying to understand you, Manfred, but when you talk like that I must admit that you do sound a bit crazy."

He turned away from her. Her voice was becoming faint. When he turned back – and this he did only because his neck was starting to cramp – he saw that she had taken the children and gone. Doubtless, she would be back at some point, but if she never returned, if he never saw his children again, he'd have enough anxieties and pressures – shifting the weight of the world from shoulder to shoulder, striving constantly to balance it, never quite managing, knowing that one wrong movement and the whole thing would come tumbling down, the earth would collapse from his back to the floor and shatter into a thousand pieces and he'd be known in myth and legend as the failed Atlas –that he wouldn't miss them. Not just that he wouldn't, but couldn't! It wasn't that he was without emotion, incapable of love. Far from it! No, it was the weight of the world that had stretched his soul to such capacity that there was no longer any room for love. Under the weight of the world, Manfred saw, love was the first thing to go.

A young doctor came in and looked at his chart. He said, "Things look good but we'll keep you for a few days, for observation." He said if Manfred hadn't had the kind of comprehensive health insurance provided for under his employee health plan, he would never have been admitted. But under the circumstances, they didn't mind keeping him a few days, for observation. Manfred looked at the doctor. He was barely thirty. His training was in medicine. What could he possibly understand about the weight of the world?

"It's the weight of the world," he said. "If you want a diagnosis, that's it, the weight of the work. It's pressing down on me."

The doctor nodded. And nodded again. Then he shoved his hands in the pockets of his white coat and said, "We'll take some X-rays." And he left.

X-rays? Thought Manfred. What good are X-rays? I haven't broken anything, there isn't a bullet lodged in my body; what good are X-rays? But he decided to be a good patient. If they wanted X-rays they could have X-rays. He wasn't going to tell them how to go about their business. The phone rang beside his bed. He picked it up. It was Gretchen. She wanted to know how he was doing, whether there was anything she should bring from home, she was planning on coming by this evening. He told her not to bother, that there was nothing for her to bring, that the crises were too numerous to even contemplate and yet he felt he had to contemplate them all. What could she possibly bring from home?

She said she wasn't going to bring the children, the way he was acting. He said fine and they hung up. She called back almost immediately. "I want you to know I still love you, if that means anything to you." He said of course it did, but he knew about love, about love being the first thing to go.

A nurse came and said it was time for X-rays. She led him down the hallway, to the elevator, down to the first floor, down another hallway, to a room. She told him to wait. Presently, a technician summoned him and made him sit at various angles while a large camera on a huge swinging arm took photographs. Sometimes Manfred smiled when the pictures were taken. The technician saw this and said, "You don't have to smile, they're not that kind of pictures." Manfred knew they weren't that kind of pictures, he wasn't an idiot. He'd had X-rays before. He told the technician, "If it's all the same to you I'd just as soon smile."

The next day he was sitting in his bed, three fat pillows propping him up. Gretchen was telling him about the children, about how they wanted to know what was wrong with Daddy, about how she didn't know what to tell them because frankly she didn't know herself. She was going on in this manner when the young doctor burst in into the room, trailed by a team of doctor-looking types, all of them frowning terribly. Gretchen put her hand to her mouth.

The young doctor held the developed X-ray pictures. He looked at Manfred for a long moment before finally saying, "You're right. I thought you were mad, or at least wildly off-balance, but you're right. These X-rays confirm it."

"What are you talking about?" asked Gretchen.

The doctor held the X-rays up to the light. "You see?" he said. "You see this spherical shape right here? That's not part of the human anatomy. That shouldn't be there. It shouldn't be there, but it is."

"What is it?" asked Gretchen, a catch in her voice.

"Well it's…" And here the young doctor looked around at the faces of his colleagues before turning back to Manfred and Gretchen. "It's the world."

"What?"

"It's the world. We don't know how else to explain it. It's the world. The planet Earth. If you look closely you can see the shapes of parts of continents. Look, here, Africa, there is the Horn, and here is the Cape of Good Hope."

Gretchen blanched. She looked like she was going to be sick.

The doctor continued: "And if we look at this X-ray we can see Florida, Cuba and the Dominican Republic. It's quite remarkable, really. We don't know how to explain it. Except…"

"Except?"

"Except as your husband has suggested."

"What do you mean?"

"He's bearing the weight of the world."

"Thank God," said Manfred, who turned away from this commotion and looked out the window.

The doctors conducted a series of tests. The young doctor was replaced by an older one who was said to be a specialist in the field. When Manfred asked which field exactly, this new doctor muttered something about universal biology and refused to be pinned down any further. Manfred was analyzed from every direction – his pores and orifices were probed, his blood taken, his hair split, his stool and urine examined, his DNA code isolated, his molecular structure broken down – but aside from a slightly elevated blood pressure, nothing seemed out of the ordinary. Until, of course, one consulted the X-rays or the ultrasounds or the various radiological scans which all revealed what the naked eye could not see – the world pressing down upon his back.

A television news crew conducted an interview:

"How does it feel to bear the weight of the world?"

"It does not feel good."

"Is it a heavy as one might expect?"

"Heavier."

"How is this affecting your sex life?"

"It presents a challenge."

"Do you have any advice for the children who might be watching?"

"Work hard at school. Be good to your parents."

Priests and theologians visited to determine if he was the Messiah, or the New Messiah. But they were unimpressed with his pronouncements – which were generally complaints about the pain and the inadequacy of his meds – and felt that while he may be shouldering the burdens of the world, he ought not be bowed down to. They instructed their pupils to continue worshipping, or not worshipping, as before.

Gretchen continued to make regular visits, though without the children, as she'd warned. And she advised him that she was now represented by a lawyer. There was a book deal pending. He didn't care and told her so. She nodded and quoted him verbatim in her journal, which she was keeping for the forthcoming book: "He told me he no longer cared."

Within days, bruises began to appear across his back. The imprint of Australia was unmistakable.

His blood pressure was rising. His breathing was becoming strained. There was talk of hooking him up to a respirator. Therapists told him not to worry, not to take it all so personally. Naturopaths prescribed a steady diet of herbal tonics. Incense was lit. But the plight of the human race was having an adverse effect on his health. And not worrying about it just wasn't in the cards. When the doctor – the specialist – next came round, Manfred told him he wanted to be cured. He wanted to be relieved of this burden. It was becoming too much to bear. It had long ago become too much to bear. Now he was at the breaking point.

But the specialist said, "Maybe the problem is that you're not strong enough. You need to strengthen your leg and back muscles. That will make the burden easier to shoulder." And the specialist supervised as Manfred lifted weights and pulled levers and added protein to his diet. But it seemed that every ounce of strength he gained was offset by the weight of a thousand new problems added to the already unwieldy mass – from Delhi to La Paz, Moscow to Hiroshima, from a mudslide to a bankruptcy, an adultery discovered to a bike stolen, a political assassination, a dog lost, a child struck sick, a bus over a cliff, a plea denied, a failure of justice, a worker fired, an insult, a slap, a wound – it was too much. Hairline fractures began to appear along the bones in Manfred's back. His spine was compressing.

"I want someone else to bear the burden," he said. "I've done my bit. Someone else can do theirs."

The doctors agreed that it was a reasonable request. Advertisements were place in newspapers around the world. Most of the responses wanted to know how much the position paid. No one, it seemed, was willing to do this for free. And why should they? The trouble was, no one was willing to foot the bill, certainly not while Manfred was doing the job for nothing. In desperation, Manfred turned to the doctors. "One of you," he pleaded. "One of you must take this on."

But they begged off, citing their commitment to science, to their other patients, and to golf. His back now bore a deep concave impression, Asia featuring prominently, the bruise of India like a giant mole above his kidneys. And his kidneys: all his organs were being pushed down and towards the front of his body as the weight of the world grew heavier. Ribs were cracking. Hemorrhaging was imminent. Gretchen brought the children round to say goodbye to Daddy. The nurses who'd been caring for him could no longer enter his room with dry eyes. But no one – no one! – was prepared to take on the weight of the world. They'd sooner bear witness to his decline, mourn his passing, than relieve him of his burden. And who could blame them, he thought – even as thought itself was becoming difficult, with the pressure mounting along the base of his skull. Who could blame them, and they didn't even know the half of it!

He asked for more tranquilizers and his request was granted.

At four in the morning, the night nurses heard a violent crashing sound. They ran to Manfred's room, as the sound had come from there. But when the lights were turned on, they saw that Manfred was no longer there. Neither, for that matter was his bed. A large round hole had appeared in that section of the floor that had previously supported Manfred and his bed. As the nurses leaned over the perforated tiling, they saw that the hole continued on the floor below and on the floor below that. And when the emergency staff and scientists and military personnel arrived on the scene and cordoned off the area, they saw that the hole continued through the basement of the hospital. And when the mining company officials arrived with their machinery, they announced that the hole continued further into the earth than any of their equipment could go. No one knew what had become of Manfred, or his bed. Or the weight of the world.

That morning, in a small village on the Malabar Coast, Sunil was mending a hole in his fishing net when he felt a crushing blow across his back.

I AM A
SPECIAL BOOBY

GAIL PRUSSKY

she could forgive him for not looking like his profile picture, but why did he have to bring his brother along?

the male ulbert carries the eggs
ON HIS head for the entire 2-year
gestation period, while the female
mocks him and laughs. Then, when
the eggs finally hatch, he kills her.

EDNA WAS
HAPPIER THAN
SHE'D BEEN IN
YEARS. NOBODY
HAD THE HEART
TO TELL HER
THAT FLUFFY
WAS A
WOLVERINE.

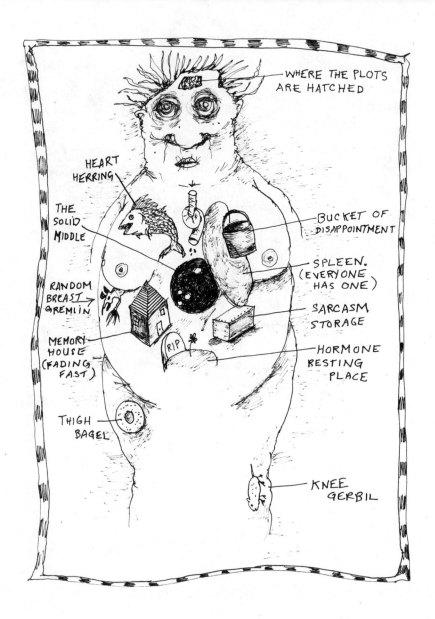

THREE STIKES AND YOU'RE OUT

LINDA ROGERS

I like baseball. Three strikes and you're out. How clear is that – rules, cut and dried, a perfect covenant, *à la grisette*, Jonathon Swift's poeticized/satirized ho, a piece of jerky in her little grey dress?

> *And, thy beauty thus dispatch'd*
> *Let me praise thy wit unmatched*
> *Set of phrases, cut and dry*
> *Evermore thy tongue supply.*

My mind travels fast, faster than fastballs and agile tongues – from *grisette* to ball(s), ball to diamond, a song *Diamonds Are a Girl's Best Friend*, and so on.

The first strike came through the bay window, beveled glass blasted to kingdom come, at least as far as the dining room and, as luck would have it, the kitchen, because the pantry door was open. It was a sunny afternoon. Light leaked in the window and the hole in the window and, of course, it refracted in the lethal bits that penetrated the Martha Stewart wallpaper and slipcovers and the oil painting of his mother, turning his living room into a veritable disco ball.

He never found the ball or the kid who threw or hit the ball, even though he ran directly outside, naked, as it happens, because he had just emerged from the shower, and had a look around. I should say a myopic look, because he hadn't put in his contact lenses. No kid, no ball, no mother dragging kid by the ear to apologize, no contacts. That would be four balls, a walk.

Because he prided himself on logic, he deduced from this lack of forensic information that the beautiful explosion in his living room was caused by a bullet. This is what he told the cops: "I was standing in the window [actually showing his wet/naked/fragrant self to the young Adonis drinking a gin and tonic on his porch across the street] and someone shot at me. Luckily he missed." Did the cop smirk as he wrote this down in his book? Did he roll his eyes when a careful search failed to turn up bullets or balls of any description?

"Were you singing?" the cop asked, a leading question. He apparently wants to be a lawyer and takes every opportunity to practice his clever-in-court theatricals. Windows break when the fat soprano sings.

No runs, no errors. Nothing. The cop left and he was alone with his fears, his undisciplined King Charles spaniel and a sideboard filled with bottles of single malt Scotch. He had a few and then slept like a baby infused with Phenergan.

"It could be car," his cleaning lady, Magda, a Bosnian War survivor, suggested the next morning. "I very scared when car make bang." Magda cleaned up what was left of the glass. ("Oh, Mama in paradise," she said, pulling a glinting sliver out of his mother's right eye, which was appropriate because that is where all of Magda's family now resided, thanks to the sharpshooters in Sarajevo. His mother was probably in hell. He would be willing to bet on that, no prayer on her lips when the drain had been successfully circled).

He agreed, the last thing he needed was to freak out his cleaning lady, who, because of language barriers, didn't realize other cleaning ladies were getting minimum wage, plus car-fare, plus lunch.

His dog, who normally thought the world was her big green latrine, refused to go outside and she relieved herself in the bathtub. She also ran and hid under the bed every time the phone rang.

One of those calls was from me. I had ordered a new suit, a bartender and catering for two hundred for the launch party. He was publishing my book on erotic Inuit art, *How to Make Love in a Snowsuit*, and my copy edit was long overdue.

"I can't talk; someone is trying to kill me and my dog is pissing in the bathtub," he said, before hanging up. Trans-lation: the copy edit had met a similar obstruction to the one that made a necessity of daily enemas and prune juice. I decided to cancel the bartender and the catering and wear the Hong Kong suit to a family wedding.

Have you noticed the world is ass over teakettle? We have had four major seismic events in the Ring of Fire over the past year, a hurricane has flattened New York and New Jersey, a bunch of billionaires have spent trillions on an election that didn't return as much as a loaf of bread, and Barney's in New York is featuring an anorexic size zero five-foot-eleven-inch Minnie Mouse in Jimmy Choo heels and a Vera Wang dress in their *tweeners* display this Christmas.

So who cares if my book comes out? Well, me for one. I spent three freezing years living in igloos, researching sex in sealskins, and polar bears with six legs.

Let me explain. I have in my small collection of aboriginal art a carving of a six-legged polar bear. The sculptor, who was grateful to a missionary for saving his soul and uniting him with his one true love in a Christian marriage, rewarded him with a sculpture of two mating bears. This makes sense. Were we not instructed by the gospels to go forth and multiply? However, the priest rejected the gift, praising the carver's skill but insisting he could not own a piece of pornographic art. The carver, a practical man, took back the sculpture, shaved off the head and forelegs of the male bear, leaving a female with six legs.

Now, doesn't that interesting artifact deserve the attention of the literate public?

Unlike my publisher, I do not have opiate dreams. Mine are of the pragmatic, straight-up archetypal variety. That is, when I am not in too deep a sleep to remember them. After the phone call, I dreamed about polar bears jumping from melting floe to floe, and, come to think of it, whence cometh that particular flow? My dictionary says it is from the Norwegians, who, after they die of cold, are sent out to sea in burning boats. Perhaps someone will send my publisher a burning boat.

And whence cometh the melt? That is another story, perhaps enhanced by my desire for publication, the devil sacrament that uses up the sacred wealth of trees. Pity the polar bears, balancing on shrinking floors, and not a rock in sight. So went my dream, and then I woke up. Perhaps the bay window was penetrated by a rock, and that would also fall into the deliberate column, deliberate but not so dangerous as a bullet.

"Maybe it was a rock," I'd ventured in my next call. "Maybe the guy across the street was offended by your nakedness."

"Not a chance," he said, and went through the list of famous and beautiful men he had slept with. "I've never been rejected."

"How is the edit coming?" I came right out with it. He sighed and I saw my pages melting like ice floes, my book sinking into a cold Arctic sea.

Months passed. I heard that the editor had edited out the most alarming assassination options and accepted the randomness of fate. He had opened his curtains, unlocked his front door and taken his disobedient dog for walks in the urban jungle half a world away from my vanishing tundra and the nuisance grounds that provided me with so much priceless material.

I phoned again. "Can't talk," he said, "I've been traumatized by a home invasion…" before putting down the receiver.

His Facebook account reported that a window washer had entered through the door on the second-floor balcony adjoining his bedroom, got into bed and fallen asleep. The editor had arrived home late after an egregious literary event, a book launch (not mine, needless to say), and got between the sheets without taking off his clothes. He assumed the other warm body under the covers was his dog and that was true, but his dog was just one of two warm bodies.

When he called 911, he reported a rape, but the story changed when the same officer who wanted to be a lawyer arrived with his partner, an attractive martial artist called Brenda, who was sleeping with him although both were married to other people. I mention this because it gives a certain *frisson* to the interview. In a subsequent call, my editor reported their conversation.

"You arrived home drunk."

"Yes."

"You took a cab, I assume."

"Uh…"

"I'll be checking."

"Am I the criminal here?"

"You might be. Did you walk the dog?"

"No."

"Wouldn't she have needed to go out?" The cop who wants to be a lawyer was once in the dog unit. He knows how much dogs need *eaties* and *walkies* when their owners arrive home at 10 p.m. after being gone all day.

"I think I told you last time that my dog has been peeing in the bathtub."

"Yes, you did."

"I took off my shoes and fell into bed."

"Then what?"

"I had a dream."

"Yes?"

"I dreamed my dog was dying and I had to give her mouth-to-mouth resuscitation."

"And you woke up kissing your dog on the mouth," Brenda guessed. She was learning vicariously.

"No, it wasn't my dog. It was the man who was in bed with my dog."

"And that man was...?"

"The window washer I hired on my way out the door yesterday morning."

"Then what?"

"Then he raped me."

"How did he do that?"

"The usual way."

"I'm sorry?"

"He penetrated me."

"I thought you were fully dressed."

"I must have undressed in my sleep. I'm a thrasher."

"You thrashed your clothes off, and then the window washer raped you."

"Yes."

The partner of the cop who wanted to be a lawyer lost it at this point and, since she had lost her validity in the interview process, he helped her out to the car. Then they went for coffee.

"They never came back," he told me. "I'm sure he's sleeping with his partner. I heard her tell him she wanted to be in a monotonous relationship."

"When was that?"

"While they were looking under the bed for the window washer."

I am a big admirer of John Irving, who really gets the congruency of sex and death, baseballs in the forehead, penises bitten off during car fellatio. Perhaps my editor has bigger fish to fry, major popular novelist kinds of fish, and this is code for lost. "I have to see a man about a dog." Dogs, to me, à la Vermeer, conjure domestic fidelity, integrity, loyalty, all good things I expect from humans as well as canines. I am confused. Perhaps his dog is also confused. I doubt she's in on it, which constitutes animal cruelty, in my opinion, and my wife agrees with me.

My grandfather used to say that to me about his mysterious disappearances. I didn't know whether he'd gone to the bathroom, gone to make a bet on dogs or horses or gone to get in some putting practice. He certainly didn't mean, "I'm about to get into bed with a man and a dog."

I put my new summer suit in the closet, drank all the Champagne (it was the kind with the jar stopper lid and we are going to use the bottles for vinegar, Christmas gifts. I doubt I will send one to my editor, but perhaps I should.

Vinegar would be appropriate, but probably too much money to post). My wife, who shared the Champagne and the loneliness of the endless nights I'd slept in the igloo a thousand miles away, suggested the shooter/window washer might be another writer. We were now approaching the situation as a shaggy dog story, vaudeville, a Sutra with endless twists. We'd taken to role-playing, changing characters – sometimes I was the male cop, sometimes the window washer, and always my editor. She was always the dog.

We made a joke out of ten years of my life.

I made one last call late in November, tongue ready to either give him a verbal lashing or lick the stamps for the box that held the last bottle of vinegar. He picked up the phone after nine rings and paused. If I weren't the caller and he the callee, I would have hung up. Those pauses never augur well. Most often it is someone in Asia who wants your money. I think he was identifying the number on his phone. I heard him manning up. Then I heard the dog barking. I made note of the timbre so I could encourage my wife to get perfect canine intonation during our next pantomime.

"I was out walking the dog," he said.

"That's good," I said. "So everything's back to normal again."

"N-n-n-no," he answered. "Not at all. I was just shot at in the park."

"Shot at? Are you dead then?" I like the idea of talking to zombies. It has the warm bullshit feel of a Caribbean breeze.

"Yes. No. I was wearing my cashmere coat and it must have stopped the bullets."

"Ah." I wondered if that coat represented my share of his block grant, but pushed that thought back.

"What did it feel like?" I covered the receiver with my hand and told my wife to pick up in the kitchen.

"Like a dull poke."

"A dull poke?" My mind went to the purple vibrator one of my wife's friends used to beat up her unfaithful same-sex partner.

"Maybe it was canes. Were you blocking the sacred path?" I have been to his house. It adjoins a convent, which is now a rest home for elderly nuns.

"That's ridiculous. The nuns adore us."

"Just a thought. She might have left a love offering on the convent lawn. Did you phone the cops?"

"Of course, I went into the public toilet and called them on my cell."

"And?" I was thinking that was dumb. What if he'd been pursued in there, *if* being the big question?

"Nothing. I got the smart-ass cop who wants to be a lawyer."

"And what did he say?"

"Three strikes and you're out."

I could hear my wife snorting in the kitchen. She couldn't help herself. I married her for her uncontrollable laughter.

"That sounds about right."

From now on, I'm going to write fairy tales.

PECULIAR PRACTICES IN ALBERTA

(Possibly Related to the Oil Boom)

LEON ROOKE

I went to the supermarket and a woman wearing see-through shoes shot her hand into mine and began dragging me into Meats. Susy was the name pinned on her white blouse.

I would have gone with her into Meats had not another woman, Rosy, taken my other hand and pulled me into Poultry. What's that? I asked Rosy, and was told that was a machine for defrocking birds. Until then I had never known they did on-site plucking.

"That's a giant turkey," she said when she was where I was next looking. "It won the Founder's Award. Are you ready?"

(I wasn't nearly ready but with practiced foreplay she corrected this oversight briskly.) When we were done she said, "They are expecting you in Bakery.

"Bakery?"

"Lots of action in Bakery," she said. "Dairy, Frozen Foods, okay, too. If I were you I'd avoid Fresh Vegetables."

"Does this go on here all the time?" I asked.

"Most days," she said, "when we're not in a panic. Do you remember those days when our nation was busy snatching furry creatures? In there, it is often like that. We yank people off the street if we're in the mood for sexual activity. It's like those eighteen months down south when we had the Pony Express. Rush, rush, rush!"

My fine white suit dissolved into ash in that long moment during which I could formulate no reply.

Bakery was calling. "Are you ready?" this beautiful woman shouted. "We don't have a lot of time. It's not like you got to know your Heidegger."

THE TOWER OF BABEL

JONATHAN GOLDSTEIN

After the flood, man's relationship with God changed. Where once there was disinterest – a sort of "you go your way, we'll go ours" attitude – there was now distrust. The generations after Noah did not know when their time might come to be wiped out.

Noah had said the people of the Earth were evil, that God had to get rid of them and start over, that God had made some kind of mistake – either in killing them or in creating them in the first place. There were different versions.

After the flood, God had given man the rainbow. It was a gift and a symbol – a promise that this kind of thing would never happen again. Back then there wasn't much in the way of entertainment so when a rainbow came along, it was the closest you got to a drive-in so the tendency was to try to enjoy. But despite its flash, when humans looked upon the rainbow, rather than feeling reassured, they felt a bit like God was trying to dupe them, like he was saying, "Let's forget about all this nasty genocide business and enjoy the pretty colors."

Man did not take God at his word, and it was this lack of trust that Mibzar played on. Mibzar was the youngest son in a family of butchers who worked in Babel.

"I had a dream," Mibzar said to his neighbours. "And in this dream, a new rain came and it made the old rain look like an old lady making pee-pee."

For Mibzar, if it wasn't a prophetic dream, it was head-aches, goiters, or excruciating groin pain – anything so long as he had something to yak about, and he was his favourite topic of conversation. Yakking about himself was what came natural to him and he believed it was a talent that would lead him to bigger and better things, better things than simply delivering meat at the butcher shop. And so he stood outside the shop and as people walked by, Mibzar yakked.

"In a dream last night, I saw monkeys underwater," Mibzar cried. "I don't know how much more of this I can take. I have a very sensitive soul. My skin is sensitive, too. I apply oint-ments of aloe half a dozen times a day and still I have psycho-somatic anal welts the size of bees."

He saw that speaking about himself only drew a small crowd, but when he added a twist of flood talk – offered up in high-flown language – more people came to listen and they stayed longer.

"Have you ever seen a tiger underwater? That you should see. Its spine twisting and nails scratching? A tiger, even in his last breath, will try to eat a tuna swimming by because he must obey his calling. But man has a higher calling. Man has things like compassion and kindness. We can only hope that from way up there the Almighty can see that."

Flood debate and speculation was popular in those days. People were still trying to make sense of the whole thing. It was Mibzar's belief that had Noah been more articulate in explaining his conversations with God, he could have made people better understand the consequences of their behavior.

And so, Mibzar believed, the flood was largely due to Noah's incompetence as a public speaker.

"I have spoken with God," Mibzar imagined Noah saying, "and He hath commanded me to build an ark. It shall be such and such cubits long, and such and such cubits high and blah blah blah blah."

People were either asleep by the time he was done talking, or back to sodomizing goats and chickens. Mibzar knew that people need a little song and dance. You have to build empathy, otherwise you turn them off.

No, there had to have been a classier way to go about it, a better way to grab people's attention. Mibzar would have included himself in the story – to humanize it. He'd have told them what he ate for breakfast on the day he spoke to God – how the figs he'd consumed were doing a number on his bowels. And most importantly, he would have opened with a joke.

"Do you have any idea what it's like talking to God?" he would have asked in a manner that was warm and conversational. "You think you have a problem speaking in front of a crowd? Try addressing the Creator of the Universe. Build an ark? You got it. Tell me to cut the skin at the fore of my willing-and-able cane and I'll do it!"

It was with his powers as a public speaker at his command that Mibzar undertook what he decided would be his true calling. He would pitch the people of Babel on the idea of building a great monolith. A tower whose top echelons, in the event of another flood, they could flee to. He would oversee its construction and call it "the Tower of Mibzar."

When he first waved over the crowd passing outside the front of his family's butcher shop, Mibzar knew he would need a strong opening line.

"God killed your grandpa," he said. "Don't let him kill your kids. Rainbows and lollipops are one thing, but what I'm proposing is *security*."

"Is that off the rump or a cutlet?" asked a soft-headed roofer named Emile as he peered into the butcher shop.

"This has nothing to do with meat," screamed Mibzar, and one of his brothers came outside and shot him a look that said "Pipe down."

"Look," continued Mibzar, making his voice calm, "I would not even presume to know what the Almighty is thinking. That would be preposterous, but we do have imaginations. It is the way the Fat One in the Sky constructed us, and so we imagine. And I will tell you this: it is my *imagining* that on the day He drowned the whole world, He could not have been feeling very good about himself. It just isn't the behavior of a very self-actualized Almighty. All I'm saying is, who knows what goes through This Guy's head? He's whimsical!"

Mibzar explained his idea for the tower and as he spoke, the crowd around him grew, and as it grew, he became emboldened, explaining it through metaphor, saying it was not so much a prayer to God as it was a prayer to man – a celebration of their humanness. And also their penises.

Along with all of this celebrating, Mibzar offered something else as well: the world's first insurance policy. It would help them sleep better at night. And for Mibzar, it gave him the sense of importance he'd been after his whole life.

The people of Babel were smitten with the idea of a tower and they set to work on it with vigor and purpose. One shift worked all through the morning and another worked through the night. Because of various chronic pains, Mibzar could not actually perform any manual labor, but he stood off to the side for hours, watching the workers as they toiled. When their pace slackened, he threw a few inspirational words their way and, where he saw fit, he peppered his talk with personal anecdotes – about his lifelong battle with foot odor or his childhood fancy for girls with crooked teeth.

On the day he had to stand on his tiptoes to reach the blossoming tower's tops, he did a hand-clapping jig that was so pure and unself-conscious that those around him were embarrassed to watch.

"The tower's shade alone will provide a spectacular get-away for a midafternoon siesta," he said, his buttocks gyrating behind him.

In the months that followed, whenever it started to rain, everyone would scramble up the tower laughing like children. Wheee, they'd yell, whizzing up the steps. They knew that whoever got the highest had the best chance of surviving the flood, so there was a fair bit of good-natured jostling.

As the tower grew taller, it could be seen in nearby towns. Curious neighbouring villagers came to check it out and once Mibzar explained it all to them in his back-slapping way – making generous mention of his difficult relationship with his father and his problems with mucus in the morning – soon enough, they were immigrating to Babel to work on the tower and take their place in history. And the higher it got, the farther news of the tower spread – and news was spreading far, for now the tower almost poked straight into the clouds.

At night when Mibzar dreamed, it was no longer terrible images of the flood that he saw; it was of himself, ascending the tower. At the very top, he would step onto Heaven's carpet.

"I love what you've done with the place," he'd say to God. Even in dreams, even when standing before the Creator of the Universe, he knew to open with something casual.

The tower slowly grew and as it did, there never seemed any good reason to stop. Everyone was working well together. From Babel and beyond, they all felt like brothers working toward a common goal, and that goal, which had begun as a mere escape ladder, had now become something else – something less easy to define. It had something to do with being more than just a workaday human. It had to do with questing after the infinite. Flood or no flood, they knew their time on Earth would only last so long, and after that – eternal darkness. But with the tower, they'd leave their mark.

As the men worked, Mibzar watched. Making speeches had become exhausting, and so he took to wearing a whistle around his neck, which he blew into to make his wishes known. One toot meant work faster, two toots meant work faster still, and three toots meant send for the lad who scrubs my feet.

Mibzar took to perching himself at the top of the tower and watching the world below. He felt like he could actually *breathe* up there.

"Sometimes it is simpler to gaze upon bald spots than faces," he thought. "Faces always need to be talked to."

Things looked so small down there. The butcher shop, where he had toiled thanklessly for so many years, the site of all his humiliations and petty triumphs – as puny as an ant hill.

"I can crush it with a finger," he said, lifting a pinkie to his eyes.

Mibzar wondered if that was a little how God felt sometimes. Crushy. He wondered, too, if He might like how the
tower was bringing the two of them closer together.

He wanted to stay up there all day, in silence, just thinking his thoughts while looking down and allowing his joyous
laborers to carry him ever higher, ever closer to God.

But it was on one particularly glorious day of fraternal
labor that Mibzar, watching from on high, noticed something
was not right. Whereas usually the harmonious sound of men
happily working together could be heard – cries of "pass me
that bucket of mortar, friend" and "throw me a pickax, my
bosom" – now all he could hear were sounds that were gar-
bled, weird, more animal than human. What's more, the jum-
ble sounded panicked – terrified, even.

Mibzar raced down the tower's steps and with his whistle,
summoned one of his foremen. Mibzar looked at him quizzi-
cally.

"*Quelque chose de bizarre s'arrive*," said the foreman.

Annoyed by the man's insubordinate gobbledygook,
Mibzar blew his whistle at three men hauling rocks on their
backs. The men dropped their loads and trotted over.

"*¿Qué pasa?... ¡Qué raro! ¿Qué está saliendo de mi boca?*"
said the first man.

"*Hakka Nee-ay shong dong teeyong nee oy eyow*," said the
second.

"*Sento come ho mangiato il fungo magico*," said the third.

Mibzar tore the whistle from around his neck and
spoke.

"*Alk-tay ormal-nay!*"

Upon hearing the strange sounds that escaped his lips,
Mibzar covered his mouth as though having emitted a long
series of burps. Waiting a few seconds, he tried again.

"*Ut-whay e-thay ell-hay is-way oing-gay on-way?*" he cried. It was as though there was a hand in his mouth, bending and curving his tongue against his will.

For a long while, none of the men dared to speak. For Mibzar, it was the first time in his life that his mouth felt like an enemy. The men all stood staring at one another, not knowing what to do. Finally, Mibzar broke the silence. Looking into the heavens, he said in a very quiet voice: "*Od-Gay, ou-yay in-way.*"

And as he stared up at the tower, the noonday wind blew through the whistle in his hand in gusts that sounded like high-pitched laughter.

During the days that followed, in the absence of a common language, there was a lot of awkward bowing and smiling – people trying to make themselves understood by talking really loudly and slowly – but it did no good, and after only a week, work on the tower ground to a complete halt. In resigned silence, everyone packed up his tools and journeyed back to his home.

It was hard to return to tending sheep and planting vegetables, though. The work they had done on the tower awakened new hungers in them, hungers they had never known before. They now wanted to create things in the world that were bigger than they were – that would outlast them and instill wonder in the generations to come.

And so they cooked up new ideas. Not high things (they had learned their lesson and wouldn't be opening that can of worms any time soon) but other things. Li wanted to build the world's longest wall; Costa wanted to build a place where hundreds of people could sit in a circle and watch marvelous events; and Bastet, a real cat person, wanted to sculpt the world's biggest feline.

In the months after the men and women of the neighbouring towns left, because of how inexperienced they were, most of Babel's tower crumbled away. In the very end, out of the whole thing, only one floor remained – the ground floor – and it was here that Mibzar made his home, opening the world's first language school. Inside, he taught Aramaic as a second language. Mibzar was the kind of teacher who always kept the students way past the end of class, continuing to yak away about himself, or whatever else it was that pleased him.

WILLARD AND KATE

BARRY CALLAGHAN

Willard Cowley lived with his wife Kate in a sandstone house. There was a sun parlour at the back of the house and the windows of the parlour opened on to a twisted old apple tree.

"Everything alters," he often told her, "under the apple tree. One by one we drop away." He was a well-known scholar, big boned and tall, with closely cropped grey hair. "It's the job of wizened old teachers like myself," he said, smiling indulgently at his students, "to tell the young all about tomorrow's sorrow." He was officially required to stop teaching, to retire. He was sixty-five. Kate came down to his office. "You needn't have come," he said, but he was comforted to see her. She said the sorrowful look in his eye made him even more handsome than he was. "A lady killer, Willard, that's what you are."

"I've never felt younger," he said, as they walked home together.

As the weeks went by, they went for a long walk every day, and he talked about everything that was on his mind. "A mind at play," he said to her one afternoon, "and I don't know whether I've told you this before, but it is not a question of right or wrong, really – a mind at play is a mind at work." She had soft grey eyes and a wistful smile. "Yes, you've told me that before, Willard, but I adore everything you tell me, even when you tell me twice." They often stopped for a hot chocolate fudge sundae at a lunch counter that had been in the basement of the Household Trust building since their childhood. She loved digging the long silver spoon down into the dark syrup at the bottom of the glass.

"You and your sweet tooth," he said. "It'll be the death of you."

"Someday you'll take death seriously," she said.

"I do. I do," he said.

"How?"

"I think I'd like to die somewhere else."

"Wherever in the world would you like to die?"

"It's strange," he said, "we've always lived in this city but now I think I'd be happier somewhere else, out in the desert."

"There's no ice cream in the desert," she laughed, softly humouring him.

"Well, it's only a daydream," he said. "It's not how I dream at night."

"What do you dream at night?"

"About you," he said.

"But I'm always right here beside you."

"Yes, yes," he said, "but think of where we could go in our dreams, think of what it would be like watching wild she-camels vanish into the dunes."

She threw her arms around his neck and said, "Yes," kissing him until they were out of breath.

"What a couple of crazy old loons we are," she said.

"Thank God," he said.

Her eyesight was failing, so at night he began to read the newspapers to her. They got into bed and he read to her as she lay curled against his shoulder. "Oh, I like this," he said. "'A politician is like a football coach. He has to be smart enough to understand the game and stupid enough to take it seriously.'"

"I like that too," she said, laughing. "I don't like football but I like that."

"That's why you'll never be a politician," he said, "thank God." He linked his hands behind his head, letting his mind wander, suddenly perplexed because he couldn't remember the name of the pharaoh at the time of Moses. He heard her heavy breathing. Before turning out the light, leaning on his elbow, he looked down into her face, astonished that she had fallen so easily into such a sound sleep because in her younger years she had often wakened in a clammy sweat, panic-stricken, mumbling about loss, about eyes that had not opened, saying she could hear her own screaming though she was not making a sound. He couldn't imagine what dreadful fear had welled up within her during those nights, what darkness she had sunk into, and he wondered how she had managed over the years to stifle that fear, tamp it down. Perhaps in her fear she had gotten a dream-glimpse of their stillborn child. He had forgotten why they had never tried to have another child. He only knew he had never wanted another woman. This gave him sudden joy and a sense of completion in her. He was close to tears as he looked into her sleeping face, afraid that she would go down into a darkness where she would not waken and he whispered:

> Child, do not go
> into the dark places
> of the soul,
> there the grey wolves whine,
> the lean grey wolves...

In the morning, after he had two cups of strong black coffee, he read the newspapers aloud. Any story about old ruins and the past lost in the dunes of time caught his eye. A few months before he'd retired he had written in *Scholastics: A Journal of New Modes* that the psalms of David were actually based on a much older Egyptian sacred text, now almost entirely lost. This meant that David was just a reporter of what he had heard somewhere on the desert trails, and so Willard was pleased one morning to read in the paper that nearly all the archaeologists at a conference in Boston had agreed that the Bible was not history, that no one should pay any historical attention to anything written before the Book of Kings. "The whole thing," he said to Kate, "may just be theological dreaming. The whole of our lives, our ethical and spiritual lives, may be a dream. A wonder-filled dream in which we defeat death by turning lies into the truth." When she asked him how a lie could be the truth, and how everything that was true could be a dream, he said, "I think that maybe all through history we have become our own gods in our dreams. We create them and then they turn around and taunt us. Maybe Christ on the cross is really a taunting dream of death and redemption, a dream in which Christ has to stay nailed to the cross because we don't dare let him come back to us again. We don't dare let him come back and live among us like a normal man because then there'd only be a dreamless silence out there without him in it, a great dark silence." As he said this he felt a lurch in the pit of his stomach, a slow opening up of an old hollow deep in himself, but this hollow didn't frighten him. It was an absence that he had long ago accepted, just as he had accepted the absence of children in their life. He had learned to live with this absence but he could not bear to see Kate in pain. One morning when he was wakened by her moaning in her sleep he felt a frightened pity as he looked down into her sleeping face, pity that she had had to suffer her own attacks of darkness, attacks of absence, in her sleep. He touched her cheek and whispered, "Kate, you're my whole life. Thank God."

One afternoon, when the apple tree was in bud and the hired gardener, who had tattoos on his arms, was cleaning out the peony beds, Willard laughed and pointed at the gardener. He told Kate that he'd been studying a book of maps of the Middle East that a friend had given him years ago, and he'd discovered that there was a small city near the Turkish border that was called, after Cain's nephew, Enos, and since the men there had always marked themselves with tattoos, he said, "The mark of Cain was probably just a tattoo."

"You mean Cain's pruning our rose bushes?"

"Yes."

"Willard," she said, "you are a notion," and she smiled with such genuine amused pleasure and admiration that tears filled his eyes. He held her hand, breathing in the heavy musk of the early spring garden.

"With you, Kate," he said, "I always feel like it's going to be possible to get a grip on something really big about life before I die. I'm very grateful."

"Oh, no," she said. "No one in love should be grateful."

"I can't help it," he said, and felt such an ache for her that he had to take several deep breaths, as if he were sighing with sudden exasperation.

"Don't be impatient," she said.

"I'm not. I was just suddenly out of breath."

"And soon you'll be telling me you're out of your mind."

"That goes without saying," he said, laughing.

"That's what everybody says happened to Adam and Eve," she said. "That she drove Adam out of his mind because he wanted the apple and she ate it…"

"And look at us now."

"A couple of old lunatics," she said, lifting his hand to her lips. "And that's not gratitude, that's love, Willard. You've always been the apple of my eye."

He stood beside her with tears in his eyes.

"Some day," she said, brushing his tears away with her hand, "I'll tell you what I really think."

"I bet you will," he said.

"Yes."

To distract her, to hide his emotions, he riffled through a sheaf of papers on a side table. "You know what? You'll never guess," he said, fumbling the papers. He was excited. He wanted to please her. "I've come across the most wonderful creation story…"

"Creation?"

"Yes, yes," he said, flattening a piece of tawny onionskin paper on the table. "Professor Shotspar translated this for me years ago, from a flood story. It was written down somewhere around 1800 BC, in Akkadian, which in case you don't know is one of the oldest languages in the world, and it's exactly the same flood you'll find in *Gilgamesh*. But this is about the gods and how they got around to creating man – Lullu, they called him. How do you like that? And it's about how they created all of us so we'd knuckle under and do their dirty work, their mucking up…

When the gods, before there were men,
Worked and shed their sweat,
The sweat of the gods was great,

The work was dire, distress abiding.
Carping, backbiting,
Grumbling in the quarries,
They broke their tools,
Broke their spades
And hoes...
Nusku woke his lord,
Got him out of bed,
'My lord, Enil, your temple wall is breached,
Battle broaches your gate.'
Enil spoke to Anu, the warrior.
'Summon a single god and make sure he's
put to death.'
Anu gaped
And then spoke to the other gods, his brothers.
'Why pick on us?
Our work is dire, our distress abiding.
Since Belet-ili, the birth goddess, is nearby,
Why not get her to create Lullu, the man.
Let Lullu wear the yoke wrought by
Enil.
Let man shed his sweat for the gods.'"

"Maybe that's where *he's a lulu* comes from," she said, laughing.

"That's good," he said. "Damned good. I guess we're a couple of lulus."

A week later they were sitting in the sunroom parlour having a glass of dry vermouth. There had been a heavy pounding rain during the night and it was still raining. The garden walk was covered with white petals pasted to the flagstone. He should have noticed that Kate was growing thin, eating only green salads, Emmenthal cheese, and dry toast. At first, sipping her vermouth, she'd grown giddy, and then, as if sapped of all energy, she said, "I'd love to be sitting somewhere down south in the hot sun." He turned to her and said, "But you've never liked the sun." She was sitting in a heavily cushioned wicker chair with her eyes closed. He touched her hand. She didn't open her eyes. He went back to reading Conrad, a novel, *An Outcast of the Islands*. Suddenly he stood up, staring into the stooping branches of the apple tree, bent by the weight of the pouring rain, and then, just as abruptly, he sat down.

"Listen to this," he said: *"There is always one thing the ignorant man knows, and that thing is the only thing worth knowing; it fills the ignorant man's universe. He knows all about himself…"*

Willard dropped the book.

"What's the matter?" she asked, opening her eyes.

"Can't you see?"

"See what?"

"If I seem to know so much about everything, maybe that's only a kind of ignorance. Maybe I don't know anything about myself."

"Don't be silly," she said sternly.

"Silly?" he said. "I'm deadly serious."

He sat staring out the window, into the downpour as tulip petals in the garden broke and fell. He stared at the headless stems. She rose and went upstairs and took a hot bath. She lay in the water a long time, slipping in and out of sleep, until she realized the water was cold and she was shivering. When she came back downstairs he was still sitting by the window, facing the drenched garden.

"Willard, for God's sake, what's the matter? You've hardly moved for hours and hours."

"I don't know," he said. "It's a kind of dread, or something like that. A dread…"

"It's silence, that's what it is."

"I suppose it is. The vast silence. Maybe we live in silence forever. Maybe when we die that's all we are to hear. Silence. The word is dead. Maybe that is what hell is."

The next morning she didn't get out of bed. He brought her tea, but she only drank half the cup. "Perhaps it's a touch of flu," she said, but she had no temperature and no headache. Her hands were cold. He sat holding and rubbing her hands. She smiled wanly. "Oh, I missed our good talks yesterday," she said.

"It was only a pause," he said, trying to be cheerful.

"That's right," she said, and she closed her eyes.

"It was a hard day on the garden, too," he said.

"Yes."

"All this dampness, it's not good, not healthy."

"No."

"It gets into the bones."

"Yes."

"Dem bones, dem bones, dem dry bones…" he sang, trying to be gay.

"Dem dry bones…" she whispered.

"Did you know, Kate," he said, leaning close, seeing that she was drifting off into sleep, "that they've started digging near to where most people think the garden of Eden was, and there's an actual town that was there around 6000 BC? And that's a fact," he said, wagging his finger at her as she lay with her eyes closed, "because there are so many ways of dating things now, what with carbon 14 and tree rings, dendrochronology they call it, when they cut across a tree and read the rings. And then of course they match it with an older tree, and that tree with an older tree, all the way back to the bristlecone pine, 5,000 years ago, in fact even longer. And then…"

She was sound asleep, smiling in her sleep. Her smile bewildered him. He had never seen her smile in her sleep. He wondered what secret happiness, found in sleep, had made her smile.

One week later she was taken to hospital. She had a private room and a young doctor who spoke in a hushed monotone with his hands crossed inside the sleeves of his smock. "It's a problem of circulation," he said. "The blood's just not getting around."

"Oh dear," Willard said, and sat in the bedside leather easy chair all day and into the early evening until Kate woke up and said, "You shouldn't stay here all this time."

"Where else should I be?"

The day she died, her feet and lower legs were blue from gangrene. And in great pain she'd quickly grown thin, the skin taut on her nose, her eyes silvered by a dull film. She panted for air, rolling her eyes. "Willard, Willard," she whispered and reached for him.

"Yes, yes."

"Talk to me."

"Yes, Kate."

"There. Talk to me there."

"Where is there?" he asked desperately.

After her cremation, to which only a few old scholars came and none of his former students, Willard wandered from room to room in the house talking out loud. He kept calling her name, as if she might suddenly step in from the garden, smiling, her hands dirty from planting. In the late afternoons he sat by the open parlour window, talking and

reading and gesturing. But then early one evening he got confused and said, "What did I say?" He couldn't remember what
he had said, and when Kate did not answer, the dread that
he'd felt the month before, the fear that the hollow he'd so
easily accepted was really a profound unawareness of himself,
seized him in the chest and throat so that he was left breath-
less and thought he was going to choke. He was so afraid, so
stricken by his utter aloneness, that he began to shake uncon-
trollably. He sat staring at her empty chair, ashamed of his
trembling hands. He was sure he heard wolves calling and
wondered if he was going crazy. He decided to get out for
some air, to go down to the footbridge that crossed over the
ravine and then come back.

Later that week, Willard went for a long walk in the downtown streets, along streets that they had walked, but he
couldn't bring himself to go into the lunch counter. All the
faces reflected in the store windows as he passed made his
mind swirl, but when he stepped through the subway turn-
stiles, to the *thunk* of the aluminum bars turning over, he told
Kate out loud and as clearly as he could that he was now
absolutely sure, as he had promised her, that he was on to
something big, a simple truth, so simple that no one he knew
had seen it, and the truth was that all the great myths were
based on lies. He'd actually been thinking, he'd said to her
during the short cremation procedure, that to live a great
truth, it is probably necessary to live a great lie. "After all," he
said excitedly, as he stepped through the last turnstile, "the
Jews were never in Egypt. There was no Exodus. The
Egyptians were fanatical record keepers and the Jews are
never mentioned, and the cities that the Jews said they built,
they did not exist. They were not there. There was no parting
of the sea, no forty years of wandering in the desert… I mean,

my God," he said, shaking his long finger as he forgot where he was going and didn't see that people were staring at him as he went back down an escalator, "what does anyone think Moses was doing out there for forty years? Forty years. You can walk across the Sinai in two days. And Jericho, there was no battle. No battle took place because there were no great walls to tumble down. There was no city there back then, not at that time," and he threw up his arms, full of angry defiance, standing on the tiled and dimly lit platform of the St. George subway station.

"Sorry," Willard said to a cluster of women who were staring at him, "I'm very sorry." He hurried back to the escalator, travelling up the moving stairs, craning his neck, eager to get out into the sunlight. "I just don't know what I'm going to do, Kate," he said in a whisper. "Talking to you like this, I forget. It's so fine, I just plain forget, people looking at me as if I were some kind of loony."

It was painful for him to stay at home all day. He kept listening for her voice in the rooms, embarrassed by the sound of his own voice. He sank into grim, bewildered silence, sometimes standing in the hall in a trance, a stupor, certain that he was losing his mind. Sometimes he slept during the day and once dreamed that he was walking on his shadow, as if his shadow was always in front of him, a shadow made of soot. It whimpered with pain. He stomped on his shadow till he was out of breath. He was afraid it was the soot of a scorched body. He heard her voice, and saw her sitting with her elbow on the windowsill, picking old paint off a glass pane. She was feverish and kept calling for ice. "Ice is the only answer." He woke up terrified. He locked their bedroom door and made his bed on the sofa in the library. For a week he slept on the sofa, drinking several glasses of port, trying to get to sleep. He could see from the sofa a hem of light under the bedroom door. He'd left the light on, a bedside reading lamp that she'd given him for his birthday, a porcelain angel with folded wings. On two evenings he was sure that he heard her voice in the bedroom, a voice so muffled that he couldn't make out the words. Then one night while he was keeping watch on the hem of light, half tipsy, half asleep, it went out. He was panic-stricken. He took it as a sign that she was in trouble, that she was really going to die, and he fumbled with the old key, trying to get it into the lock, whispering. "Hold on Kate, hold on, I'm coming," cursing his own stupidity and cowardness for trying to close off the bedroom. Willard felt ashamed, as if he had betrayed her. When he got into the room, breathing heavily, he discovered that the bulb in the lamp, left on for so long, had burned out. He had seldom cried before, and only once in front of her. Now, standing before her dressing-table mirror, he discovered that he was dishevelled and haggard and he was crying. He began to sing as cheerfully as he could:

> If I had the wings of an angel,
> over these prison walls I would fly,
> I'd fly to the arms of my poor darling,
> and there...

He moved close to himself in the mirror and curled his lip with contempt. "You're a coward," he said, and then lay down and fell asleep on their bed. In the morning he dressed with care, putting on an expensive Egyptian-cotton shirt and camel-hair jacket. He went out into the bright noon hour and found he was relieved to be walking again with a sudden jaunt in his stride, downtown among the crowds. He began to sing: *I'll take you home again, Kathleen...* But then he grew suddenly wary and stopped singing, trying to make sure he heard himself before he spoke out loud. He kept looking for himself in store windows to see if he was singing or talking at the top of his voice.

In the Hudson's Bay underground shopping mall, he came to a halt so abruptly that an old woman was unable to avoid bumping into him, and spilled her bag of toiletries. He didn't notice. He stared at a portly black man standing by the check-out counter. The black man was talking into a cellphone, and farther along the mall, another man had a cellular phone close to his cheek. Willard realized that for weeks he'd seen people all over the city talking and nodding into phones and no one paid any attention to them. "Nobody knows who they're talking to," he cried. "Maybe they're not talking to anyone," and the old woman, picking up her rolls of Downy Soft toilet paper scattered around his feet, looked up and said, "You're not only rude, you're crazy," but he hurried off.

At Rogers Sound Systems a young salesman, with a Jamaican accent Willard had trouble understanding, tried to interest him in the latest models of cellphones. Willard was surprised at how compact the phones were. When the salesman said, "Look, this one even has its own built-in flashlight," Willard said, "A phone is a phone. How complicated can that be?" The salesman shrugged. "In that case, we have older models on sale, half price."

Willard bought one of the sale-price models. When the salesman tried to advise him, saying, "About all those old-fangled buttons, man—" Willard cut him short with, "Never mind. I think I can figure out a phone." He strode out of the store and set out for home, eager to get talking to Kate.

As soon as he got to the footbridge he tapped a green button and, holding the phone close to his ear like an old walkie-talkie, began telling Kate an old joke he'd heard years ago:

"How these two old ladies had promised each other that the first one to die would come back and tell the other what Heaven was like, so after Sadie died Sophie waited and waited, and just when she gave up, Sadie appeared in a halo of light and Sophie said, You came back, so what's it like? And Sadie said, You get up in the morning and eat and then you have sex, and then it's sex before breakfast and afterwards sex, and before lunch and then lunch and more sex and sex before a snack before goodnight and then sex, and Sophie said, Sadie... Sadie, this is Heaven! But Sadie said: Heaven, who's in heaven. I'm a rabbit in Wisconsin." He laughed and laughed but with the phone tucked against his cheek, so that no one paid any attention to him. "Oh, I'm in fine fettle," he said. "This walking clears the lungs."

Willard stood on the footbridge over the ravine. He had never stopped to look down into the ravine before. He'd always been in a hurry to get home, his head tucked into his shoulder against the wind. He was surprised at how deep the ravine actually was, and how dense and lush the trees and bush were. The city itself was flat, all the streets laid out in a severe military grid, but here was the ravine, and of course there were ravines like this one that ran all through the city, deep, dark, mysterious places, running like lush green wounds through the concrete, the cement surfaces, and he felt sheepish. "All these years, and I've never been down in the ravines. Who knows what goes on down there. Can you imagine that, Kate?" He began to walk slowly home. He looked up and down the street. "All this is beginning to trouble me. Everything's beginning to trouble me," he said. "Everything seems to be only the surface of things. Everything is not where it's supposed to be. I mean, Abraham was always Abraham, some kind of old desert chieftain from around the

River Jordan, but that's probably not true. All the actual references that I can find say he lived in Heran, in Anatolia, and that's a place in southern Turkey, close to where Genesis says Noah's ark ended up, settled on Mount Ararat, and that's not in Jordan, that's in eastern Turkey. The whole thing seems more and more like a Turkish story, a Turkish delight," and he laughed and quickened his pace, "because Abraham's descendent, a man called Dodanim, became the Dodecanese Islands, and a guy named Kittim is really Kriti, which is Crete, and Javan is really the Aegean, and Ashkenaz… Everyone knows the Ashkenazi are from north of the Danube. The whole thing, the whole story, took place somewhere else farther north. It's not a desert story at all, that's why the Jews weren't seen in Egypt…they weren't there, they were out on the edge of the world."

He was so out of breath from talking and walking at the same time that he had to stop walking. He had a cramp in his wrist from clutching the cellphone to his cheek. He was relieved. There was no one on his street of tree-shaded homes. He put the phone in his jacket pocket. Then he suddenly shuddered and choked back tears. All his talk, he felt, was wasted. He was alone. He was alone in a well of silence. "Jesus," he said, "even Sadie came back and said something." He felt abandoned, he wanted to hear what Kate thought of all his talk, all his daring insights. A man coming around the corner with his dog on a leash hesitated because Willard looked so frantic, but Willard shouted, "And a good day to you." The man hurried on.

Around noon on Easter Sunday, Willard put on a lightweight tweed suit that he hadn't worn for years. He went across the footbridge and strode along Bloor Street, revelling in the strong sunlight. He hadn't been out of the house for days because he'd been working in his study on several cuneiform texts. He'd hardly eaten. He'd done very little talking to Kate, but now he felt fresh and bold and self-confident as he walked among well-dressed women.

"It's a wonderful day" he said to Kate, holding the phone close. "And I've got wonderful news. I've finally figured this thing out, yes ma'am... The answer's right there in what looks like a contradiction that's built in at the beginning, right there at the start of Genesis, where God says he's made man in his own image, and then, in the second chapter, there's no one around. Everything's empty. So whoever he'd made has flown the coop."

As the red light changed to green at Church Street, he stepped off the curb, saying, "The whole place is empty, man is gone and what that means is that for nearly a million years, man trekked around chasing animals, naming them, hunting them, but suddenly he got smart. Ten thousand years ago he got smart. He wanted a garden. And a closed garden is something you've got to cultivate. And man shows up in Genesis again, and he was Cain the cultivator, who'd taken off from the old happy grazing grounds of Eden to work the earth in a new place, the new civilization where there was nothing. That's what the new Eden was, not a paradise of two witless souls lying around under an apple tree, but Cain, the tattooed man who had the courage to build a closed garden, a city out there on the edge of the world. Cain the civilized man, the marked man..." and Willard raised his arms, facing into the sun. The women in their Easter outfits shied away from him. "That's when man became magnificent, Kate. That's when he went into the dark to create his own world, to create himself. That's the first time he had the guts to take his own word for everything."

"Oh yes, yes," a tall, lean woman with big owl glasses said. "Oh yes." She was smiling eagerly. He quickly brought the phone closer to his ear. He wanted to be left alone. He wanted Kate. He waved the woman with the owl glasses away and as he did so, his thumb slipped on to a red button. He had never pressed the *red* button before, but now he suddenly heard Kate. She was calling him. "Willard, Willard, what's been the matter with you?"

"It's you!"

"Of course it's me."

"I knew you were there. I knew it," he cried triumphantly.

"You knew? You knew where I was!"

"No. Where are you?" he whispered, stepping through a crowd of women on the sidewalk.

"I'm here. Right where I said I would be. I've been screaming at you for weeks, and you didn't hear a word."

"I never dreamed that all I had to do was touch the other button. I never did that. I never heard you."

"But I heard you," Kate said. "Can you imagine what it's been like listening and listening and I couldn't say a word…"

"But I never thought…" he said.

"That's all you've been doing, Willard," she said, calming down. "Thinking."

"I've been talking to you."

"A blue streak, I'd say."

"Don't be upset," he said.

"I have a right to be upset," she said. "Sitting here like a dumb bunny for weeks."

"Never mind," he said.

"I mind. And locking our bedroom door, that did not help. I was yelling so loud at you I thought I would die. I was hoarse for two days, I lost my voice."

His thumb was sore from flicking back and forth. "We're just wasting time talking like this," he said.

"Time is not my problem," she said.

"I have been dying to know for weeks what you think."

"What I really think?"

"Yes."

"Truly?"

"Yes."

"I think you are," and she paused, and then with quiet gravity, "simply magnificent. I can't imagine living without you. I hang on every word."

"You do?"

"I would never lie to you."

"Thank God you're still alive," he said.

"Nobody wants to die," she said.

THAT DAY I SAT DOWN WITH JESUS

on the Sun Deck and a Wind Came Up and
Blew My Kimono Open and He Saw My Breasts

GLORIA SAWAI

When an extraordinary event takes place in your life, you're apt to remember with unnatural clarity the details surrounding it. You remember shapes and sounds that weren't directly related to the occurrence but hovered there in the periphery of the experience. This can even happen when you read a great book for the first time – one that unsettles you and startles you into thought. You remember where you read it, what room, who was nearby.

I can remember, for instance, where I read *Of Human Bondage*. I was lying on a top bunk in our high-school dormitory, wrapped in a blue bedspread. I lived in a dormitory then because of my father. He was a religious man and wanted me to get a spiritual kind of education, to hear the Word and know the Lord, as he put it. So, he sent me to St. John's Lutheran Academy in Regina for two years. He was confident, I guess, that's where I'd hear the Word. Anyway, I can still hear Mrs. Sverdren, our housemother, knocking on the door at midnight and whispering in her Norwegian accent, "Now, Gloria, it is 12 o'clock. Time to turn off the lights. Right now."

Then scuffing down the corridor in her bedroom slippers. What's interesting here is that I don't remember anything about the book itself except that someone in it had a club foot. But it must have moved me deeply when I was sixteen, which is some time ago now.

You can imagine then how distinctly I remember the day Jesus of Nazareth, in person, climbed the hill in our backyard to our house, then up the outside stairs to the sundeck where I was sitting. And how he stayed with me for a while. You can surely understand how clear those details rest in my memory.

The event occurred on Monday morning, September 11, 1972 in Moose Jaw, Saskatchewan. These facts in themselves are more unusual than they may appear to be at first glance. September's my favourite month; Monday, my favourite day; morning, my favourite time. And although Moose Jaw may not be the most magnificent place in the world, even so, if you happen to be there on a Monday morning in September it has its beauty.

It's not hard to figure out why these are my favourites, by the way. I have five children and a husband. Things get hectic, especially on weekends and holidays. Kids hanging around the house, eating, arguing, asking me every hour what there is to do in Moose Jaw. And television. The programs are always the same; only the names change! Roughriders, Stampeders, Blue Bombers, Whatever. So when school starts in September I bask in freedom, especially on Monday. No quarrels. No TV. The morning, crisp and lovely. A new day. A fresh start.

On the morning of September 11, I got up at 7, the usual time, cooked Cream of Wheat for the kids, fried a bit of sausage for Fred, waved them all out of the house, drank a second cup of coffee in peace, and decided to get at last week's ironing. I wasn't dressed yet but still in the pink kimono I'd bought years ago on my trip to Japan – my one and only overseas trip, a $200 quick tour of Tokyo and other cities. I'd saved for this while working as a library technician in Regina, and I'm glad I did. Since then, I've hardly been out of Saskatchewan. Once in a while a trip to Winnipeg, and a few times down to Medicine Lake, Montana, to visit my sister.

I set up the ironing board and hauled out the basket of week-old sprinkled clothes. When I unrolled the first shirt it was completely dry and smelled stale. The second was covered with little grey blots of mould. So was the third. Fred teaches junior-high science here in Moose Jaw. He uses a lot of shirts. I decided I'd have to unwrap the whole basketful and air everything out. This I did, spreading the pungent garments about the living room. While they were airing I would go outside and sit on the deck for a while since it was such a clear and sunny day.

If you know Moose Jaw at all, you'll know about the new subdivision at the southeast end called Hillhurst. That's where we live, right on the edge of the city. In fact, our deck looks out on flat land as far as the eye can see, except for the backyard itself, which is a fairly steep hill leading down to a stone quarry. But from the quarry the land straightens out into the Saskatchewan prairie. One clump of poplars stands beyond the quarry to the right, and high weeds have grown up among the rocks. Other than that, it's plain – just earth and sky. But when the sun rises new in the morning, weeds and rocks take on an orange and rusty glow that is pleasing. To me at least. I unplugged the iron and returned to the kitchen. I'd take a cup of coffee outside, or maybe some orange juice. To reach the juice at the back of the fridge my hand passed right next to a bottle of dry red Calona. Now here was a better idea.

A little wine on Monday morning, a little relaxation after a rowdy weekend. I held the familiar bottle comfortably in my hand and poured, anticipating a pleasant day. I slid open the glass door leading to the deck. I pulled an old canvas folding-chair into the sun, and sat. Sat and sipped. Beauty and tranquility floated toward me on Monday morning, September 11, around 9:40.

First he was a little bump on the far, far-off prairie. Then he was a mole way beyond the quarry. Then a larger animal, a dog perhaps, moving out there through the grass. Nearing the quarry, he became a person. No doubt about that. A woman perhaps, still in her bathrobe. But edging out from the rocks, through the weeds, toward the hill, he was clear to me. I knew then who he was. I knew it just as I knew the sun was shining.

The reason I knew is that he looked exactly the way I'd seen him 5,000 times in pictures, in books and Sunday School pamphlets. If there was ever a person I'd seen and heard about, over and over, this was the one. Even in grade school those terrible questions. Do you love the Lord? Are you saved by grace alone through faith? Are you awaiting eagerly the glorious day of his Second Coming? And will you be ready on that Great Day? I'd sometimes hidden under the bed when I was a child, wondering if I really had been saved by grace alone, or, without realizing it, I'd been trying some other method, like the Catholics, who were saved by their good works and would land in hell. Except for a few who knew in their hearts it was really grace, but they didn't want to leave the church because of their relatives. And was this it? Would the trumpet sound tonight and the sky split in two? Would the great Lord and King, Alpha and Omega, holding aloft the seven candlesticks, accompanied by a heavenly host that no man could number, descend from heaven with a mighty shout? And was I ready? Rev. Hanson in his high pulpit in Swift Current, Saskatchewan, roared in my ears and clashed against my eardrums.

And there he was. Coming. Climbing the hill in our back-yard, his body bent against the climb, his robes ruffling in the wind. He was coming. And I was not ready. All those mouldy clothes scattered about the living room, and me in this faded old thing, made in Japan, and drinking – in the middle of the morning. He had reached the steps now. His hand touched the railing. His right hand was on my railing. Jesus's fingers were curled around my railing. He was coming up. He was ascending. He was coming up to me here on the sundeck.

He stood on the top step and looked at me. I looked at him. He looked exactly right, exactly the same as all the pic-tures: white robe, purple stole, bronze hair, creamy skin. How had all those queer artists, illustrators of Sunday School papers, how had they gotten him exactly right like that?

He stood at the top of the stairs. I sat there holding my glass. What do you say to Jesus when he comes? How do you address him? Do you call him *Jesus*? I supposed that was his first name. Or *Christ*? Remembered the woman at the well, the one living in adultery who'd called him *Sir*. Perhaps I could try that. Or maybe I should pretend not to recognize him. Maybe, for some reason, he didn't mean for me to rec-ognize him. Then he spoke.

"Good morning," he said. "My name is Jesus."

"How do you do," I said. "My name is Gloria Johnson."

My name is Gloria Johnson. That's what I said, all right. As if he didn't know.

He smiled, standing there at the top of the stairs. I thought of what I should do next. Then I got up and unfolded an-other canvas chair.

"You have a nice view here," he said, leaning back against the canvas and pressing his sandaled feet against the iron bars of the railing.

"Thank you," I said. "We like it."

Nice view. Those were his very words. Everyone who comes to our house and stands on the deck says that. Everyone.

"I wasn't expecting company today." I straightened the folds of my pink kimono and tightened the cloth more securely over my knees. I picked up the glass from the floor where I'd laid it.

"I was passing through on my way to Winnipeg. I thought I'd drop by."

"I've heard a lot about you," I said. "You look quite a bit like your pictures." I raised the glass to my mouth and saw that his hands were empty. I should offer him something to drink. Tea? Milk? How should I ask him what he'd like to drink? What words should I use?

"It gets pretty dusty out there," I finally said. "Would you care for something to drink?" He looked at the glass in my hand. "I could make you some tea," I added.

"Thanks," he said. "What are you drinking?"

"Well, on Mondays I like to relax a bit after the busy weekend with the family at home. I have five children, you know. So, sometimes after breakfast I have a little wine."

"That would be fine," he said.

By luck I found a clean tumbler in the cupboard. I stood by the sink pouring the wine. And then, like a bolt of lightning, I realized my situation. Oh, Johann Sebastian Bach. Glory. Honour. Wisdom. Power. George Frederick Handel. King of Kings and Lord of Lords. He's on my sundeck. Today he's sitting on my sundeck. I can ask him any question under the sun, anything at all, he'll know the answer. Hallelujah. Well now, wasn't this something for a Monday morning in Moose Jaw? I opened the fridge door to replace the bottle. And I saw my father. It was New Year's morning. My father was sitting at the kitchen table. Mother sat across from him. She'd covered the oatmeal pot to let it simmer on the stove. I could hear the lid bumping against the rim, quietly. Sigrid and Freda sat on one side of the table, Raymond and I on the other. We were holding hymn books, little black books turned to page one. It was dark outside. On New Year's morning we got up before sunrise. Daddy was looking at us with his chin pointed out. It meant, Sit still and sit straight. Raymond sat as straight and stiff as a soldier, waiting for Daddy to notice how nice and stiff he sat. We began singing. Page one. Hymn for the New Year. Philipp Nicolai. 1599. We didn't really need the books. We'd sung the same song every New Year's since the time of our conception. Daddy always sang the loudest.

The morning Star upon us gleams:
How full of grace and truth His beams,
How passing fair His splendour.
Good Shepherd, David's proper heir,
My King is heav'n Thou dost me bear
Upon Thy bosom tender.
Near-est. Dear-est. High-est. Bright-est,
Thou delight-est still to love me.
Thou so high enthroned a-bove me.

I didn't mind, actually, singing hymns on New Year's, as long as I was sure no one else would find out. I'd have been rather embarrassed if any of my friends ever found out how we spend New Year's. It's easy at a certain age to be embarrassed about your family. I remember Alice Olson, how embarrassed she was about her father, Elmer Olson. He was an alcoholic and couldn't control his urine. Her mother always had to clean up after him. Even so, the house smelled. I suppose she couldn't get it all. Anyway, I know Alice was embarrassed when we saw Elmer all tousled and sick-looking, with urine stains on his trousers. Actually, I don't know what would be harder on a kid – having a father who's a drunk, or one who's sober on New Year's and sings "O Moring Star"? I walked across the deck and handed Jesus the wine. I sat down, resting my glass on the flap of my kimono. Jesus was looking out over the prairie. He seemed to be noticing every-thing out there. He was obviously in no hurry to leave, but he didn't have much to say. I thought of what to say next.

"I suppose you're more used to the sea than to the prairie."

"Yes," he answered. "I've lived most of my life near water. But I like the prairie too. There's something nice about the prairie." He turned his face to the wind, stronger now, com-ing toward us from the east.

Nice again. If I'd ever used that word to describe the prairie, in an English theme at St. John's, for example, it would have had three red circles around it. At least three. I raised my glass to the wind. Good old St. John's. Good old Pastor Solberg, standing in front of the wooden altar, holding the gospel aloft in his hand.

In the beginning was the Word
And the Word was with God
And the Word was God
All things were made by him;
And without him was not anything made
That was made.

I was sitting on a bench by Paul Thorson. We were shar-ing a hymnal. Our thumbs touched at the centre of the book. It was winter. The chapel was cold – an army barracks left over from World War II. We wore parkas and sat close together. Paul fooled around with this thumb, pushing my thumb to my own side of the book, then pulling it back to his side. The wind howled outside. We watched our breath as we sang the hymn.

> In thine arms I rest me, Foes who would molest me
> Cannot reach me here; Tho the earth be shak-ing,
> Ev-ry heart be quak-ing, Jesus clams my fear,
> Fires may flash and thunder crash,
> Yea, and sin and hell as-sail me,
> Jesus will not fai-l me…

And here he was. Alpha and Omega. The Word. Sitting on my canvas chair, telling me the prairie's nice. What could I say to that?

"I like it too," I said.

Jesus was watching a magpie circling above the poplars just beyond the quarry. He seemed very nice actually, but he wasn't like my father. My father was perfect, mind you, but you know about perfect people – busy, busy. He wasn't as busy as Elsie, though. Elsie was the busy one. You could never visit there without her having to do something else at the same time. Wash the leaves of her plants with milk or fold socks in the basement while you sat on a bench by the washing machine. I wouldn't mind sitting on a bench in the basement if that was all she had, but her living room was full of big soft chairs that no one ever sat in. Now Christ here didn't seem to have any work to do at all.

The wind had risen now. His robes puffed about his legs. His hair swirled around his face. I set my glass down and held my kimono together at my knees. The wind was coming stronger now out of the east. My kimono flapped about my ankles. I bent down to secure the bottom, pressing the moving cloth close against my legs. A Saskatchewan wind comes up in a hurry, let me tell you. Then it happened. A gust of wind hit me straight on, seeping into the folds of my kimono, reaching down into the bodice, billowing the cloth out until, above the sash, the robe was fully open. I knew without looking. The wind was suddenly blowing on my breasts. I felt it cool on both my breasts. Then as quickly as it came, it left, and we sat in the small breeze of before.

I looked at Jesus. He was looking at me. And my breasts. Looking right at them. Jesus was sitting there on the sundeck, looking at my breasts.

What should I do? Say "Excuse me" and push them back into my kimono? Make a little joke of it? Look what the wind blew in, or something? Or should I say nothing? Just tuck them in as inconspicuously as possible? What do you say when a wind comes up and blows your kimono open and he sees your breasts?

Now, there are ways and there are ways of exposing your breasts. I know a few things. I read books. And I've learned a lot from my cousin Millie. Millie's the black sheep in the family. She left the Academy without graduating to become an artist's model in Winnipeg. A dancer too. Anyway, Millie's told me a few things about body exposure. She says, for instance, that when an artist wants to draw his model he has her either completely nude and stretching and bending in various positions so he can sketch her from different angles. Or he drapes her with cloth, satin usually. He covers one portion of the body with the material and leaves the rest exposed. But he does so in a graceful manner, draping the cloth over her stomach or ankle. Never over the breasts. So I realized that my appearance right then wasn't actually pleasing, either aesthetically or erotically – from Millie's point of view. My breasts were just sticking out from the top of my old kimono. And for some reason that I certainly can't explain, even to this day, I did nothing about it. I just sat there.

Jesus must have recognized my confusion, because right then he said, quite sincerely I thought, "You have nice breasts."

"Thanks," I said. I didn't know what else to say, so I asked him if he'd like more wine.

"Yes, I would," he said, and I left to refill the glass. When I returned he was watching the magpie swishing about in the tall weeds of the quarry. I sat down and watched with him.

Then I got a very, very peculiar sensation. I know it was just an illusion, but it was so strong it scared me. It's hard to explain because nothing like it had ever happened to me before. The magpie began to float toward Jesus. I saw it fluttering toward him in the air as if some vacuum were sucking it in. When it reached him, it flapped about on his chest, which was bare now because the top of his robe had slipped down. It nibbled at his little brown nipples and squawked and disappeared. For all the world, it seemed to disappear right into his pores. Then the same thing happened with a rock. A rock floating up from the quarry and landing on the breast of Jesus, melting into his skin. It was very strange, let me tell you, Jesus and I sitting there together with that happening. It made me dizzy, so I closed my eyes.

I saw the women in a public bath in Tokyo. Black-haired women and children. Some were squatting by faucets that lined a wall. They were running hot water into their basins, washing themselves with white cloths, rubbing each other's backs with the soapy washcloths, then emptying their basins and filling them again, pouring clean water over their bodies for the rinse. Water and suds swirled about on the tiled floor.

Others were sitting in the hot pool on the far side. Soaking themselves in the steamy water as they jabbered away to one another. Then I saw her. The woman without the breasts. She was squatting by a faucet near the door. The oldest woman I've ever seen. The thinnest woman I've ever witnessed. Skin and bones. Literally. Just skin and bones. She bowed and smiled at everyone who entered. She had three teeth. When she hunched over her basin, I saw the little creases of skin where her breasts had been. When she stood up the wrinkles disappeared In their place were two shallow caves. Even the nipples seemed to have disappeared into the small brown caves of her breasts.

I opened my eyes and looked at Jesus. Fortunately, everything had stopped floating.

"Have you ever been to Japan?" I asked.

"Yes," he said, "a few times."

I paid no attention to his answer but went on telling him about Japan as if he'd never been there. I couldn't seem to stop talking about that old woman and her breasts.

"You should have seen her," I said. "She wasn't flat-chested like some women even here in Moose Jaw. It wasn't like that at all. Her breasts weren't just flat. They were caved in, as if the flesh had sunk right there. Have you ever seen breasts like that before?"

Jesus's eyes were getting darker. He seemed to have sunk farther down into his chair.

"Japanese women have smaller breasts to begin with, usually," he said.

But he'd misunderstood me. It wasn't just her breasts that held me. It was her jaws, teeth, neck, ankles, heels. Not just her breasts. I said nothing for a while. Jesus, too, was not talking.

Finally I asked, "Well, what do you think of breasts like that?"

I knew immediately that I'd asked the wrong question. If you want personal and specific answers, you ask personal and specific questions. It's as simple as that. I should have asked him, for instance, what he thought of them from a sexual point of view. If he were a lover, let's say, would he like to hold such breasts in his hand and play on them with his teeth and finger? Would he now? The woman, brown and shiny, was bending over her basin. Tiny bubbles of soap drifted from the creases of her chest down to her navel. Hold them. Ha.

Or I could have asked for some kind of aesthetic opinion. If he were an artist, a sculptor, let's say, would he travel to Italy and spend weeks excavating the best marble from the hills near Florence, and then would he stay up night and day in his studio, without eating or bathing, and with matted hair and glazed eyes, chisel out those little creases from his great stone slab?

Or if he were a curator in a large museum in Paris, would he place these wrinkles on a silver pedestal in the centre of the foyer?

Or if he were a patron of the arts, would he attend the opening of this grand exhibition and stand in front of these white caves in his purple turtleneck, sipping champagne and nibbling on the little cracker with the shrimp in the middle, and would he turn to the one beside him, the one in the sleek black pants, and would he say to her, "Look, darling. Did you see this marvellous piece? Do you see how the artist has captured the very essence of the female form?"

These are some of the things I could have said if I'd had my wits about me. But my wits certainly left me that day. All

I did say, and I didn't mean to – it just came out – was, "It's not nice and I don't like it."

I lifted my face, threw my head back, and let the wind blow on my neck and breasts. It was blowing harder again. I felt small grains of sand scrape against my skin.

Jesus, lover of my soul, let me to thy bosom fly.
While the nearer waters roll, while the tempest
Still is nigh...

When I looked at him again, his eyes were blacker still and his body had shrunk considerably. He looked almost like Jimmy that time in Prince Albert. Jimmy's an old neighbour from Regina. On his twenty-seventh birthday, he joined a motorcycle gang. The Grim Reapers to be exact, and got into a lot of trouble. He ended up in maximum security in PA. One summer on a camping trip up north we stopped to see him – Fred and the kids and I. It wasn't a good visit, by the way. If you're going to visit inmates you should do it regularly. I realize this now. Anyway, that's when his eyes looked black like that. But maybe he'd been smoking. It's probably not the same thing. Jimmy Lebrun. He never did think it was funny when I'd call him a Midnight Raider instead of a Grim Reaper. People are sensitive about their names.

Then Jesus finally answered. Everything seemed to take him a long time, even answering simple questions.

But I'm not sure what he said because something so strange happened that whatever he did say was swept away. Right then the wind blew against my face, pulling my hair back. My kimono swirled about every which way, and I was swinging my arms in the air, like swimming. And there right below my eyes was the roof of our house. I was looking down on the top of the roof. I saw the row of shingles ripped loosed from the August hail storm. And I remember thinking, *Fred hasn't fixed those shingles yet. I'll have to remind him when he gets home from work. If it rains again the back bedroom will get soaked.* Before I knew it, I was circling over the sundeck, looking down on the top of Jesus's head. Only I wasn't. I was sitting in the canvas chair watching myself hover over his shoulders. Only it wasn't me hovering. It was the old woman in Tokyo. I saw her grey hair twisting in the wind and her shiny little bum raised in the air, like a baby's. Water was dripping from her chin and toes. And soap bubbles trailed from her elbows like tinsel. She was floating down toward his chest. Only it wasn't her. It was me. I could taste bits of suds sticking to the corners of my mouth and feel the wind on my wet back and in the hollow caves of my breasts. I was smiling and bowing, and the wind was blowing in narrow wisps against my toothless gums. Then quickly, so quickly, like a flock of waxwings diving through snow into the branches of the poplar, I was splitting up into millions and millions of pieces and sinking in the tiny, tiny holes in his chest. It was like the magpie and the rock, like I had come apart into atoms or molecules, or whatever it is we really are.

After that I was dizzy. I began to feel nauseated, there on my canvas chair. Jesus looked sick too. Sad and sick and lonesome. *Oh, Christ,* I thought, *why are we sitting here on such a fine day pouring our sorrows into each other?* I had to get up and walk around. I'd go into the kitchen and make some tea. I put the kettle on to boil. What on earth had gotten into me? Why had I spent this perfectly good morning talking about breasts? My one chance in a lifetime and I'd let it go. Why didn't I have better control? Why was I always letting things get out of hand? *Breasts.* Why wasn't it Lucille? Or Millie? You could talk about breasts all day if your name was Millie. But Gloria. Gloria. Glo-o-o-o-o-o-o-oria. I knew then why so many Glorias hang around bars, talking too loud, laughing shrilly at stupid jokes. Making sure everyone hears them laugh at the dirty jokes. They're just trying to live down their name, that's all. I brought out the cups and poured the tea. Everything was back to normal when I returned except that Jesus still looked desolate sitting there in my canvas chair. I handed him the tea and sat down beside him.

Oh, Daddy. And Phillip Nicolai. Oh, Bernard of Clairvoux. Oh, Sacred Head Now Wounded. Go away for a little while and let us sit together quietly, here in this small space under the sun.

I sipped the tea and watched his face. He looked so sorrowful I reached out and put my hand on his wrist. I sat there a long while, rubbing the little hairs on his wrist with my fingers. I couldn't help it. After that he put his arm on my shoulder and his hand on the back of my neck, stoking the muscles there. It felt good. Whenever anything exciting or unusual happens to me, my neck is the first to feel it. It gets stiff and knotted up. Then I usually get a headache, and frequently I become nauseous. So it felt very good having my neck rubbed.

I've never been able to handle sensation very well. I remember when I was in grade three and my folks took us to the Saskatoon Exhibition. We went to see the grandstand show – the battle of Wolfe and Montcalm on the Plains of Abraham. The stage was filled with Indians and pioneers and ladies in red, white and blue dresses, singing *In Days of Yore from Britain's Shore*. It was very spectacular but too much for me. My stomach was upset and my neck ached. I had to keep my head on my mother's lap the whole time, just opening my eyes once in a while so I wouldn't miss everything.

So, it felt really good having my neck stroked like that. I could almost feel the knots untying and my body becoming warmer and more restful. Jesus, too, seemed to be feeling better. His body was back to normal. His eyes looked natural again.

Then, all of a sudden, he started to laugh. He held his hand on my neck and laughed out loud. I don't know to this day what he was laughing about. There was nothing funny there at all. But hearing him made me laugh too. I couldn't stop. He was laughing so hard he spilled the tea over this purple stole. When I saw that I laughed even harder I'd never thought of Jesus spilling his tea before. And when Jesus saw me laugh so hard and when he looked at my breasts shaking, he laughed harder still, till he wiped tears from his eyes.

After that we just sat there. I don't know how long. I know we watched the magpie carve black waves in the air above the rocks. And the rocks stiff and lovely among the swaying weeds. We watched the poplars twist and bend and rise again beyond the quarry. And then he had to leave.

"Goodbye, Gloria Johnson," he said, rising from his chair. "Thanks for the hospitality."

He leaned over and kissed me on my mouth. Then he flicked my nipple with his finger, and off he went. Down the hill, through the quarry, and into the prairie. I stood on the sundeck and watched. I watched until I could see him no longer, until he was only some dim and ancient star on the horizon.

I went inside the house. Well, now, wasn't that a nice visit? Wasn't that something? I examined the clothes, dry and sour in the living room. I'd have to put them back in the wash, that's all. I couldn't stand the smell. I tucked my breasts back into my kimono and lugged the basket downstairs.

That's what happened to me in Moose Jaw in 1972. It was the main thing that happened to me that year.

from

KING LEARY

PAUL QUARRINGTON

The brothers of St. Alban the Martyr started putting together the boards. They were usually a quiet bunch, but they got even quieter, all of them rushing around with hammers in their hands and nails sticking out of their mouths. The only thing us lads heard from them was pounding out in the playing field, pounding and the occasional grunt. I personally thought the monks were crazy, and I'll tell you why: they laid out the boards in a circle. A huge and, as far as I could tell, perfect circle. I even asked Brother Isaiah about it. He just grinned and fastened his strange eyes on my left shoulder. "Have ye not known?" he asked me. "Have ye not heard? It is he that sitteth upon the circle of the earth that bringeth the princes to nothing." That's the kind of answer I used to get from Brother Isaiah. So anyway, they laid out the boards in a circle, and around the beginning of December they raised them. The monks took the old horses off the cart. It took the horses and sometimes six or seven brothers to raise each section of board. The weather stayed pleasant for a week or two, the sun all biting and bright even though the trees were naked as firewood. We all waited; the monks prayed.

On Christmas Eve the temperature fell about forty degrees. The brothers rushed out with buckets and hoses. They stayed out there all night, and to keep themselves amused they sang. They sang strange songs with words I didn't understand. All night long the monks watered the world, and the winter air turned the water to ice. Blue-silver ice, hard as marble. On Christmas morning the round rink was ready. Brother Simon was out there skating, his face even uglier, reddened by lack of oxygen, his carbuncles polished by the stinging wind. For a huge, monstrous man he sure could dance out there on the ice! He had some figure-skating moves, dips and twirls, his arms raised slightly, the hockey stick acting as a balancing pole. And as I watched him, Brother Simon the Ugly became airborne. It seemed he was up there for a whole minute, and during that time he pirouetted lazily. This stunt robbed me of my breath and made my knees quiver... I said to myself, Leary, if you could do that, no one could ever stop you. It took me some months to learn to skate like Brother Andrew the Fireplug. I call it Bulldogging. Miles Renders, who is currently coaching the Toronto Maple Leafs, calls it "achievement through perseverance and mental imaging," and I say that one of the reasons the Leafs are faring so poorly is that Renders would call Bulldogging something like that...

One night, I couldn't sleep. There was a full moon, and it filled the window across from my cot, and for some strange reason I could make out all the mountains and craters. The moon was a strange colour, too, a silver like a nickel had been flipped into the sky.

Then I heard the sounds, the soft windy sweeping of hockey sticks across ice. At first I thought I was dreaming, but then I recalled that I never did dream to speak of. I moved across to the window, soft on my feet so as not to wake the other delinquents. The moon was so bright that I do believe I squinted up my eyes. I have never seen it like that since.

I could see the rink, and I could see the shadows moving on it. The monks were playing a little midnight shinny. It quickened my heart. I threw on some clothes and flew outside.

There were five of them. I watched from a distance at first. I couldn't understand what sort of game they were playing. The action would move erratically within the circle, and sometimes the five would split so that three men would rush two, or four would rush one, and then sometimes the five of them would move in cahoots, the idea seeming to be to achieve a certain prettiness of passing. Then a man would break from the pack, and another man would chase him around the circle, and as quick as that happened they'd rejoin the three in the centre. There were no goal nets on the ice. Just five men, a puck, and a lot of moonlight. They played in silence. I moved closer.

Simon the Ugly was the easiest to pick out, because he was the biggest. He was dancing, jumping into the air, and sometimes I could see his monstrous frame silhouetted against the trout-silver moon. Theodore the Slender cut a shadow so fine that it was hard to pick out, but I could tell him from the quick, precise movements of his twiggy arms as he took a shot. And Andrew the Fireplug, it was he who was likeliest to make a break for the boards, to drift like gun smoke around them. I watched him scoot off with the puck, and then I watched a man slip up easily behind Andrew and relieve him of the rubber. That was Isaiah the Blind. I could scarcely credit it. Playing goaler is one thing – I mean, at least Isaiah was standing still between the pipes, and you could always convince yourself that he was simply the luckiest son of a bee ever – but here he was skating around like a madman, stealing pucks, passing and receiving, and the moonlight was sitting on his dead eyes like it does on the still surface of a lake…

I have never in my life seen such a good goaler as Brother Isaiah, and I have seen everyone from the Chicoutimi Cucumber to that tall slender fellow who looked like a schoolteacher and played so well for the Montreal Canadiens. Yet I am convinced to this day that Brother Isaiah was blind as a bat, though he denied it. Isaiah might occasionally admit to being "a tad shortsighted," but you'd have to catch him walking into a brick wall. The other monks couldn't get a shot by him. Isaiah would just reach out and grab them in his glove (and gloves back then didn't amount to much), or else he'd get the toe on them, or the chest in front of them, or bang them away with his stick. Brother Simon the Ugly tried to jimmy one by him, dancing right up to the goal crease, flipping the puck off his backhand as he made one of his ballerina twirlabouts. Brother Isaiah flicked it away with his wood. Then Andrew the Fireplug comes barrelling along the wing, taking out a couple of bystander brothers just for style, and he unleashes a slapshot even though the damn thing isn't even invented back then! Brother Isaiah the Blind raises his left shoulder maybe a quarter inch and the rubber is dancing harmlessly behind the net.

But there was Brother Theodore the Slender standing in the centre of the huge silver circle, and his eyes were popped open all the way and his mouth had ceased working. In front of him was a puck. Brother Theodore brought his stick back real slow, and then, with a motion that cut the air like a knife, Brother Theodore whacked the rubber…and it didn't even look like he was trying.

Theodore the Slender gave me the gam on shooting, which is this: shooting is more mental than physical. You just practice so much that you can feel the puck, like the blade of your lumber was the palm of your hand, and then you just inner-eye that puck into the back of the net. "See it there first," Brother Theodore was wont to say, "and then put it there." In other words, *wham, bingo*.

"Metaphysical Beaver" by Gustave Morin

AFTERWORD

CANADIAN WRY

BARRY CALLAGHAN

I live in a perplexing country, a country that is a hotbed of rest. I find it hilarious, an exercise in deadpan slapstick at an undertaker's convention.

The first thing is this: Robertson Davies said, "Our condition is stuporous; dully contented and stuporous." Wrong. Absolutely. We Canadians are never who we appear to be. Deception, sometimes self-deception, is our genius. We may appear to be stuporous, we may appear to be boring, but in fact, we're zany and make no sense at all.

I came to understand this several years ago, in the days of Leonid Breshnev, when I was in Leningrad trying to get to know a woman. She was watched by the secret police. I was watched by the secret police. It was grim. It was impossible. So I came home, and at the airport in Toronto, I had an epiphany. There, in front of me, was a Mounted Policeman, all in red and blue and yellow stripes. Like everyone in this world, we have our secret police, but suddenly I thought – what other people would dress up their secret police in scarlet coats, put campfire boy hats on their heads and have them ride around on horses wagging lances at the wind, calling covert action a musical ride? Then I thought, what other country's serious ideologues on the radical left would call themselves the WAFFLE, a word that means a total inability to take a position and hold to it, so that absolutely no one would take them seriously? What other country's serious ideologues on the radical right would form a new group and call it the Canadian Reform Alliance Party – CRAP – meaning pure shit – so that no one could take them seriously? Then I looked at the roots of our history. What other country could dissolve into a duality – French and English – after a nineteen-minute musket skirmish 200 years ago on a ratty field outside Quebec City and make both inept generals who got themselves killed into heroes? Such heroism is a deception. In fact, the whole land as it lies on the map is a deception: huge, bigger than the United States, but almost empty because the mass of the few million folk who live in cities strung like a necklace along the 49th parallel, cling to the border by their fingernails, as if the parallel were a window ledge on America, on the world.

So, that world on the other side of the window likes to think we're boring, likes to think we win more bronze medals than anyone else on the face of the earth. But here's the trick. Here's the laugh. We love people to think we're boring. We've raised being boring to a wacky art form. And why? Because it pays off.

Take our most successful prime minister, William Lyon MacKenzie King, our leader through the Second War. King held power longer than any other Western politician in the past century. How did such a pudgy, mundane-looking little man do it? And he was pudgy and parsonish. And little. The truth is, he did it deliberately. He was shrewd and self-effacing, and he told one of his friends in Cabinet that the secret to holding power was to make every speech as boring as possible because then no one would ever remember what he had said and hold it against him. Almost twenty-two years in power, droning on and on over the airwaves, leading us through the war and the only phrase that stuck to him – a slogan thought up to define a domestic crisis – was "Conscription if necessary but not necessarily conscription." Seemingly balanced, nobody knew what it meant, so our soldiers went off to die. King smiled. Meanwhile, he was crazy as a loon.

He talked about economic policies to his dead mother, consulted his dog on matters of state, sought signs from Franklin Delano Roosevelt in his shaving cream in the morning mirror, and in the evening he did missionary work with local street prostitutes, trying to convert them to Christianity, and then – confronting mortality – he built his own little garden temple to himself from the stone remnants of old bank buildings. He was a choice one, *fol dol di die do,* but not so rare; after all, we're the only people anywhere who ever took the radical right-wing Social Credit economics of the poet Ezra Pound so seriously that we've elected several Social Credit governments – and we knew clearly what we were doing. We called them the Funny Money Party because when they went broke they just cranked up the presses and printed more dollars. When we grew tired of them we elected radical socialists, or rather, faux radicals, because they betrayed socialism by imposing wage controls on the very civil servants and teachers who had elected them.

So there we are, WAFFLING like mad one day, full of CRAP the next, droning on in the middle of the road, telling the world that this is our special gift, a gift for the middle, a gift for compromise, a gift for running while standing still. What can anyone make of our chief droners and men of the middle over the years – moving as we did in Ottawa from a prairie populist prime minister, John Diefenbaker, whose national dream was to "green" the Arctic as the Israelis had greened the desert, to the lisping internationalist, Lester Pearson who – it's true – won the Nobel Peace Prize, but it's a good thing he never had to go to war because on the one day the Red Phone rang in his office, he couldn't find it. He was watching a baseball game and didn't know where the war phone was. He'd hidden it away in a desk drawer. Only to be followed by an expert canoeist, the ascetic and acerbic Pierre Trudeau who, after dating Barbra Streisand and Margot Kidder, took a flower child in tow to the marriage chamber. All seemed to be bliss, there seemed to be a fine monkish air of decorum in Bytown, until his wife showed up bra-less for supper with Fidel Castro, her nipples bare through a sheer blouse, and then she took to dancing at Studio 54 in New York and hung out for a weekend in a Toronto hotel with all the Rolling Stones. To inflict even more pain on the proud Trudeau, we tossed him out of office, making a man called Joe Who our prime minister – a man who'd never in his life had another job – but then, cruel as we are, we let him keep the job for only nine months. Then we put Trudeau back in office. Before he quit, Trudeau the disciplined intellectual, the man of exquisite taste and manners, had actually given the Western part of the nation the finger, had told French taxi strikers to eat shit, and had told parliamentary back benchers that they were "nobodies" and one of them to fuck off ("fuddle duddle"), yet when he died, the people went into a paroxysm of praise and lament, even in Quebec (where else but in Canada could you have a Revolution that was Quiet? Where else but in Canada would a federal government support a *séparatiste* party – the Bloc – whose only policy is to destroy federalism? Where else but in Canada would the leader of such a *séparatiste* party be treated as if he were a Right

Honourable member in good standing and not Benedict Arnold?)

As for Quebec as a whole...well, not even the French from France understand the Québécois, so scrupulously determined to preserve their *pure laine* culture – especially the pure woolliness of it all. They have enacted laws to guard their language, so that inspectors with measuring sticks go from store to store to make sure that the lettering on signs in French is larger than the lettering in English on English signs by at least a centimetre, and when the oh-so-secular Québécois cry *vierge, hostie, ciboire, tabernacle,* they seem to be chanting tidbits from the old catechism. In fact, they are cursing along the lines, in English, of *bugger off, suck this, my sweet ass.* The scatological is hidden inside the sacramental.

Who knows this? Do they want anyone to know? Not necessarily; who else in the world can walk up to you and, as far as he's concerned, call you a suckhole to your face and smile as you cross yourself, believing you have just been blessed? Clever, we're clever as we cling to the ledge of the world, muttering that we have no identity, that we have no history. Again, so that no one will blame us, or hold us to account for anything, we never tell the Americans that they have tried to invade us twice – and tried through their whiskey merchants and cowboys to steal our West. But we gunned down their booze merchants and defeated their federal armies. We chased those armies back across the border – and the second time (during the war of 1812) we marched south and burned their capital city. To make things look good, like nothing had happened, Washington painted their charred government house white – and we have refused to rub it in – or give ourselves a belligerent history – by telling them that we're responsible for the White House.

Our determination to show a flat billboard face to the world marks our musical culture, too. None but a Canadian rock band – the greatest of all – would have called themselves – with simple, splendid, self-deprecating arrogance – The Band. Not surprisingly, the second greatest, as true Canadians, called themselves The Guess Who. No one but a Canadian would have carried on like Glenn Gould – the silver bullet among interpreters of Bach and Beethoven, a musician who was a great natural showman – seated on a dilapidated chair as if it were the edge of the abyss, wrapped in his scarf as he played with mittens on his hands. He was the toast of the concert halls, but what did he do? Dismissed it all as vaudeville, dismissed public performance as if it were as irrelevant as the appendix, and refused to ever play in public again, a recluse tinkling to no one but machines in closed recording studios, a true Canadian, a powerful presence, a studied absence.

So, what's the advantage of all this dodging, all this disdain for the glitter, let alone the glitz, of stardom? Well, we have – for all our need for law and order (and we have cities like Calgary in which brawling and free-booting businessmen will not cross against a red traffic light even in the emptiness of 3 o'clock in the morning) – a remarkable freedom.

In the United States, upright citizens suffer through a House Un-American Activities Committee because they not only know who they're supposed to be – good homogenized patriotic, hand-over-the-heart Americans – but they insist on it. Such a committee in Canada would be laughable. If anyone ever suggested a Senate Un-Canadian Activities Committee, the nation would fall on its face laughing. We still refuse to agree on what the words to our national anthem are. We don't know who we are and we don't want to. That way

we don't have to be anybody's anything. It is a terrific freedom. People can curse us for being wrong, or vulgar, or stupid
– but not un-Canadian. In fact, since we don't have to be anybody's anything, we can pretend to be everybody else, and if
we make a mistake, *they* take the blame.

Our largest corporations got very rich during the Viet
Nam War, several got rich in South Africa (do those Canadians who supported sanctions against South Africa and the
Afrikaners know that the architetcs of apartheid took as their
model for control and oppression our brutal system of "homeland" reserves, do they know that many Afrikaner intellectu-
als believe that the only people in the world that they share a
vision of righteous isolation with are the Québécois? Does
anyone among us ask why that might be so?). Know it or not,
many of our corporations are still getting profoundly rich in
South and Central America, but when is the last time you
saw or heard of an anti-Canadian demonstration in the
streets of Santiago? We're so clean we squeak, the sound the
sullen mouse makes beside the lumbering elephant. Haw!
The Americans are our whipping boys, we blame them for
our economic failures and cultural woes – while, if they
think about us at all, it's to assure us that we are lucky to be
out mingling among them.

And actually, we are: not so much lucky, but among them.
We're insidious infiltrators inside their system. Do you know –
do they know – that nearly 40 percent of their major television
reporters around the world and commentators at home are
Canadian? It's true. Every night we tell millions of Americans
how to see the world, how to see their wars and their movie
stars and heroes and bums, their dreams achieved and broken.
And if Americans ever laugh at their own insanity, Canadians
control the scripts. On the loneliest night of the American

week, the television program *Saturday Night Live* is a joke conceived of and produced by Canadians. Think of the Canadian
comics – Jim Carrey, John Candy, Dan Akroyd, the SCTV
McKenzie brothers, Mike Myers, Martin Short, Tommy
Chong, Samantha Bee and the Atomic Fireballs…the list goes
on and on, Canadian laughter at American expense. As for
expensive performers, think of the singer Céline Dion – who
speaks French, who sings in English, who has become the
Queen of Las Vegas with the Cirque du Soleil, the most imag-
inative circus in the history of the world, as her Court – and
who knows or cares that she's Canadian, let alone Québécois?
To the world, she's a nobody from nowhere except that she's a
star, a celebrity, and if celebrity is now the opium of the people, then she – the perfect Canadian – is a citizen of the world.

As such, this archetypal Canadian – no matter how public – is invisible – he is that no one who is everyone from
nowhere, a man like Rich Little…the most skilled show-biz
impersonator in American history. Having no voice of his own,
he has had everyone else's – male or female – and he "did"
everyone else, as they say, perfectly. Patrons in Las Vegas and
the power folk in the White House preferred him to the real
thing. In half an hour, when he performed in the intimacy of
the White House, they got John Wayne talking to Richard
Nixon, Sylvester Stallone talking to Ronnie Reagan, Bill
Clinton talking to the Pope.

"Boffo," as they say in *Variety*, the American showbiz bible,
because you see you pick up a few tricks while clinging to the
ledge of the world. You learn how to amiably draw no public
attention to yourself while secretly having your own way.
Canadians (those Mounties, never forget those Mounties)
could be the world's greatest secret agents. Who knows? A
secret agent is secret. But remember our man in Iran dur-

ing the Carter years, during the Iran hostage crisis, the biggest story in the world – and our ambassador, Ken Taylor, actually freed American hostages and got them out of the country. He explained to a flabbergasted and thankful America – when asked – that to get the Americans out of Iran he had only to "disguise them as Canadians."

Sound and fury behind a bland face.

We take pride in our Blue Beret peace keepers (how bland in the theatre of war can peacekeeping be?). But that role is actually long gone, ever since the Serbian-Croatian War, gone since the battle of the Medak Pocket (1993) in which our boys, after days of ferocious fire-fighting, drove the Croat troops back into their own territory. Fierce. Many Blue Berets came home emotional wrecks. Who knows? Who has heard of the Medak Pocket, a battle that changed entirely our fighting sense of ourselves in this global village we call our peace keeping home.

It was that global villager, Marshall McLuhan (what a perfect Canadian - the secret conservative adored by a New York advertising world that he abhorred), who came closest to the point about our nationally (psychically) divided selves when he said that English Canada leapt directly from the eighteenth century into the twentieth century, skipping the romantic assertion of self so central to the nineteenth century, while Quebec – as counter culture to the nation – lives in the self-aggrandizing nineteenth century as if that century were an *arrondissement,* dreaming of an independent national orbit, knowing such a state can never be. It's hilarious in its contradiction. Deadpan. Slapstick. We stand astride life as if it were a seesaw, balancing, waiting.

The prime minister, Wilfrid Laurier, who forecast that "The twentieth century shall be the century of Canada", was wonderfully Canadian in that he was right when he was wrong – and absolutely so. That is, he was right if Samuel Beckett touched any chord in the contemporary heart, and we know that he did. Being two cultures in one country, both waiting for the century to be ours, we are like Beckett's two tramps by the side of the road, watching in amazement as the Pozzos and Luckys of this world pass through our lives, and we wait. Bland-faced, we wait, and wait, and shrug and make self-deprecating jokes and sly probes – as McLuhan would have it. The probative Trudeau's most characteristic gesture, after completing a comic pirouette behind an august person like the Queen, was a shrug. You can't get any more contemporary – any more tragically comic – than that shrug, a shrug we take to the grave.

The defining saint in our history is the Jesuit, Jean de Brébeuf – who shrugged as he was tortured and burned to a crisp at the stake. His skull, saved from the ashes, is now an object of worship – but worshipped in a way that accommodates our divided, duplicitous Canadian mind. There are two Brébeuf skulls on display – one Brébeuf skull (right half *bone*, left half *wax*) in Quebec, and another Brébeuf skull (left half *bone*, right half *wax*) in Ontario. Who's to know?

As for secret laughter, one of the Anglo-Saxon world's favourite humorists is our Stephen Leacock, master of the comic light touch, with a tinge of blackness around the edges, a little like a requiem mass card. Our own secret agent of small-town laughter. But almost no one in Canada – or anywhere else – knows how he went to his grave. It was, you see, the tradition in his family to be buried in a plain, good old Canadian pine box, but he'd bought a huge oak and brass-handled job. Heavy, heavy, heavy, and burly men carried it to the hole not knowing – no one knew – that he'd had himself cremated. They sweated and heaved under the weight but inside, having the last laugh, Leacock was only ashes in a little glass bottle cradled on a satin puff. It is the final comfort we crave, ashes on a satin puff, watched over by a scarlet man, waiting, who may be the police.

THE CONTRIBUTORS

"Aislin," Mosher, Terry of Montreal has used the pen-name AISLIN for the past fifty years working as a cartoonist mainly for the *Montreal Gazette*. He has also freelanced for many other publications including *Maclean's*, the *Toronto Star*, *Time Magazine* and the *New York Times*. Mosher's latest collection, *From Trudeau to Trudeau: Fifty Years of Aislin Cartooning*, is his forty-ninth book. In 2012, Aislin was inducted into the Canadian Cartoonists' Hall of Fame as part of the eighth Annual Doug Wright Awards for Canadian Cartooning. Along with fellow cartoonist Serge Chapleau of *La Presse*, Aislin received the Hyman Solomon Award for excellence in public policy journalism in 2015.

Amprimoz, Alexandre was born in Rome, brought up in Gabon, and settled in Canada. He was a noted philologist, poet, critic, translator, writer and programmer, who also taught a course on Modern Languages, Literatures and Cultures at Brock University in Ontario until his death in 2012. His books include *A Season for Birds: Selected Poems by Pierre Morency* (as translator), *Venice at Her Mirror: Essays by Robert Marteau* (as translator), and the books *Nostalgies de l'ange* and *Too Many Popes*. He was awarded the Palmes Académiques, and was nominated several times for the Pushcart Prize.

Armstrong, Bob of Winnipeg is a speechwriter and humorist. He is the author of a comic novel about stay-at-home fathers, *Dadolescence*, a comedy, *Noble Savage, Savage Noble*, about Voltaire and Rousseau, some 1,700 speeches for Manitoba's last four Lieutenant Governors, and 280,000 words of environmental impact reports. He sometimes posts stuff at bobarmstrong.ca.

Atwood, Margaret of Toronto is a poet, essayist, novelist, inventor, environmental activist. She has won the Booker Prize, the Governor General's Award twice, and has received many other awards and honorary degrees from around the world. Her books of poetry include *The Journals of Susannah Moodie, Procedures for Underground, True Stories, Morning in the Burned House,* and her two-volume *Selected Poems.* Her novels include *The Handmaid's Tale* – the source for the U.S. television series by the same name – *Alias Grace, Surfacing, The Edible Woman, Oryx and Crake, MaddAddam, Life Before Man, The Robber Bride,* and *Blind Assassin.* Her short story collections include *Bluebeard's Egg, Good Bones, Moral Disorder* and *The Stone Mattress.*

Borkowski, Andrew of Toronto is a writer whose short story collection *Copernicus Avenue,* set in Toronto's post-war Polish community, won the 2012 Toronto Book Award. It was also a finalist for the Danuta Gleed Literary Award for short fiction. His journalism has appeared in the *Globe and Mail, Quill & Quire, TV Guide,* and the *Los Angeles Times.*

Boulton, Marsha of Harriston, Ontario, is the fifth woman and the first shepherd to receive the Stephen Leacock Medal for Humour. She began telling stories about her transition from city girl to farmer on CBC Radio's *Fresh Air.* Those stories formed the backbone of the award-winning, four-book *Letters from the Country* series. A former *Maclean's* magazine editor, her journalism has appeared in her journalism has appeared in *Toronto Life, Chatelaine, Canadian Business* and the *Wool-growers' Cooperative Magazine*. Three anecdotal Canadian history books, headlined *Just a Minute*, evolved from her work on the televised *Heritage Minutes*. A memoir, *Wally's World, Life with Wally the Wonder Dog*, has been published internationally in many languages.

Bramer, Shannon of Toronto is a poet and playwright. *Precious Energy*, published this year, is her fourth collection of poetry. Her plays, *Monarita, The Collectors* and *The Hungriest Woman in the World*, have appeared in juried festivals across the country. Bramer regularly conducts poetry workshops in schools and is the editor of *Think City: The Poems of Gracefield Public School*. *Climbing Shadows* is her illustrated collection of poetry for young children.

Callaghan, Barry of Toronto was born in that city where, in 1972, he founded the landmark literary journal, *Exile, A Literary Quarterly* (now *ELQ* magazine), and in 1975 the publishing house Exile Editions. The Afterword to this volume, "Canadian Wry," was originally commissioned by *Punch*, London, in 1985 (updated for this collection). He received the inaugural W.O. Mitchell Award for "mentoring young writers and a body of work of his own." Callaghan's works include *The Black Queen Stories, A Kiss Is Still a Kiss, Between Trains, The Hogg Poems, Hogg: The Seven Last Words, Barrelhouse Kings: A Memoir,* and three volumes of his collected journalism and articles, *Raise You Five, Raise You Ten* and *Raise You Twenty* – the latter will be re-issued in 2018 as a revised edition. *All the Lonely People: Collected Stories* (autumn 2018) gathers the majority of his short fiction. Also in 2018 is his edited volume, *What the Hand Sees*, a comprehensive perspective on the life and works of internationally exhibited Canadian artist Claire Wilks.

Morley Callaghan was born in Toronto. His earliest short stories appeared in Paris where he was an important part of the literary milieu of 1929 – the great gathering of writers in Montparnasse that included Ernest Hemingway, Ezra Pound, Gertrude Stein, F. Scott Fitzgerald, and James Joyce. His short stories stand as classics of the form. His novels include *Strange Fugitive, Such Is My Beloved, It's Never Over, The Many Coloured Coat, More Joy in Heaven, The Loved and the Lost, A Time for Judas, Our Lady of the Snows,* and the four-volume *Collected Short Stories of Morley Callaghan*. Father of poet, novelist, and publisher, Barry Callaghan, he died in 1990.

Clarke, Austin is Barbadoes-born and was a long-time Toronto resident (1959 until he died in 2016). He was a novelist, poet, short story writer, essayist, social activist and diplomat who won the Giller Prize for his novel, *The Polished Hoe,* in 2002. Among his many works are *The Survivors of the Crossing, The Meeting Point, The Origin of Waves, Choosing His Coffin, Love and Sweet Food* (which won the James Beard Award for Food Writing), *There Are No Elders, The Prime Minister, Growing Up Stupid Under the Union Jack, Pig Tail'n Breadfruit, More* (which won the City of Toronto Book Award), and *They Never Told Me.* He also received the Order of Canada, the Governor General's Award for Fiction, the Commonwealth Writers' Prize, and the W.O. Mitchell Award.

Dandurand, Anne of Montreal says she was born in good company, with her twin sister Claire Dé. Having worked as an actress, journalist, union activist and screenwriter, she is also the author of eight books of short stories and novels, some translated. For past twenty years she has also been a sculptor.

Dé, Claire of Montreal was born in the good company of her twin sister, Anne Dandurand. She has been a stage set and costume designer, playwright, short story writer of the collection *Desire as Natural Disaster*, literary translator, freelance magazine writer, and an author for many other sources of pay-for-hire writings. Being at a loss for numbers and business, she has managed to stay poor all the while, but had fun all the way.

Dewar, James of Port Perry, Ontario, writes short fiction and poetry and has been published in several anthologies and literary journals. He is author of *The Garden in the Machine*. He teaches fiction and poetry workshops throughout the Metropolitan Toronto area and internationally via www.inkslingers.ca, and is host of the reading series, Hot-Sauced Words.

Feldman, Jamie of Alberta Bridge, Nova Scotia, received her M.Phil in Creative Writing from Trinity College, Dublin. Her fiction has appeared in *Canadian Stories, The Big Jewel, Every Day Fiction*, and Silver Birch Press' *Alice in Wonderland Anthology*, among others. Her plays have been performed internationally at the Atlantic Fringe, King's Theatre Annapolis Royal, and Short+Sweet: Sydney/AU Festival. She is a past writer in residence in Flojtstunga, Iceland.

Ferron, Jacques, after a brief spell as a young man in the Canadian Army, practiced as a country physician in the

Gaspé, Quebec. In 1948, he settled in Montreal, establishing a medical consulting office on the city's South Shore. Ferron, from this base, led a very public life, contributing to medical and literary journals while taking an active part in politics. In 1963 he founded his own party, the Rhinoceros Party, designed for the purpose of satirizing the federal political system (some time or other in the '70s, he appointed Barry Callaghan as the English leader for a term of one year – "a position in which he would have nothing to do and no one to speak to"). As a playwright and essayist, novelist and short story writer, Ferron took on in his fiction the multifaceted aspects of his cultural heritage. His first collection, *Contes du pays incertain*, won the Governor General's Award for Fiction in 1962. In 1977, the Quebec government awarded him the Prix Athanase-David, and he was named an honorary member of the Union des écrivains québécois in 1981. The best of his short fiction is available in *Tales from an Uncertain Country and Other Stories*, translated by Betty Bednarski, herself a prize-winning translator. Ferron died in 1985.

Gervais, Marty of Windsor, Ontario, is author of numerous books of poetry and history. At the time of publication, he is the Poet Laureate of the City of Windsor, Ontario. He has been awarded the Queen's Silver Jubilee Medal for contributions to the community, is a professor of publishing at the University of Windsor, and is the publisher of Black Moss Press. His works include, *A Show of Hands; Boxing on the Border, From America Sent: Letters to Henry Miller, To Be Now: Selected Poems, Afternoon with the Devil: Growing Up Catholic in a Border Town,* and *The Rum-Runners.*

Gluckman, Darren of Toronto placed third in the *Toronto Star*'s 1996 short story contest and in 1999 published a collection of stories, *The Weight of the World*, which was shortlisted for the Upper Canada Brewing Company Writer's Craft Award. He has written a screenplay, numerous magazine profiles, while also reviewing scripts for the CBC's *movies&miniseries* department. Latterly, he has worked as a city prosecutor, employment lawyer, and as a policy advisor for the provincial government.

Goldstein, Jonathan was the host and creator of *Wiretap* which ran on the CBC for eleven years. His new podcast, *Heavyweight*, has been listed as one of the best of 2016 by Itunes, *The Atlantic Monthly*, *The Guardian* and other publications. He's the author of several books, including a novel, memoir and collection of short stories.

Hayward, Steven of Colorado Springs, Colorado was born in Toronto and is the author of two novels, *The Secret Mitzvah of Lucio Burke* (which won the Grinzane Cavour Prize in Italy, 2006), *Don't Be Afraid*, the short story collection *Buddah Stevens and other stories* – which won the Upper Canada Writers' Craft Award in 2001 – and most recently, *To Dance to the Beginning of the World: Stories*. He holds a doctorate from York University in Shakespeare and Literary Theory, and currently teaches creative writing at Colorado College in the United States.

Maheux-Forcher, Louise was born in Montreal in 1929. Maheux-Forcier studied music in Quebec and Paris before attending the University of Montreal. In 1959, she turned from a career in music to writing, and produced five novels:

Amadou, L'Etejoyeuse, Une forget pour Zoe, Paroles et music, and *Appasionata.* "The Carnation" is taken from a story collection, *En routes lettres.*

Marshall, Helen of Cambridge, England, is a lecturer in Creative Writing and Publishing at Anglia Ruskin University in Cambridge, England. Her first collection of fiction, *Hair Side, Flesh Side* won the Sydney J. Bounds Award in 2013, and *Gifts for the One Who Comes After,* her second collection, won the World Fantasy Award and the Shirley Jackson Award in 2015. In 2016, she won the $5,000 Carter V. Cooper Award for Best Short Story by a writer at any career point (that story, plus a previous shortlisted story while an emerging writer, appeared in Exile Editions' annual *CVC anthology Series*).

McFadden, David of Toronto was born in Hamilton, Ontario and is a poet, fiction writer, and travel writer. He has served as an editor with Coach House Press. His numerous books include *What's the Score?* – which won the Griffin Poetry Prize in 2013 – *A Knight in Dried Plums, On the Road Again, The Art of Darkness, Why Are You Sad? Intense Pleasure, A New Romance,* and *The Poet's Progress.*

Miscione, Christine of Hamilton, Ontario, is a fiction writer, with an MA in English Literature from Queen's University. Her work has appeared in numerous literary journals. In 2012, her short story "Skin, Just" won the $10,000 Carter V. Cooper Award for Best Short Story by an emerging writer. Her first collection of short stories, *Auxilliary Skins,* appeared in 2013, and went on to win the ReLit Award. She followed that with a novel, *Carafola.*

Morin, Gustave says he is a werewolf and a ferris wheel, the demon-barber of concrete in Canada, the maker of a "few poetry," and the author of a number of books in and out of print, including *The Etcetera Barbecue* and *A Penny Dreadful*.

Paterson, Mark of Lorraine, Quebec, is the author of the short story collections, *A Finely Tuned Apathy Machine* and *Other People's Showers*. He is a past winner of *Geist* magazine's Literal Literary Postcard Story Contest and the *3Macs carte blanche* Prize.

Prussky, Gail of Mono Mills, Ontario, says that after leading an "average" unassuming life for some years topped off by a decade as a Toronto hard-drug addiction therapist, she moved from the city to retire in the country where she suddenly began to draw, paint and write. She has exhibited at several galleries in recent years. Her first book of drawings, poems and stories, *Broken Balloons*, with an introduction by David Cronenberg, was published in 2016.

Quarrington, Paul, born and raised in Toronto, was a novelist, playwright, screenwriter, filmmaker, musician and educator best known for his novels *King Leary*, *Whale Music*, *Galveston,* and *The Ravine*. He won the Stephen Leacock Award in 1988 and the Governor General's Award in 1989. He died in 2011.

Rogers, Linda of Victoria, B.C. is a broadcaster, teacher, journalist, poet, novelist and songwriter. She has received the Stephen Leaock Poetry Prize, the Reuben Roise Poetry Prize (Israel), the Dorothy Livesay Award for Poetry, the Hawthorne Prize, the Saltwater Festival Prize, the People's Poetry Prize, and most recently was co-winner of the Gwendolyn MacEwen Poetry Prize. Her works include *Queens of the Next Hot Star, Singing Rib, Woman at Mile Zero, Letters from the Doll Hospital, The Empress Letters, Muscle Memory* and *Homing: New and Selected Poems,* and most recently, the novel, *Bozuk.*

Rooke, Leon of Toronto, was born and raised in Roanoake Rapids, Virginia and after a time as a Freedom Rider and a stint in the US military he came to Canada where he has distinguished himself as a prolific author. His numerous novels and short story collections include *Fat Woman,* which was nominated for the Governor General's Award for Fiction, *The Birth Control King of Upper Volta, Shakespeare's Dog,* which won the Governor General's Award for Fiction, *A Bolt of White Cloth, Sing Me No Love Songs I Say You No Prayers, Oh! Twenty-Seven Stories, Hitting the Charts: Selected Stories, Fabulous Fictions & Peculiar Practices* and *Wide World in Celebration and Sorrow.* His other awards include the Canada-Australia prize, the W.O. Mitchell Award, the CBC Fiction Award, and two ReLit Awards.

Roorda, Julie of Toronto is the author of the novel *A Thousand Consolations,* as well as *Courage Underground, The Eleventh Toe, Floating Bodies, Naked in the Sanctuary,* and *Wings of a Bee.* Her story, "How to Tell If Your Frog Is Dead," was included in the 2014 Journey Prize Anthology.

Rosenblatt, Joe was born in Toronto, but has lived in Qualicum Beach, British Columbia, for decades. He has written more than twenty books of poetry, several autobiographical works, and a novel. His *Topsoil* won the Governor

General's Award for Poetry. He is also a gallery-exhibited artist – many of his works are in permanent collections in public galleries and academic institutions in Canada. His books include *Bumblebee Dithyramb*, *The Sleeping Lady (Sonnets)*, *Poetry Hotel: Selected*, *The Voluptuous Gardener*, *Parrot Fever*, *The Lunatic Muse*, *Escape from the Glue Factory*, *The Joe Rosenblatt Reader*, *Snake City*, and *Hoggwash: The Callaghan and Rosenblatt Epistolary Convergence*.

Sawai, Gloria was born in Minnesota, grew up in Canada, and was educated in Alberta and Minnesota before settling in Canada where she taught at Grant MacEwen College in Edmonton. Her play for young people, *Neighbour*, was published in 1981. She won the Governor General's Award for Fiction for *A Song of Nettie Johnson* (2000). She died in 2011.

Shaw, Matt of Toronto was raised in southwestern Ontario and lives in Toronto. He received the Journey Prize for short fiction in 2005, and is the author of a collection of short stories, *The Obvious Child*. With Barry Callaghan, he edited and introduced an anthology of Toronto tales, *The Stories That Are Great Within Us*.

Uppal, Priscila of Toronto is a poet, fiction writer, memoirist, essayist, playwright, and Professor of English at York University. Among her publications: poetry, *Sabotage*, *Traumatology*, and *Ontological Necessities* (Griffin Poetry Prize finalist); the novels *The Divine Economy of Salvation* and *To Whom It May Concern*; the memoir *Projection: Encounters with My Runaway Mother* (Writers' Trust Hilary Weston Prize and Governor General's Award finalist); the collection of short stories *Cover Before Striking* and the play *6 Essential*

Questions. She was the first poet-in-residence for Canadian Athletes Now during the 2010 Vancouver and 2012 London Olympic and Paralympic games. Her second play, *What Linda Said,* recently had its World Premiere at SummerWorks. For more information visit *priscilauppal.ca*

Wallin, Myna of Toronto has two published books: a collection of poetry, *A Thousand Profane Pieces,* and the novel *Confessions of a Reluctant Cougar* – longlisted for the ReLit Award in 2010. Her poetry has won Honourable Mentions in both the CV2 2-Day Best Poem Prize 2009, and in the Winston Collins/Descant Prize for Best Canadian Poem 2010. A poem of hers hung at the AGO in a 2014 exhibit entitled, "Why (Not) Paintings of Poets?"

White, Karen Lee of Victoria, is an Indigenous writer and playwright living on "the rock'" (Vancouver Island), British Columbia. In 2017, she was awarded a Hnatyshyn Foundation REVEAL Indigenous Arts Award. Her short stories and poetry have been published in a Manitoba textbook, ezines, magazines and literary journals, and a body of work includes the cd of her music, *Dance Away.*

Wood, Heather J. of Toronto is the author of the novels *Fortune Cookie* and *Roll With it,* and is the World Fantasy Award nominated editor of the *Gods, Memes and Monsters* anthology.

Zolf, Larry, was born in Winnipeg and settled in Toronto. He was, for all of his adult life, a national presence: as a reporter, television personality, raconteur, gadfly, pundit among the punditti, stand-up comedian, friend and pal to several prime ministers and as many low-lifes. He was by his own declaration *The Schnozz, the Prince of the Proboscis.* In other words, he lived and died by his nose for a good story, whether it was fact or fiction, anecdote or leak for attribution. His last book, published just before he died, was a memoir, *The Dialectical Dancer*, with an introduction by Peter C. Newman. He died in 2010.

The Editor

Meyer, Bruce of Barrie, Ontario, is the author and co-author, or editor of more than sixty books of poetry, short fiction, non-fiction, literary journalism, and portrait photography. His broadcasts on *The Great Books* were heard nationally on the CBC and were followed by *The Golden Thread: A Reader's Journey Through the Great Books.* He was the inaugural Poet Laureate of the City of Barrie where he teaches at Georgian College, and at Victoria College in the University of Toronto.

PERMISSIONS

Aislin (Terry Mosher)
The cover illustration, and the two illustrations that accompany the Preface and the story "Queen Elizabeth Visits the Elks Hall" are copyright and reprinted by permission of Aislin. All rights reserved.

Alexandre Amprimoz
"Saint Augustine" is from *Too Many Popes*, Exile Editions, 1990. Copyright the Estate of Alexamdre Amprimoz. Reprinted by permission of Exile Editions. All rights reserved.

Bob Armstrong
"Undelivered Letters Home" is copyright Bob Armstrong, 2017. First time published by permission of Bob Armstrong.

Margaret Atwood
"Salome Was a Dancer" (with accompanying drawing by Margaret Atwood), "King Log in Exile" and "It's Not Easy Being Half-Divine" are from the collection *The Tent*, by Margaret Atwood – copyright 2006, O.W. Toad Ltd. Reprinted by permission of the author and McClelland & Stewart, a division of Penguin Random House Canada Limited. All rights reserved.

Andrew Borkowski
"The Lesson" is from the collection *Copernicus Avenue*, by Andrew J. Borkowski, published by Cormorant Books, Toronto, copyright 2011, Andrew J. Borkowski. Reprinted with the permission of the publisher. All rights reserved.

David McFadden

"The Cow that Swam Lake Ontario" is excerpted from *The Art of Darkness* by David McFadden, copyright 1984 by David McFadden. Reprinted by permission of McClelland & Stewart, a division of Penguin Random House Canada Limited. All rights reserved.

Bruce Meyer

"Preface: Behind Those Beaver Teeth" is copyright Bruce Meyer, 2017. First time published by permission of Bruce Meyer. All rights reserved.

Christine Miscione

"Timourous in Love" is excerpted from *Auxiliary Skins*, Exile Editions, 2013. Copyright Christine Miscione. Reprinted by permission of Exile Editions. All rights reserved.

Gustave Morin

The collage "Metaphysical Beaver" that accompanies the Afterword "Canadian Wry" is copyright and reprinted by permission of Gustave Morin. All rights reserved.

Mark Paterson

"The Canadian Accent" is copyright Mark Paterson, 2017. First time published by permission of Mark Paterson. All rights reserved.

Gail Prussky

"The Story of Weasel Tossing, Drawings" is excerpted from *Broken Balloons,* Exile Editions, 2016. Copyright Gail Prussky. Reprinted by permission of Exile Editions. All rights reserved.

Paul Quarrington
"King Leary" is excerpted from *King Leary*, Doubleday Canada Limited, 1987. Copyright and reprinted by permission of the Estate of Paul Quarrington. All rights reserved.

Linda Rogers
"Three Strikes and You're Out" is excerpted from *The Carter V. Cooper Short Fiction Anthology Series: Book Four*, Exile Editions, 2014. Copyright Linda Rogers. Reprinted by permission of Exile Editions. All rights reserved.

Leon Rooke
"Critics' Take on the Premier Showing of Tank's Documentary of the Closing Eye," "Narcissistic Eb and Lucky Flo," "Peculiar Practices in Alberta (Possibly Related to the Oil Boom)" are from *Fabulous Fictions & Peculiar Practices*, The Porcupine's Quill, 2016. Copyright Leon Rooke. Reprinted by permission of The Porcupine's Quill. All rights reserved.

Julie Roorda
"'Til Death" is copyright Julie Roorda, 2017. First time published by permission of Julie Roorda. All rights reserved.

Joe Rosenblatt
"When Monsters Smoked" is excerpted from *Escape from the Glue Factory*, Exile Editions, 1985, 1987. Copyright Joe Rosenblatt. Reprinted by permission of Exile Editions. All rights reserved.

Gloria Sawai
"That Day I Sat Down with Jesus on the Sun Deck and a Wind Came Up and Blew My Kimono Open and He Saw My

Breasts" is excerpted from *A Song for Nettie Johnson,* Coteau Books, 2001. Copyright and reprinted by permission of the Estate of Gloria Sawai. All rights reserved.

Matt Shaw
"Talmud" is excerpted from *The Obvious Child,* Exile Editions, 2007. Copyright Matt Shaw. Reprinted by permission of Exile Editions. All rights reserved.

Priscila Uppal
"Conspiracy" is copyright Priscila Uppal, 2017. First time published by permission of Priscila Uppal. All rights reserved.

Myna Wallin
"Canadoll" is copyright Myna Wallin, 2017. First time published by permission of Myna Wallin. All rights reserved.

Karen Lee White
"Queen Elizabeth Visits the Elks Hall" is copyright Karen Lee White, 2017. First time published by permission of Karen Lee White. All rights reserved.

Heather J. Wood
"Revulsion" is copyright Heather J. Wood, 2017. First time published by permission of Heather J. Wood. All rights reserved.

Larry Zolf
"The Ping-Pong Affair" is excerpted from *The Dialectical Dancer,* Exile Editions, 2010. Copyright Barbara Diakopolou: the Estate of Larry Zolf. Reprinted by permission of Exile Editions. All rights reserved.

ACKNOWLEDGEMENTS

The editor and the publisher thank the following individuals for their time and efforts in bringing this anthology to fruition: Betty Bednarski, Patrick Crean, Darcy Ballantyne, Marsha Boulton, Betty Clarke, Darlene Madott, Marc Côté, Alice Major, Karen Wetmore, Marilyn DiFlorio, Nina Callaghan, Peter Budd, Dana Francoeur, Lawrence Wong, Alicia Dercole, Kerry Johnston, and Katie Meyer – and to Corey Redekop who initiated the process. A special thank you to all who demonstrated the grace that is the hallmark of good humour that made this book possible.

BM

THE EXILE BOOK OF ANTHOLOGY SERIES

ONE TO FOURTEEN

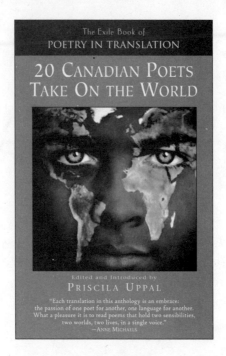

The Exile Book of
POETRY IN TRANSLATION

20 CANADIAN POETS
TAKE ON THE WORLD

Edited and Introduced by
PRISCILA UPPAL

"Each translation in this anthology is an embrace:
the passion of one poet for another, one language for another.
What a pleasure it is to read poems that hold two sensibilities,
two worlds, two lives, in a single voice."
—ANNE MICHAELS

20 CANADIAN POETS TAKE ON THE WORLD

EDITED BY PRISCILA UPPAL

A groundbreaking multilingual collection promoting a global poetic consciousness, thisvolume presents the works of 20 international poets, all in their original languages, alongside English translations by some of Canada's most esteemed poets. Spanning several time periods and more than a dozen nations, this compendium paints a truly unique portrait of cultures, nationalities, and eras."

Canadian poets featured are Oana Avasilichioaei, Ken Babstock, Christian Bök, Dionne Brand, Nicole Brossard, Barry Callaghan, George Elliott Clarke, Geoffrey Cook, Rishma Dunlop, Steven Heighton, Christopher Doda, Andréa Jarmai, Evan Jones, Sonnet L'Abbé, A.F. Moritz, Erín Moure, Goran Simic, Priscila Uppal, Paul Vermeersch, and Darren Wershler, translating the works of Nobel laureates, classic favourites, and more, including Jan-Willem Anker, Her-man de Coninck, María Elena Cruz Varela, Kiki Dimoula, George Faludy, Horace, Juan Ramón Jiménez, Pablo Neruda, Chus Pato, Ezra Pound, Alexander Pushkin, Rainer Maria Rilke, Arthur Rimbaud, Elisa Sampedrín, Leopold Staff, Nichita St˘anescu, Stevan Tonti´c, Ko Un, and Andrei Voznesensky. Each translating poet provides an introduction to their work.

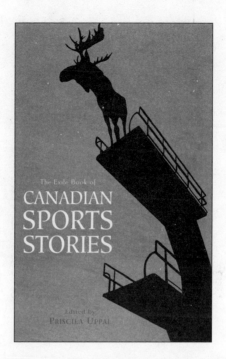

The Exile Book of
CANADIAN
SPORTS
STORIES

Edited by
PRISCILA UPPAL

CANADIAN SPORTS STORIES

EDITED BY PRISCILA UPPAL

"This anthology collects a wide range of Canada's literary imaginations, telling great stories about the wild and fascinating world of sport… Written by both men and women, the generations of insights provided in this collection expose some of the most intimate details of sports and sporting life – the hard-earned victories, and the sometimes inevitable tragedies. You will get to know those who play the game, as well as those who watch it, coach it, write about it, dream about it, live and die by it."

"Most of the stories weren't so much about sports per se than they were a study of personalities and how they react to or deal with extreme situations…all were worth reading"
—4/5 Star Review, goodreads.com

Clarke Blaise, George Bowering, Dionne Brand, Barry Callaghan, Morley Callaghan, Roch Carrier, Matt Cohen, Craig Davidson, Brian Fawcett, Katherine Govier, Steven Heighton, Mark Jarman, W.P. Kinsella, Stephen Leacock, L.M. Montgomery, Susanna Moodie, Margaret Pigeon, Mordecai Richler, Priscila Uppal, Guy Vanderhaeghe, and more.

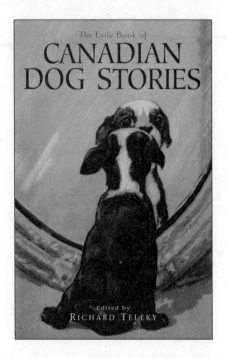

CANADIAN DOG STORIES

EDITED BY RICHARD TELEKY

Spanning from the 1800s to 2005, and featuring exceptional short stories from 28 of Canada's most prominent fiction writers, this unique anthology explores the nature of the human-dog bond through writing from both the nation's earliest storytellerssuch as Ernest Thompson Seton, L. M. Montgomery, and Stephen Leacockand a younger generation that includes Lynn Coady and Matt Shaw. Not simply sentimental tales about noble dogs doing heroic deeds, these stories represent the rich, complex, and mysterious bond between dogs and humans. Adventure and drama, heartfelt encounters and nostalgia, sharp-edged satire, and even fantasy make up the genres in this memorable collection.

"Twenty-eight exceptional dog tales by some of Canada's most notable fiction writers... The stories run the breadth of adventure, drama, satire, and even fantasy, and will appeal to dog lovers on both sides of the [Canada/U.S.] border." —*Modern Dog Magazine*

Marie-Claire Blais, Barry Callaghan, Morley Callaghan, Lynn Coady, Mazo de la Roche, Jacques Ferron, Mavis Gallant, Douglas Glover, Katherine Govier, Kenneth J. Harvey, E. Pauline Johnson, Janice Kulyk Keefer, Alistair Macleod, L.M. Montgomery, P.K. Page, Charles G.D. Roberts, Leon Rooke, Jane Rule, Duncan Campbell Scott, Timothy Taylor, Sheila Watson, Ethel Wilson, and more.

NATIVE CANADIAN FICTION AND DRAMA

EDITED BY DANIEL DAVID MOSES

The work of men and women of many tribal affiliations, this collection is a wide-ranging anthology of contemporary Native Canadian literature. Deep emotions and life-shaking crises converge and display the Aboriginal concerns regarding various topics, including identity, family, community, caste, gender, nature, betrayal, and war. A fascinating compilation of stories and plays, this account fosters cross-cultural understanding and presents the Native Canadian writers reinvention of traditional material and their invention of a modern life that is authentic. It is perfect for courses on short fiction or general symposium teaching material.

Tomson Highway, Lauren B. Davis, Niigonwedom James Sinclair, Joseph Boyden, Joseph A. Dandurand, Alootook Ipellie, Thomas King, Yvette Nolan, Richard Van Camp, Floyd Favel, Robert Arthur Alexie, Daniel David Moses, Katharina Vermette.

"A strong addition to the ever shifting Canadian literary canon, effectively presenting the depth and artistry of the work by Aboriginal writers in Canada today."

—Canadian Journal of Native Studies

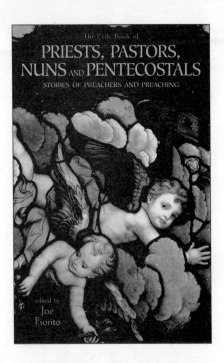

PRIESTS, PASTORS, NUNS AND PENTECOSTALS

EDITED BY JOE FIORITO

A literary approach to the Word of the Lord, this collection of short fiction deals within one way or anotherthe overarching concept of redemption. This anthology demonstrates how God appears again and again in the lives of priest, pastors, nuns, and Pentecostals. However He appears, He appears again and again in the lives of priests, nuns, and Pentecostals in these great stories of a kind never collected before

Mary Frances Coady, Barry Callaghan, Leon Rooke, Roch Carrier, Jacques Ferron, Seán Virgo, Marie-Claire Blais, Hugh Hood, Morley Callaghan, Hugh Garner, Diane Keating, Alexandre Amprimoz, Gloria Sawai, Eric McCormack, Yves Thériault, Margaret Laurence, Alice Munro.

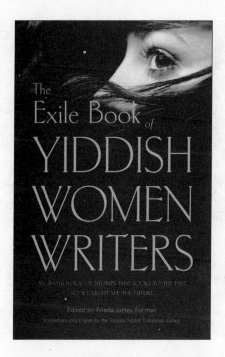

The
Exile Book of
YIDDISH
WOMEN
WRITERS

AN ANTHOLOGY OF STORIES THAT LOOKS TO THE PAST
SO WE MIGHT SEE THE FUTURE

Edited by Frieda Johles Forman
Translations into English by the Toronto Yiddish Translation Group

YIDDISH WOMEN WRITERS

EDITED BY FRIEDA JOHLES FOREMAN

Presenting a comprehensive collection of influential Yiddish women writers with new translations, this anthology explores the major transformations and upheavals of the 20th century. Short stories, excerpts, and personal essays are included from 13 writers, and focus on such subjects as family life; sexual awakening; longings for independence, education, and creative expression; the life in Europe surrounding the Holocaust and its aftermath; immigration; and the conflicted entry of Jewish women into the modern world with the restrictions of traditional life and roles. These powerful accounts provide a vital link to understanding the Jewish experience at a time of conflict and tumultuous change.

"This continuity…of Yiddish, of women, and of Canadian writers does not simply add a missing piece to an existing puzzle; instead it invites us to rethink the narrative of Yiddish literary history at large… Even for Yiddish readers, the anthology is a site of discovery, offering harder-to-find works that the translators collected from the Canadian Yiddish press and published books from Israel, France, Canada, and the U.S."
—*Studies in American Jewish Literature*, Volume 33, Number 2, 2014

"Yiddish Women Writers did what a small percentage of events at a good literary festival [Blue Metropolis] should: it exposed the curious to a corner of history, both literary and social, that they might never have otherwise considered." —*Montreal Gazette*

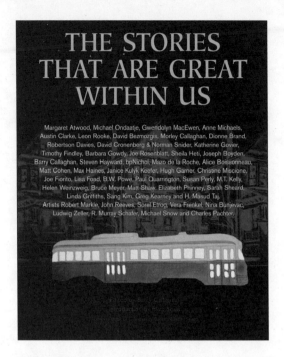

THE STORIES THAT ARE GREAT WITHIN US

EDITED BY BARRY CALLAGHAN

"[This is a] large book, one to be sat on the lap and not held up, one to be savoured piece by piece and heard as much as read as the great sidewalk rolls out…This is the infrastructure of Toronto, its deep language and various truths." —*Pacific Rim Review of Books*

Among the 50-plus contributors are Margaret Atwood, Michael Ondaatje, Gwendolyn MacEwen, Anne Michaels, Austin Clarke, Leon Rooke, David Bezmozgis, Morley Callaghan, Dionne Brand, Robertson Davies, Katherine Govier, Timothy Findley, Barbara Gowdy, Joseph Boyden, bpNichol, Hugh Garner, Joe Fiorito and Paul Quarrington, Janice Kulyk Keefer, along with artists Sorel Etrog, Vera Frenkel, Nina Bunjevac, Michael Snow, and Charles Pachter.

"Bringing together an ensemble of Canada's best-known, mid-career, and emerging writers…this anthology stands as the perfect gateway to discovering the city of Toronto. With a diverse range of content, the book focuses on the stories that have taken the city, in just six decades, from a narrow wryly praised as a city of churches to a brassy, gauche, imposing metropolis that is the fourth largest in North America. With an introduction from award-winning author Matt Shaw, this blends a cacophony of voices to encapsulate the vibrant city of Toronto." —*Toronto Star*

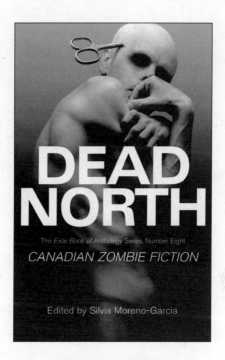

DEAD NORTH:
CANADIAN ZOMBIE FICTION

EDITED BY SILVIA MORENO-GARCIA

"*Dead North* suggests zombies may be thought of as native to this country, their presence going back to Aboriginal myths and legends…we see deadheads, shamblers, jiang shi, and Shark Throats invading such home and native settings as the Bay of Fundy's Hopewell Rocks, Alberta's tar sands, Toronto's Mount Pleasant Cemetery, and a Vancouver Island grow-op. Throw in the last poutine truck on Earth driving across Saskatchewan and some "mutant demon zombie cows devouring Montreal" (honest!) and what you've got is a fun and eclectic mix of zombie fiction…" —*Toronto Star*

"Every time I listen to the yearly edition of *Canada Reads* on CBC, so much attention seems to be drawn to the fact that the author is Canadian, that being Canadian becomes a gimmick. *Dead North*, a collection of zombie short stories by exclusively Canadian authors, is the first of its kind that I've seen to buck this trend, using the diverse cultural mythology of the Great White North to put a number of unique spins on an otherwise over-saturated genre."—*Bookshelf Reviews*

Featuring stories by Chantal Boudreau, Tessa J. Brown, Richard Van Camp, Kevin Cockle, Jacques L. Condor, Carrie-Lea Côté, Linda DeMeulemeester, Brian Dolton, Gemma Files, Ada Hoffmann, Tyler Keevil, Claude Lalumière, Jamie Mason, Michael Matheson, Ursula Pflug, Rhea Rose, Simon Strantzas, E. Catherine Tobler, Beth Wodzinski and Melissa Yuan-Ines.

FRACTURED:
TALES OF THE CANADIAN POST-APOCALYPSE

EDITED BY SILVIA MORENO-GARCIA

"The 23 stories in *Fractured* cover incredible breadth, from the last man alive in Haida Gwaii to a dying Matthew waiting for his Anne in PEI. All the usual apocalyptic suspects are here – climate change, disease, alien invasion – alongside less familiar scenarios such as a ghost apocalypse and an invasion of shadows. Stories range from the immediate aftermath of society's collapse to distant futures in which humanity has been significantly reduced, but the same sense of struggle and survival against the odds permeates most of the pieces in the collection… What *Fractured* really drives home is how perfect Canada is as a setting for the post-apocalypse. Vast tracts of wilderness, intense weather, and the potentially sinister consequences of environmental devastation provide ample inspiration for imagining both humanity's destruction and its rugged survival." —*Quill & Quire*

Featuring stories by T.S. Bazelli, GMB Chomichuk, A.M. Dellamonica, dvsduncan, Geoff Gander, Orrin Grey, David Huebert, John Jantunen, H.N. Janzen, Arun Jiwa, Claude Lalumière, Jamie Mason, Michael Matheson, Christine Ottoni, Miriam Oudin, Michael S. Pack, Morgan M. Page, Steve Stanton, Amanda M. Taylor, E. Catherine Tobler, Jean-Louis Trudel, Frank Westcott and A.C. Wise.

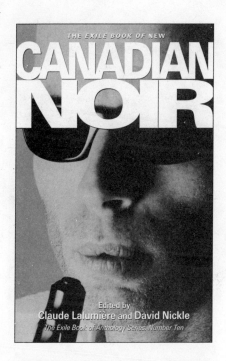

THE *EXILE BOOK OF* NEW

CANADIAN NOIR

Edited by
Claude Lalumière and David Nickle
The Exile Book of Anthology Series, Number Ten

NEW CANADIAN NOIR

EDITED BY CLAUDE LALUMIÈRE AND DAVID NICKLE

"Everything is in the title. These are all new stories – no novel extracts – selected by Claude Lalumière and David Nickle from an open call. They're Canadian-authored, but this is not an invitation for national introspection. Some Canadian locales get the noir treatment, which is fun, since, as Nickle notes in his afterword, noir, with its regard for the underbelly, seems like an un-Canadian thing to write. But the main question *New Canadian Noir* asks isn't "Where is here?" it's "What can noir be?" These stories push past the formulaic to explore noir's far reaches as a mood and aesthetic. In Nickle's words, "Noir is a state of mind – an exploration of corruptibility, ultimately an expression of humanity in all its terrible frailty." The resulting literary alchemy – from horror to fantasy, science fiction to literary realism, romance to, yes, crime – spanning the darkly funny to the stomach-queasy horrific, provides consistently entertaining rewards." —*Globe and Mail*

Featuring stories by Corey Redekop, Joel Thomas Hynes, Silvia Moreno-Garcia, Chadwick Ginther, Michael Mirolla, Simon Strantzas, Steve Vernon, Kevin Cockle, Colleen Anderson, Shane Simmons, Laird Long, Dale L. Sproule, Alex C. Renwick, Ada Hoffmann, Kieth Cadieux, Michael S. Chong, Rich Larson, Kelly Robson, Edward McDermott, Hermine Robinson, David Menear and Patrick Fleming.

The Exile Book of Anthology Series
Number Eleven

playground
of
LOST
toys

Edited by Colleen Anderson and Ursula Pflug

PLAYGROUND OF LOST TOYS

EDITED BY COLLEEN ANDERSON AND URSULA PFLUG

A dynamic collection of stories that explore the mystery, awe and dread that we may have felt as children when encountering a special toy. But it goes further, to the edges of space, where games are for keeps and where the mind plays its own games. We enter a world where the magic may not have been lost, where a toy or computers or gods vie for the upper hand. Wooden games of skill, ancient artifacts misinterpreted, dolls, stuffed animals, wand items that seek a life or even revenge — these lost toys and games bring tales of companionship, loss, revenge, hope, murder, cunning, and love, to be unearthed in the sandbox.

Featuring stories by Chris Kuriata, Joe Davies, Catherine MacLeod, Kate Story, Meagan Whan, Candas Jane Dorsey, Rati Mehrotra, Nathan Adler, Rhonda Eikamp, Robert Runté, Linda DeMeulemeester, Kevin Cockle, Claude Lalumière, Dominik Parisien, dvsduncan, Christine Daigle, Melissa Yuan-Innes, Shane Simmons, Lisa Carreiro, Karen Abrahamson, Geoffrey W. Cole and Alexandra Camille Renwick. Afterword by Derek Newman-Stille.

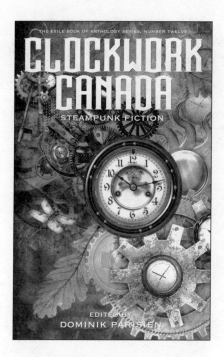

CLOCKWORK CANADA:
STEAMPUNK FICTION

EDITED BY DOMINIK PARISIEN

Welcome to an alternate Canada, where steam technology and the wonders and horrors of the mechanical age have reshaped the past into something both wholly familiar yet compellingly different.

"These stories of clockworks, airships, mechanical limbs, automata, and steam are, overall, an unfettered delight to read." —*Quill & Quire*

"[*Clockwork Canada*] is a true delight that hits on my favorite things in fiction – curious worldbuilding, magic, and tough women taking charge. It's a carefully curated adventure in short fiction that stays true to a particular vision while seeking and achieving nuance." —*Tor.com*

"...inventive and transgressive...these stories rethink even the fundamentals of what we usually mean by steampunk." —*The Toronto Star*

Featuring stories by Colleen Anderson, Karin Lowachee, Brent Nichols, Charlotte Ashley, Chantal Boudreau, Rhea Rose, Kate Story, Terri Favro, Kate Heartfield, Claire Humphrey, Rati Mehrotra, Tony Pi, Holly Schofield, Harold R. Thompson and Michal Wojcik.

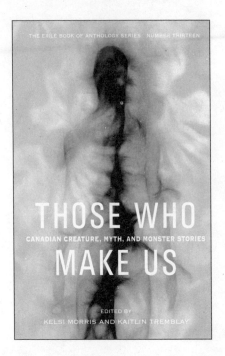

THE EXILE BOOK OF ANTHOLOGY SERIES NUMBER THIRTEEN

THOSE WHO
CANADIAN CREATURE, MYTH, AND MONSTER STORIES
MAKE US

EDITED BY
KELSI MORRIS AND KAITLIN TREMBLAY

THOSE WHO MAKE US: CANADIAN CREATURE, MYTH, AND MONSTER STORIES

EDITED BY KELSI MORRIS AND KAITLIN TREMBLAY

What resides beneath the blankets of snow, under the ripples of water, within the whispers of the wind, and between the husks of trees all across Canada? Creatures, myths and monsters are everywhere…even if we don't always see them.

Canadians from all backgrounds and cultures look to identify with their surroundings through stories. Herein, speculative and literary fiction provides unique takes on what being Canadian is about.

"Kelsi Morris and Kaitlin Tremblay did not set out to create a traditional anthology of monster stories… This unconventional anthology lives up to the challenge, the stories show tremendous openness and compassion in the face of the world's darkness, unfairness, and indifference." —*Quill & Quire*

Featuring stories by Helen Marshall, Renée Sarojini Saklikar, Nathan Adler, Kate Story, Braydon Beaulieu, Chadwick Ginther, Dominik Parisien, Stephen Michell, Andrew Wilmot, Rati Mehrotra, Rebecca Schaeffer, Delani Valin, Corey Redekop, Angeline Woon, Michal Wojcik, Andrea Bradley, Andrew F. Sullivan and Alexandra Camille Renwick.

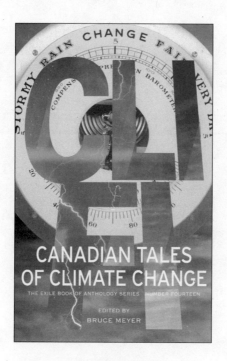

CLI FI:
CANADIAN TALES OF CLIMATE CHANGE

EDITED BY BRUCE MEYER

In his introduction to this all-original set of (at times barely) futuristic tales, Meyer warns readers, "[The] imaginings of today could well become the cold, hard facts of tomorrow." Meyer (Testing the Elements) has gathered an eclectic variety of eco-fictions from some of Canada's top genre writers, each of which, he writes, reminds readers that "the world is speaking to us and that it is our duty, if not a covenant, to listen to what it has to say." In these pages, scientists work desperately against human ignorance, pockets of civilization fight to balance morality and survival, and corporations cruelly control access to basic needs such as water....The anthology may be inescapably dark, but it is a necessary read, a clarion call to take action rather than, as a character in Seán Virgo's "My Atlantis" describes it, "waiting unknowingly for the plague, the hive collapse, the entropic thunderbolt." Luckily, it's also vastly entertaining. It appears there's nothing like catastrophe to bring the best out in authors in describing the worst of humankind. —*Publishers Weekly*

George McWhirter, Richard Van Camp, Holly Schofield, Linda Rogers, Sean Virgo, Rati Mehrotra, Geoffrey W. Cole, Phil Dwyer, Kate Story, Leslie Goodreid, Nina Munteanu, Halli Villegas, John Oughton, Frank Westcott, Wendy Bone, Peter Timmerman, Lynn Hutchinson Lee, with an afterword by internationally acclaimed writer and filmmaker, Dan Bloom.

Exile's $15,000 Carter V. Cooper Short Fiction Competition

FOR CANADIAN WRITERS ONLY

$10,000 for the Best Story by an Emerging Writer
$5,000 for the Best Story by a Writer at Any Career Point

The shortlisted are published in the annual *CVC Short Fiction Anthology* series and many in *ELQ/Exile: The Literary Quarterly*

Exile's $3,000 Gwendolyn MacEwen Poetry Competition

FOR CANADIAN WRITERS ONLY

$1,500 for the Best Suite of Poetry
$1,000 for the Best Suite by an Emerging Writer
$500 for the Best Poem

Winners are published in *ELQ/Exile: The Literary Quarterly*

These annual competitions open in November and close in May.
Details at:
www.ExileEditions.com
www.ExileQuarterly.com